THE SPELL

THE SECRET OF SPELLSHADOW MANOR
6

BELLA FORREST

CHAPTER I

ALEX FELT A SHOCK RUN THROUGH HIS BODY AS HE put himself between Aamir and the first swell of the sentient, silver tide. It recoiled, leaving Alex with a sensation so unbearably cold that it burned, shivering through his veins like icy rocket fuel. It wasn't something he had expected, given the mist's Spellbreaker origins, but he knew he had intervened between predator and prey.

The mist paused only for a moment before surging forward again, though this time it avoided Alex, bending around him the way the same poles of a magnet repelled one another. Alex wanted to block the branching flow, but the shock of the mist's initial strike had left him rooted to the spot, the slightest movement leaving every cell screaming in agony.

There was nothing for him to do but stand his ground. He opened his arms wide around Aamir, knowing he wouldn't evade the oncoming mist, not if it meant his friend's life. The first tendrils slithered past his own legs, the twisting silver tips coiling instead around Aamir's ankles like snaking vines, drawn by the magic within him. Alex could almost sense how desperate it was to snatch at Aamir's essence and drag it from the very depths of his body. The thought sent a pang of panic through him.

Looking up into the eyes of his friend, Alex saw tiny silver flecks appear in Aamir's dark brown irises, and the faintest sparks of silver rose through the skin of his face. The mist was taking hold of him.

Bracing himself, Alex closed his eyes and clutched at the center of his anti-magic, building it into a powerful shield around his body, until the silvery mist snapped back with a jarring whoosh, the shield shocking it. The Great Evil hadn't expected a Spellbreaker to sour the taste of mage essence.

Seizing the opportunity, Alex lunged forward, pushing Aamir toward the door, though every limb and muscle rallied against him. A guttural cry bellowed from the back of his throat, the pain in his body so intense he thought he might implode. For a brief second, everything went black, and though his vision returned rapidly, tiny black dots seemed to dance in the center of his eyeballs. Grimacing against the agony, he looked toward Aamir, making sure the older boy was as far from harm's way as he could be. Aamir stared back, like a puppet with its strings cut, his eyes blank, though the silver flecks had begun to fade.

Staggering back, Aamir grasped for the handle of the pit door that had closed behind them during the ensuing chaos, and pulled it open. Alex turned back to the pit, knowing the mist wouldn't hold off for more than a couple of seconds. He could feel it building behind him again, readying for another strike.

"RUN!" Alex roared, catching sight of Elias, who was still hauling an unconscious Virgil along the floor. Alex cursed under his breath; they couldn't leave the Head here, not after what had happened. Something had gone terribly wrong with the counter-spell, that much was clear, but if they were to stand any chance of fixing the mistake he'd made, they would need to keep Virgil alive.

The only problem was, every part of his body felt as if it were crumbling, every tiny motion more agonizing than the last, and he had a sinking feeling that he wouldn't be able to help drag Virgil from the room, even if he wanted to. As soon as the mist rushed back toward the door, they were done for—Alex would be frozen to the spot, Aamir would be engulfed, and it was yet to be seen what might happen to Virgil. Elias might be all right, Alex reasoned—Elias always found a way to survive.

But instead of rushing back toward Aamir, the mist peeled off in the direction of the Head, slithering across the floor until it reached the unconscious man's dangling legs.

"He's too fat!" Elias shouted, trying and failing to drag Virgil's body across the floor. "Can I get a hand here?"

"I can't! The mist did something to me!" Alex hissed, the pain overwhelming. He could only watch as the mist separated into long wisps shaped like the hands of a silver skeleton. The fingers clawed at the vulnerable flesh of the white-haired hybrid, evidently trying to get at whatever remnant of mage-kind remained within him. Alex gasped, not knowing what it would mean if the mist managed to take Virgil's magical half from him—would it even stop at half, Alex thought, or might it develop a taste for the anti-magical half as well?

Alex forced one foot in front of the other, each step knocking the breath out of him, but then he suddenly became aware of a movement behind him. Turning, an expression of horror fell across his face. Aamir was running toward the pit, his eyes focused on Virgil and the misty snakes snapping at the Head's heels. Ducking, Aamir grasped Virgil's arm and yanked it around his shoulder. It was a split-second movement, and one that Alex couldn't prevent. He wanted to yell at his friend for his heroic stupidity, but Elias and the older boy were already hurrying back toward him at breakneck speed, the weight now shared between them. Alex tried to move, gritting his teeth against the pain, but each movement was too slow, too ineffective.

"I still can't move!" Alex called out.

Elias's teeth glinted in a grin. "Brace yourself!"

4

The shadow-man's vaporous arm caught Alex square in the back, sending him hurtling in the direction of the exit. It was just the encouragement his body needed, the icy stiffness inside him shattering upon the impact of the shadow-man's shove, the strange frost splintering, giving him his movement back.

He didn't waste another moment. Racing toward the door, Alex yanked it fully open and ushered the other two ahead of him, slamming the thick door shut behind them, just in time to hear a great tidal wave of mist crash against it, the vibrations shuddering through his hands, though he pulled them away sharply.

Even then, Alex didn't dare take a moment to pause. He wasn't naïve enough to think that the door would hold back the silver mist for long. It would figure out a way through the cracks and crevices. It would find every single mage and suck the life out of them until they were empty shells.

"We have to get to the others," gasped Alex, the pain all but gone from his bones. "Can you carry Virgil?" he asked, glancing between the shadowy form of Elias and a panting Aamir.

Aamir nodded. "We've got him."

"We have to get out of here before that mist escapes," said Alex, though he knew he was stating the obvious. The severity of the situation was clear to everyone present, but it wasn't an easy thing to process. Though there was no time to dwell on what had happened, Alex couldn't help but feel foolish—he had been too confident, too sure of himself, and it had ended in disaster. Why he had thought the spell would be easy, he no longer knew. After retrieving the book and passing all the tests required of him, he supposed he had thought his "worthiness" would see him through to victory, but it had needed more. The spell had needed something he hadn't given it, and now it was up to him to figure out what that missing piece was, while hoping he didn't make another catastrophic error.

"Well, are we going or not?" Elias asked, his silky voice tinged with a note of uncharacteristic fear.

Without another word, they hurried through the rock-hewn hallway and up the staircase, emerging breathlessly into the private library, which already held so many nightmares for Alex. He tried not to look at the spot where he'd found Ellabell after Elias's scaremongering, and pressed on past it, out into the wide hallway of the Head's quarters. They ran through the main body of the school, sprinting over the broken ends of the golden line that had once kept the hallways safe from prying eyes.

Alex skidded to a halt as a pained grunt echoed in the corridor behind him. Snapping his head back to find the root of the sound, he saw Aamir crumple to the ground, Elias sagging as his hold on Virgil was knocked off balance. Aamir's face twisted in a mask of agony, his arms gripping his stomach. It was a position Alex had seen his friend in before, but this didn't seem like a curse. No, this was something else entirely.

"What's the matter?" Alex asked, rushing to Aamir's side.

"Something… burning… inside me," he panted, beads of sweat appearing across his forehead.

"Do you feel cold?"

Aamir shook his head. "No… very hot… like I'm… on fire," he gasped.

Alex turned to Elias for help, half expecting a sassy remark or a shrug of his vaporous shoulders. Instead, the shadow-man dropped Virgil on the ground and swept over to Aamir's hunched form, allowing his wispy hands to pass through the older boy's skin. Alex frowned, unsure of what Elias was trying to do. It looked to him like the shadow-man was rummaging around inside Aamir's body, but it was hard to tell whether the movements were intended to heal or hurt. Alex hesitated, debating whether or not to step in and stop him. He decided to hold himself back and let the shadow-man continue. It soon became apparent that whatever his rummaging technique was intended for, it seemed to be working. A moment or two later, Aamir visibly relaxed, the pain fading from his face.

"What did you do?" Aamir asked, catching his breath.

Elias gave the shrug that Alex had been waiting for. "A bit of this, a bit of that. I wouldn't want to give away state secrets," he purred, though it was evident he felt pleased with himself.

"What was wrong with him?" Alex demanded, not in the mood for any of Elias's games.

Elias sighed. "Some of the mist got into his system—his magic is all jangled up inside him, spreading through his squishy bits like oil on water. He'll be fine once it all finds its way back to where it ought to be." He turned to Aamir, who was looking up at him with a pained expression. "Though, I wouldn't go using your magic for a while, old boy—not unless you want to end up putting on a rather remarkable fireworks display, with yourself as the main event."

A smile curved his wispy mouth, but his heart didn't seem to be in it. Though he knew Elias would never admit it, Alex was sure the truth was that the shadow-man was just as spooked by the whole incident as the rest of them.

"How long should I avoid using it?" Aamir asked, his brow furrowed with concern. Alex didn't blame him; it wasn't every day a person got told they might explode if they did something that came naturally to them.

Elias shrugged. "Until you feel normal again… Maybe start small, see what happens," he teased.

"The mist is probably spreading already. We've got to go," said Alex, cutting Elias's amusement short. "Aamir, I'll help Elias with Virgil. You go on ahead," he insisted, nodding toward the darkened hallways of the school.

"You make it sound like I'm a virgin," Elias purred.

Alex flashed him a bemused look. "*What?*"

"You make it sound like I've never seen this happen before," the shadow-man elaborated. "I know what that stuff does. I've seen it with my own eyes… when I had proper eyes. I have seen havens fall before—you're the one who has no idea what's coming."

"You saw the havens fall?" Aamir asked.

Elias tilted his head in a languorous nod. "Comes with the territory of my chosen career, I'm afraid. But story time can wait. We need to be moving on." He grinned, returning to his perpetually vague, annoying self.

In any other situation, Alex would have asked to hear more. It was infuriating, being fed such juicy morsels of information, but there were too many innocent souls still within the walls of Spellshadow, and he couldn't allow himself to think about anything else until they were safe. This was his fault, after all, and their lives were his burden to bear.

The buzz of chatter and the scuff of footsteps echoed down the corridor, and though Alex dreaded what was to come, the sound filled him with a strange sense of relief. His friends, his former classmates, and people he'd never even met were waiting in those halls. Soon, he would have everyone gathered together, where they could begin the evacuation of Spellshadow Manor.

It was time for another haven to fall.

CHAPTER 2

A LEX TOOK AAMIR'S PLACE, PICKING THE LISTLESS
Virgil back up with Elias's help, before racing
toward the sound of people. He turned the corner
of a particularly ivy-swamped corridor to see Helena,
Ellabell, Natalie, and Jari standing a short way off, at the
head of a large congregation of Spellshadow students. There
were Stillwater students too, and though Alypia's magic had
faded at the elite school, it was still easy to pick out who was
who—there was an otherworldly beauty to the Stillwater
youth, even now, that the outside-world folk did not quite
possess.

Alex was surprised to see Catherine de Marchmont

sitting in the alcove of a shifting hallway window, the land-scape behind her showing a dark, dreary moor, a fine spray of rain washing over the gnarled roots of ancient trees. Her eyes were rimmed with red, her pretty face pale and drawn. It was evident she'd been crying, and Alex felt a pang of guilt, seeing her distress. Jun Asano had died at his hand, though his intentions had been honorable. If he hadn't stepped in, he was certain Jun would have killed Natalie, but that fact didn't make him feel any better. The memory still haunted him, and he knew the weight of Jun's life would rest on his shoulders for a long time to come.

Two other black-cloaked professors stood to one side, their heads hung low in shame. They wore the same tired expression that Catherine did, and Alex wondered if it was because Helena had removed their curses, the way she had done with Aamir. Glancing down at the edges of their cloak sleeves, he saw that the golden lines that had once encircled their wrists were gone. Remembering the toll it had taken on Aamir, he found himself feeling even sorrier for the three chosen ones, who had been wrangled into doing the Head's bidding.

As Alex and the others approached, the three new pro-fessors stared at the unconscious Head, a mixture of terror and disgust flashing across their faces. Alex almost breathed a sigh of relief; such a look could only mean one thing—these three, at the very least, were free of the Head's influence. Old feelings of fear, the kind Alex and his friends had once felt, appeared to have replaced false sentiments of worship. Alex just wished it was in better circumstances that they had been returned to their former selves.

It was Natalie who saw them first.

"Alex! Aamir," she said, with a hint of surprise. He guessed she hadn't expected Virgil to be returning. In truth, none of them had. They had been so sure of everything going right... a foolish assumption, in hindsight.

"We have to get out of here. Now," Alex said.

"What happened?" Helena chimed in, her eyes glancing across the peculiar party of four. Elias, rather than running off in his usual manner, had remained, his vaporous form floating just above the flagstones, the Head's arm alarmingly visible through the shifting shadows of his neck. Alex caught the silver-haired girl's suspicious glance, and knew there would be questions later, when they made it out of Spellshadow.

"It all went wrong," Alex said bluntly. The blood drained from their faces.

"The spell didn't work?" Ellabell asked, her eyes wide.

"Something was missing," Alex replied quickly. "It was all going fine, and then... I don't know what happened, but the ground began to shake, and..." He paused, not quite knowing how to phrase the next part. "The Great Evil... it's coming for us," he said, his heart heavy. The hallway had gone so silent that every single word carried with crystal-clear clarity, bouncing off the stone walls. Even though many of the other students had little idea of what he was talking about, the fear that rippled through the congregation was unmistakable.

Alex met the eyes of those in the group. "The mist is rising, and we need to be as far from here as possible."

"Isn't it gonna spread to the other havens?" Jari asked.

Elias was the one to answer. "Not if essence is still being poured into the pits at the other havens," he said grimly. "I know because I've seen it. That'll keep the mist at bay... for now."

"But there is no more essence at Stillwater," Helena said, her voice shaking.

"Then we need to go to Falleaf, and hope Hadrian can do something to help us," Alex said. "Is this everyone?"

The group looked at one another, scanning the faces for anyone who seemed to be missing. A minute passed before a voice spoke up.

"This is everyone," it confirmed, though Alex couldn't see who had said the words.

"Good, then I'm going to need you all to come with me," Alex insisted. He knew Hadrian wouldn't be too happy at the sight of so many of them, but that was his tough luck. Alex wasn't going to leave anyone to die.

"I can't come with you to Falleaf," Helena said suddenly.

"Of course you can! Come on, it'll be fine," Jari jumped in, touching Helena's arm.

Helena shook her head. "If what you say is true, Alex,

I need to take whatever essence we have left and bring it to Stillwater. If I can keep the Great Evil at bay there, we will be keeping our options open. Julius will find out what we've done with Venus, and if we only have one place to run to, the king will come down on us like a raging tempest," she explained. "More importantly, I still have people there. I will not leave them to a fate like this, not if I can prevent it."

A moment of tense silence passed in the group. If it had been his own people, Alex knew he would have done the same. Before he could speak, members of the Stillwater party began to announce their unyielding loyalty to Helena, their voices rising in a stirring chorus of support.

"We will return with you! We will make our school safe!" one cried.

"We stand with you, Helena," another said.

"We'll follow you!" shouted a third.

Helena smiled. "I shall be returning to Stillwater immediately—anybody who wishes to join me is more than welcome, but the others must follow Alex. He will lead you to a safer place."

With that, the group split into two, though the returning Stillwater group was far smaller—less than half the army Helena had brought with her. The rest huddled with the Spellshadow students, not daring to meet Helena's gaze, though it was clear the young woman understood their reluctance entirely.

"Here," said Ellabell, handing Helena the somewhat

emptier bag of Falleaf essence.

"Thank you," Helena said, then turned to Alex. "Now go. We'll try to meet you at Falleaf afterward. I'll see you all soon."

Helena and her downsized army sprinted toward the Head's office, where the portal would be lying open. Alex watched them go for a moment before projecting his voice over the crowd.

"Follow me," he shouted, lugging along the still-unconscious Virgil. The Head groaned as they began to move, but Alex ignored it, hoping the royal would have the decency to stay knocked out until they reached Falleaf.

A nervous energy trailed Alex, with the congregation keeping pace with him as they hurried through the hallways. As Alex began to tire, Natalie and Jari took the place of himself and the shadow-man, the latter seemingly using their gesture of kindness as an excuse not to help any longer.

"I'll see you there," purred Elias, before disappearing into the darkness of the rafters.

"You'd better," Alex muttered.

They poured out across the front steps of the manor, ignoring the scattered bodies that lay on the front lawn. Alex turned in time to see Catherine de Marchmont's red-rimmed eyes glance toward the spot where Jun Asano had fallen, but she dropped her gaze a second later, evidently unable to bear the sight.

A few members of the group cowered as Storm

reappeared, dropping down onto the grass beside them with a loud chirrup of indignation. It was clear she hadn't appreciated being left to her own devices while everyone else disappeared inside the stone walls of the manor, where she couldn't follow.

Alex smiled, reaching a hand up to stroke the downy feathers on the side of her face. "Sorry, girl, we've gotten ourselves into a bit of trouble," he whispered.

The Thunderbird gave a low, anxious coo.

"It's okay, we're getting everyone out," he said, before clambering up onto her back. She opened her enormous wings, startling the nearby students, but Alex stopped her. "No, Storm, we just need to walk for now, toward the Falleaf portal," he explained. With a bristle of the feathers at the top of her head, she folded her wings back in and began walking as instructed, in a strangely hypnotic motion, Alex riding on her back. It was clear it wasn't natural to her, but she was doing it anyway. Alex smiled at the thought—he had grown exceptionally fond of his Thunderbird.

With him leading the way on his peculiar steed, the rest of the group followed, though they picked up speed as a great rumble tore through the ground, making several students stumble. The mist was rising, and they needed to get to Falleaf fast. Almost running now, they hurried through the desolate gardens with their tumbledown walls and warped trees, the fountains mossed over, the flowers long since withered.

Reaching the broken section of the outer fortifications, Storm flew over the wall and landed neatly on the other side, just as another quake shook the ground, chunks of wall tumbling down. The students ducked out of the way, prompting the group to push and shove their way through the gap.

"Single file!" Alex yelled, but nobody was listening. Behind them, debris was falling from the walled gardens, the ancient fountains cracking, and the manor, just visible in the distance, was shaking. The sound of breaking glass and splintering rock filled their ears.

Bigger students trampled smaller ones, forcing Alex to jump down from Storm and join his friends as they struggled to pull the squashed students from the gap in the wall, while more stampeded through. It was a mess, everybody out for themselves. There had to be around fifty students trying to push their way out of the walled garden, and though some called for order, the panicked screams and pained cries drowned them out.

"Storm, can you help?" Alex asked, desperate now. There was a small boy trapped at the very bottom of the gap, his hand just visible, but nobody could get to him and people continued to run over him, pushing him farther and farther down into the crevice.

Storm chirped her response. Taking a step back, she braced herself, puffing out her feathered chest. A beam of ice came hurtling out of her mouth, her wings arched behind her for support. The ice thundered into the side of the stone wall, a short distance from the initial break in the fortifications, cracking it apart like the shell of an egg. As it came tumbling down, the scared students peeled away from the smaller exit, sprinting through the larger break instead. Seizing the opportunity, Alex hauled the small boy out of the wreckage, quickly checking that he was okay. Remarkably, he was, with just a few scrapes and bruises to show for it. His friends came running up, taking over from Alex, giving him the chance to hop onto Storm's back and continue their exodus.

"With me!" he called, picking up the pace again. Reaching the top of the hill, a few of the students turned back to the manor to see the first wisps of something silver rising into the air. The ground shook again, more violently this time. One of the manor's towers fell, hitting the ground with an earth-shattering bang. The students couldn't tear their eyes away; Spellshadow had been a weird sort of home to them for so long that to be leaving no doubt felt strange. Alex shared the feeling—it wasn't easy to leave a place of apparent safety, to step into the unknown. However, there was no time to think any farewell thoughts they might have— they could do that later, when they were somewhere safer. Barking at them to move, Alex ushered them down the slope of the hill, coming to a halt as they reached the very edge of the smoking field.

"Wait!" Alex called, knowing this would not be a simple

crossing, thanks to the wispy snakes that Virgil had placed beneath the scorched earth. He gestured to Natalie and Jari, and they managed to get Virgil up onto Storm's back, practically draping the skeletal man around the bird's neck, so the pair of them would be free to race across the treacherous expanse of barren wasteland. Alex wished he could take them all on Storm, but as it was, there was no more room. Turning, he addressed the group. "We need to run for that tree-line over there, do you understand?" he said, watching the congregation closely for any weak links who might need more help.

The group nodded, more than fifty faces staring at him in abject horror.

"I need you to run as fast as you can, without looking back, okay?" he added.

The group nodded again, more anxiously this time.

"If you fall, get up and keep going. If a friend falls, pick them up and keep going. Do not stop, do not wait, do not pause, do not rest until you have reached the woods on the other side," he insisted. "Now, GO!"

The students sprinted across the smoking field, some faster than others, but none daring to look back, just as Alex had instructed.

With one eye on the darting students, Alex got onto Storm's back, pinioning Virgil between himself and Storm's neck. With the Head securely in place, the Thunderbird stepped back, taking a run up, before rising into the air.

Glancing down at the charging army of scared students, he hoped they would all make it across in one piece. For a moment, his gaze was pulled backward toward the manor, where the silver glitter of the mist was rising from the roof like smoke, seeking out souls to feed its insatiable hunger.

CHAPTER 3

THE SMOKING SNAKES SLITHERED UPWARD FROM THE cracked, dry earth, sensing the pounding of feet above. Alex saw a few of the students glance at the wispy creatures, their eyes wide in horror, but they did not falter, turning their gaze straight ahead toward the trees, their legs carrying them across the smoking field. Vaporous fangs opened wide, the snakes snapping at the heels of the fleeing students, but none of them managed to make contact. Alex felt a wave of relief when the first of the students disappeared behind the blockade of sickly-looking tree trunks, followed a few moments later by the next few, and the next, until only the stragglers remained.

Billy Foer and Catherine de Marchmont trailed the rest of the runners, two snakes right on their tail, the serpents' mouths stretching in readiness for the bites they longed to take. The first was just about to close its foggy fangs on the ankle of Billy Foer when Ellabell rushed forward, grabbing the boy by the arms and hauling him into the trees, leaving the serpent to recoil, slithering backward with what Alex could swear was a look of disappointment on its vapory face.

Catherine, however, simply stopped, only a few yards shy of the tree-line. Alex frowned, wondering what she was doing—there was a smoky snake blocking her way, but if she was smart, she could dodge out of its way. But it seemed as if all the fight had left her, body and soul.

"Catherine, run!" Natalie yelled, but Catherine only stared at her blankly. A few students even tried to reach out and grab her, but the snakes blocked their way. Seeing that she had no exit, a sudden light came back to her eyes, but it was too late. The vaporous serpent behind her clamped its jaws around her leg, the other snake joining in, biting down hard on Catherine's arm. She let out a blood-curdling scream, but there was nothing anyone could do to help her, and though she fought, it was clear there was no escape for her. As a sickening tag-team, the serpents dragged her across the cracked earth, though Alex had no idea where they kept their intense strength, considering their smoky appearance. With a vicious tug, they pulled her into a hole in the ground that was much too small. She screamed all the while, until she suddenly went silent, the echo of her final scream shivering through the air toward the shocked students, the light in her eyes extinguished. Yanking and dragging with appalling vehemence, the serpents continued their foul game, until their prey disappeared beneath the earth.

"Keep... Keep going!" Alex urged, though he knew it would be hard to get over the scene they had just witnessed. He could hardly believe it himself. Grief-stricken and confused, he realized she must have paused, believing she wanted to give up, only to change her mind a fraction of a second too late. He tried to push the image of her final moments to the back of his mind as he urged Storm to descend into a tiny clearing he'd spotted in the woods. There would be time to mourn later, once they were away from the threat of the silver mist.

With a last flap of her wings and a ripple of muscle, the Thunderbird elegantly dropped to the ground. As she landed, the crowd of students appeared through the woods, horror written across their faces.

"Is everyone okay?" Alex asked, dismounting the Thunderbird.

"No physical injuries," Natalie answered, looking queasy.

Alex nodded, glancing around at the shell-shocked group. Their fear seeped toward him, heightening the worry in his own veins. "I know what you've all just seen is terrible, and I promise, we'll honor Catherine later, but right now we need to get going. Aamir, you know where the portal is, right?"

"This way," Aamir said, leading the group.

As they departed, Alex turned to the Thunderbird. "Can you meet us at Falleaf? Hide beside the cave until I can come and find you," he instructed, trying to wrestle the unconscious Virgil from her back.

Storm's bright eyes glanced over Alex, and a chirp of understanding trilled from her beak. With a rush of limbs and wings, she took off again, soaring over the sickly woods, casting a shadow on all those below, and then disappearing with a crack like thunder.

Knowing she was safely on her way to Falleaf, Alex took off after the others, dragging Virgil along. It still surprised him how heavy the Head was, considering his slight frame and skeletal appearance, and it was tough going as he pulled the man along.

The woods gave way to a larger clearing with a stone circle of obelisks in the center. In the middle of that circle, a portal glimmered, showing the autumnal leaves of Falleaf House, though it was a different view from the one Alex had seen from the walls of Kingstone. This led into a deeper, darker part of the forest around Falleaf, but there didn't seem to be any signs of soldiers in the immediate vicinity, which made Alex feel a small flicker of relief.

Aamir, Jari, Ellabell, and Natalie were standing at the rear of the student group, marshaling the progress of the procession of students stepping through the portal. Nobody wanted a repeat of what had happened at the walled garden. Some were reluctant, having never seen a portal before, and not knowing what the world was beyond, but Alex could hear the comforting words of his friends reassuring them.

"You are all going to be just fine. The person in charge here is nothing like the Head—he will keep us safe," Aamir promised.

"Come on, it's just a little step, dude!" Jari encouraged.

"That's it, just straight through and you'll be fine," said Ellabell, flashing her brightest smile.

"See, they are all fine, and you will be too," Natalie insisted calmly, pressing a firm hand against the backs of the more reluctant students.

With the last person through, the only thing left to do was step through themselves. Alex glanced back, and though the woods blocked the manor from view, he could see the coil of silver mist rising over the spot where the manor ought to be, its tendrils twisting into the air, sniffing out its prey. With any luck, Alex hoped, it would go hungry today.

"Need a hand?" Jari quipped, before coming over to take up Virgil's other arm. With the Head decidedly more balanced, and Alex's shoulders giving a sigh of relief, they took their steps through the portal, into the realm of Falleaf. The temperature dropped instantly, the forest chillier than the woods of Spellshadow, though it looked like warm sunlight was trying to peek through the thick canopy. A few of the Stillwater students, used to constant warmth and sunshine, began to shiver.

As they stood in the cool glade where they had come out of the portal, Alex's mind wandered toward the idea of the fifth haven. It seemed like the best place to take so many people, though he was certain the suggestion wouldn't go down well. Yet, he found himself thinking about the clear, crisp air of Starcross, and its seemingly idyllic landscape. Surely, if it had been one of the five fallen havens, it ought to have been smothered in a blanket of mist, but it wasn't. Did that mean the mist ebbed and faded over time, after it had done its deadly sweep of the place? With no mage essence left to taste, had it retreated? It was a question he'd have to save for Ceres—she knew more about the fifth haven and its secrets than anyone.

"I'm going to leave you all here while I go and find the man in charge, to ensure safe passage through these forests. While I'm gone, keep yourselves as hidden as possible and your eyes peeled for anything strange that might look like a trap. Listen to what these guys have to say, too," he added, gesturing toward his friends.

The group made noises of anxious agreement, some of them retreating into the darkest recesses of the glade, their bodies morphing with the shadow into nothingness, the camouflage remarkable. Alex just hoped it would be enough to fool any passing soldiers.

"What are we going to do with *him*?" Aamir asked, nodding at Virgil.

Alex grimaced. "I'm going to have to leave him here. Can

26

you manage?"

The four remaining friends glanced at one another, their hesitant expressions mirror images of Alex's own.

"We will do what we can," Natalie said, finally.

"Though that's not exactly saying much," a silky voice purred from the shady boughs of a giant oak. Elias rippled down the twisted trunk, his teeth glinting. "Which is why you'll be pleased to know I've come to join the party," he added, splaying out his arms while shaking his shadowy fingers—the weirdest jazz hands Alex had ever seen.

As much as he hated to admit it, Alex was pleased to see that Elias had returned. No matter how powerful his friends were, and how weak Virgil was in his current state, they all knew how unpredictable the Head could be. With Elias's assistance, they stood a better chance of being able to keep the Head under control, at the very least.

"Do you think you'll be able to manage *him*?" Alex smiled wryly, trying hard not to roll his eyes in the direction of the shadow-man.

Ellabell gave a short, sharp laugh. "If he tries anything, he'll have me to answer to," she muttered.

"And here I was thinking we were friends now," Elias taunted, swooping close to Ellabell. The move was clearly intended to frighten her, but her face remained a stoic mask, her nerves unperturbed by the shadow-man. Whatever terror she had formerly felt in his company, it was clear it no longer had a hold over her.

"You and me?" Ellabell sniffed. "Never in a million years."

Elias grinned. "Looks like we'll be just fine."

"Do you think Hadrian can fit all of us in the treehouses, maybe make it look like a new intake of students?" Aamir said.

Alex shook his head. "I've got a different idea in mind," he admitted. "If I let these people stay here and join the Falleaf students, I'm just sending them into more of the same—more of what they've already been through. I won't do that."

"You want to send them through the cave?" Aamir pressed.

Alex nodded. The fifth haven was the only truly safe place he could think of, though he knew the suggestion wouldn't go down well. It was going to be a tricky sell, especially as there were so many. Hadrian and Ceres were determined to protect the isolation of Starcross and the freedom of its inhabitants, but surely, Alex reasoned, these people deserved the same chance at freedom?

"I'd better get going," said Alex solemnly. "Which way is it?"

Aamir smiled. "That way," he said, pointing between two trees. "Keep going straight, and you'll come to the clearing with the pagoda."

With a brief farewell, Alex departed, darting through the deep forest, keeping his eyes and ears out for any buzzing sounds, or anything strange that lay in his path. As luck would have it, he had become somewhat adept at avoiding the Falleaf traps, and managed to weave through the trees and undergrowth with relative ease. It was almost a relief when he saw the glint of the pagoda's top, and the water gardens surrounding the base of the striking building. However, having never approached the pagoda from this side before, Alex saw that the distance between the tree-line and the back of the pagoda was far wider than it had been on the other side, and there were two bands of soldiers standing between him and the hidden doorway that led into the structure.

Ducking down, he crept past the first group, freezing as a twig snapped underfoot. Fortunately, the soldiers were so engrossed in their own conversation that they didn't seem to hear it. He paused for a second, to make sure they hadn't heard, but they had descended into a conversation about one of their wives. Realizing it was safe to move, though he still didn't dare to exhale, Alex carried on, scouring the space between the trees and the pagoda for a suitable spot to sprint across.

There was a slightly narrower passage just ahead, but a group of soldiers was standing too close by. Although they had their backs turned, that didn't make it any less dangerous. Glancing between the two bands of soldiers, Alex took a deep breath and ran for it.

A shout went up, but he didn't stop to see if it was him they were shouting after. Barreling toward the door at the back of the pagoda, the lock of which was still broken, he slipped into the cellar and ran up the dank steps, not pausing for anything. He tore past the kitchens, grabbing a scarlet uniform on the way and yanking the top half on, just in case he came across anyone unsavory. Up and up he went, ducking into doorways whenever a soldier turned in his direction, until he finally reached the top floor. To his relief, there were no soldiers standing guard at the door.

Catching his breath, he knocked, then stepped in and closed the door firmly behind him. Hadrian was standing by the window, talking with Vincent, but he turned sharply as Alex entered, a look of surprise on his face. Alex glanced at Vincent, wondering how the necromancer came to be there. The last time he'd seen him was at Spellshadow Manor, though he now realized he hadn't seen the peculiar man amongst the student exodus. Somehow, the mysterious necromancer had slipped away, returning to Falleaf before any of them.

"Alex? What are you d-doing here?" he asked, his brow furrowed with anxiety.

"It's a long story," Alex gasped. "You might want to sit down."

"Do you wish me to make myself scarce?" the necromancer asked, the black veins in his face pulsing slightly. "Or can I stay to hear about the shenanigans you've evidently managed to mix yourself up in? I must say, that absolutely has to be a record—I only saw you a mere handful of hours ago, yet here you are, plainly in some form of trouble?"

Alex shook his head. "No, you can stay. You might be able to help, actually," he said, gesturing toward the central table. Even though he didn't know how Vincent had arrived here, Alex was glad to see him—the necromancer was undeniably useful in all sorts of situations. The deep black of his veins had faded ever so slightly, and, by the looks of it, he and Hadrian had become firm friends in the brief time they'd known one another, or co-conspirators at the very least.

"I'd prefer to stand," Vincent said, smiling.

Hadrian began to wring his hands as he walked over to the low table and sat down. Alex sat opposite, dreading the conversation that was to follow.

Hadrian sighed heavily. "What h-happened?"

"The spell went wrong. The mist got loose, and I had to evacuate Spellshadow Manor. I have over fifty people waiting in the forest, by the portal, who need your help," Alex replied, trying to keep the anxiety from his own voice. "I know what you're going to say—we should integrate them into the students here, and make it look like you were doing Julius's bidding, but I won't do that. I won't have them out of the frying pan and into the fire."

Vincent gave a sharp intake of breath. "Oh dear," he muttered. "I am afraid I departed shortly after helping that silver-haired young woman retrieve that device. I sensed that my dear Agatha was in some distress, but it also seemed prudent to inform Hadrian of what was occurring at Spellshadow—that is what I did, but had I known the danger you were in, I would not have tarried so long."

Hadrian gulped loudly. "The spell w-went wrong?"

"Yes. Something happened, and the mist got released," Alex repeated. "That's not the most important thing right now. There are people who need your help, Hadrian. I need you to provide us with a safe route through the forest, and into Starcross. I'm not leaving here until you agree."

"Y-You realize the s-situation you are p-putting m-me in?" Hadrian asked, his nervous tic going into overdrive.

Alex nodded. "I do, but they deserve protection while we figure out how to do the spell again. This is all my fault, and I need your help, so nobody else suffers for that mistake. You agree with me, right, Vincent?"

Vincent raised his hands. "I think it is best I remain out of this one, Alex. This is neither my domain nor my jurisdiction, so I would not feel proper offering up my perspective. Hadrian must do whatever he deems best."

"You s-still have the b-book?" Hadrian asked.

Alex patted the satchel still slung around his body. "It's not leaving my side for a moment."

"T-Two tries l-left," Hadrian muttered, almost to himself. Alex grimaced, having almost forgotten the caveat of the spell's limited attempts. Still, if he could pore over the book again and maybe pry some information out of Virgil when he awoke, he was confident he could try again and succeed.

"They're out there, vulnerable, and they need you," Alex pressed. "Can I count on you?"

For a long time, Hadrian said nothing, though from time to time he looked at Vincent, as if seeking approval. The necromancer wasn't particularly forthcoming, his face remaining a webbed canvas of neutrality. Alex didn't speak either, watching and waiting for the white-haired man to come to a decision. At this point, there was nothing left for Alex to say, and he was scared he might end up begging on his knees. If Hadrian wouldn't help, then they were lost.

At long last, the royal opened his mouth to speak. "I s-suppose you haven't l-left me with m-much choice."

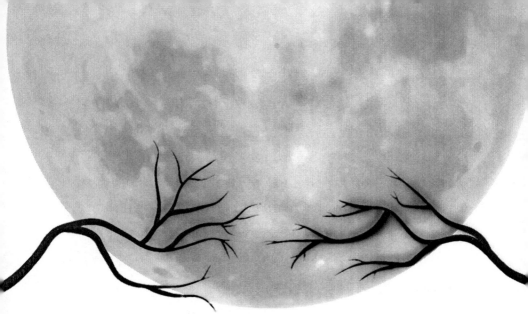

CHAPTER 4

HADRIAN AND VINCENT FOLLOWED ALEX BACK through the forest, though nobody had much to say. It was clear to Alex that Hadrian wanted to ask him all about the spell, and what had gone wrong, but the truth was, Alex was still trying to figure that out himself.

"I knew it w-was a bad idea," said Hadrian suddenly.

Alex cast a sideways glance at him. "What choice did we have?"

"You should have j-just left that s-spell alone," Hadrian murmured.

"I am not certain this line of discussion is exactly helpful, dear Hadrian," Vincent chimed in, evidently trying to mediate.

"You'd have been happy with that?" Alex remarked sourly, ignoring Vincent. "You'd have been happy for everything to just stay the same, the cycle repeating endlessly, until no more babies were born with magical ability, and the essence all ran out? I suppose you figured you'd be dead by then, or something?"

After the forceful show Hadrian had displayed when Alex had tried to get the survivors to join the cause, Alex had thought that, perhaps, there was more to the nervous royal than met the eye. He had thought that, maybe, Hadrian had fire in his belly after all, when it came to the injustices of the magical realms. Now, it seemed Alex had been mistaken. Hadrian was just afraid—a coward, nothing more, never wanting to rock the boat. It was hard to believe Hadrian and his sister, Ceres, could be such polar opposites. Alex had a feeling Ceres was the kind of woman who would never back down from a fight, if someone else was suffering.

"You think I'm a w-weakling." Hadrian laughed bitterly. "You think I'm a n-nervous wreck with no moral compass, but you're m-mistaken. You wouldn't be the first to think so, b-but you *are* mistaken. I care… I really care. I want the change you seek, but I also know the r-risks."

"They're worth taking, if this is the alternative," Alex replied, gesturing to the leafy world around them. True, it looked beautiful, but its core was rotten.

"I know, Alex. I t-truly do know—it's just hard for me to

35

change m-my ways, after so long l-living the same life, being made to kneel and scrape in the s-sight of the king." Hadrian sighed. "You forget, the survivors wouldn't even b-be alive if I hadn't r-risked everything to get them out."

Alex frowned. For some reason, whether it was the wringing of the man's hands or the stammer in his voice, he had forgotten all the good Hadrian had actually done, within the constraints around him. It couldn't have been easy defying a man like Julius, stowing away students in secret, and keeping it that way all these years. Alex thought back to his visit to the fifth haven, and remembered the age of some of the people there. Hadrian really had done a great thing, and he had kept those people safe for a long time. It was only natural the anxious royal would be worried, Alex realized, when all that hard work was threatened by something that may not even work, but could never be taken back.

Alex smiled apologetically. "I imagine a lot of people have given you a hard time?"

"Not so many, but those who h-have don't hold back," Hadrian replied, a sorrowful look in his eyes. "My sister tells me all the t-time what a failure I am f-for not doing more. I suppose she's right... but I d-did all I thought I could do."

"Remember, Hadrian, your sister speaks from a place of passion—she is not always in control of her words, or the way in which they tumble from her mouth," Vincent said, offering up some comfort to the battered royal.

"And, hey, you're helping us now," Alex added, softening

toward Hadrian. "That *is* doing more."

When Alex, Vincent, and Hadrian emerged through the shade of the trees, the crack of a branch went off like a gunshot in the silence of the forest, and the students in the clearing scattered like disturbed rats. Peering into the darkness, all Alex could see were beady eyes staring at him from the gloom, the fear tangible.

"It's just me," Alex announced. "And this is Hadrian, the guy who is going to help us. The guy next to him is—"

"I am Vincent, for those who were, perhaps, wondering. I am also here to offer my assistance, though I am afraid I am not quite the grand fromage," Vincent interrupted.

Natalie snorted with laughter from the back of the group. Figures slowly began to unfurl from the shadows, moving forward on shaky limbs. The four friends approached Alex, Vincent, and Hadrian, though they didn't bring Virgil with them. A shift of something even darker than the forest shade told Alex that wherever the Head was, tucked back there in the dim light, Elias had handled the situation.

"Alex tells me y-you're in need of shelter," said Hadrian. "It is a pleasure to meet you, and a p-pleasure to see familiar faces again. I only wish it w-were under happier circumstances," he added, going down the line, shaking hands with the four friends. He had yet to meet Natalie and Jari, but he shook their hands all the same, smiling warmly.

"Hadrian has kindly agreed to let us go through to meet with his sister," Alex explained.

The royal nodded, his stammer fading as he addressed the gathered group. "My sister, Ceres, will be able to take care of you, and keep you safe. I know you must all be cold, tired, and hungry, but you will soon be out of danger," he promised. The metamorphosis was peculiar to Alex—one moment, Hadrian had been wringing his hands with anxiety; the next he had become an authoritative leader, a voice of comfort to the weary troops. Alex wondered if this was the way his own students saw him.

"Monsieur Hadrian, a few of these students are injured after the battle we had at Spellshadow. Does your sister have medical facilities?" Natalie asked, pointing toward a cluster of individuals curled up in various states of fitful slumber between the twisting roots of an enormous tree.

"She is fully equipped to assist with all kinds of ailments," Hadrian confirmed. Alex knew it had to be true, given the state in which the survivors must have come through to Starcross, not to mention their lifelong treatment after they'd had half their essence taken away. "If you'd like to follow me, all of you, I can lead you to her. You will have to be as quiet as you can possibly be, and do exactly as I instruct."

The congregation moved forward, evidently impressed by the manner of Hadrian, who was a million miles away from the Head and Headmistress they had all known in their time at the havens.

"Aren't you forgetting something?" a sultry voice barked from the back of the clearing.

"Ah, I forgot to mention that," said Alex, turning apologetically toward Hadrian.

The nervous royal frowned. "What?"

"I had to bring Virgil with us," Alex explained. "If we're going to try the spell again, we need his help still. There was no way we could leave him there."

Elias heaved the dangling figure of Virgil forward, throwing him haphazardly onto the grass, where he landed in an unconscious heap.

"He certainly looks as if he has seen better days," Vincent remarked, eyeing the limp man with curiosity.

Hadrian sighed heavily. "My sister won't be happy about it, but I can see why you had to bring him. It's funny, the way that man always seems to dodge the worst of things," he mused. "Do you need help carrying him?"

Alex shook his head. "No, we've got this," he said, as Jari hurried to pick up one arm and Natalie moved to take the other.

"Where would you all be without me?" Elias grinned, before twisting up into nothingness. The forest of Falleaf was an easy spot for the shadow-man to disappear into, without a trace. Regardless, Alex could still feel Elias's presence lingering around him. He felt like he was being watched, but knew the surveillance was coming from within him, pulsing at the center of the piece of soul he'd accidentally stolen.

The students trailed after Hadrian, treading carefully. It seemed the royal was taking the long way around, circling the whole forest before coming back toward the place where Alex knew the cave stood, hidden away in a distant section of the woods. Using the slender device that picked out traps, and ensuring that any bands of soldiers were suitably diverted by stern words of broken snares, Hadrian escorted them to the cave without incident. However, Alex knew that was the least of their worries. They still had Ceres to contend with.

"Come on through, but you'll have to be aware of space— it might get a little cramped," Hadrian instructed, before opening the narrow door that covered the cave entrance and hurrying inside. The group followed, though the royal was right: it was a little cramped with so many inside.

"Very good, keep on heading through, push right down to the very end of the cave," Vincent urged, though he remained outside the cave's entrance, to keep watch.

Hadrian was saying much the same thing inside. "Yes, that's right, you need to follow me, right through to the very end of the cave. Come on past the shelves, and keep on coming until you've gone as far as you can go," he shouted, so everyone could hear.

Jari bounded up to the entrance and slipped through the doorway, followed closely by Aamir. The rest of the students came after, with Alex, Ellabell, and Natalie bringing up the rear, calming any hesitation, to ensure that nobody got cold feet.

It was strange to enter the cave again, and it wasn't long before Alex began to feel the half-familiar sensation of the essence calling to him. It was magnetic, drawing him toward the bottles on the shelves, though he knew they contained only a fraction of the person they had been dragged from, unlike the Kingstone essence, which could be felt a mile away. The pulse that emanated from these was still weak, and somehow sad, though the other students walked past the bottles with disinterest, their focus firmly on Hadrian.

"It's so weird in here," whispered Ellabell. "I don't think I'll ever get used to this place."

Alex knew what she meant. "It's because it's full of lost souls," he said, half to himself.

As they moved farther into the cave, the walls began to press inward, the pathway bottlenecking in places once they got past the shelves of essence. Slender creepers twisted up the rock face, with tiny white flowers peppering the vine. The petals were smooth and velvety with a bright yellow center, almost like a daisy. It was hard to believe anything could grow in here, but Alex supposed nature always found a way of thriving, even in the darkest of places.

Before long, the large group had collected in a small expanse at the farthest end of the cave, where the narrow path of the cave's walkway gave way to a slightly more open space. An enormous stalactite hung down from the cave's roof, with a tip forged from sapphire. Pausing here, Hadrian made a show of hiding something from sight, a shape that was sticking out of the wall. Alex peered around the nervous royal, and saw he had his hand upon a big, rough-cut gem that

BELLA FORREST

resembled a lotus flower. Casting an anxious glance back at the group, Hadrian pushed the gem in. With a loud, rumbling scrape that panicked the students into thinking another quake was happening, a large section of wall slid away, though it was clear now that it was a thick screen of painted wood, made to look like rock. It wasn't as convincing when it was tucked away to the side, but Alex knew it had looked just like the real thing moments before. Now, it revealed the familiar glow of a portal, and, beyond it, Alex could see the beautiful land he had scouted from Storm's back. Even at this distance, he could almost feel the crisp, cool air and the warm sunlight on his face. Of all the havens he had encountered, this was the only one that truly felt like a haven to him.

Alex hung back until the last of the students had stepped through to the new land, following the lead of a sensible Aamir and an exuberant Jari. With only Alex and the two girls left to step over the threshold into Starcross, he gestured for them to go on ahead.

"I just want to have a quick word with Hadrian first," Alex explained, glancing at the nervous royal. To soften the blow of bringing all these people to Starcross, he wanted to try to persuade Hadrian to come with them, even though it seemed the royal had no intention of doing so whatsoever. It was almost as if he feared the portal to Starcross, not daring to get too close. Perhaps what lay on the other side was too tempting an escape from the responsibilities of Falleaf.

"We'll wait," said Ellabell, and Natalie nodded.

"No, really, you go on ahead, it's—" He never got to finish his sentence, as vibrations began to shake the cave, and the sound of feet pounding the stone echoed off the walls. Alex turned sharply in the direction of the narrow passageway, bracing himself for whoever, or whatever, was incoming. A split second later, Vincent appeared in the narrow passageway, running down through the cave, a panicked expression on his face. To Alex's surprise, Helena was following, and there were others, just visible behind her, all of them hurtling toward the portal.

"What's the matter, Vincent?" asked Ellabell.

The necromancer came to an abrupt halt just in front of them, his brow beading with sweat. "It is exceptionally bad news, I'm afraid," he gasped, clutching his chest.

Helena ran up behind him, the exertion barely affecting her. "It's Julius," she explained bitterly. "We'd just jumped through the portal back to Stillwater when we saw him arrive—it was like lightning in the distance, and I just knew it was him. He descended on us out of the blue. We turned tail and went straight back through to Spellshadow, following your tracks... but there's nothing I can do for the rest of them—those still trapped at Stillwater, suffering who knows what at his hand." Her face twisted in a furious grimace.

"How did you avoid the mist?" Alex asked.

"Some of us didn't," said Helena, shaking her head sadly. "It had started to roll out and was seeping through the floor, but there were a few corridors that were clear, and we used those. It still got a few of us though." Her eyes glittered with un-spilt tears.

"I'm so sorry," Alex whispered.

"Julius is going to find us," she warned. "Wherever we go, he will follow us, until we have nowhere left to run."

It was a terrifying thought, made all the more horrifying by the fact that Alex knew she was right. Julius would follow them to the ends of the earth. They had his wife, they had defied him, they were a thorn in his side—it was only a matter of time before he caught up. But, at least for now, he had no idea where they were.

For the time being, they were a tentative step ahead.

CHAPTER 5

AFTER ENSURING THE REMAINDER OF THE Stillwater army was through, Alex and the girls followed, stepping into the idyllic realm of Starcross Pond. Hadrian paused in front of the portal.

"Vincent and I will stay behind. If we hear anything, we'll l-let you know," he said. The nervous royal looked perplexed, as if the weight of what was happening had just sunk in.

Alex nodded. "We'll do the same, but could you do me one last favor before you go?"

Hadrian frowned. "What is it?"

"If you walk around the forest outside the cave awhile, you'll see my Thunderbird—she should have arrived by now," he explained. "You might have to call her name to coax her out. She's called Storm. If you just tell her where I've gone, so she can follow, that would be great."

"Tell her where you've gone?" Hadrian repeated, incredulous.

Alex nodded. "I know it sounds strange, but she's a clever bird. She'll understand."

"Very well, I shall s-send your Thunderbird to y-you."

"Oh, where are we going, by the way?" Alex asked, realizing they'd need to know. He'd only seen Starcross from the air before, and had no idea where this field was in relation to the survivors' camp.

"Follow the r-river, and k-keep it to your righthand side. It w-will lead you to Ceres," Hadrian said. With that, the nervous royal pressed what Alex presumed to be the lotus-shaped gem, and the false wall slid back across the portal entrance, hiding it from anyone who might accidentally wander into the cave.

"Thank you!" Alex called through, feeling bad for the amount of pressure he'd loaded onto Hadrian's shoulders.

The group gathering on the emerald-green field had grown considerably with the arrival of the Stillwater students. Alex had been sure Ceres would accost them before they even set foot through the portal, but she was nowhere to be seen. He headed to the front of the group, where Jari and Aamir were trying to allay the fears of a few fraught individuals. They would have to follow the river that glittered just ahead, where the banks sloped down to meet the babbling water, until they found the survivors' camp.

"Not much farther to go," Alex promised, shouting to the gathered group. It was as Hadrian had said upon meeting them all in the Falleaf glade: they were all hungry, cold, and tired, with many of them injured. If they didn't reach a safer place soon, they would lose their resolve entirely.

Alex led the way across the field, which was fringed by regal-looking eucalyptus trees that rose to monstrous heights around the edges, their silvery trunks gleaming in the low afternoon sunlight. After clambering over a fence, they set off across another field, this one brimming with row upon row of vivid lavender, the scent so overpowering it almost stung the nostrils. Alex kept the river to his right, using it as his compass, though his eyes flitted toward the distractions all around, from the graceful flap of a "cabbage white" butterfly, half remembered from his grandfather's butterfly collection, to the sprawling wildflowers that seemed to take up every available patch of land. Across the river, fields of poppies stretched along the bank, the delicate scarlet heads dancing in the breeze, carefree and flourishing.

It didn't seem like the kind of place that had once been overtaken by the mist, but then again, Alex wasn't sure exactly what type of fallout had occurred in its wake. Did the Great Evil affect plants and animals in the same way as mages? Did it leave whole realms to wrack and ruin? Or did it simply kill and move on, like a rabid disease, sinking away once there was nobody left to consume?

"What is this place?" Ellabell asked, her blue eyes wide with awe, the bronze sunlight on her face making her look more beautiful than Alex had ever seen her.

"This is Starcross Pond," he replied, reaching for her hand. "There used to be a castle here somewhere, but it fell with the rest of the havens that didn't make it."

"It does not seem very fallen to me," Natalie commented.

Alex shook his head. "No, it certainly doesn't."

Such idle thoughts were cut short by the sight of strangely shaped figures moving toward them in the distance. They appeared small at first, but quickly grew larger, as if they were moving at a great speed. The earth shuddered beneath Alex's feet. He froze, wondering if they had just made a colossal error. What if Julius had somehow guessed where they had gone, and was charging toward them this very minute, having trapped them exactly where he wanted them? It seemed unlikely, but Julius was an unlikely sort of man, prone to being dangerously unpredictable; it was part of his power, part of what drove people to fear him.

"Get ready for a fight!" Alex bellowed. They were standing in a field full of blackberry bushes, and though he knew the spiny leaves wouldn't provide much cover, they were better than nothing.

Panic rippled across the faces of the group, but they rallied, moving into a rough formation, lifting their hands in the direction of the oncoming aggressors. Some dove for the cover of the blackberry bushes, curling up into balls at the bases of the plants, but most stood ready to fight, awaiting Alex's orders. Alex and his friends took to the front line, standing side by side, while they waited for the approaching individuals, whose numbers seemed to be expanding by the minute.

As they neared, Alex realized why their silhouettes had seemed so peculiar. They were riding horses—but these horses were no ordinary steeds. They were gigantic, muscle-bound beasts, built like draft horses, but taller and broader than any Alex had ever seen, with manes that streamed with feathers and beads. The entirety of their eyes were colored an alarming shade of white, though the centers seemed to glow with a pearlescent light that made Alex feel suddenly cold.

"What are they?" Jari gasped, voicing Alex's own question.

"Kelpies," whispered Helena. "I didn't think there were any left in the wild. I have only seen them in the royal stables," she added, looking just as awestruck as Jari.

So, Alex thought, *these are the creatures Julius threatened to have his wife ripped apart by.* Seeing them in the flesh made the idea of such a torture all the more horrifying; they looked like they could tear a bear apart in five seconds flat, so he could only imagine the mess they'd make of a weaker human.

Something in the back of his mind made him remember stories of these creatures, told by his grandmother when he'd asked for a particularly spooky tale. They were found in Celtic folklore and were said to be terrible water spirits who rose from lakes, rivers, and streams to entice local children to jump onto their backs. Once on, the children would always find they were stuck and could not get down again, no matter how they struggled. With the trap securely snapped shut, the Kelpies would walk back into the water, drowning their quarry and savoring the souls of the departed. Though, it was said, if a person could get hold of a Kelpie's bridle, that Kelpie would do the bidding of whoever controlled it.

Alex wondered how much truth there was in that tale, because these thundering beasts seemed to be very much under the control of their riders, of which there seemed to be about twenty.

Ceres was one such rider, her Kelpie speeding along the fastest, leading the cavalry charge. It pulled up short with a ferocious snort, just before it would have trampled Alex and his friends. He peered into the squad that had arrived, hoping to see the friendly face of Demeter, but the redhaired teacher wasn't with them.

"Alex?" Ceres snapped, a look of displeasure on her face. "What are you doing here? And who are all these people?" she asked, glancing across the large group. Behind her, the rest of the Kelpies pulled up, their riders giving firm tugs on the reins. In their hair, they all wore beads and feathers that corresponded to those on the manes of their mounts, and none of them looked pleased—neither animal nor human.

"I'll tell you everything, but first, we need help," Alex replied calmly. "Hadrian let us through. He knew you wouldn't let us suffer any more than we already have. These are evacuees from Spellshadow Manor and Stillwater House, and I am begging you to offer them your protection."

Ceres glowered at Alex with her one good eye. "You didn't think to ask first?"

"There wasn't time, Ceres," Helena cut in, her voice piercing through the pounding of settling hooves.

Ceres scrutinized the silver-haired young woman. "Helena, is it? I haven't seen you since you were a little girl," she mused. "I hope you aren't as similar to your mother as you look."

Helena flinched at the mention of her mother, who was still stuck in the cells at Stillwater. Alex glanced at her, wondering whether to step in or not. It wasn't something they'd had a chance to talk about yet, but surely she was worried about Alypia, given that Julius had descended upon the place.

"I am nothing like my mother," Helena hissed.

"Then we might get along," said Ceres, with a wry half smile upon her face. "What happened? If you can't give me the long version, give me the short one," she demanded, turning back toward Alex.

"There was a battle at Spellshadow. We managed to overcome Virgil, as you can see," Alex began, gesturing toward the still-unconscious Head. "But something went wrong with the spell, and the mist escaped. We had to evacuate. Helena wanted to return to Stillwater, but Julius was already there. This is the only place that's truly safe for us now. If we stay at any of the other havens, Julius will inevitably find us." He let the last part go unspoken: *and kill us all.*

Ceres's gaze settled on the frightened faces before her. Alex could read the thoughts in her eyes. They had done nothing wrong, nor had they done anything to deserve the position they were in. They were sheep left for the slaughter.

"You shouldn't have brought them here. My brother should never have allowed it," Ceres murmured after a drawn-out silence, shaking her head. Alex had a sinking feeling in the pit of his stomach that she was about to turn them away. "But, since you are all already here, I suppose I wouldn't be a particularly good Samaritan if I made you go back. Follow me," she said, with a heavy sigh.

"Thank you, Ceres," said Alex.

Ceres glared at him. "You and I will speak more later. I am only doing this because I could never live with myself if I didn't, but make no mistake—I am not pleased," she growled, turning her vast steed around and steering it the direction they had come.

The Starcross cavalry trotted at a slow pace, allowing the evacuees to keep up, but every so often the blank face of a Kelpie would turn, and Alex would feel a tremor of fear run through him as its white eyes stared him down, nostrils flaring, with hot jets of steam ushering forth from them. These were not domestic, friendly creatures, and it left Alex in awe of how Ceres and her squad of mounted riders had managed to control them.

After a long walk, longer than Alex had imagined it would be, they arrived at the edge of the encampment he had visited before. The tents billowed in the breeze, and the makeshift shanty homes creaked, but it still looked as beautiful as the first time Alex had seen it. There was something peaceful about the place that Alex couldn't put his finger on—perhaps it was the absence of royal influence, Ceres being the exception.

Pausing beside the river, the riders dismounted, keeping hold of the leather bridles that they unbuckled from the Kelpies' faces. They kept these in their hands, while the gigantic beasts trotted down the sloping banks and back into the water, disappearing beneath the surface with a froth of bubbles.

So the tale has some truth, Alex thought to himself, watching Ceres strap the Kelpie bridle to her belt. He imagined the creatures' watery abode was why he hadn't seen them before; Ceres hadn't had time to summon them when Alex had descended upon Starcross last time.

"You may follow Beulah and Conleth," Ceres instructed, gesturing toward two of her fellow Kelpie riders, a dark-haired woman and man. "Except for you, Alex, and your friends. You will follow me—and you can bring that *thing* along too," she added, nodding to the limp figure of Virgil, her tone carrying a warning.

The rest of the congregation hurried away after the riders, who seemed more affable now that they were down from their savage steeds. Alex stifled a gulp as he and the other five followed Ceres toward the large tent at the far edge of the shantytown, where he had been reprimanded by her before. The heavy scarlet material still flapped in the breeze, and the yellow flag perched at the top still rippled wildly.

Once they were all inside, Ceres turned on them immediately. "You realize he will come after you, don't you?" she remarked curtly. "I've spoken to you about this before—I *warned* you about this before, but you wouldn't listen, would you? Now, he's definitely going to find us. We have his wife, and we have the people who took her. He'll sniff us out like the wolf that he is. You understand that, right? You knew that the minute you stepped through that portal."

Everyone shuffled uncomfortably, not daring to look up at the fierce glare of the short-haired woman. It was true, Alex thought, they *had* known what they were doing by coming here, and yet they had done it anyway.

"There was no other—" Alex began, but she cut him off sharply.

"Don't you give me that crap, Alex," she snarled. "You could have integrated them into the Falleaf students. They would have been safe there, while you tried the spell again. It would have been a temporary measure, but no, you just had to be the hero."

"He was trying to do what he thought was best," Ellabell interrupted.

Ceres shot her a dirty look. "This wasn't it, sunshine," she barked, turning back to Alex. "You didn't want them to suffer anymore, and I get that, but you have put more lives in jeopardy than you know. They wouldn't have had to suffer for long, but now you've added untold horror for everyone here—*them* included."

Alex leveled his gaze at Ceres, the tension so thick it would break any blade that tried to cut it. He knew that, in hindsight, there might have been easier options, but they were here now, and there was no changing that. Julius was coming—it was just a matter of when. If they were all going to survive his arrival, they were going to need each other.

"Then I guess we'll have to put up a fight," he whispered, his gaze unwavering.

Ceres gave a bitter smile. "What choice have you given us?" she muttered, echoing words he had heard her brother speak, barely a few hours before. "Who knows, maybe we've been hiding too long... Maybe it's time something brought us out of our rabbit holes, to fight the wolf that put us here." She crossed her arms with a sigh, her expression grim.

Alex shuddered, feeling the presence of that very wolf sniffing them out as they spoke.

CHAPTER 6

T HEY NEEDED AN ARMY.

Ceres informed Alex that she would be arranging a public meeting shortly, to ask the opinion of the survivors. Any who wanted to fight would be permitted to, and any who wanted to hide would be taken far from the camp to set up another somewhere safer, where Julius might not seek them out.

With that decided, and Ceres in a decidedly less volatile mood, she showed the six friends to two spare tents, where they could rest and recuperate, though she insisted she take Virgil and lock him away where she could keep an eye on him.

"The last thing we want is for him to sneak off and tell Julius everything," she remarked, snapping her fingers to capture the attention of two Kelpie riders from earlier. They picked up Virgil, their muscled arms making the Head look lighter than a loaf of bread, and hauled him away.

"When he wakes up, I might need to talk to him about the spell—" Alex began.

"If you want to see him, come and find me first," Ceres said with a glare, letting Alex know, once again, who was in charge.

"Of course," Alex murmured, before heading into the tent that had been designated for the boys.

The tent was sparsely decorated, with a few roll-mats on the floor, a pile of motheaten blankets, and a couple of benches set up in a square around a central fire. It was here that Alex headed, lying flat on his back on one of the benches, staring up at the billowing yellow fabric of the roof. It had been a long day by anyone's standards, and it still wasn't over. Above all, he wanted to talk to Elias, but the shadow-man wasn't offering his company.

"I think your beastie has arrived!" exclaimed Jari, who was peering out of the tent flap.

Alex sat up. "Huh?"

"Your bird, dude. I think she's arrived." Jari grinned.

Wearily, Alex wandered over to the spot where Jari stood, and looked out. There was a commotion up ahead, where a large crowd had gathered. Looking closer, Alex could make out the silky, striking silver feathers of Storm, and saw her beak snapping at over-curious hands.

Alex smiled, pleased to see that she'd weathered the journey. Hurrying outside, he weaved through the crowd, heading toward the center, where she stood. Storm chirped when she saw him, and the crowd dispersed, whispering among themselves as Alex petted the creature on the side of her neck, as if she were any domestic animal.

"You made it," he whispered.

She chirruped loudly.

"I suppose we'd better put you somewhere safe," he said, leading her through the crowd toward the tents where they were staying. There was a shady spot just behind, with a few low-hanging willows draping their leafy fronds across a sun-dappled expanse. "How's this?" he asked.

Storm dipped her head and gave a throaty coo of approval.

Alex grinned. "Then I suppose I'll leave you to it," he said, watching as the Thunderbird moved off beneath the willow tree, where she hunkered down on her haunches and settled herself in the cool shade, like any nesting bird might. Resting her chin on her fluffy, feathered breast, her eyes closed, and soon, all that could be heard from beneath the willows was the soft cooing snore of a mighty Thunderbird. None of the crowd dared to follow her there, though some peered around the edge of the tent to catch a glimpse.

Knowing she'd be safe enough, Alex returned to the tent.

Jari and Aamir had gone off to explore the rest of the camp, so Alex was left alone with his thoughts. He took up his spot on the bench. This time, however, he didn't lie down. Instead, he pulled the satchel from his shoulder and lifted the flap, pulling out the thick book inside. He almost hated the feel of it as he brought it out onto his lap. This was the thing that had caused them so much suffering, and yet they still needed it. He was just glad he'd had the foresight to snatch it up before they'd made a run for it; otherwise, they'd really be in trouble.

Folding out the pages at the back, Alex forged a thin gauze of anti-magic and placed it over the glyphs, watching as they rearranged themselves into proper letters and sentences. Even now, the novelty had not quite worn off.

He scanned the text to find what he had missed, to uncover what had caused the catastrophe at Spellshadow. However, as his eyes glanced down at the page, he got something of a surprise. Where, before, the lettering had been clear and easy to read, now the words had faded, the ink less bold, the wording harder to make out. It was like someone had left the pages out in the sun too long.

"One failed attempt," a voice whispered in his ear. Alex jumped, nearly dropping the book. Elias cackled as his wispy form floated onto the bench.

Alex scowled and scooted as far away from the shadow-man as he was able. "Did you know this would happen?"

Elias gave a careless shrug. "It's rather obvious, isn't it? If you fail again, the words will continue to fade. On the third and final try, the book will return itself to its cozy little home in the vault."

"But what went wrong? We missed something—how could we have missed something?" Alex ran a hand through his hair in frustration.

Elias looked suddenly uncomfortable, his shadowy lips pursed, his galactic eyes shifty.

"What do you know, Elias?" Alex asked, his tone accusatory.

"Yogodarongblod," Elias muttered.

Alex blinked at him. *"What?"*

"You got the wrong blood."

Alex turned sharply in the shadow-man's direction. "The wrong blood?"

Elias nodded his wispy head. "It had to be the blood of the ruler, the blood of the one who sits on the throne."

"And you didn't think to say this *sooner*?" Alex growled.

Elias held up two dark fronds. "Hey, don't go blaming me! I didn't know until the mist rose. Until that moment, I thought we were dandy."

Alex had been wracking his brains, and hadn't even fathomed that the blood was the issue, until Elias had mentioned it. Now that it had been spoken aloud, it made complete sense. Venus's blood wasn't the same as the blood running in Julius's veins, and his was the blood of the ruler. Venus, as his wife, had married into the title—she had not been born to it, as Julius was.

"So we have to get our hands on the king's blood," Alex murmured.

"If you can move close enough to the guy without him sucking the life out of you, yes," Elias said, rather unhelpfully.

Alex sat up straighter, struck with a sudden thought. "Well, we do have leverage—Venus."

"You may have his wife, but what exactly do you plan to do with her? I wouldn't really consider Julius the deal-making sort," Elias purred.

"It's our best shot—heck, it's our only shot right now," Alex said, pausing thoughtfully. "We could offer him his wife back in return for a vial of blood. Getting rid of the Great Evil is in his best interest, anyway. There's no reason for him to refuse."

"I think you underestimate how much our dear king enjoys doing things on his own terms," the shadow-man tutted, waggling a shadowy finger.

Alex clutched the edge of the bench, trying to rein in his irritation. "Would you stop with the endless pessimism? Or at least offer up a better idea, if you're going to be so critical about everything."

"What can I say? I'm a realist," Elias replied blithely. "But don't point the finger at me when it all goes awry. If you manage it, I'll eat my own hat."

"You don't have a hat," Alex remarked.

Elias grinned. "Precisely—*that* is how confident I am."

"Confident in my failure? How very uplifting of you,

Elias. Remind me never to ask you to give a pep talk," Alex muttered.

"Well then, you'll be pleased to know you're about to get a brief reprieve from my glorious presence," Elias said, smiling.

Alex frowned. "What do you mean?"

"Since you believe I am not pulling my own weight—not that I weigh a whole lot," he cackled, "I have decided that a book hunt is long overdue. You require answers, and I shall seek them out. Should only take me a few days, perhaps longer... Depends what else I find on my travels," he said, with a sly wink.

"Why do you need books?" Alex asked, not quite following.

Elias sighed. "After all this time, you still don't see the glory of literature. Everything is in books—people can't help but write things down. Every little thing. If someone has successfully done this spell before, even if it only happened once about a million years ago, I will find it, and I will figure out if there's anything else you did wrong, or anything else you need to know, to ensure it doesn't go wrong again. So, *ciao* for now, Alex Webber—don't miss me too much!" he taunted. With that, the shadow-man disappeared in a swirling vortex, leaving Alex alone with his thoughts.

Leaning his elbows on his knees, Alex was still trying to process his options when Aamir and Jari walked in wearing awkward smiles. Jari was munching on a handful of what looked like pecans, presumably found on his and Aamir's exploration of the camp food stores.

Alex gave an apologetic wave. "Have you been waiting outside the tent?"

"We didn't want to interrupt your chitchat. Sounded intense!" Jari said through a mouthful of snacks.

"How much did you guys hear?" Alex asked, slightly embarrassed. Elias always made him feel like a petulant child, and he didn't like to think of his friends seeing him as anything but calm and collected.

"Only a little," Aamir said, at the same time Jari announced, "Pretty much everything."

"Great," Alex replied drily.

"At least we know what needs to be done, right?" Aamir asked with an apologetic look.

"Yep, just need to strike a deal with the devil," Jari said. "Easy peasy."

Alex stood up. "Well, there's one more thing I need to do, to make sure I haven't overlooked anything important with the spell." Even though Elias had gone to do just that, Alex couldn't rely on the shadow-man being back in time, and, with Spellshadow exploding in a cloud of silver mist, they didn't have the luxury of waiting anymore.

Aamir raised an eyebrow. "You want to talk to Virgil?"

As always, it surprised Alex how perceptive the older boy could be; he had assumed he hid his thoughts well, but it seemed he wore his heart on his sleeve more often than not.

"Exactly. Virgil has gone through this four times now, counting our most recent failed attempt," Alex said with a sigh. "So if anyone knows the pitfalls, or has any ideas, it's him."

"I bet he'll give you a hard time," Jari commented. "I wouldn't feel like talking to the person who hijacked my brain and almost got me killed. Although you could always just rummage around in his head if he doesn't cooperate." He waggled the fingers of his free hand.

"We can come with you, if you'd like," Aamir offered.

"He might be more open to talking if it's one-on-one," Alex said, hoping that would be the case. Neither Jari nor Aamir seemed surprised at his response.

"Have fun," Jari said, flashing a peace sign.

"And do let us know what you find out," Aamir added with a knowing look.

Alex promised he would and assured them that he would be back soon, although he knew he had a somewhat bad habit of leaving his friends out of the loop. He just didn't want to drag them into making tough choices, not if he could spare them the mental anguish he was going through when it came to the counter-spell. This wasn't exactly a "problem-shared, problem-halved" kind of event.

If he wanted to talk to Virgil, he would first need to find Ceres. The vividly remembered image of her riding the Kelpie had also given him an idea.

Heading out of the tent, he turned toward the spot

where he had left Storm sleeping, and emerged between the narrow passageway that led between the girls' tent and the boys'. Sitting on the low fence that ringed the back of the two makeshift shelters was Ceres, her one good eye gazing intently at the sleeping Thunderbird, who was nesting beneath the shadow of the willow trees, oblivious to her watcher. Ceres turned as Alex approached, a serene look on her face; it was an expression he hadn't seen on her before, and it knocked him slightly off guard. He had been expecting the brutal, no-nonsense Ceres, but this one was different.

"She's something else." The short-haired royal spoke first.

Alex nodded. "She certainly is."

"Where did you find her?" Ceres's attention moved back to the resting Thunderbird.

"She found me," Alex laughed, though her interest made him curious. "How did you find your Kelpies?"

Ceres smiled. "Through a similar experience. They were thriving here when we arrived. I didn't expect anything to be alive, and then there they were... beautiful creatures, just trotting around on the riverbanks."

"Aren't they dangerous?" Alex asked, not sure he'd call those monstrous beasts beautiful. Imposing, perhaps, but not beautiful.

"All wild things are dangerous, Alex. Your Thunderbird is dangerous, but she trusts you, and you trust her, and there is a partnership between you. People who don't understand that unique bond would seek to domesticate her, but she should never be tamed. That's where they went wrong, way back when—trying to domesticate creatures that should always be wild..." She trailed off wistfully, before snapping back toward Alex. "Anyway, what did you come out here for? Were you looking for me?"

Alex nodded. "I need to speak with Virgil."

"I thought you might." Ceres sighed. "Come with me. He should be awake by now."

Alex did as he was told, trailing Ceres through the encampment, walking past the curious eyes that watched them as they went. A few people whispered furtive words as he passed, though he tried hard not to hear what they were saying.

"I hear he's a Spellbreaker," one muttered under their breath.

"I hear he's something else entirely—neither mage nor Spellbreaker," another breathed.

Before long, they had reached the outskirts of the camp, moving past the spot where Alex had landed on that first visit. Ceres was showing no signs of stopping, though she paused for the briefest moment at the edge of the riverbank before crossing over to the other side, wading through the knee-high water without hesitation. Alex followed, feeling the cold squelch of water in his shoes as he hurried up after her. They appeared to be keeping to a worn-out track that led along the perimeter of a gaudy poppy field, where the flowers bloomed in a variety of different shades, some unfurling blue petals, others showing off purple ones, with the occasional white flower popping up between the bolder variants.

They came to a halt at what looked like an ancient windmill, though the sails had long since broken off into a heap of splintered wood at the base of the structure. Two sentries stood at either side of the entrance. They straightened to attention as Ceres approached.

"How are the prisoners?" she asked.

"One is asleep, one is awake," said the sentry on the right.

"Which is doing which?" Ceres enunciated.

"The lady is asleep, the gentleman is awake," said the sentry on the left.

Ceres smiled. "Very good. Thank you. My friend and I are in need of an audience with the gentleman—we won't be long."

The sentries opened the heavily bolted door and gestured for them to enter.

Inside the windmill, the air was stagnant, though the floor was clean and the walls were devoid of grime. Sunlight shone in through thin, slit windows, pooling on the flagstones in two long rectangles that crossed in the center. Around the circular room were four large, heavy-duty cells, the iron bars reinforced with twisting vines of gray ivy, and the dull glow of a protection spell or two. Inside two of these cells were Virgil and Venus, though, upon closer inspection, it was clear that Venus was asleep in hers, breathing softly where she lay, curled up on a rather soft-looking mattress, a thick blanket tucked around her chin. Virgil, however, was not so quiet.

"Not you again! Can't I get a moment's peace?" Virgil hissed, smacking the iron bars hard with the palms of his hands. "If you think you can make me do that spell again, you're out of your mind," he added, his expression furious.

"Good to see you're awake and ready to chat," said Alex, more confident now that Virgil was behind bars.

"I won't do it, Webber," Virgil retorted.

"We got you out, remember? You'd be dead if it wasn't for us," Alex reminded him, recalling the way the silver mist had surged toward the Head and his magical half.

"I almost died because you used me as a puppet, in a spell you were woefully unprepared for!" Virgil snapped back.

Alex felt a surge of shame and annoyance at that statement, but he tried to keep his tone measured. He didn't want to argue with the Head; he just wanted to talk.

"And that's why I'm here. That's why I saved you. That's why... That's why I need your help, Virgil."

"I suppose he put you up to this too, looking at me with your doe eyes—or doe eye, I should say," Virgil sniped, turning his attention to Ceres, but she seemed unruffled by his words. Instead, she simply stared at Virgil for a moment, something strange passing between them, his fury calming, before she opened her mouth to speak.

"Come on, Virgil, I know you want the same things we do," she said softly. "When we were kids, we used to play together. Do you remember? You, me, and Hadrian. When your sister was cruel, I stood up for you, and when Julius tried to hurt my brother and I, you stood up for us—do you remember?"

A thoughtful expression fell across Virgil's face. "I think I still have the scar," he whispered.

"When the war ended, you said you hadn't wanted to follow Julius's orders. Both you and Hadrian hated the thought of running the schools," Ceres continued. "The two of you only did it so somebody worse wouldn't step in—somebody who would relish the task of torturing and killing children. My brother was made to remember that recently, that he was never in this for the long haul, or for the nature of the job. I'm asking you to remember that too." Ceres stepped forward, and to Alex's utter shock, she grasped Virgil's skeletal hands through the bars.

The movement seemed to take the Head by surprise too, his strange eyes glancing down at Ceres's hands holding his, as if nobody had ever touched him before. When he looked back up at her, his eyes were filled with tears, though they refused to spill down his cheeks. For the first time, Alex felt like he could see a glimpse of the Virgil that lay beneath the bony façade—a scared man, out of his depth, treading water the only way he knew how. And, though Alex couldn't begin to forgive the things Virgil had done in the name of saving his own skin, he could, at the very least, begin to understand.

CHAPTER 7

"WHAT DO YOU WANT TO KNOW?" VIRGIL asked, a look of defeat on his face.

Alex glanced at him in surprise. "Really?"

The Head shrugged. "Why not. I'm not getting out of here anytime soon—let's just say I'm feeling charitable." The clipped edge to his voice had returned, and his eyes were once again bone dry, but there was a new softness in his posture, brought on by Ceres's coaxing. Alex cast a grateful nod in the one-eyed royal's direction. She nodded in return, then left to join the sentries by the door, leaving the two of them alone with a sleeping Venus in the cell nearby.

"How much do you know about the spell?" Alex began. "I don't know how conscious you were in the pit, but, needless to say, the spell went haywire."

"Spellshadow Manor has fallen to the mist?" said Virgil, furrowing his pale brow. He seemed both saddened and relieved by the news.

Alex nodded.

"Do you know why yet?" Virgil asked.

"I've read over the book, but Elias said it might have had something to do with the blood we used," Alex explained.

Virgil gave a tight laugh. "Let me guess—you used dear queenie's over there, instead of Julius's?"

"How did you know?" Alex asked, suspicious.

"I made the same mistake, the first time," said Virgil.

Alex wanted to curse under his breath. What had happened at Spellshadow could have been avoided, if he had only tried to pry more information from Virgil beforehand. It was obvious now—he'd had a veritable fountain of information right in front of him, and he simply hadn't bothered to use it. Not enough, anyway.

"And the other times?" he asked.

Virgil shrugged. "It's hard to say. I've tried to imagine what more I could have done, but I've never managed to come up with the answers."

"I don't imagine you tried very hard." Alex snorted.

Virgil flashed him an angry look, showing a pain in his eyes that Alex had never seen before. It was almost as if Alex had physically struck the man. For a long while, Virgil said nothing, though a whole spectrum of emotion rippled across his skeletal, sunken face. Finally, he began to speak. His voice was tight, like he was combating a great feeling he could not ignore.

"You might not believe me when I say this, but I really did endeavor to do the spell to the best of my ability, when Julius demanded it of me. I was prepared to sacrifice my life for the good of others—not that it was much of a life," Virgil said quietly, his eyes taking on a far-off look. "I never wanted to fail. I gave it everything, followed the spell to the letter, and each time it went awry. The first time, Snowthorn Temple fell, as Spellshadow will undoubtedly have done now, though two havens had already fallen to the silver mist by then, given that we had nothing in place to prevent it.

"At Snowthorn, the mist surged up and engulfed everyone—those who escaped ran to other havens, seeking sanctuary. When it failed the second time, at Summerfire Hall, that haven had already been evacuated. With the third... Well, you know how it goes by now." He sighed remorsefully. "After that, the book returned to the vault, and Julius changed tact. He knew the Great Evil could be restrained by the essence of mages, and so he implemented the schools and Kingstone, for just such a purpose. I was made Head as punishment, no doubt, for my failure—sent to seek out unknowns from the outside world and train them up, only to end their lives." He paused, his chest rising and falling quickly, the words taking a visible toll on him.

Alex was speechless. Never in a million years had he thought he would begin to sympathize with a man like Virgil, but here he was, feeling a pang of something close to it. For some reason, he believed Virgil; he believed that the Head had tried his best, but had failed anyway. The pain in the skeletal man's voice was not something that could be easily faked.

"But you don't know where you went wrong, exactly?" Alex pressed, wanting to know more.

"I have my theories," replied Virgil, his eyes gleaming.

"Tell me everything," Alex said.

"In the first attempt, the problem was the blood. I didn't know how important it was to have exactly the right blood, and Julius refused to give it to me, citing the sanctity of blood such as his, so Venus volunteered. I thought it would be fine—I read the text the same way you must have," he explained. "In the second attempt, I think I must have fumbled a line somewhere. The blood was correct, but halfway through the spell, I misread a line... It had faded by that point, I believe," he said, looking at Alex curiously, as if for corroboration.

"The book has faded for me too."

"Indeed... Well, I fumbled the line, and the mist rose again," Virgil continued. "Then, the third attempt failed, but there was nothing amiss. I would stake my life on it, that I had completed the spell precisely as instructed. The blood was right, the words were right, the motions were right, but the earth rumbled all the same, and out poured the silver mist. It has plagued me for years, that last attempt. I have gone over it countless different ways, looking at it from every angle, but I promise you, I can think of nothing that I did wrong."

Alex frowned. "Surely, you must have done something wrong, though?"

"I must have, but I can't think what—for decades, as I say, I haven't been able to come up with the answer," Virgil murmured, his expression thoughtful. "Once, I thought I had it, but I wasn't able to try it again. Too much time had passed, and Julius wasn't interested."

"What did you think it might be?" Alex pressed, excited by the prospect of positive information.

The Head flashed a cold smile in Alex's direction. "That depends."

"On what?"

"On whether you're planning to make me your mind puppet again," Virgil said, his voice menacingly low.

Alex paused, not knowing what to say. They both knew the truth of the matter, and Virgil had exposed it. There was no way Alex could deny it, and he doubted he could convince Virgil to do it of his own accord.

"Your silence speaks volumes," murmured Virgil, a half-amused smile on his face.

"I guess it depends on whether you'd do it willingly, without my... mental assistance," Alex replied, trying to call the royal's bluff.

Virgil smiled, pulling the skin taut over the protruding bones of his features. "You'd like that, wouldn't you?"

"Is that a yes?" Alex asked evenly.

"I'll tell you what…" He paused, clearly wanting to leave Alex on tenterhooks. "I will think about it. Upon my word as someone who, in truth, wants what you want, I shall think about it. After all, I have lived a long time with my guilt— who knows, perhaps I'll have an epiphany." A strange, sad expression passed over his face that Alex couldn't quite understand. Perhaps the Head actually did feel remorse for the things he had done, and the ghosts that lay in his wake.

Ceres approached them, hands on her hips. "We should be heading back," she said to Alex. "I have a meeting to attend in the central square, and I'd rather not leave you here unsupervised."

Alex didn't want to leave, not with the carrot Virgil had just dangled in front of him, but he knew he had no choice. Ceres would demand he follow, and he reasoned it was better not to cause a fuss. However, he was certain he would return to pick up this conversation where it had left off.

"Until next time," murmured Virgil, still smiling that elusive smile.

"Until next time," Alex echoed, before following Ceres from the windmill. As he passed Venus's cell, he saw that she was still sleeping, looking so peaceful beneath the blanket. Although… He looked closer, noticing that her breathing had slowed, the snuffling sound of her slumber easing off.

She wasn't asleep at all—she had been listening to every word, though for what reason, Alex couldn't be sure. He just hoped it wasn't something sinister. Venus was an anomaly to him. He couldn't quite place where her loyalties lay, or which way her moral compass pointed. The only thing he knew for certain was that she was stronger than she looked, and could endure Julius's wrath. Maybe one day she would reveal her true colors, one way or the other.

The walk back was a silent one, both Alex and Ceres deep in thought. He glanced at her now and again, wondering if she was going to speak, but she never did. Alex, for one, didn't want to get too excited about the prospect of Virgil doing the second attempt at the spell, in case it came to nothing, but he couldn't help feeling the tiniest flicker of hope that the Head might truly come around to the idea.

There was a commotion when Alex and Ceres returned. Someone was running across the fields, and the riders were mounting their Kelpies to cut the figure off, strapping on the bridles that kept the bulky, terrifying creatures obedient.

"Stop!" Ceres bellowed, her voice carrying across the crowd that had gathered.

The riders turned.

"Ceres! We tried looking for you—there's an intruder, just come through the portal," said the closest rider, a young woman in her twenties with flowing, dark blond hair.

"Sorry, I got tied up," Ceres apologized. "No need to ride out. That's my brother."

The young woman turned to look at the figure, who was fast approaching. "Hadrian?"

Ceres nodded. "Many of you haven't seen him for a very long time, but yes, that's him. I'd question what he's doing here, but I think I might have an inkling," she remarked, flashing an accusatory look in Alex's direction.

Although Alex felt slightly guilty, he was distracted by what Ceres had said about many of them not seeing Hadrian for a long time. Perhaps, Alex thought, that meant Hadrian had never set foot in Starcross himself; he just ferried the weary survivors over the border, where Ceres and her mounted band of merry men saw to the rest. It was the perfect hiding place, if it was secret even from the one who brought the people through. But now, thanks to Alex, Hadrian had evidently been forced to break his self-imposed distance.

They waited patiently for him to arrive, the riders letting their steeds return to the water, bridles strapped firmly back to their belts. As Hadrian neared, it was clear this messenger wasn't coming with good tidings.

"It's b-bad news," Hadrian gasped, sprinting the last few meters to where Alex and Ceres stood.

Ceres placed her hand on her brother's back, rubbing it gently. "What happened?"

"Julius has f-finished with Stillwater, and h-he has c-come to Falleaf," Hadrian explained. "He is f-furious, angrier than I h-have ever seen him. I m-managed to slip away w-without being s-seen, but I n-need to hurry b-back before

BELLA FORREST

he r-realizes I am m-missing," he stammered, his eyes wide
with fear. "He knows s-someone is r-responsible for t-tak-
ing his wife, and h-he won't s-stop until he f-finds out who
d-did it. I w-will divert h-him as m-much as I c-can, but you
should s-still be safe if you s-stay here. He doesn't know anything about it y-yet, and I p-plan to keep it that w-way!"

"Why did you come, Hadrian?" Ceres asked softly. "Were
you followed?"

Hadrian shook his head. "I m-made sure I w-wasn't. I
had to k-keep you updated, as p-promised."

"Here, let me at least take you back to the portal, before
you collapse from exhaustion," Ceres suggested, calling her
Kelpie from the river. Hers was the biggest of the herd, standing almost a foot taller than Alex, its shoulders rippling with
muscle, its hooves the size of dinner plates. Still, the one-eyed
royal hopped up like it was a pony, and pulled Hadrian on
behind her.

"Thank you for warning us," said Alex, reaching up to
shake Hadrian's hand.

"I j-just pray he d-doesn't find you," Hadrian replied, his
stammer worse than ever.

Still gripping Hadrian's hand, Alex leaned in close to the
royal's ear. "Set up a parlay—set up a meeting between me
and Julius. I want to negotiate."

Hadrian gazed at him in abject horror. "You're not s-seri-
ous?" he hissed.

"I'm deadly serious. If you don't set the meeting up, I'll

78

come anyway. If the meeting is a go ahead, leave a letter at the portal door… I'll check for it every day," Alex whispered.

Ceres charged off before Hadrian had a chance to answer, which suited Alex nicely. Now, the nervous royal would have no time to argue—though now that Alex thought about it, he wasn't as sure of himself. It had been an impulsive request, borne from the glimmer of an idea that was formulating in his head.

If Julius was at Falleaf, that presented a window of opportunity Alex couldn't ignore. In order to attempt the spell again, they needed Julius's blood, and the only way to get that was from the man himself. Alex wasn't an idiot—he knew he could never overcome someone as powerful as Julius, not unless he wanted to become a pile of goop on the floor. Nor did he think he could get close enough to steal some, which would undoubtedly have the same result, as Elias had implied. No, the only way to get the blood in a large enough quantity was to do something even more stupid, perhaps—he would have to negotiate with Julius, for as much as he dared.

Elias had said that Julius was the kind of man who did things on his own terms. Even if Julius and Alex called a truce while the spell was performed, Alex knew that when the dust had settled and the Great Evil was gone, the king would likely continue the removal of essence for his own sick pleasure, or to see how else it could benefit his relentless desire for power. The outcome would be the same if they stole the blood. Julius wouldn't care, as long as the mist was purged. But, if

Alex negotiated terms and garnered the release of all the students in return for the removal of the Great Evil, they might know true freedom. The dwindling number of magical babies would no longer matter, nor would the threat of death continue to loom over the mage world. That, surely, was tempting for anyone… even Julius.

CHAPTER 8

FTER WATCHING CERES AND HADRIAN RIDE AWAY, Alex felt a sense of trepidation. *Maybe I was too hasty,* he thought, but it wasn't important now. The deed was done. He planned to go to the portal as dawn was rising each morning, to check for any messages, though the trek there would undoubtedly be a long one. He just hoped he could sneak away without anyone noticing him.

Just then, a figure burst through the crowd, bounding toward Alex. The red hair was unmistakable.

"Alex!" Demeter cried. "While the cat's away, the rats will hide!" he added, though Alex wasn't sure what that was supposed to mean. Still, it brought a smile to his face.

"Demeter," Alex replied, greeting the ex-teacher warmly. "I was wondering where you'd gotten to."

"Indeed, I heard some strangers had arrived, and I knew it could only be you guys. I was up at the farm, helping out."

"There's a farm?" Alex asked, incredulous.

"Oh yes, they have everything here—it's quite the operation. My Ceres is one hell of a woman." He sighed, flashing Alex a borderline inappropriate wink.

Alex laughed. "She really is a firecracker."

"Venus is still locked away. I've made sure of it," Demeter said.

"Yeah, I've just gone to see her." Alex paused. "Well, not her exactly. Virgil is here too. I had a few questions for him. The spell failed."

Demeter's expression suddenly became somber. "Where are the others?"

"They're all okay," Alex assured him. "We've been given two tents to stay in, up at the back of the camp. I was just heading back there, if you want to join me?"

"Delighted to!" Demeter grinned, before following Alex through the camp. The crowd that had gathered to see Hadrian's arrival had dispersed somewhat, but a few eyes still followed the pair as they made their way through, Alex deliberately keeping his head down so as not to draw too much attention.

The group of five was sitting outside in front of a fire, where a pot of something delicious smelling was boiling.

Alex's stomach rumbled for the first time in a long while. With so much going on, he'd pretty much forgotten about such luxuries as eating a good meal.

The group turned, their discussion halted, but when they saw who was with Alex, their faces morphed into expressions of sheer joy. It was a feeling Alex shared; it was always good to see Demeter, who brought his unique brand of calm happiness to any room. Though Alex knew that the auburn-haired man was capable of mood-changing magic, he was never quite sure if it was his special skill or just the ex-teacher himself that made everyone feel at ease.

After greetings had been made, and Demeter had caught up with the events that had led them all here, they sat down to the meal Aamir had prepared. Alex had never known it before, but the older boy was an exceptional cook, and had apparently raided the camp spice store in order to cook the evening's dinner.

"Is there chicken in this?" Alex asked.

Aamir shrugged. "Don't think so. I asked for a bunch of raw, mostly vegetable ingredients for this stew, but they came pre-chopped and mixed up together. Looks like some kind of poultry, though, doesn't it?"

Alex had a sudden urge to go and check on Storm.

"I'd say this was anything but a poultry meal!" Demeter joked, which made the whole group laugh. The joke itself was terrible, but the laughter was a beautiful, treasured sound, which Alex had forgotten could even exist. There had been so much seriousness that it seemed they'd all held off on joy. But now, here at Starcross Pond, where everything felt just that little bit safer, it seemed like the right time to rediscover some levity.

After eating the delicious food, which had been bulked up by a fresh green salad that Ellabell had prepared from the camp allotments, and some soft, salty sweet potatoes that Natalie had been roasting under the coals of the fire, they lay back and looked up at the stars beginning to dot the early night's sky. They twinkled in the hazy dark blue, and, just for a moment, Alex almost believed he was on a camping trip somewhere with his friends, far away from any of this. It was a nice feeling, ruined only by the knowledge of what he had arranged with Hadrian. Tomorrow morning, he would have to go to the portal and see if the nervous royal had done as he'd asked. In truth, he wasn't sure which outcome he'd prefer.

As dawn broke, Alex slipped out of the tent and hurried along the back of the encampment. It was easier than he had expected, given that most of the camp was still fast asleep. Jari and Aamir had been snoring soundly when he'd left, undisturbed by the soft sound of his bare feet creeping across the tent floor. He'd only dared put his shoes back on once he was out of the makeshift home, though his feet got damp on the dew-soaked grass, making him shiver slightly. The sun was only just rising, and its rays were yet to cast their warm glow upon the earth. As Alex walked, he could see his breath in the air in front of him, and pulled his sweater a little tighter to keep out the morning's chill.

A few people were milling around the central square, a rudimentary center point to the camp with a well in the middle, the perimeter forged from a rickety fence. The other inhabitants were dressed for hard labor, their boots thick, their sweaters even thicker, with scarves and bandanas wrapped around their heads. Many of them were carrying tools, a couple lugging spades and pitchforks over their shoulders, but none of them acknowledged Alex as he slipped past.

He kept an eye out for familiar landmarks. The blackberry bushes came and went, as did the lavender fields, until, finally, Alex found himself heading toward the outcrop of rocks where they had stumbled through the portal the day before. From this side, the portal itself continued to glow, the surface rippling like a pool, though it showed only rock behind it, where the false wall had been drawn across.

At first, it didn't look like anything was different, but when Alex approached, he noticed something resting on the trampled earth beside the portal. It was a wooden box, the top decorated with golden inlay in the shape of a crown. Alex's heart seized in his chest. He knew the symbol could only mean one thing.

Crouching, he picked up the box and held it for a moment, his hands trembling. Taking a deep breath, he flipped open the lid. There was a small scroll of thick cream vellum inside, tied with a scarlet ribbon that stood out vividly against the pale background. With shaky fingers, he untied the ribbon and opened the scroll, tucking the box under his arm.

Dear Evasive, Vexing Stranger,

I am not usually one for taking requests, but Hadrian tells me you would like to meet, so that you and I might have a parlay. Whilst I do not know you, you intrigue me. As such, I have decided that I shall agree to your desire for an audience, so we might have ourselves something of a negotiation. Fear not, I shall listen, and I shall consider. Who knows, perhaps we seek the same objective? Perhaps you'll find me on a particularly giving sort of day, though I must say, capturing my beloved wife was a mistake. However, should I hear your reasoning, forgiveness is not entirely out of the question. I expect you to practice your excuses in the interim before our meeting. Fail to prepare, prepare to fail. I can appreciate time and effort, and I do love a good speech.

I wait, in anticipation of your arrival, no later than midday tomorrow. I presume you know the way? Oh, and while I am certain you are not working alone, I would request that you come to meet me by yourself. I will not tolerate others intruding on our conversation. In fact, if I hear even a whisper of your accomplices, our meeting is off, and you can be sure such insolence will not go unpunished. The nuisance you have caused me is not the work of one man alone. After all, no man is an island. However, you stand representative for the aggravation you have caused.

Yours in expectation,

King Julius

P.S. I cannot abide tardiness. Be late, and I shall execute you on the spot, even though Hadrian has counseled me against such rashness.

Alex re-read the note several times, hardly believing that it had come from Julius's own hand. The pompous tone definitely belonged to the king, and though there was lenience within its words, there was a warning too. It was clear that Alex had annoyed the king, but maybe, just maybe, he would be prepared to listen if Alex could offer something that couldn't be ignored. And the price Alex planned to ask for was so small, in the grand scheme of things. A couple hundred captives released in return for a kingdom free of fear—free of the Great Evil.

Then again, Julius was a known psychopath. Perhaps such an offer wouldn't be nearly tempting enough for a man like him. After all, why would he give up his playthings when he loved to torture? Alex shuddered, knowing he had to remain confident in the fact that Julius couldn't force him to do the spell, even if he wanted to. His mind was a Spellbreaker mind, off limits to mage-kind. If Julius wanted the Great Evil gone, there would have to be some bargaining, and Alex firmly hoped the king knew that.

Looking back into the box, Alex saw another compartment underneath the first, which contained another piece of vellum, though this one bore no writing. A miniature, slender quill lay beneath it. Steadying his hand, Alex wrote his reply in his neatest handwriting:

Dear King Julius,

It is most kind of you to contemplate my request, as I know you are a very busy man, with plenty on your plate these days. As such, I would be delighted to accept an audience with you, and I assure you, I shall come prepared, and I shall come alone. Expect me at midday—I will not be late.

Yours in anticipation,

The Evasive, Vexing Stranger

Curling the scroll back up and placing it in the main compartment, Alex set the box back down by the side of the portal. He pocketed the king's letter. His reply seemed polite enough, though he hadn't been able to help himself from putting a few sly remarks in there, hidden among the propriety. Julius probably abhorred rudeness, but Alex had a feeling he could get away with sarcasm, at least when it came to a man who took himself so seriously.

With the box set back down, Alex took off across the fields, racing for the camp. The sun was getting higher in the sky overhead, and he knew the others would be rising soon, if they had not done so already.

All around him, birds began to sing, harmonizing in a late dawn chorus, and the chirp of grasshoppers could be heard in the long grass that grew among the wildflowers. This place was a true sanctuary, and he wanted to protect it. No matter what happened, he wouldn't give the secret of this realm away, not even on pain of death. He owed the survivors that much.

Slowing his pace, he walked across the last of the fields until he could see the camp emerging in the near distance. Smoke was rising from a few of the structures, with breakfast underway for many of the encampment dwellers.

Unseen, he moved around the perimeter, keeping to the edges until he saw the familiar sight of the willow trees, with Storm resting underneath. He wandered up to her, and her bright eyes gazed up at him. She chirped loudly in welcome, and he stayed with her awhile, sitting up against the soft feathers of her wings, contemplating the steps that had brought him here. His old life seemed to belong to someone else, and, not for the first time, he wondered what he would even do if he managed to get home. How could someone continue with normality after going through so much?

"No use in thinking about that just yet," he said, patting Storm's neck.

She gave a low coo that sounded almost sympathetic. He smiled, still in awe of this beautiful beast, who had put her trust in him and allowed him to become a part of her world. It was like Ceres had said—Storm was a wild animal, never destined to be tamed, but their bond was undeniable. He thought about Leander Wyvern, and how he must have felt about his own Thunderbird, Tempest. Had they shared moments like this, man and beast, once upon a time?

Brushing himself off, he walked over to the gap between the two tents where his friends were, and slipped into the narrow passageway. Ellabell was already up and about, boiling something in a pot dangling over the fire they'd used last night. She was crouched low on the ground, blowing into the embers, trying to get the flames to rise, although she didn't seem to have the natural chef's talent Aamir possessed.

"Don't you have a spell for that?" Alex asked, amused.

Ellabell turned in surprise. "There you are, Alex! When I woke up, you weren't in your bed—everything okay?"

"You went into the boys' tent to check on me?" Alex asked, a quirk of a smile upon his lips.

Ellabell flushed a little, the pink highlighting the freckles around her nose. "I was about to make some breakfast, and wanted to see if you'd like some," she mumbled. Alex stepped forward, and she put her arms around his waist, the action as natural as a sigh. "You didn't answer my question, Alex."

He nuzzled her hair, which somehow smelled of wildflowers. "I think it'll be okay."

"What do you mean?" she pressed, leaning away from him, a peculiar, worried expression passing over her face.

"Let's get everyone out here," said Alex solemnly. "I have something I need to tell you all."

CHAPTER 9

WITH EVERYONE GATHERED, ALEX SETTLED DOWN to tell them the plan. Jari rubbed his eyes sleepily, having been rudely awoken, but the girls looked remarkably fresh-faced. They sat around the fire, clutching cups of coffee flavored with cinnamon—another of Aamir's unexpected culinary delights. As Alex began, an anxious air fell across the group.

"When Hadrian arrived here yesterday, I asked him to do something for me," said Alex. "I asked him to send a message to Julius so that we could arrange a meeting and negotiate terms. Julius sent a letter back this morning, agreeing to meet with me, and I plan to go ahead with it."

A gasp rose from the group.

"Do you have a death wish?" Helena spoke first, shaking her head in disbelief. "That man is insane. He'll kill you as soon as you're near him."

Alex smiled. "He won't. I'm too valuable, and what I have to offer will be too tempting for him not to hear me out."

"That is a bold assertion, Alex," Aamir remarked. "You know Julius's mind doesn't work like other people's. He might not care what you are, or what you can do. I hope you considered that fact."

Alex nodded. "I've thought of every possible scenario."

"Yeah, and each one ends up with you *dead*, dude," Jari said, looking equally incredulous.

"I really don't think so," Alex replied. "He might be angry about Venus, but, at the end of the day, he wants what we want. As long as the Great Evil is around and the magical realm is having fewer magical children, his kingship is in jeopardy. Who wants to be king over nothing? Or, worse, who wants to be king over a sea of corpses, once the mist gets loose because there's no more essence to feed the Great Evil?"

"I think Julius just might prefer the latter," Ellabell said, a stern look on her face. Alex could understand her sudden shift in mood; he hadn't spoken to anyone about what he planned to do. Heck, he hadn't really spoken with himself about what he planned to do—it had been impulsive, but it felt like the right path.

Alex looked down into his empty coffee mug. "I think

this is the only option we have. We know now that the blood was the problem with the first spell attempt, and if we're going to do it again, we need Julius's blood anyway. If I can get Julius to give us his blood willingly, then that's one less thing to worry about. Otherwise, how do you suggest we take it from him?"

This one seemed to stump the group, who glanced at one another with uncertain looks. It had been hard enough to get the blood from Venus, and that had been a spur-of-the-moment plan. Retrieving it from Julius without him knowing was more or less out of the question. Even getting near him would be impossible without him sounding an alarm or executing them on the spot. Julius was far stronger than any mage they had encountered. A face-to-face meeting in a civilized setting was the only way, as far as Alex could see.

"Why didn't you tell us what you were planning?" asked Natalie, eyeing Alex with a disappointment that made him quickly jump to his own defense.

"It just happened. I saw an opportunity, and I seized it. Once Hadrian had left, I couldn't take it back."

"And when are you supposed to be meeting with him?" Ellabell cut in, her voice wavering.

"Tomorrow at midday."

"Are you definitely going to go?" Natalie pressed.

"I think I have to," said Alex.

Jari gave a tight laugh. "I think you're an idiot."

"I'm not feeling too smart myself, right now." Alex smiled

wryly, knowing he probably should have consulted his friends first. However, another feeling stirred within him—a sense of panic, of fear that they might try to come with him. He had arranged this fool's errand, and he would see it through on his own.

"You know we're coming with you, right?" Ellabell said, confirming Alex's fears.

He shook his head vehemently. "Julius told me to come alone. In the letter, he specifically said that if I bring anyone along, there'll be trouble and the meeting will be off."

"Why would he want you to come alone? Surely, he'd want as many of us there as possible, so he could deal with us all in one fell swoop," Aamir reasoned, making Alex wince at the thought.

"I've got no idea—those were just the terms he set," Alex said with a shrug. "Maybe he really is open to a discussion?"

Natalie snorted. "Please, Alex. Even if he hears you out, what reason does he have not to imprison you?"

"This arrangement would benefit him more than anyone else," Alex insisted. "Once the Great Evil is gone, he won't have any use for essence. I'll make him see how much his kingdom will adore him, once they discover that the threat has been vanquished because of him. He loves flattery, and I can flatter with the best of them." He tried to lighten the mood, but it was clear that nobody was impressed.

"You think we're just going to let you walk into the lion's den without any backup?" Helena spoke, putting on a firm tone. "Do you not know any of us by now?"

Alex sighed. This wasn't what he had wanted to happen, and, now that it was happening, he wished he'd just kept the meeting to himself. As immoral as it might have been, at least he would have been sure of everyone's safety. After almost losing Aamir to the mist, he simply wasn't prepared to put anyone else in the line of fire, not when he could get the task done by himself. Now, he realized it would be difficult to head to the meeting without the others trying to follow.

"You can't be thinking about running off on your own, Alex Webber," remarked Ellabell, flashing him a chiding look that made his cheeks flush pink. "I say we take a vote on it. As I see it, we have three options: Alex doesn't go at all, Alex goes with us as backup, or Alex goes alone."

Alex cut in, not wanting the decision to be taken out of his hands. "Look, I know you all want to help, but it'll put us in more danger if we defy Julius's wishes," he said, meeting the eyes of each of the five. "I'm going alone, and that is final." He stood defiantly.

"Sit down, dude, you're not going anywhere—this is bigger than just you," Jari said.

"Fine... but don't I get a say?" Alex asked, Jari's words forcing him to sit back down on the fireside bench.

Natalie shook her head. "You are too biased. This decision is between the five of us. We have heard your side of the argument, and we shall take it into account in making our decision."

Alex sat back, dreading how the vote was going to go.

Ellabell went first. "I think we should go with him. It's stupid for him to go alone, given what we know about Julius. He'll just kidnap him and force him to do the spell. If he's going, he needs backup and an escape route, should things go south," she said firmly. "So, my vote is he goes, but he goes with us."

Aamir was second. "As much as I hate to say it, I believe Alex should go alone. Julius is a volatile man, but I think Alex could be right. Maybe, just maybe, he is willing to strike a deal. There will never be an opportunity like this again, to retrieve that blood so simply. I know I must sound naïve, but I have a feeling in my gut that Julius genuinely wants what we want, in the grand scheme of things. Why rock the boat by defying the king's wishes? That's more likely to get us killed than anything else."

The older boy spoke a lot of sense, and Alex flashed him a grateful look, though Aamir's features remained a blank canvas, giving little away.

Jari chimed in third. "Are you insane? I can't believe you just said that. You vote he goes alone?"

Aamir nodded. "That is my vote."

"I think you're mad. Of course we have to go with Alex—we can't just leave him to that lunatic. No way, José. I'm with Ellabell—I vote he goes, and we go with him," said Jari simply, giving Aamir a rough shove in the shoulder.

Natalie was next. "Hmm… Well, I am afraid I do actually

agree with Aamir. Either Alex goes alone, or Alex doesn't go at all. I realize they are two uncompromising options, but they are the only two I feel we should be thinking about. I do not feel the king will kill Alex, or force him to do anything, when Alex is already offering to do the spell. There would be no point," she explained. "This is a win-win situation for Julius, and if we tag along, we threaten to ruin that. I vote he goes alone."

And so, the deciding vote fell to Helena, who shifted uncomfortably in her seat.

"There are pros and cons to each side of the argument," she began softly. "I can see the benefits of Alex going alone, and I can see the benefits of us going with him. However, knowing you all as I know you, and knowing my grandfather the way I do, I cannot, in good conscience, let Alex go alone. I vote we go with him."

It wasn't the result Alex had wanted to hear, but he was relieved they had at least reached a consensus. Three against two—they were all going to Falleaf together. Aamir and Natalie glanced at the others, who looked back. There was tension still, between the two sides. Alex just hoped it would dissipate in time for their departure. Not that he was planning on actually letting them go through with him. He still had a few ideas up his sleeve.

"Okay, decision made," said Ellabell, her relief evident. "We leave for Falleaf in the morning, as a group."

"Yeah, so don't try anything funny, man—we've got our

eyes on you," warned Jari, doing spooky wide eyes in Alex's direction.

With that, the group disbanded, but for the rest of the day, Alex constantly felt like a shadow was following him. No matter where he went, he felt watchful eyes on him, keeping tabs on his whereabouts. It was exasperating, but he understood why. In their shoes, he'd have done the same.

Seeking solitude, he disappeared across the riverbank, toward the windmill, though he slowed as he saw the guards standing sentinel at either side of the entrance. They wouldn't let him in without Ceres, and he didn't feel like going to find her just so he could speak with Virgil again. Besides, the Head probably hadn't come up with an answer yet—Alex had a feeling the skeletal man was keeping him waiting on purpose. Again, Alex couldn't blame him. He had intruded upon the Head's mind, and forced him to do something he would otherwise not have done, in precarious circumstances that had almost gotten him killed. Why would he give Alex an answer straightaway, just so he could rest easy?

Instead of heading up to the entry, Alex turned right and walked along a narrow path covered in crushed shells and tiny pieces of gravel. It was well worn, and Alex soon found out why. Ahead lay the allotments, and the farm that Demeter had spoken of. In fact, the auburn-haired man was there, wrangling with some small creatures that looked a lot like boars, though they had six tusks going up the length of their snouts and large, floppy ears that flapped as they ran from their keeper's grasp. Ceres was there too, laughing at the scene, a broad smile lighting up her face. Giving up, Demeter wandered over to where Ceres sat perched on the corral fence. His hands were muddy from wrestling with the boar-like creatures in the dirt.

"Don't you dare!" Alex heard her cry as Demeter lunged to smother her face in the muck. Ceres squealed, trying to wriggle free of him, but he just held her tighter, pulling her in for a kiss that Alex didn't feel he ought to be spying on.

Embarrassed, he returned the way he had come, wondering what it would be like to have a relationship that seemed as carefree as theirs did. Out in the real world, could he and Ellabell play around like that, laughing like they had no worries? He hoped so, and yet he wasn't sure he'd ever get to find out.

On the walk back, he realized something—the only way to evade his friends, and travel alone to Falleaf, was if he left when they least expected it. Sure, they'd definitely be anticipating a sly move, maybe thinking he'd go at dawn like he had that morning, but if he did it when they had been claimed by sleep, perhaps he'd get away with it.

Yes, thought Alex, *in fact, I could go now, and hide out in the forest at Falleaf until morning.*

That settled it. With that firmly in his mind, he set off back the way he had come and allowed himself to think of the meeting itself, and how he might persuade Julius to see things from his perspective. He knew he was going to have to flatter the king and make him see how beneficial all of this would be for him, if he would just give them a small amount of his blood. It would be the quickest and cleanest of Julius's kills, and he could do it without lifting a finger. That was what Alex knew he needed to focus on—how easy and noncommittal the act would be for the king, but how good it would make him look to his royal citizens.

As Alex crossed back over the riverbank, the group of five was waiting for him on the other side.

"Thought you'd like a bit of company," chirped Jari.

"Aamir has something delicious cooking, if you're hungry?" Ellabell added, smiling.

"Just wanted to check you weren't feeling any desires to go for a jog," Natalie teased.

Alex realized, with absolute certainty, that he wasn't going anywhere by himself. Even if he tried to slip away in the early hours of the morning, he had a feeling they would be setting up sleeping shifts to prevent him from doing just that. They weren't stupid, and as much as he loved them for that, he wished that, just this once, they would let him keep them out of harm's way.

The atmosphere of the group improved as day led to evening and evening wore on into night, with Alex even relaxing a little as he feasted on some roasted figs, dripping in honey, that Aamir had cooked for their dessert. Full and content, he stood up, the fire dancing against everyone's faces, casting strange shadows.

"Right, well, I'm exhausted—I'm going to hit the hay," he said, waiting to see how the news would go down. Surprisingly, nobody seemed bothered, or questioned why he wanted to go to bed so early. It confirmed his suspicions that they had already set up watches to make sure he didn't slip away.

Ellabell smiled sweetly. "Goodnight."

"Sleep well," added Jari, grinning.

Lying back on his roll-mat, staring up at the yellow fabric of the tent, Alex pulled the blanket tight around him and pretended to sleep. As he lay there, he could hear the chatter and laughter of his friends, still sitting around the campfire. For a sad moment, he felt completely alone—excluded from the group, peering in from the outside. Brushing the feeling off, he turned over, squeezing his eyes shut. Wasn't solitude what he'd been seeking, after all?

An hour or so later, he heard Aamir and Jari enter the tent, milling about before settling down on their roll-mats to sleep. With one eye open, he glanced over at where they had lain down, but saw that Aamir was, in fact, sitting in a chair by the tent flap instead. He waved at Alex, a cheeky grin on his face.

"Sweet dreams," he teased, and Alex turned over with a frustrated sigh.

At around three in the morning, the adrenaline successfully keeping him awake all night, Alex unfurled, sitting up slowly. Pausing, he listened closely to the sounds around him, but the soft snoring sounded genuine. Pleased, Alex crept past Jari and Aamir and ducked out of the tent flap, only to see Natalie sitting directly in front of him, facing the tent entrance from the fireside bench, the flames flickering behind her.

"Back to bed, if you would be so kind," she said, smiling. "I would hate to have to wrestle you to the ground."

He had been caught. Undoubtedly, no matter what time he tried to creep out, someone would be waiting for him. Briefly, he considered using his anti-magical travel to zip over to the cave entrance, but there wasn't enough room inside the tent, and he didn't feel like getting himself tangled in the fabric.

Grumbling under his breath, Alex backed away and returned to his roll-mat, where he lay down, closing his eyes and allowing sleep to come. There was no use fighting it anymore. There was no way he was going back to Falleaf on his own. Smiling to himself, he realized it had likely never been a possibility. Never had he felt luckier, and more exasperated, to have such good friends.

CHAPTER 10

T HE GROUP ROSE EARLY, EATING BREAKFAST AROUND the fire, joking with Alex about the previous night's escape attempts. From the clock attached to one of the bigger buildings that sat around the central square of the camp, they could see that it was only ten a.m., meaning they still had plenty of time before they needed to set off for Falleaf. Still, Alex was adamant about leaving earlier than they needed to, remembering Julius's words about what would happen if he was late.

"Are we ready?" he asked, picking up the satchel with the book in it. He planned to take it to the cave and leave it hidden there, with instructions for the others to bring it back to

Ceres should anything go awry. He didn't feel right leaving it at Starcross, nor did he think it wise to take it to the negotiation, in case Julius decided to snatch it.

The others nodded, so they headed out of the camp, walking along the outer perimeter. Passing Storm, Alex wished he could take her with him, but there was no reason to throw her in harm's way too. He could only imagine what Julius would do if he saw a Thunderbird—he'd no doubt want to add her to some awful menagerie he had, or perhaps he'd make some horrifying taxidermy out of her. Either way, it wasn't something Alex wanted to dwell on. No, she was definitely safer at Starcross.

The morning sun was warm on their faces as they passed through the fields of wildflowers, followed by the rows upon rows of blackberry bushes, and then into the fields of lavender, the strong scent startling their nostrils. It was an oddly enjoyable walk, despite the challenge that lay ahead. Birds wheeled above, and scurrying creatures hopped and sprinted across the grass, ducking into the shade of nearby woods when Alex and his friends passed by. Things were almost ordinary in this realm, as close to the outside world as any realm he'd seen.

They were setting foot onto the final field, the shape of the rocky outcrop visible just ahead, when the thunder of hooves shook the ground beneath their feet. Alex whirled around, catching sight of a dust cloud rising in the near distance, and the unmistakable forms of four charging Kelpies emerging from the haze. They were moving at a rapid pace, and gaining on them fast.

Alex didn't know whether to run for the portal or stand his ground, and in the end the group simply waited, with bated breath, for the horsemen to arrive. There was no way they could have reached the portal before the horses got there, and Alex knew that only the guilty ran. If Ceres wanted to know where they were going, then he would tell her. It seemed only right, after the reluctant kindness the short-haired woman had shown them.

As they neared, Alex saw that Demeter was riding beside Ceres, sitting astride a Kelpie equally terrifying looking as hers, with two others, whom Alex didn't recognize, riding behind. Once the four riders had pulled their steeds to a halt, the Kelpies snorted hot air from their nostrils and pawed the ground with their hooves. Somehow, they appeared to have grown in size since the last time Alex saw them, their white eyes staring him down.

"Stop right there!" Ceres bellowed, her eyes as furious as those of her steed.

Alex lifted his hands in a gesture of surrender. "What's the matter?" he asked.

She jumped down from her horse, landing neatly on the ground. "You know exactly what the matter is, Alex," she spat, striding up to where the group stood. "There are rumors flying around that you're headed to see Julius."

"Who told you that?" Alex countered.

"Never mind who told me—is it true?"

Alex nodded. "It is, but if you'll hear me out, I'll tell you why."

"I don't need to hear you out; this is a stupid, reckless thing to do," she snarled, evidently not in the mood for negotiation. "Not to mention the fact that you're putting my people in danger—more than you already have. Don't you care about anything other than your ridiculous 'mission'?" Her chest heaved with emotion, her eyes narrowing. Demeter and the other two riders stayed where they were, though the auburn-haired man flashed a questioning look at Alex.

"It's not ridiculous if it means they can be free," Alex replied calmly. The last thing he wanted to do was get into a mudslinging match with Ceres, given the tight schedule they were on. It had been ten when they'd left, but the walk over had taken at least half an hour, and would be much the same on the other side, from cave to pagoda.

"Listen to yourself!" Ceres barked. "You think going to Julius will do you any favors? You think he'll just roll over and give you what you want? I *know* Julius a damn sight better than you do, and I know you won't come back from Falleaf if you step through that portal."

Helena stepped forward. "He's my grandfather, Ceres. I think I know him a lot better than you do. He'll see the benefit in what we're trying to do. Everyone will love him, and that's exactly what he wants most." She spoke softly, looking Ceres dead in the eye.

Ceres scoffed. "You weren't there when war broke out. You weren't there when he implemented the essence system, with such a look of glee on his face—you'd think he'd just been given the best gift in the world. You don't know him at all, girl, and you're a fool if you think you know him better than I do."

Helena's cool façade slipped slightly at Ceres's sneer, and the two royals looked tense, almost poised for a fight. Before either could make a move, Alex stepped in, wanting to defuse the situation as quickly as possible.

"You both know him well enough to think that he just might hear me out," he said. "We don't want to fight you, Ceres. You're our ally. But, please, don't stand in our way. I know I've said it before, but I'll repeat it until I'm blue in the face, if it'll make you see sense. This is the only way we can get what we need to do the spell that could end *all* of this suffering."

Ceres shook her head. "You're idiots. Young, stupid idiots. We were doing just fine until you came along, and you are set to ruin everything," she snapped.

Natalie stepped up beside Helena and Alex. "If you think protecting a small portion of people who've had half their souls torn out is 'doing just fine', I think it might be you who is the idiot," she said coolly, though Alex instantly wished she hadn't.

"What did you just say to me?" Ceres whispered, a hint of menace in her voice.

Natalie looked alarmed by the change in tone. "What I meant to say is… If you think what's going on now is okay, you have a very warped view of the world."

"This world *is* warped," Ceres snarled. "You just haven't been around long enough to see it. You are *not* getting through that portal, if stopping you is the last thing I do!"

With that, she lunged forward, an orb of magic spiraling from her hands and heading toward the group at breakneck speed. It caught Jari in the leg. He fell to the ground with a hard thump. Aamir ran to him, helping him up, as the others moved to intercept Ceres. Natalie and Helena worked on the offense, sending wave after wave of shining bursts, with Ellabell attempting to shield them against Ceres's onslaught of golden orbs.

The two riders behind Demeter jumped down and sprinted to their leader's aid, sending bolts of energy toward Ellabell's ankles. They were strong, despite the fact that they must have been two of her half-soul survivors, but Alex dispensed with one of them swiftly, letting his anti-magic coil around her legs, causing her to stumble forward and fall flat on her face. Only Demeter remained astride his Kelpie.

Jari took out the other rider, slamming a barricade of magic into the man. It knocked him out, rendering him useless on the ground, unmoving, though still breathing. Jari flashed a grin in Alex's direction. At least now, there was only the one-eyed royal to contend with, though that wasn't much of a consolation. Ceres was ferociously strong, as Alex had imagined she would be. Her hands were moving so fast that Alex couldn't even see them, let alone the direction in which her magic was flowing. A few orbs hit him, and though they didn't have nearly as much impact as they had on the others, it still felt like a heavyweight boxer had punched him hard, the blows winding him.

Jari was up and fighting again, though Aamir hung back, given his reduced ability where magic was concerned. Alex made sure he got between any blasts of magic and the older boy, not wanting to aggravate his situation, as none of them knew what might happen if he really got hurt. The three girls were holding their own, however, forming a powerful trifecta, their magic mingling into one jet of supreme energy, before it was sent surging toward Ceres. The one-eyed royal managed to dodge most of their attacks, and the shield she had set up around herself was proving pretty much impenetrable, the golden glow of it glittering around her body like a shroud. Wave after wave of magic rushed from her palms, whizzing across the grass.

With a cry of pain, Ellabell crumpled to the ground, only to stand up again a moment later, her face contorted in agony but her resilience undamaged. Natalie got hit in the arm, but she simply continued to conjure with just the one hand. Helena was the most impressive, her hands moving almost as fast as Ceres's, dispensing attacks just as quickly, the bronze bristle of them crackling through the air like fireworks. Still, nothing seemed to affect Ceres. Being a royal, she was already infinitely more talented and able than Alex and his friends, with the slight exception of Helena, but she had experience on her side too—real, battle-hardened experience.

In truth, Alex wasn't sure how they were going to win this, and they were running out of time. If he was late in meeting Julius, he knew he may as well not bother going. It would signal almost certain death.

A spinning javelin of raw, golden energy sliced through the top of Helena's chest, just by her collarbone, cutting straight through her into the grass behind. It pierced through the shield Ellabell had put up as if it wasn't even there. Helena gasped, her eyes going wide, her body frozen. Natalie and Ellabell both grasped for her as she began to topple over, and it was precisely the moment Ceres had been waiting for. With their guard down, she raised her hands to strike, building a twisting orb in the center of her palms.

Alex rushed forward, forging a sword of anti-magic in his hands, only to catch sight of Demeter. The auburn-haired man had slid from the back of his Kelpie and was walking up to his beloved, his movements slow and silent. Ceres was so engrossed in her fight with the group that she didn't even see him until it was too late. Breaking apart her shield with his own powerful magic, he rested his hands gently on the sides of her head, and wove silvery strands through the skin of her temples, into her mind. Her one good eye went blank as she fell limp in his arms. Demeter caught her, sinking to the ground and holding her tenderly to him, while he continued to weave the mind-control magic into her brain, halting her fighting spirit.

"Go," he whispered, looking up at Alex and the others, his expression glum. "And make sure it's worth it."

They didn't need telling twice, with the sands of time slipping away at an alarming rate. Natalie and Ellabell gathered up a recovering Helena, and they all sprinted for the portal. There was a familiar-looking, lotus-shaped gem on this side of it, which Alex hadn't noticed before. Pressing it in, they watched as the false rock face slid back, allowing them through to the cave beyond. They hurried in, not wasting a moment more.

Alex wished he had a way to check the time. Through the thick canopy of trees, he could see that the sun was a little higher in the sky, but he didn't know what that meant—were they already too late?

Knowing they'd have to chance it, they continued through the forest, running as fast as they could, avoiding any traps that sprang up along the way. Even so, Alex knew it was taking them far longer than he'd like. They came to the edge of the forest, the pagoda rising in front of them. Koi carp swam lazily in the pools of the water gardens, the petals of the pink and white lotus flowers swaying gently in the breeze that rippled the surface of the ponds. The calm scenery did little to slow Alex's racing pulse, however, especially once he caught sight of the soldiers.

There were more military personnel than usual, due to

the celebrity staying within the walls of the pagoda, but Alex knew they would be expecting him. The others, however, were not exactly welcome guests.

"You're going to have to hide yourselves outside, in the trees, but close enough that you can help if I get into trouble. A few of you can maybe hide up on the walkway of the top floor, if you're careful—the guards don't patrol the walkways, so if you keep low and climb fast, you should be okay," he whispered, pointing toward the open wooden balconies that surrounded each floor. They were only accessible from the pagoda windows, or if someone was a very good climber, so Alex knew the guards had little reason to patrol there. "If anything happens, I'll send a spear of anti-magic out through one of the windows. That'll be your signal to help, and for us to get the hell out of dodge, okay?" he added rapidly, knowing he was really cutting it close.

"We've got this," said Aamir confidently. "Go on, before you really are late."

Alex nodded, waiting a moment until his friends had gone a little farther up the tree-line before emerging into the bright sunlight, where everyone could see him. To his right, he saw Jari and Helena dart across the gap between the trees and the cellar, without incident. The sight gave him some degree of comfort, and he steeled himself as he continued his walk forward.

"Halt! Who goes there?" A soldier came forward, pointing a nasty-looking saber in his direction.

Alex cleared his throat. "I am Alex Webber. I have an audience with the king."

The soldier gave him a cruel smile. "Ah, so you're the one we've been expecting? I thought you'd be bigger," he said mockingly. "Well, I suppose you'd better come with me." With that, he marched toward the front entrance of the pagoda—a beautiful, carved archway with two iron double doors, painted a deep, sea green. Alex smiled despite himself, realizing he'd never actually come through the front door of this place before.

He could smell rice and onions cooking in the kitchens as he followed the guard through the doorway and into a grand reception hall with countless golden statues arranged around the room, shaped like foxes, raccoons, and the turtle-like kappa—creatures of folklore. They stared at him with eyes of precious jewels as he was directed toward the stairs.

"Fifth floor. The king is awaiting you," the soldier sneered.

Alex paused. He had presumed he'd be meeting with Julius on the top floor. Still, if anything went wrong, his friends would be close enough to come to his aid. He hoped so, anyway.

He had just climbed the stairs to the fifth floor when he saw a familiar figure turning the corner, heading straight for him. His head was low, and he was wringing his hands. It wasn't until he was almost upon Alex that Hadrian looked up. Once he did, and saw Alex standing there, a look of pure,

113

unadulterated horror flashed across his face.

"What are you d-doing here?" he asked. "Oh no, no, n-no, this is b-bad—this is very b-bad."

"Julius asked me to come," Alex said, frowning. All his previous good feelings had fallen away at the sight of Hadrian's expression. Perhaps all this had been a colossal error in judgment.

"No, no, n-no, why would you c-come here!" Hadrian hissed. "This wasn't part of the p-plan."

Alex furrowed his brow with worry. "What do you mean? This *was* the plan."

"No, no, n-no, dear me, I didn't think y-you were r-reckless enough to actually c-come! Have you l-lost your m-mind?" Hadrian hissed. "Did anyone s-see you?"

"A soldier sent me up," Alex replied.

Hadrian let out a long, exasperated sigh. "Well then, I g-guess there's n-nothing for it. You're g-going to have to s-see him now. He's b-been placing b-bets all morning on whether y-you'd actually show up. I c-can't believe y-you have." He shook his head and led Alex to a door at the far end of the hallway.

"The letter told me to come here," said Alex, incredulous about what he was hearing. He replayed the letter over in his head, wondering if he'd missed some subtle warning, telling him not to come after all.

"I know it did, b-but I didn't expect y-you to actually d-do what it asked," Hadrian muttered. "Well, no, that's not t-true. I knew you'd c-come if he c-called, I just h-hoped you wouldn't."

"Sorry, Hadrian," Alex said. "I had no choice. I have to try."

Hadrian sighed, cracking half a smile. "I k-know. He's w-waiting for y-you." He opened the door and gestured for Alex to enter.

It was a room Alex was fairly sure he'd seen before, with tapestries on the walls that appeared to move as a person walked past them, shifting to another image, showing another panel in the tale it was trying to tell. A clock sat on the mantelpiece above the fireplace at the nearest end of the room. It read eleven fifty-five. He had just made it.

At the end of the room sat a throne, which looked as if it had been dragged in here purely for the purpose of this meeting, so Julius could really put on a show. It was gigantic and garish, with twisting golden vines making up the frame, each one embellished at the top with a jewel the size of Alex's fist. Plush, red velvet cushions lay at the bottom of the vines, and atop those cushions sat Julius, a smug expression on his face.

"The stranger, I presume?" purred Julius. "Just in time, I see."

Alex nodded. "Yes, Your Royal Highness," he replied, remembering his manners. "Though my name is Alex Webber."

"We've met before, haven't we?" the king said quietly, a suspicious look in his eyes.

"Yes, Your Royal Highness. We have met twice before."

"Twice?" Julius snapped.

Alex inhaled deeply, calming his nerves. "Yes, Your Royal Highness. Once at Kingstone Keep, and once here, when I served you and your lady wife, the queen."

Julius got up and prowled toward Alex, coming nose to nose with him, the way he had done at Kingstone. "Ah yes, now I remember you," whispered the king.

CHAPTER II

A SECOND LATER, JULIUS MOVED SHARPLY AWAY AND began to pace, walking up and down the lengths of tapestry. Alex didn't dare speak until spoken to, and so he stood there silently, awaiting the king's next words.

"You know, I loathe it when things are stolen from me," Julius said quietly, pausing to look at a tapestry depicting a great battle, Thunderbirds flapping in the sky, the glint of magic and anti-magic clashing. "I do not tolerate thieves, and *you* are a thief, are you not?"

Alex took a deep breath. "Not in the way you would think, Your Royal Highness. I have not stolen anything of yours with the intention of keeping it. I firmly intend to give it back. I suppose I am more of a… racketeer than a thief."

Julius smiled. "A good word. I like it. And what makes you a racketeer? I already know of your blackmailing exploits where that nervous wreck Hadrian is concerned, but if you think you can blackmail me, in the same way you have done him, you are sorely mistaken."

Alex tried not to let his bemusement show on his face. Blackmail? Alex guessed it must have been a ruse Hadrian was using, in order to keep up the pretense of being allied with Julius. If Alex was the bad guy, Hadrian could continue to be neutral in Julius's eyes, giving him the opportunity to see and hear things he otherwise wouldn't be able to. Once again, Alex marveled at the resourcefulness of the anxious royal, who somehow always seemed to be one step ahead.

"I would never think to blackmail you, Your Royal Highness. Hadrian is a different creature entirely—like chalk and cheese, the pair of you could not be more different if you tried," Alex replied. "Blackmailing a man like Hadrian is easy. Blackmailing a man like you would not be."

Julius suddenly sped in Alex's direction, circling him. "So, is it a ransom you want? Think very carefully about your reply."

The to-and-fro of Julius was unsettling, with Alex never knowing if the king was going to lunge toward him or drift away. The man was like a shark, stalking its prey, sizing it up before going in for a bite.

"No ransom either, Your Royal Highness. I took your

property; I admit to that. I took the queen, without your consent, and for that I am sorry. But I took her for a very good reason," Alex began, aware that Julius was now behind him, breathing down his neck. "I took her because I needed to broker a deal with you, and I believed her to be a valuable bargaining chip. I needed to get your attention, so we might meet like this. You would not have met with me if I were some nobody who mattered little to you. The truth is, I wanted to matter to you—I had to matter enough that you would agree to this." Alex gestured between himself and the king.

Julius smiled, puffing out his chest a little. "Well, you have certainly gained my attention, though whether you will keep it remains to be seen," he remarked, laughing coldly in Alex's face.

"I wanted to strategize like a king," Alex ventured. "I wanted to think the way a leader would think. So, I stole Venus from you and took her hostage, because that is what a leader would do. With her in my grasp, I now have something to offer you in return for what I want, where before I didn't. Are you familiar with Sun Tzu's *The Art of War*?" he asked, taking a gamble.

Julius nodded. "I know it well. I have read it many times," he replied proudly, his eyes glancing at Alex with curiosity.

"Excellent. Then you will be familiar with the quote, 'If you know both yourself and your enemy, you can win numerous battles without jeopardy'?"

Another eager nod. "I know it very well. I can recite much

of that book by heart, I have studied it so intently," Julius replied, though Alex had a feeling the king was embellishing the truth slightly. Still, it was clear Alex had his interest.

"Then you must understand why I did what I did. I had to meet with you, to know you, and know where your weakness lay, so we both might win the battle we seek to fight, without anyone having to die or any war being waged," Alex pressed on, pausing as Julius flew toward him, raising a hand as if to strike. Alex trembled, watching a swirling orb of magic appear beneath the king's palm, preparing for it to smash down on his face.

"You think I have a weakness?" the king spat, his spittle flying across Alex's face.

Alex shook his head. "No, no, that's not what I meant. Of course you have no weakness—you are the strongest, most powerful man in the magical realms, and undoubtedly beyond," he said hurriedly, conscious of the heat of the swirling magic on his face. "I simply meant that I had to take something you cared about, to make you care about getting that property back. It was my way of knowing how to get to you, so we could talk—that is all I meant," he added, hating the fact he was referring to Venus as "property".

For a moment, Julius kept the burning ball close to Alex's face. Then he drew it slowly away and wandered toward a bookshelf, his index finger scraping along the spines. "I see. You were strategizing, as you say, using ideas from Sun Tzu's fine text?"

Alex nodded. "Indeed, Your Royal Highness. That is what I was doing."

"Very shrewd," said Julius, evidently impressed. "So, what is it you want to put on the table, in exchange for my wife's safe return? Though, I think you put too much weight on how much I care for her. If she returns to me tainted in any way whatsoever, any deal we might make is terminated, effective immediately. Is that understood?" he warned, though it was clear in his eyes how much he actually did care for his lost "property".

"I understand, Your Royal Highness, but I assure you she is being safely kept and treated well," Alex said. For the briefest instant, he thought he saw a wave of relief pass over the king's face, but it was gone as soon as it had appeared.

Storming over to his throne and sinking back down into the plush velvet cushions, Julius waved his hand in Alex's direction. "Go on then, get on with it. What is it you want? I can't guarantee I'll give it to you, or that you will even leave this room alive, but you have intrigued me enough that I will listen to what you have to say," he said, unsettling Alex even more.

What if it didn't even matter? What if Julius heard him out, but simply didn't care about the future of the magical realms, so long as he got to be king of whatever remained? Gulping quietly, he hoped his friends were in place, to help him if things quickly turned sour.

"In essence, Your Royal Highness, I want what you want,"

121

Alex began. "I want to see an end to the Great Evil, and the scourge it has caused upon this land. I have the power and the ability to do that, but in order to succeed, I need your blood. A small amount of it, that is all. In return for doing the spell, or getting my volunteer to do it, in this case, and returning your wife to you unharmed, I would ask only that you promise to release all the students from the havens and allow them to return to their families, be they in the outside world or another magical place. If they wish to study, then make those havens real schools, with no death waiting for them at the end of their school days," he suggested, coming to the end of his proposal. "That is all I ask in return for ridding the world of the Great Evil, and giving back your wife. Though, I should point out, you will receive the accolade of such a task. You will be named the one who destroyed it, and rid the magical realms of it forever, allowing everyone to live in safety and security, once and for all."

Julius said nothing for a long time, tapping his slender fingers against the bejeweled armrest. His eyes narrowed as he scrutinized Alex. The silence was deafening, and Alex knew he'd prefer anything to the awful tension he felt gathering in his chest. At any moment, he knew Julius could end his life, and he couldn't stop thinking it was about to happen. There was something about the king that instilled that kind of fear in a person; there was an unpredictable, antsy, psychotic quality that emanated from him in terrifying waves.

"I admire your gumption, Alex Webber." He almost

hissed the name. "I suppose there is bravery in you coming here and asking these things of me," he said, flicking small, fast-moving darts of golden magic in Alex's direction, smirking as they sailed past Alex's shoulder. It was like a game, to see how close he could get the dart to Alex, without actually hitting him. "I wish you hadn't stolen my property first, but I can see bravery in that too, now you have explained it to me. Perhaps a deal of this kind might not be so bad. I can certainly see how it could work in my favor," he mused, a dart zinging beneath Alex's ear.

Alex tried not to flinch, but he had to duck out of the way of another dart as it narrowly missed his eye. "It would be entirely in your favor, Your Royal Highness. Your people will be free, and they will adore you for getting rid of the evil that has loomed over them for so long. The cost to you is low, in comparison. A few hundred people, in return for your realm fully restored to you."

Julius nodded thoughtfully, chuckling to himself as a dart skimmed the skin of Alex's neck. A tiny, almost imperceptible snowflake drifted down onto Alex's shoulder.

"Why should I trust a Spellbreaker?" Julius sneered, throwing another dart that made impact with Alex's chest. It hit him like a freight train, surprising him, given the dart was so small. He gasped for air as it was knocked from his lungs. Julius laughed.

Clawing back his breath, Alex rallied. "You can trust me… because I want… what you want. I want the realms free, and I want my friends free. Unity is power, as Sun Tzu says… and the only way to achieve freedom is by uniting with you."

Julius ceased throwing darts. "Very well. I have listened to your terms, and I am willing to bargain with you, but I have points of my own," he said, a touch of menace in his voice. "As I said, if my wife is returned tainted, our deal is instantly off. I presume you are getting Virgil to do the dirty work?"

"Virgil has volunteered, yes, Your Royal Highness."

Julius cackled. "You got Virgil to volunteer? Perhaps your powers of persuasion are better than I thought!" He guffawed, flinging another dart for good measure. "Anyway, where was I? Ah yes, upon the point of freeing the students. I shall agree to it. However, if you fail in the spell and it results in the destruction of another haven, your life will be forfeit. I will do anything in my power to ensure the Great Evil is destroyed, but it will be you doing the spell next, if you fail this time."

"If that happens, will the students still walk free?" Alex asked anxiously.

Julius glanced at him thoughtfully. "Yes, why not. You've caught me at a generous moment." He flashed a cold grin. "So, I take it you agree? My wife and your destruction of the Great Evil, one way or another, in return for a vial of blood and the freedom of the havens' students?"

Alex knew he didn't have much choice. "I agree to your terms."

Julius sprinted toward Alex, making Alex certain he was

about to get an orb of energy in the face, but the king skidded to a halt just shy of him, sticking out his hand for Alex to shake. Though his palms were sweaty and his fingers were trembling, he took the king's proffered hand, and endured the roughest handshake he'd ever experienced.

"Hadrian!" Julius bellowed, returning to his throne.

The nervous man appeared at the door. "Your Highness?"

"Fetch the leeches and vial," he instructed, and Hadrian disappeared again with a low bow. It was clear Julius had prepared for this visit, having no doubt already known what it was Alex was coming for. Alex realized he must have known the potency of his blood, even before Alex began to make a deal.

Hadrian re-entered a minute later, pushing a cart with a box and several glass bottles on top. They rattled loudly as he moved, jangling Alex's nerves. The nervous royal didn't dare look at Alex as he pushed the cart toward the king. Once he reached Julius, he took up the box and lifted the lid, pulling out a single, slimy-looking leech that Alex knew would soon grow fat with the blood of the king.

"Anywhere, Your Royal Highness?" Hadrian asked, his hands shaking.

Julius nodded. "Neck is probably best," he said. Hadrian obliged, placing the vile creature on the king's pale neck, where it latched on and began to suck.

It became quite awkward for everyone involved, standing there, watching the blood being sucked from Julius's neck, especially as the king began to whistle a tune, like it was the most normal thing in the world. For some unknown reason—probably nerves—it gave Alex the giggles, and he had to force himself to push the laughter down, snatching his gaze away from the comical scene of Julius on the throne, a leech attached to his neck, Hadrian holding the slimy end of the critter.

At long last, just as Alex thought he might burst, Hadrian removed the leech. There was a knife in the box too, which the anxious royal plucked out. He slid the sharp end into the leech, creating a small hole, from which he squeezed the blood, letting it drip into the vial. Alex counted nine drops before Hadrian stoppered the bottle. Enough for one attempt, but likely not two—just as Julius had no doubt engineered it.

"Hand it to the boy," Julius instructed.

Hadrian hurried toward him and handed over the vial, a look of excitement on his face. Alex felt that same excitement; they were almost done, and Julius had agreed to the terms. There was one caveat, but Alex had expected some kind of curveball. All in all, the meeting had been a success.

"Now, when can I expect my wife to be returned to me?" asked Julius curtly.

Alex smiled. "I hope you won't mind, but myself and my friends will keep Venus as collateral until your end of the bargain is upheld. Even if I should fail, my friends will hold her until you do as you've promised," Alex said, his eyes glancing toward the window.

Immediately, he realized the huge mistake he'd made.

Julius's expression morphed into a mask of abject fury. "Are they out there?" he roared, shooting a glare toward where Alex had glanced. "Are your friends out there, waiting like little snakes, ready to strike at your command? Did you think you could take me down?" he screamed. "How *dare* you? How dare you come here before me, ask me for all these things, when all the while you were disobeying my one rule! Come alone, I said. Have you brought your little friends along? If you have, they will not live. None of you will!" he shouted, conjuring much larger spears of energy in his hands.

"No, no, I meant nothing by it," Alex lied. "Your Royal Highness, I am here alone. I was just looking out there because they are waiting for me, but not nearby, not here."

"Liar!" Julius screamed. "You dare defy me! I will make you pay, you worthless wretch!"

Alex turned to Hadrian for help, but Hadrian was nowhere to be seen, though he had been there mere moments before. He caught sight of something shadowy moving close by, but he couldn't make out the figure. Whoever it was who had spirited Hadrian away, their face was pale, and Alex was almost certain he could see the telltale black veins of a necromancer. Presumably to keep Hadrian from the king's wrath, and to keep the hope of a plan alive, Vincent had stepped in. Alex just wished he had stepped in to spirit him away, too.

Alex ran for the flimsy windowpanes that lined the gallery. Building an orb of anti-magic in front of him, he let it surge forward, smashing the glass of several windows in one precise blast. The energy exploded in the sky beyond, giving the signal that would bring aid. He knew he needed to get out of there, and fast, before Julius could get hold of him.

Without another moment's thought, he vaulted over the sill, his leg catching on a shard that was sticking up. Ignoring the stab of pain, he clambered down the side of the building, using the ancient structure's wooden formation to his advantage; there were footholds and handholds everywhere, the climb an easy one. Looking up, he saw Helena and Jari scrambling down the side of the building from the sixth floor, like rats running from a flood. As Julius poked his head out, sending a bolt of magic toward Alex, the duo above him dropped magical bombs of their own, the blasts landing squarely on Julius's head. The king recoiled, ducking back inside. Helena and Jari hurried past the open window.

Julius appeared again, firing a furious artillery down at them. Trying to climb and dodge waves of magic was no simple feat, and once or twice Alex felt a blast knock into him, causing a flurry of snowflakes to drift down to the ground below. A new ache pulsed through his veins. One spear hit Helena square in the shoulder, causing her to lose her grip on the plank of wood she had been clinging to. Alex could do nothing to help, forced to watch as she plummeted to the earth. Just shy of the ground that would have undoubtedly flattened her like a pancake, a cushion of glistening golden light appeared, breaking her fall. The safety net had been forged by the quick-thinking Natalie.

Seeing the net's success, Jari pushed away from the building, landing on the cushion of energy just in time to break his fall. It was a quick way down the side of the pagoda, but Alex knew that kind of cushion wouldn't help him.

There was only one other option.

Bracing himself against the wooden slats, he pushed off as hard as he could, and felt the air rushing around him as he fell. Less than a minute later, he splashed into the closest pool in the water gardens below, the icy water enveloping him, before he resurfaced with a sharp intake of breath. Fortunately, it had been deeper than he'd thought, and he hurried to the edge, pulling himself out. His feet squelched as he sprinted for the tree-line, desperately trying to count how many of his friends were running alongside him.

Let there be five, let there be five, let there be five, he prayed.

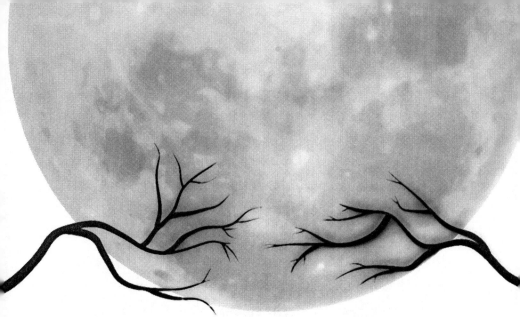

CHAPTER 12

A LEX WAS THE FIRST TO ARRIVE, CRASHING THROUGH the narrow doorway into the sanctuary of the cave. He crouched on the ground, panting, keeping one eye on the entrance in case anyone who shouldn't tried to enter. Thinking back on what had just happened, he realized how close they'd come to succeeding. Julius had been willing to negotiate, and it had failed because he'd brought his friends along, knowing he shouldn't. A simple error, and it had all gone wrong.

After tearing through the forest with bands of soldiers in hot pursuit, he had managed to lose them by clambering up one of the tall oaks and waiting there in the shadows until the danger had passed. He'd lost the others in the chaos, though he'd caught glimpses of Helena and Aamir through the trees, running and hiding, just as he was. The others, he wasn't so sure about.

All he could do was sit and wait, and hope that Julius wouldn't discover the secret cave.

Time went by with agonizing slowness, but still no one appeared at the doorway. Glancing down at his leg, he saw a tear in his trousers, the fabric colored a rusty red where the shard of glass had caught him unawares, but the wound beneath was only minor, the blood already drying. Satisfied he hadn't gouged a hole in his flesh, Alex began to run through every possible scenario in his head, knowing how badly this could play out. Just as he was picturing everyone dead at Julius's hand, a figure crept in through the entrance, peering around with furtive eyes.

"Jari?" Alex whispered from his hidden vantage point.

"Alex, is that you?" Jari replied.

"Yeah. Is anyone else with you?"

"No, it's just me," said Jari, shaking his head.

The blond-haired boy walked over to where Alex sat and sank down beside him, holding his head in his hands.

"Did you see anyone else?"

"No," Jari muttered miserably. "Ellabell was running near me for a while, but then she disappeared. I haven't seen anyone else—I hid under a pile of branches, and just closed my eyes until all the soldiers had run past me."

"I was up a tree," said Alex.

Jari shook his head. "What happened?"

"Julius suspected I wasn't alone, and he just went mad," Alex explained, not wanting to lay blame at anyone else's door.

"We should have known he'd go psycho! What did we think we were doing, going there in the first place?" Jari grunted in annoyance, punching the wall. "We should've listened to Natalie and Aamir."

Alex was about to reach out and comfort his friend when another scuffle by the entrance distracted them. They waited with bated breath as a figure emerged. The gleam of her silver hair gave her away instantly, and though Alex was pleased to see Helena safe and sound, part of him wished there were another girl standing there.

"We're over here!" said Jari, his eyes wide with delight at the sight of the beautiful young woman.

Helena peered into the darkness. "Who?"

"Alex and Jari," Jari replied, looking a little crestfallen that she hadn't known him by the sound of his voice. In any other circumstance, Alex would have been amused by Jari's puppy love, but now wasn't the time for levity. Not with half their party still missing.

"Just you two?" Helena asked, her voice heavy with sadness.

Alex nodded. "For now."

She joined them against the wall, where the trio sat in

somber silence, their eyes fixed on the entrance, hoping for another of their number to come rushing through it.

Their hopes were answered twenty minutes later, when Aamir and Natalie stumbled through, looking flustered and pretty beaten up. The older boy was holding Natalie up, her arm around his neck, her knee bent as though it hurt to put weight on it. Aamir himself had a bruise appearing around his eye, and his still-healing hand was bleeding afresh, with a few new cuts and scrapes appearing in livid gashes all the way up his arm. The rest of Natalie's appearance wasn't much better, her shirt torn, the bleeding wounds beneath saturating the fabric. Her lip had swollen, and a trail of blood meandered down her chin. Whatever had happened to them, it hadn't been pretty.

"We're over here," said Alex, getting up to help them. Natalie winced when Alex put his arm beneath hers. She moved with a definite limp, her forehead creasing in agony as she settled down on the floor, stretching out her damaged leg.

"What happened to you guys?" asked Jari, coming to the aid of Aamir, who could barely hold his hand up.

"Soldiers," explained Natalie, with a sharp intake of breath.

Aamir nodded. "They ambushed us, but we put up a good fight. We managed to get away and hide in a hollow, but not before they got a few good blows in," he said, clearly trying to make light of it.

"Is Ellabell not here?" Natalie asked, looking around for the missing girl.

Alex shook his head, feeling anxiety swell inside him. "No, she's not back yet."

"I'm sure she'll be along soon," Aamir said reassuringly, though there was uncertainty in his dark brown eyes.

Alex couldn't rest, pacing up and down, one eye constantly on the entrance. He had seen Ellabell from his spot in the tree. She had been running, and the soldiers had been far enough behind her that she should have been okay. But, if that was the case, where was she? Was she hiding out, like he had done, just waiting for an opportune moment to sneak out and head for the cave? Or was she out there, injured and alone, needing their help? One particularly nightmarish thought crept into his head—all he could think about was Julius getting his paws on her, holding her hostage the same way he was holding Venus hostage. He hoped more than anything that wasn't the case.

"If she's not back in the next half hour, we have to go looking for her," Alex said suddenly, unable to bear the weight of his own poisonous thoughts anymore. No matter which way he tried to envisage things, they were always the worst-case scenario.

"Aamir and Natalie can't go anywhere like this, Alex," Helena replied, glancing at the two wounded warriors.

Alex grimaced. "Fine, then you, me, and Jari will have to go looking for her. I'm not leaving her out there if she's in trouble—even if I have to go on my own, I will."

This time, nobody spoke up about joining him. It was clear that nobody had the energy to argue, nor did they want to leave one of their own out there with an army of soldiers after her. If it came to it, Alex knew he could count on them.

A short while later, there was another disturbance at the cave entrance, though the person who entered was not the one Alex had been hoping for. Agatha was standing in the dim light, her wild eyes trying to make out the shapes of Alex and his friends.

"Alex, my darling, is that you?" she asked, rushing to embrace them all, even Helena, whom Agatha had never even met. "Oh my dears, what a to-do! You must all be so frightened. Well, fear not, everything is in hand and old Agatha is here to set things right. I found a little something on my way here that I think you might enjoy," she added, giving them all a dramatic wink before slipping back out of the cave entrance. She reappeared a moment later, cradling Ellabell in her arms, carrying her with surprising strength.

Alex and Jari rushed forward to take the limp girl from Agatha's arms.

"Is she okay?" Alex asked, brushing a loose strand of hair back from Ellabell's face. She looked peaceful, as if she were sleeping, and there didn't appear to be any visible marks or bruises on her, aside from a couple of scrapes on her hands.

Agatha nodded. "Goodness, yes, she's quite well. I gave her a little something to help her sleep is all—she'll be right as rain in no time, my cherubs."

"Where did you find her?" Alex pressed.

"Hadrian put us up in a quaint little cavern in the middle of the woods. Quite out of the way; you wouldn't know it was there unless you knew to look, and it's surrounded by about a gazillion of those pesky boobytraps, so nobody ever bothers with our secret little abode," she explained, punctuating every few words with a flourish of her hands. "Mind you, poor, dear Ellabell stumbled on us, though not before she'd walked into one or two of those traps I mentioned. She had quite the shock, but she'll be okay."

"How did you know to bring her here?" asked Helena, her tone revealing her suspicion of this strange woman.

Agatha grinned. "Aha! I'm a perceptive old coot! I see you, coming and going, thinking this place is a great secret. I come down here sometimes to see who might creep out. I figured you beautiful creatures would be here!" she cried, enveloping Helena in a warm hug that seemed to make the girl extremely uncomfortable.

"Is Vincent with you?" Alex asked, remembering what he'd seen in the gallery.

"Not with me, no, but he got back not too long after Ellabell stumbled upon our cozy wee home. He's always disappearing off up to the pagoda. From what I gather, he had to do a spot of backside-saving up there today, yes? He sends his apologies, by the way, Alex, for not being able to get you out," she said solemnly.

Alex frowned. "Yeah, I've been wondering why he did that. One minute, Hadrian was there, the next he'd vanished."

"Goodness, you're a sharp flint!" Agatha exclaimed, throwing her arms wide. "The thing is, it's so very important that Hadrian continues to seem like a neutral party, but it's even more important that he stay alive, given the information he's been gathering. Of course, if the king thought the bunch of you were in cahoots, he'd decapitate the poor, nervous lad in a heartbeat."

That, Alex could understand.

"You were saying…?" he prompted, not wanting the old hippie to get too carried away with other thoughts.

"Ah, yes, where was I?" She paused, tapping her chin thoughtfully. "Yes, backside-saving! How could I forget?" she chuckled. "So, Vincent came back just after poor wee Ellabell had her run-ins with the traps, but it wasn't safe for Hadrian to come himself, otherwise he would have—he's ever so fond of all of you. All of us are, you adorable cherubs!"

Alex's heart skipped a beat. "Is he okay?"

"Who, Hadrian? Yes, right as rain! Ooh, what a right old mess you've made of your handsome face!" she cried, looking at Aamir. "You must allow me to have a look at that swelling before I go. And you, mademoiselle—something tells me you're suffering beneath that stoic veneer of yours? Well, you can't fool old Agatha, no indeed!" she added, swooping down to where Aamir and Natalie sat before they could say a word of protestation.

There were bottles of vibrant liquids and tiny boxes filled with herbs and powders all about her person, and she whipped them out after scrutinizing the pair's injuries more closely. In a pestle and mortar that seemed to appear from nowhere, the old hippie crushed up a bit of this and a bit of that, dampening it with a drop or two from a few bottles. Once it was blended into a thick paste, she rubbed it on Aamir's eye, and smoothed it over the cuts and bruises the two of them had obtained during their fight with the soldiers. She even forced Natalie to slather it on her swollen lip, with a warning not to lick it off or she might grow horns. Nobody was sure if the old woman was joking or not—even her cackle didn't clarify anything.

Once that was done, she put the bottles and boxes away before holding out a single pill in the palm of her hand. She offered it to Natalie, who eyed it suspiciously.

"Swallow this, and that leg of yours will be good as new!" Agatha encouraged.

Tentatively, Natalie picked up the pill and placed it on the end of her tongue. With a grimace, she swallowed it down in one gulp.

"Superb! I am so glad I ran into you all. Well, I must be off—undoubtedly our paths shall cross once more. Vincent sends his love! I'll tell him you send your love back, or else he'll sulk." Giving a theatrical wave, she grinned at the six friends, and then she was gone, the whirlwind passing out of the cave as if it had never even been there.

Alex looked at the glass bottle in his hand, holding it up to the sliver of light that glanced in from outside. The viscous liquid slid thickly from side to side, and Alex knew he'd hit the jackpot. Although he'd made a mistake, they still had the blood, and nobody had died. Not yet, anyway. He was glad to hear Hadrian hadn't suffered any undue consequences as a result of what had happened; he just hoped the nervous royal's double agenting wouldn't become too much for him to handle.

The only problem was, that tiny error had cost them a fairly good deal. In his hand, Alex still clutched the vial of blood, though what it now stood for, he didn't know. After what had just gone down, it was likely that Julius's deal was off the table, with no room for further negotiation. If Alex wanted peace, he was going to have to prove it by getting the spell right.

In the words of Sun Tzu, he hadn't known his enemy. Now, if he failed, he wouldn't be getting any more blood. This was his only shot.

CHAPTER 13

A SOMBER AIR SETTLED ACROSS THE GROUP AS THEY moved through the cave, Alex and Jari taking it in turns to carry Ellabell, while Aamir and Natalie helped one another along. Agatha's treatment had done wonders, but it wasn't an instant fix by any means. The group was broken, and though they had the vial, it was clear nobody felt particularly positive. Alex had yet to explain just why Julius had lost his temper, but it didn't matter—they all knew that any deal they might have had, had been obliterated.

After retrieving his satchel from behind one of the bottle shelves, the book thankfully still inside, Alex pressed the lotus gem in the small chamber at the end of the cave.

Solemnly, the group headed through to the rolling fields of Starcross, though Alex was surprised to find the near distance devoid of Kelpie-riding aggressors. He had been pretty sure that Ceres would be awaiting their return, given the way they had left things, but there was no sign of the one-eyed royal. Still, he knew that meeting would come soon enough; the leader of Starcross would be eager to know how things had gone, even if she hadn't agreed with them going. Alex sighed, knowing just how badly that was going to go down.

Regardless, Alex knew he had to carry out the second spell attempt as soon as possible, in case Julius came searching for them. If he could complete it, successfully, he hoped he would find himself back in the king's favor. There might be hope for a peaceful conclusion after all.

Re-entering the camp, they noticed that a few suspicious eyes followed their movements toward the tents they were staying in. Alex couldn't blame them. Undoubtedly, they'd seen the riders go out that morning, and had managed to put two and two together. Glancing around, he felt a wave of guilt wash over him. It was true, what Ceres had said: he had put these people in unimaginable danger, and, after what they'd all been through, he didn't have strong enough words to tell them how sorry he was.

I'll make it up to you all, he promised, silently.

Turning the corner that led up to their tents, Alex saw that Ceres was waiting beside the fire, perched on one of the benches, one eyebrow raised as they approached. He tried hard not to sigh, knowing this had been inevitable—he had just hoped he might have a bit more time to collect himself.

"It didn't go well, I take it?" she asked pointedly, eyeing the limp figure of Ellabell and the bruised faces of Aamir and Natalie.

Alex shook his head. "Afraid not... Please don't say 'I told you so.'"

She smiled tightly, as if those words were already on her lips. "What happened?" she asked, gesturing toward the benches around her. Jari took Ellabell into her tent, while the rest of the group sat down.

"It was going well," Alex began, "but then he turned. Julius guessed I'd brought people with me, when he had specifically told me to come alone."

Ceres frowned. "Then why on earth didn't you go alone?" she barked. It was a question Alex had been trying not to ask himself, not wanting to lay blame on anyone else for what had happened. They had thought they were doing the right thing in coming with him, and he knew he'd never have escaped without them. Whether or not things would have gone smoothly without them there at all, he'd never know.

"We decided it wasn't safe," Alex said, finally.

"I suppose he'd have found some excuse to fly off the handle, even if you had gone alone," mused Ceres with a shrug. "You realize you should never have gone at all, don't you?" she added curtly. It was strange—Alex had expected her to be far angrier than she was. He suspected he had Demeter to thank for this slightly peeved version of the one-eyed royal, instead of the howling banshee she had every right to be.

"I thought you'd be screaming at us from the rooftops," chirped Jari, who had returned from the tent.

Ceres flashed him a warning look. "Don't get me wrong, I am beyond furious with everything the lot of you have done since coming here," she said simply, her tone cold. After a long pause, in which she appeared to be taking slow, deep breaths, she continued. "But Demeter took the time to explain your reasoning, once I'd forgiven him for his devious trick by the portal, and though I'm not happy about it, I can see your intentions are good. Maybe one day you *will* grant us the freedom we've been searching for."

"Where is Demeter, anyway?" Natalie asked, wincing as she tried to stretch out her leg.

"I asked him not to be here. I don't want him clouding my mind," Ceres explained, her tone growing harsher by the second. "You have, once again, brought Julius another step closer to us. You've put us all in very real jeopardy, for the sake of a deal that went awry. You have come back with nothing, but we stand to lose everything," she snarled.

Aamir smiled. "Actually, we have come back with something."

"What?" Ceres snapped.

"Alex managed to retrieve the blood he needs to perform the second spell attempt," Helena added, before Alex could speak for himself.

A curious expression fell over Ceres's face. "Well then, I suppose all is not lost," she muttered. "Don't mistake my words for forgiveness, though. Until that spell is done and the Great Evil is gone, you will not have my blessing. You have caused us enough trouble. It better be worth it." She glowered at them all, her gaze settling on Alex. "I guess this means you and I have a visit to make?"

Alex nodded. "If you're happy for us to go ahead, then we should try to be as quick as possible."

"I am not happy about any of this, Alex," Ceres reiterated sharply. "But Demeter has made me see that I may as well let you try, especially now you have what you need. I'd say the sooner the better, if Julius is intent on finding you and punishing you, which he doubtless will be." With that, she got up, brushing imaginary dust from the legs of her leather trousers before striding off toward the windmill.

Alex gave his friends a look of nervous optimism, then hurried after her. The one-eyed royal walked quickly, forcing Alex to jog if he wanted to keep up, and they soon reached the entrance to the windmill. The guards stepped aside to let them in.

Inside, both Venus and Virgil were awake, sitting close to the edges of their cells, apparently in the midst of an intense discussion. What looked like tears were glistening in Virgil's eyes, but he looked away rapidly when Alex and Ceres entered, rubbing away whatever sorrowful evidence had been there. Alex frowned, wondering what Venus could possibly have said to him that had such a powerful effect. Whatever it was, it was clear neither of them was going to give up the secret, both of them moving over to their cell chairs.

"The wanderer returns," joked Virgil, though his voice was still thick with traces of emotion. The sound of his choked tears made Alex feel uncomfortable, as if he'd intruded on a very personal moment.

"You'll be pleased to know I come bearing a gift," Alex replied.

Virgil's face fell slightly. "The blood?" he asked softly.

Alex nodded. "The blood."

"Seems presumptuous, seeing as I haven't yet given you my answer," Virgil remarked, but one glance toward his mother made his whole manner change. "Though, with time to ponder it some more, I have decided that I will go ahead with the spell."

Alex's eyebrows shot up in surprise, but he stayed silent, in hopes that Virgil would continue unprompted. He did.

"I feel it is time I sought redemption for the terrible things I have done," the Head said solemnly, the words spoken in a voice barely above a whisper. "I was made to believe I was doing things for the greater good. I was made to feel it was my fault, and extracting essence was the only option that could prevent the deaths of even more people… I was lied to, but I am ready to atone, to fix what has been broken."

Relief flowed through Alex at those words. If, after all he had endured with Julius, he had returned to the cells to find an unwilling Virgil, he wasn't sure what he'd have done. Perhaps he would've forced him again, but then, wouldn't that make him just as evil as the king?

"You're really going to do it?" Ceres asked, incredulous.

Virgil nodded, flashing an apologetic look at his mother. "It is the least I can do… for the suffering I have caused." It seemed the skeletal man was struggling to suppress his feelings, his breathing sharp and quick. He wiped his eyes hurriedly, but Alex had already seen his tears.

After a moment of awkward silence, Alex said, "So, we have the blood. We have the book." He patted the satchel he still wore. "And we have the spellcaster. Now all we need is a place to actually do the spell." A puzzled look fell across his face; it had previously been one of the easier parts of the spell, finding a suitable pit in which to perform it, but things had become a little more complicated. He knew, without a shadow of a doubt, that Julius would be watching the other havens like a hawk, waiting for just such an opportunity to strike, meaning those pits were likely going to be risky options.

There was, however, one alternative.

"What are you thinking, Alex Webber?" said Ceres, suspiciously.

"There was a castle here once, wasn't there? Starcross Castle?" he asked, trying not to get too excited about the idea brewing in his mind.

Ceres nodded slowly. "There was… Why do you ask?"

"Well, if that castle was once the central building of this haven, it means there might just be a pit beneath it that we can use for the spell," he explained. "The other havens will be riddled with Julius's spies, but here, we can do it and he won't be any the wiser. He doesn't even know this place still exists."

Ceres eyed Alex closely, a myriad of emotions flickering in her one good eye. "I definitely like the idea of doing it somewhere away from Julius's prying eyes," she began, filling Alex with hope. "But what if it fails—what if the mist escapes? What are we supposed to do then?" she added, deflating those hopes.

Alex had been so excited about the prospect of doing the spell, now that they had everything they needed, that he had almost forgotten what could go wrong if it didn't succeed. He chastised himself for allowing his confidence to overtake his focus again. That was what had gotten them into trouble last time.

"Evacuate?" he suggested. "We've got a better chance of evacuating the people of Starcross before the spell even takes place than we do with the people at any other havens. We could get them out of the way before we start, so nobody is at risk?"

Ceres sighed heavily, her shoulders sagging.

"I know it's a lot to ask, and I wouldn't dare to ask if I didn't think this was our best shot," Alex continued softly, his voice full of regret.

Virgil chimed in. "For what it's worth, I think it's probably our best shot too."

She looked up, her face strained. "My brother will take the people here, if we are forced to evacuate. I can take them to the portal and hold them there. One of my riders will wait by the entrance of the castle for a signal—be it bad or good news, they will ride to us and tell us what has gone on," she said quietly. "No matter how quickly the mist here might be released, the Kelpies can outrun it."

"Where will Hadrian put all these people?" Alex asked, wanting all the logistics out of the way, even though he hadn't even seen the castle yet.

"There are secret places at Falleaf where he can keep them safe," Ceres explained. "In the early days of hiding students away after graduation, we started somewhere else. It's big enough to hold most, though some of the people you brought through may have to reintegrate with the Falleaf students, until you can try the spell again. If you fail a third time, we're doomed anyway." She gave a tight smile.

"Doomed?" Virgil questioned through the bars of his cell.

Ceres flashed him a withering look. "Given the essence situation, the lack of magical children being born, and Spellshadow falling to the mist, it won't be long before the Great Evil takes hold of everything. There isn't enough essence to keep it at bay anymore, unless Julius starts taking it from anyone and everyone," she said bitterly. "Even if he manages to reinstate the essence system between three havens, somehow, the cycle will never end. If this is the best chance we have, we have to take it… though I'm not happy about it," she added for good measure, though a wry smile pulled at the corners of her lips.

"You should hurry," Venus said suddenly, her charming voice surprising all of them. In all their time there, she hadn't spoken once. "The sands of time are running swiftly, and you're down to a handful of grains," she added, every word like a symphony. With that, she turned her back on the others, opening a book on her lap. Where she had obtained the book, Alex could only guess, but he knew nobody would dare take it from her either.

"She's right," Ceres agreed. "We should hurry to the castle now—scope it out, see if it's any good."

Alex nodded, and the pair left the windmill. Virgil called after them, pleading to be allowed to go too, but they ignored him as they stepped out into the warm sunlight, the gentle breeze whipping their hair. Striding ahead, Ceres led them to the edge of the riverbank, removing the glinting bridle she wore on her belt. She held it out and began to sing—the tune a low, Celtic ballad, sounding so sad and mysterious Alex felt his heart grip, despite the fact that he couldn't understand the words.

Below, the fast-running surface of the water began to stir and froth. A moment later, the slick mane of a Kelpie emerged, followed by the beast itself. It rose, bit by bit, the water drying immediately as its rough hide met the cool breeze, until it had mounted the bank and was standing in front of Ceres, beating its hooves against the hard earth. Its white eyes glared in Alex's direction, forcing him to look away, but Ceres held its gaze, her voice still singing delicately as she slipped the bridle around the beast's face and fastened it into place.

With that, she jumped up, swinging lithely onto the huge beast's back. Once she was settled, she held out a hand to Alex, who paused uncertainly. It wasn't on his bucket list to ever ride a Kelpie.

"Come on, he's fine," Ceres encouraged.

Taking a deep breath, Alex gripped Ceres's hand and allowed her to haul him up behind her. The steed's back was broader than he had anticipated, and he felt his thighs straining as he struggled to get a comfortable seat. It was nowhere near as comfortable as Storm's back. The Kelpie flicked its tail in annoyance, causing Alex to stop squirming and sit still.

"You'll get used to it," Ceres laughed, digging in her heels as the mighty beast set off at a terrifying speed, the world flashing past Alex's eyes as he clung onto Ceres for dear life. They headed toward the ruins of Starcross Castle.

CHAPTER 14

THEY TORE THROUGH THE COUNTRYSIDE, ALEX'S nerves calming as they settled into a rhythm. He hadn't seen this part of the realm before, but it was just as breathtaking as the fields they'd walked through to get to the encampment. Beautiful forests rose on either side of them, teeming with wildlife. A stag emerged, its fur a pure white, its antlers gleaming like ivory, its brown eyes watching them curiously as they passed by. Behind it, just visible in the trees, he could see the ghostly shapes of other deer, not quite as bold as their leader.

The Kelpie sprinted with ease, the heavy muscles rippling beneath Alex. If he closed his eyes and imagined he was on the back of Storm instead, the great beast didn't seem so frightening.

"You okay back there?" Ceres asked, laughing to herself.

"Just about!" Alex yelled back, his voice only just audible above the roar of the wind rushing in their faces.

Eventually, they reached the remnants of an ancient wall, the stone crumbling apart. Above it, on what might have been parapets, stood grisly gargoyles, staring them down as they approached. They looked like demons, their faces twisted, ghoulish wings covered in moss sprouting from their backs.

The castle beyond it, however, wasn't nearly as Gothic.

The Kelpie jumped easily over a gap in the wall, leading them into stretching gardens that must have once been beautiful, making Alex think of landscaped lawns containing quaint benches and stunning patches of exotic flowers. Now, the plants had overgrown, taking back their land, no longer keeping to the neat squares they'd once been grown in. Roses and violets writhed all over the stones and former fountains, blooming brightly. Wisteria hung low like willow trees, casting a purple sheen over everything it shaded from the sunlight. Giant oaks and silver birches towered above the gardens too, growing to monstrous heights, having been left to their own devices.

Everywhere he looked, Alex saw something else that pleased the eye. There were exquisite statues in a Grecian style, carved from marble, still holding their shape. Tiny figurines shaped like fairies and brute-faced gnomes hid among the foliage too, giving the castle an otherworldly air, like something out of a bedtime story. Alex half expected a princess to wander through singing a sweet song that would stay in his head for weeks, but the place was empty, its last inhabitants long gone.

As for the mist, there was none of that here. It seemed not to have touched the plants and animals, taking only the lives of those with magical blood inside their veins. A twinge of sadness prickled inside Alex as he wondered what this place might have been like before the plague of the Great Evil rose to terrorize the people here.

Up ahead, the castle came into view. It had evidently once been a glorious, regal place, surrounded by a glittering moat. A few of its golden-tiled spires were still intact, and the pure white walls still showed through the years of dirt, though the rest of it had fallen into disrepair. Great, gaping chunks had been torn out of the sides, the stained-glass windows mostly smashed in, several towers having crumbled in on themselves. Alex was about to ask Ceres why she and her people hadn't tried to make it habitable again, but it was clear this place was beyond repair, even with a hundred hands helping out.

Ceres halted her Kelpie at the edge of a drawbridge, its rickety planks leading across the moat, which still sparkled despite the wreckage it protected. They jumped down, and Ceres removed the bridle from the Kelpie's snout, hooking it back onto her belt. With a snort of its nostrils, the hulking beast arced gracefully down into the water of the moat, sinking below the surface.

"Needs a paintjob," Alex joked, looking up at the enormous building.

"Needs tearing down," Ceres replied grimly.

Sharing a glance, they walked across the rotting beams of the drawbridge, careful of their footing, and reached the other side. A heavy door of pure gold met them, with two knockers shaped like stag's heads, though one side was already wide open. They ducked inside, only to find more decay within. In the grand reception room, the marble tiles were covered in piles of debris, several statues smashed to pieces on the ground. A chandelier lay in the very center, the diamond embellishments holding their shape, unbroken by the impact of the fall from the ceiling above, though the expensive fixture lay on its side, resting where it had fallen.

More debris fell as they walked, a large chunk of rock narrowly missing Alex's head. Their very presence seemed to be upsetting the fragile balance of deterioration the castle had set in motion, and Alex knew they were going to have to find the pit quickly. Of course, where they were going to start was another matter entirely—the castle was huge.

"Any idea where the pit could be?" Alex asked.

Ceres nodded. "I've scouted out this place before. I think I remember the way," she replied, alleviating Alex's anxiety. At least someone knew where they were going.

They wandered through vacant hallways littered with

fallen masonry the size of Alex's body. Smashed windows lay to either side of them, some looking out over the beautiful gardens, others showing overgrown courtyards. There was a pond in the center of one such courtyard, and Alex could see fish the size of small dogs swimming peacefully beneath the murky surface. It always amazed him how nature could thrive in adversity and emerge from destruction.

Ceres paused beside a door at the end of a corridor filled with torn paintings of the people who had once lived here. She pushed tentatively. It gave, creaking open with a rusty groan. Beyond it was a throne room, the two thrones still standing in the middle, though they were covered in a thick layer of gray dust. A stag's head rose above the back of one, its sapphire eyes still glinting, while a doe's head rose up above the back of the other, one ruby eye missing. Alex almost made a joke about it, but held his tongue, realizing how deeply inappropriate it would be.

"Remind you of anyone?" Ceres asked, pointing at the doe, a wicked smile upon her face. Alex laughed, the tension breaking.

She moved around the backs of the thrones, searching for something underneath the throne with the stag's head on it. She gave a cry, presumably finding what she'd been looking for. Alex hurried around to see a trapdoor had swung loose in the floor, a musty, earthy scent rising from a steep set of stone-hewn steps visible beneath. They were very familiar-looking steps.

"I think this might be the place," Alex whispered, feeling as if he were in a museum.

Ceres raised an eyebrow. "Well, yeah, that's why I brought you here."

Alex flushed. "I was just agreeing with you," he said. Something about Ceres always left him on edge. Sometimes she was the smiling daredevil; other times she was the sharp-tongued warrior who made him feel like an idiot.

"Ladies first," she said, gesturing toward the open trapdoor.

Alex stepped down, descending into the earth. Ceres followed, her footsteps echoing behind him. At the bottom of the steps, there was a narrow door, but before Alex even pushed it open, he knew what he would see on the other side. He was not disappointed. A cavernous walkway led to a set of huge gates, and beyond that...

What should have been a lofty cave with a deep fissure in the center was in fact a lofty cave with no fissure whatsoever. The pit that should have been there had obviously, at some point after the mist rose, collapsed in on itself, rendering it unusable. Stepping closer, Alex saw that a golden bird lay still at the top of a pile of rubble, half buried by dirt and rock.

"Maybe the mist caused it to crumble so another spell attempt couldn't be made at the same pit," Ceres mused, crouching to grasp some of the dirt in her hand.

"You think Virgil sent us on a wild goose chase?" Alex asked, frowning.

Ceres shrugged. "Wouldn't surprise me. I'm not sure he's as eager to participate as he's claiming; he's probably trying to buy a little time. Wouldn't you, if you had to do it?" she said, her tone surprisingly compassionate.

"I don't know," Alex replied, trying to put himself in Virgil's shoes.

There was a scuffle in the shadows across the room, followed by the sound of someone clearing their throat. A figure slowly emerged, but Ceres was already sprinting over the rubble pile, barreling into the shadowy shape with all her might, taking it down before it could strike. In the confusion, Alex caught a glimpse of horn-rimmed spectacles and over-rouged cheeks.

"Ceres! Ceres, get off her—she's a friend!" he yelled, though the squat figure of Siren Mave was doing a fine job of holding off the rampaging royal. A black cloud of magic was rippling around Ceres, lifting her up and away, though her limbs were flailing and magic whipped from her hands in wild motions.

"Siren Mave, let her go! We're all friends here!" Alex cried. To his surprise, Siren Mave actually obeyed, lowering Ceres to the ground with an unceremonious thud before removing the cloud of magic.

Ceres stood up indignantly, dusting herself off. "Who is this woman?" she snapped, flashing a sour look at Alex.

"She won't do us any harm," he replied. "Sorry about that," he added, turning to Siren Mave.

She gave an awkward curtsey. "No harm done. Nice to see you've got a useful protector for once!" she remarked tartly. "Anyway, I thought I'd drop in, seeing as you're getting things all wrong again, and Elias seems to have gone AWOL. Looked like you could do with a little divine intervention." She chuckled to herself, smacking her lips.

"Elias is busy researching," Alex said, jumping to the shadow-man's defense.

"Is he now? If you believe that, you'll believe anything. He's probably swinging from a rafter somewhere, pretending to be a hammock," she scoffed.

"Anyone going to introduce me?" Ceres cut in, looking suspiciously at the squat woman.

Siren Mave stuck out a plump hand. "Siren Mave, pleased to meet you. And you must be Ceres, yes? I must say, what a wonderful operation you've got set up at Starcross—very quaint idea. Very heroic. Good while it lasted, eh?"

Ceres scowled. "What did you just say?"

"Ignore her," Alex warned. "We have bigger things to deal with."

Ceres didn't say another word, though her savage expression said everything. Siren Mave smiled before turning back to Alex.

"Now, where was I?"

Alex sighed. "I'm getting everything wrong?"

"Of course!" Siren Mave nodded vigorously. "I just thought I'd come and say you were barking up the wrong tree."

"Well, I can see that now," said Alex, pointing to the caved-in pit. "You didn't think to tell us before we came out here?"

Siren Mave shook her head. "Where would the lesson be in that? Anyway, now I have your attention, let's have a little spot of history, shall we?"

Alex shrugged, while Ceres remained silent.

"Not the most enthusiastic response, but… Well, I'll take what I can get. Both of you are right about the mist causing the pit to cave in, by the way," she began. "This is what the tales mean about a haven 'falling.' Well, that and the destruction of anyone stupid enough to stick around while the mist is rising. But, mostly, it's this. The mist rose, killing everyone, and the pits crumbled, along with the castle, given that the pit is dug into the foundations of a place."

Alex frowned. "Why would they dig a pit into the foundations?"

"Only place to put them!" Siren Mave pronounced. "You see, the pits had to be dug as close as possible to a magical building, so a containment spell could be used to get the mist below the earth. However, without essence to feed it, the mist can only be held below ground for a short period of time. All the spells in the world can't keep it at bay—aside from the obvious," she continued, flashing an amused smile that showed specks of red lipstick on her teeth.

"How come it's not here now, then?" Ceres asked, evidently too intrigued to stay silent. "The mist, I mean?"

"The big question, and one I'm glad you asked," enthused Siren Mave. "The original containment spell was already beginning to fail, but it was exacerbated by Virgil's failed spell attempts. It was around this point that Julius, in all his wisdom," she muttered sarcastically, "decided to implement the essence system. An ill-advised advisor told him it would be the best course of action, and he naturally got a kick out of the idea. So, he went ahead with it. As a result, the mist was drawn away from the peripheral havens, to be contained only within the circle forged by the four havens that are, more or less, still standing," she explained, giving Alex a knowing look. "It created a ring-like barrier around the Great Evil, keeping it in only within that circle. As such, Starcross and the other fallen havens are protected from the mist... Well, as long as that circle holds."

Alex felt a wave of panic flow through him as his mind wandered toward the mess he'd made of Spellshadow, and then thought of Stillwater. It had been a long time since the latter had had essence poured into its pit. After all, Helena had never made it back with her sack of half-essence, given Julius's abrupt arrival there. Yes, it had definitely been a while since the Great Evil had been fed from there. With Caius gone, too, at Kingstone, Alex realized it was unlikely that the keep's pit had been fed either, unless Julius had taken it into his own hands.

Alex sighed. "So the reason you're telling us this is because... if the other havens fall, then the mist will spread to places outside the circle?"

"Correct." Siren Mave smiled cheerily.

"Great," Alex replied drily.

"We're wasting time here," Ceres cut in. "We have to find a new location, and fast. I don't want Julius sniffing you out, Alex."

"We'll figure something out," Alex said with more confidence than he felt.

"Just remember, when the moment comes, ensure the spell is properly witnessed by all who are involved," Siren Mave warned, giving Alex the kind of vague comment he had come to expect from his shadowy advisors.

He wanted to scream at her, demand to know what she meant, but knew there was no point. Before he could even think about the spell, and everything it entailed, they needed a place to perform it. Without that, all of this was pointless.

Turning on his heel without another word, he raced from the derelict pit, with Venus's words running through his mind: "The sands of time are running swiftly, and you're down to a handful of grains."

He could feel each one slipping through his fingers.

CHAPTER 15

AFTER BRINGING THE KELPIE BACK UP FROM THE murky depths of the moat, Ceres and Alex raced back through the beautiful landscape, the golden sun shining down and warming their faces as they rode. Alex, however, barely even noticed the scenery, his mind was so preoccupied.

As they charged along, he couldn't help but think of the words Siren Mave had spoken as they left. As usual, her cryptic message had left him exasperated. Why couldn't they just tell him what he needed to know in plain terms? He knew why, since she and Elias had explained the curse that bound their lips, but it didn't make figuring out the puzzle any easier.

"Who *was* that woman?" Ceres asked, as they rode.

Alex smiled grimly. "I'm not sure even I know the answer to that."

"How did she get to the castle?" Ceres pressed.

"She moves between realms as she pleases," Alex explained. "I don't know how she does it, so there's no point asking me that either. She's… not exactly human, if you catch my drift?"

Ceres nodded, falling into silence. Alex could almost hear the cogs whirring in her head, as she tried to figure out the toady woman, and how she fit into all of this. The story was a long one, and it wasn't a tale Alex was in the mood to tell.

Upon returning to the camp, they headed straight for the windmill. Out of the corner of his eye, he saw Demeter, watching them from the farm, but the auburn-haired man made no move to follow.

Alex burst through the door of the windmill, striding straight toward Virgil's cell. "Did you know it was unusable?" he asked angrily.

Virgil sat up, startled. "Know what was unusable?"

"Don't play dumb. Starcross Castle, did you know it was unusable? Were you sending us on a wild goose chase?" he demanded.

Virgil shook his head, a confused look in his eyes. "No, why would I?"

"The pit has caved in. Did you do one of your spells at

Starcross Castle?" Alex pressed.

Just then, Ceres walked up and rested her hand on Alex's shoulder. "It could've just been the mist, Alex, as your strange friend said," she commented softly, evidently trying to calm him.

"Maybe so—or maybe *you* sabotaged us, sending us there to buy time," Alex countered, his gaze still firmly set on the squirming figure of Virgil.

"Step away from my son," a voice called sweetly from the other side of the room, though there was a hint of a warning in her words. Venus was standing up against the bars, her beautiful eyes piercing Alex's soul as he turned to look at her. "Your anger is misplaced. Come over here. Speak with me a while."

As much as Alex wanted to keep raging at Virgil, he found he couldn't deny the queen's request. Seemingly on autopilot, he began to walk toward her, but Ceres's hand held him back.

"Don't go up to her cell," Ceres warned, but Alex was helpless, and found himself doing as Venus had asked. He shook off Ceres's hand and took a seat on one of the low guard stools that sat beside the queen's cell.

"He did it on purpose," said Alex quietly, feeling foolish.

Venus smiled a glowing smile. "No, Alex, he didn't. When my husband took Virgil to do that awful spell, Starcross Castle wasn't one of the places he took him to. If the cave has fallen in, it has nothing to do with my son," she said firmly, her voice utterly compelling. Whatever she said, Alex instantly believed—it was impossible to resist.

"Maybe I was wrong," Alex replied shyly.

"I can see you're under a lot of stress, Alex. I know how difficult that must be for you," Venus said soothingly. "Perhaps you simply wanted to vent, and my son was the easiest target? I don't blame you. Stress can make us all do silly things sometimes."

Alex felt he could get lost in the eyes that gazed at him so intently, as if he were the only person in the world who mattered. Her smile was exquisite, her voice so musical, her tone like a lullaby. He couldn't help but be drawn by this woman, even though he could feel Ceres's burning stare somewhere behind him. He would have looked, but he was transfixed by Venus. Ceres had backed away farther, keeping her distance from the cell.

"I am quite stressed," Alex admitted, nodding slowly.

"Of course you are—who wouldn't be, in your situation? Look at you, a young man with the weight of the world on his shoulders, and after what happened at Spellshadow, I can only imagine how immense the pressure must be to get things right this time," she said, her voice so soft he was forced to lean in to hear her better. "Tell me, why are you so stressed, Alex? What is going on up there?" she asked, reaching through the bars to gently touch the side of his temple. Her touch was like an electric shock to his system, his heart pounding.

Alex dipped his head in embarrassment. "It's the spell, Your Royal Highness. I'm worried about the spell, and how much I have let my friends down," he explained. "If I hadn't made your husband angry, we'd have gotten the deal we wanted. I messed up, and now I'm trying to fix it. Only, I don't know where to do the spell—your husband will be watching all the havens, and I'm scared. I'm scared of how dangerous it will be, and how great the risks are to my friends." He didn't know what had compelled him to be so honest with her, but it felt good to tell the truth.

Venus nodded, pushing a strand of his hair away from his forehead. "No need for formalities—call me Venus," she instructed. Never had a single word sounded so thrilling to Alex's ears than her name. "And fear not, you haven't let your friends down. My husband is capricious at the best of times, always blowing hot and cold." She gave a quiet laugh that sounded like tiny bells ringing. "We can never know if your actions would have changed anything, had you done something different. Alex, dear boy, we must never dwell on the past. The future is changeable; the past is not. As for your fear, you must use it, not run from it."

"I suppose I hadn't thought of it like that," Alex murmured, his cheeks growing hot.

"Tell me, did you get the blood you needed?" she asked innocently.

Alex nodded. "I did. Julius gave it to me before he snapped."

She smiled. "Let me guess, the blood you so rudely took from me didn't work?" There was ice in her words.

"No, it didn't," Alex replied. "And I'm sorry for taking it without your permission. We were in a rush," he added, almost groveling for her forgiveness.

She flashed him an even brighter smile, stroking his cheek. "No harm done. I know your heart was in the right place, even if you misread the lines. My own son made the same mistake—it is an easy one to make. The words of that spell are so tricky, aren't they? So vague and confusing?"

"They really are," Alex replied, nodding vigorously, as if he'd just been given a treat.

"But you know them well?" she pressed.

Alex shrugged. "Well enough."

"Well enough to do the spell and succeed?" she asked, her voice making his head swim, as if he had a fever.

"I hope so," Alex said. "Although, it's Virgil who's going to do the spell."

She nodded. "I see… And you think that is fair?"

Alex frowned. "For him to do it, instead of me?"

"Yes, Alex."

"I think it's fairer for him, a man who has lived a long time and done a lot of bad things, to do it, rather than me, a boy who has barely lived, and not done anything really horrible," Alex said solemnly, feeling ashamed. He knew it must be hard for her to hear that her son was going to have to do the spell. Unbidden, an image of his own mother flashed into his mind, making him think about how she'd feel, if the roles were reversed.

Venus removed her hand from between the bars and rested it delicately on her chin, her eyes thoughtful. "You believe he should sacrifice his own life for the things he's done?"

"Only if he is willing, which he's said he is," Alex murmured, wishing she'd rest her hand on his face again.

"And you believe him?" Venus asked, making Alex pause. "Look at him, Alex. Look how frightened he is. I just want you to remember what he is giving up. I want you to remember how frightened he is, because it could be you in there, mentally preparing for something like this. He is willing, and he wants redemption, but I want you to understand that, despite what he has done, he is a person. He is someone's son— he is *my* son. I want you to be grateful for the sacrifice he is making, because it is breaking my heart," she whispered, so close now he could feel her hot breath on his ear.

Tears sprang to Alex's eyes. "I'm sorry. If there were another way, I would choose it," he breathed.

"I have no doubt you would, Alex," she said, and it sounded like she meant it. "I sincerely hope your mother gets to see you again because of the gift my son is giving," she added with a sad smile, her tone not bitter in the slightest, only hopeful.

"I hope so too," Alex replied, lowering his head.

"I love him, you know?"

Alex looked up. "Who? Julius?"

A strange glint flashed in her striking eyes. "Virgil. He is my son, and I love him dearly. We have spoken a lot in your absence, and he truly is sorry… for everything," she said, a single tear rolling down her high cheekbones. Even crying, she was the most elegant woman Alex had ever seen. "It would ease my pain to know you at least respected what he was doing, despite your differences."

"I do," Alex promised.

"And if he is scared, calm him," Venus pleaded, more tears running down her cheeks. "Don't let him die alone, please, whatever you do."

"I won't. I swear I won't."

Venus sighed heavily, letting the tears drip down her chin. For a long while, she said nothing, composing herself. Still, Alex couldn't take his eyes off her, a magnetic pull keeping him entranced. Finally, she raised her chin, her face proud, and addressed the whole room.

"Then, since I can't change his mind or yours, might I make a suggestion?" she asked, her regal tone returning.

Alex nodded. "Anything."

"My husband will not be watching Kingstone Keep quite as closely as Stillwater and Falleaf," she said. "There will be a handful of scouts, but there won't be an army."

"Kingstone?"

"Yes, Kingstone. If you're going, go now—don't linger a moment longer. Oh, and use that Thunderbird of yours, to avoid portals. That's where they will be watching," she insisted. "Remember that, as volatile as the king is, he wants what you want. If you succeed, he can be persuaded to keep his part of the bargain, regardless of how you left things. If you do not succeed, however, there will be nothing anyone can do to calm his wrath. Not even me."

Alex stared, open-mouthed, at the queen. In one fell swoop, she had eased his troubled mind. Yes, there would still be challenges ahead, but if she meant what she said, then they had a window of opportunity and a continued flicker of hope. The only problem was gauging whether she did indeed mean what she said. In that moment, Alex believed every word.

"Thank you," he whispered, standing up, although he was almost shaky on his feet.

"Leave your thanks for later," she replied, smiling. "The hard part is yet to come."

With those parting words, Alex hurried back to Ceres, who was still casting a suspicious eye over the whole scene.

"I hope you didn't say anything you weren't supposed to," Ceres chided. "As beautiful as you might think she is, she is still our enemy's wife, and she has these ways of making people say things they don't want to. I'd have warned you if you hadn't already been drawn in, like a little puppy dog—I wouldn't risk getting drawn in myself."

Alex flushed. "Hey, I was no puppy dog! I was fine—I kept my cool," he lied. "Anyway, we've got to get going. You bring Virgil; I'm going to rally the others. We're off to Kingstone!"

He didn't wait for Ceres's response as he rushed out the windmill door and into the cool air, his mind set on the tents and the friends he hoped he'd find there. Attempt number two would be underway before the day was over.

Suddenly, however, his mind felt foggy, a dull pain pulsing at the sides of his temples. Glancing back at the windmill, he realized with a start that Venus had done something to him. She must have used some kind of hypnosis spell. It had felt like Demeter's empathic abilities, only more intense, borne out of her allure. Now, he understood why Ceres had told him not to walk up to the bars—he had revealed so much and gained little in return. Was that part of her power? To learn as much as she could about everyone around her, storing it away so she might use it against them one day?

Even so, she had seemed genuine enough in her advice about using the pit at Kingstone and avoiding the portals. That was likely the best course of action, despite the source of the suggestion.

Sighing, Alex wondered whose team the queen would be on, when all was said and done.

CHAPTER 16

N EARING THE TENTS, ALEX WAS PLEASED TO SEE HIS
friends sitting around the fire. They looked up as
he approached, eager to know where he'd been all
this time. With time being of the absolute essence, he gave
them a quick rundown of events before diving into the task
at hand.

"Venus told me I should take Storm, which means only
one of you can come with me," he said. It was something he'd
been thinking about on the way over. With Virgil in tow, that
left only one other space. Although he could see the sense in
avoiding portals, since they were the spots most likely to be
guarded by Julius's soldiers, he couldn't help feeling doubt in

the back of his mind that Venus was somehow setting him up. With only three people, they could easily be captured and put into the king's custody. He glanced around, hoping to see the shadowy figure of Elias perching somewhere close by. At least with the shadow-man around, they wouldn't be quite so outnumbered. However, it appeared Elias still had not returned from his little research trip. Disappointed, Alex returned his attention to the group.

"You think you can trust her?" asked Aamir dubiously.

"I'm not sure, honestly. She seemed genuine enough," Alex replied. "And she probably has more reason to hate Julius than any of us. I know she's his wife, but you remember the way he was with her."

Aamir's expression darkened. "I hadn't thought of it like that."

"I think we have to trust her," Alex insisted. "I mean, we had to pick a haven. She just narrowed down the options."

Ellabell smirked. "I'm sure she did. I bet you'd believe anything she said."

"What's that supposed to mean?" Alex said defensively.

"Just that she's a very beautiful woman, and if she can control Julius the way you've said she can, I don't imagine you stood a chance against her charms," she teased.

"Look, we need to decide who's coming with me," said Alex, wanting the subject changed as quickly as possible. "Ceres is bringing Virgil over as we speak, and I'd like us to be ready to go when she arrives."

Ellabell chuckled knowingly, but said no more about Venus. However, before she could open her mouth to volunteer, Natalie spoke up instead.

"I would like to come with you."

Alex frowned. "Aren't you still injured?" he asked, glancing at her damaged leg.

She shook her head defiantly. "Agatha's pill has worked wonders. I am fine to run, fight, conjure—you name it."

He glanced at the others, hoping for backup. The last thing he wanted, as much as he hated to admit it, was someone who might slow them down. Natalie was strong, but if her leg was still hurt, she would be no use if they had to run from anything—soldiers, mist, Julius, any of the terrors that could chase them through the hallways of Kingstone Keep.

Aamir held up his hands. "I'm out, given my last mist encounter."

"I'd rather keep an eye on the cripple," Jari added, giving his friend a shove in the ribs.

"As much as I'd like to go... because of Virgil, I think we need to go with our strongest options. Helena or Natalie," said Ellabell, nodding at the two other young women.

"Hey, I'm not going to stand in Natalie's way if she wants to be the one to go," Helena chimed in, flashing her friend an encouraging grin. "If she says she's fit enough, she's fit enough."

Alex couldn't argue with that. "You positive you're better?" he asked Natalie.

Natalie put her hands on her hips. "Just a few aches and scrapes, but I feel just fine. Honestly."

He was about to ask again, when Ceres arrived, dragging Virgil behind her. Glancing down, Alex saw cuffs encircling the Head's wrists, the manacles entwined with gray ivy. There was a sweet sort of irony to the sight of them clamped on the skeletal man, but Alex thought better of making a remark as they approached.

"I thought I'd throw on the cuffs, just in case," Ceres explained. "Although, we likely won't be able to keep him in them during the spell, if there are things he needs to do with his hands," she added, lowering her voice so Virgil wouldn't hear. Alex nodded; he had been thinking the same thing. As much as Venus had insisted they could trust him, and Virgil himself had insisted he was ready and raring to go, as far as the spell was concerned, Alex couldn't shake the ingrained doubt he had where the Head was concerned.

"Okay. Natalie, Virgil, with me," said Alex, walking up the narrow passage between the tents, toward the shady glade at the back. Everyone followed, and as they neared the drooping willows, Storm poked her head out. She let out a delighted chirp, though it quickly turned to a trill of disgruntlement as she saw Virgil loping along behind the group. "It's okay, Storm. It's not going to be for long," Alex promised, stroking the silky feathers on the side of the Thunderbird's face.

Storm trilled again, showing her displeasure with a puff of the feathers atop her head.

Alex smiled. "I promise, it's just there and back. Then you don't have to see him again."

She turned her face away from Alex's hand, giving a sharp chirrup.

"Please? We just need to get to Kingstone Keep—can you do that?"

Her chirp turned into a coo as she relented.

"What would I do without you?" Alex grinned, stroking the sides of her face, before gesturing for Natalie and Virgil to hold their palms out flat. Storm touched her beak to the center of Natalie's hand without issue, giving a cheerful chirp. Virgil's, however, she barely deigned to touch, snatching her beak away the very second she made contact with his palm. Alex tried not to laugh at the sour expression on the Thunderbird's face. Instead, he helped Natalie onto Storm's back, followed by Virgil, who had to sit in the middle, given his restricted hands. It was going to be a tight squeeze, but it was manageable. Finally, Alex hopped up into the "driver's seat," clutching the bony protrusions of the Thunderbird's shoulders. Taking it as a sign for them to go, Storm broke into a run, tearing across the field before soaring upward in one elegant swoop, her giant wings stretching out to catch the currents of air beneath her.

Below, the others waved them off, anxious expressions on their faces. Turning away, he tried to ignore their anxiety, knowing it would only serve to feed his own. He needed to remain optimistic if this was going to work.

"Kingstone Keep," Alex whispered to Storm. "I know it's a longer way than usual, and you'll have to break through two barriers—do you think you can make it?"

She chirped loudly, puffing out her chest. Although she was a bird, Alex could hear a wavering note in her chirp that worried him. Was he asking too much of her? He had no real idea how inter-realm travel worked, but he remembered the strain it had caused her to break through to Starcross from Spellshadow. The trip to Kingstone might burn her out. As if trying to prove him wrong, Storm sped up, while Alex took a deep breath and clung on tight.

"Hang on!" Alex roared over the sound of the wind rushing past. There was an earth-shaking boom as Storm broke through the sound barrier, but still she did not slow. Her wings flapped harder and faster, building up speed. The others yelped behind him as the world stretched and distorted, and even Alex began to feel afraid as everything trembled around them. Like an airplane against a strong headwind, Storm battled the barriers between realms, forcing herself through, tearing the fabric of reality until it spiraled all around and everything looked like they'd fallen into the bottom of a kaleidoscope. Alex's teeth juddered and his bones rattled, his knuckles white where he was gripping Storm. They were tossed this way and that, Thunderbird and passengers both, Natalie reaching forward to grab Alex's arms tightly, sandwiching Virgil between herself and Alex so he wouldn't fall off.

With another boom that sounded like thunder cracking overhead, the world straightened, and they emerged into the familiar realm of Kingstone with a sharp jolt. Storm sagged as she struggled to carry them toward the keep, trying to glide to preserve energy wherever she could. Her neck dipped, and her wings slowed.

"You're doing great," said Alex, stroking her neck.

She cooed wearily, barely able to keep her head up.

A few times, they dropped out of the sky, plummeting a short distance, only for Storm to pull up at the last minute, delving into her reserves of strength to keep them in the air. Stoically, she flapped, carrying them toward their destination. Never had Alex been more pleased to see the prison as it came into sight. However, there was something amiss with the place. Squinting toward it, he noted the lack of rusty red fog floating about the structure, and the moat, with its strange lizard-like creatures, had dried up completely.

With an exhausted chirp, Storm landed on her favored turret, waiting until the trio dismounted before sinking into her nesting position, her chin on her chest, her wings tucked in. By the time they were at the top of the steps leading down into the prison, the Thunderbird was asleep. Alex smiled at her, hoping she'd be okay to fly again if they got into any trouble. What he'd just put her through had clearly been a grueling challenge, but they still had a return journey to make.

As Alex pushed the door at the bottom of the steps and crept out into the corridor beyond, he half expected to come face-to-face with a band of unruly inmates, the way he'd done the last time he'd been here. Instead, he was met with the foulest stench imaginable. It was a smell he'd only ever heard about, but never experienced with his own nostrils.

Pulling his t-shirt up over his nose, he walked into the prison itself, peering anxiously around corners in case any-one came hurtling toward him. No one did. The prison was like a ghost town, everything silent and deathly still. He even peeked into a few cells, just to see if there was anyone inside, but each one was empty. Stepping through into one of the larger common areas, he understood why.

Piles of bodies lay stacked up on the floor, tossed care-lessly like yesterday's trash. Worse than that, each body looked as if the bone and muscle had been pulled from it, the corpses floppy, ghoulish messes, the sunken faces staring upward at nothing, each expression still showing the horror of their final moments. A sea of scarlet ran beneath Alex's feet, maggots writhing across the open wounds, as blowflies buzzed around the mouths of the dead. The smell was over-whelmingly metallic and so strong that he could almost taste it.

This was Julius's handiwork.

Staring down a nearby hallway, he saw the same grue-some scene at the end of it. Bodies piled high, everything torn from within—bone, muscle, sinew, organs. Undoubtedly, the king had taken the essence too. Perhaps, Alex thought, this was Julius's quick method of extraction, removing it all at once, not caring about the mess it caused.

Nobody said a word as the trio stalked through the mass grave, leaving footprints in the congealed blood beneath their shoes. With every footstep, a swarm of green-tinged flies soared upward, flying into their faces. The trio's hands swatted wildly with palms coated in bristling energy, a frying sound hissing every so often as a blowfly got zapped.

At each floor they came to, knowing they had to descend to the subterranean levels, they found more of the same, the foul stench of death and decay growing more pungent. The murder was endless. Julius had evidently ripped through the place like a tornado, destroying everything in his path, not caring if it was male or female, young or old. There were even scorch-marks on the wall where some of them had tried to fight back, though such a thing could only be futile against a man like that.

There were no words to describe how nauseated Alex felt, knowing how these people had suffered at the king's hands. He remembered how he had broken the barrier modules on his way out, hoping to distract Julius's attention and bring him to Kingstone, to deal with the chaotic mess. Well, if Alex had known *this* was what that cleanup would entail, he'd never have broken the cylinder. One impulsive move, and all these people had died. Had he not had the spell to think about, he would have curled up in a ball right there, and remained that way for the rest of his life. Though he knew it wasn't his fault, considering nobody could predict something so abhorrent, he still felt the weight of responsibility crushing him.

Focus, he told himself, trying not to look at any more hideous corpses.

At long last, they reached the subterranean level they needed—the one with the empty cell that led to a staircase. Fortunately for them, both cell door and staircase trapdoor were already open. Alex thought that was a bit strange, but said nothing about it as they followed the narrow stairs down. Alex led the other two past the room where Natalie had crouched in her possessed state, toward the large gates at the end of the rough-hewn corridor.

He heaved himself against them, and the doors swung open with a loud creak. Expecting to see the golden bird and the pit, Alex stepped into the room, only to stagger back again as the smell hit him hard in the nostrils. The whole room emitted a rotten stench, and, as his eyes adjusted to the dim light, Alex could see why. The edges of the pit were slimy with the remnants of decaying entrails. Julius had evidently dumped everything he'd extracted into the pit at once, organic and magical alike, not bothering with any form of control or etiquette. Well, at least the Great Evil was satisfied here, Alex thought, shuddering at the mental image of Julius pouring the slops of hundreds into that gaping hole.

"We're doing the spell here?" asked Virgil, pinching his nose.

Alex nodded. "We have to."

"Are you sure we cannot go to Stillwater or Falleaf?" Natalie wondered, her eyes watering from the stench.

Alex shrugged apologetically. "I'm afraid not. It's either here or nowhere."

"Right now, I'd vote nowhere," Virgil muttered, turning to retch slightly.

"You can't do that while you're reciting the spell," Alex warned.

Virgil rolled his eyes. "Which of us do you think has more experience with this spell?" he remarked, silencing Alex. "Speaking of which, I won't be able to do the spell with these on my wrists," he said, jangling the cuffs on his wrists.

"Of course you can," Natalie countered.

"I need my hands for the spell," he insisted. "One hand needs to be on the book, and I can't do that with them pulled together like this."

"I guess not," Alex said, a little dubious. Still, he moved over to Virgil so he could undo the cuffs on his wrists. Once they were off, he threw them to Natalie, who had taken up her position by the door. Whipping the book and vial from his satchel, he reluctantly handed the two objects to the Head. "Shall we get started?"

"No time like the present," Virgil replied sourly, taking the book and vial and gesturing for Alex to follow while he approached the pit. "I hope that nasty little shadow friend of yours isn't going to turn up in the middle of this?" he said as he opened the book to lie flat on the surface of Alex's palms.

Alex shook his head, still wishing Elias *were* here. "He's otherwise engaged."

Virgil snorted. "Unsurprising—he'd always do anything to get out of hard work."

With that, Virgil pressed his own palm down on the page. Slowly, the book began to glow, before bursting into a fierce light that backlit Virgil's hand, making his skin appear to glow too. As it had done before, the writing on the pages lifted, swirling up in a spiral, and then settled in the air before them, hovering just above the pit. The large, glowing letters were paler than they had been the last time, but they were still readable, the words clear.

With a deep breath, Virgil made to begin the incantation.

Suddenly remembering Siren Mave's advice, Alex cut in, hoping to stop the Head before he spoke the first word. "A friend of mine said the spell had to be properly witnessed, by all who are involved. Does that mean anything to you?" he asked.

But it was too late. Virgil had already spoken the first word. There was no way he could pause to talk; he had to continue. Like a runaway train, there was no stopping him. With every stanza the skeletal man cleared, the earth shook. His voice rang clear and true across the cavern, the words singing smoothly toward the Great Evil.

Gradually, Virgil came to the twelfth stanza, though his eyes stared at Alex strangely. "With the blood of my enemies, I close the circle of pain," he said.

As the final word echoed across the cavern, Virgil nodded for Alex to pick up the vial on the ground. Leaving the book in Virgil's grasp, Alex did just that, ducking down to pick up the small bottle.

A second later, the book landed on the ground beside him with a heavy thud, dust flying up from the pages. Looking up in horror, Alex watched as Virgil slowly backed away from the edge of the pit, heading for the door. The skeletal man was trying to escape before he had finished the spell.

"VIRGIL, NO!"

CHAPTER 17

VIRGIL BROKE INTO A SPRINT AS ALEX SHOUTED.

"I can't finish it. I can't do it," he stammered, shaking his head, racing for the door of the pit room. Natalie cut him off, ready with the cuffs, but he feinted out of the way, leaving them to clatter fruitlessly in her hands.

Virgil struggled to pull open the heavy door, but Natalie lunged for him again, tackling him to the ground by gripping his legs. She tried to run her magic under his skin, but his anti-magic half fought back.

Alex dove for Virgil too, creating quite the pileup, though they were getting perilously close to the edge of the pit. Natalie scrambled to her feet before scooping the vial and the book off the ground, away from where the two men were brawling.

"The cuffs!" Alex yelled, still wrestling with Virgil on the ground. Natalie held out the cuffs for Alex to grab. He snatched them from her hands, and tried to shove them onto Virgil's wrists. The royal was already weak from having the manacles on the first time, but the repeated presence of the gray ivy that wound around the cuffs debilitated him further. A weak coil of hybrid magic emerged from his palms, twisting feebly past Alex's head. Alex himself could barely conjure a shield, much less fight back. Realizing it was futile, Alex threw the cuffs away, and they hit the wall with a tinny clank.

Instead, he powered through the flurry of Virgil's twisting fists, ignoring the searing pain as Virgil's weakened spells landed on him, and clamped his hands onto the sides of the Head's temples. The Head's eyes went wide in horror as Alex fed the silvery strands of his mind-control into Virgil's brain.

As his power took over, Alex felt a twinge of remorse for what he was doing. Part of him wished it didn't have to be like this, given how much their relationship had progressed, but Virgil hadn't left him with another option. There was no way he was going to give up on this opportunity, just because Virgil was scared and having second thoughts. Once again, he heard Venus's voice in his head, reminding him that Virgil was just a person, with hopes and fears like the rest of them. Like everyone else, Alex understood that the Head probably feared death too—it was the great leveler, bringing even the strongest men to their knees.

Still, they had made an agreement. One life wasn't enough of a reason to stop the spell, not when there were hundreds out there, at risk while the Great Evil continued to exist.

Maneuvering the skeletal man, Alex managed to get him to his feet, walking him slowly back toward the edge of the pit. The stench of the room had eased slightly, as Alex had become accustomed to it, but sometimes a fresh wave caught him unawares, making bile rise in his throat. This was one of those moments, though he recovered quickly. Natalie ran up with the book and the vial, and held them out, just as Alex had done before. He thanked her, before placing the Head's palm flat on the open page. For a long time, the page remained nothing but paper. Then, just as Alex was about to give up hope, a glow surged from within, growing brighter with each second, until it shone with ferocious luminescence around Virgil's hand, the golden words rising up into the air once more.

Alex breathed a sigh of relief, though he hoped this didn't mean they were on attempt number three. Virgil had never swallowed the blood, or even so much as lifted it to his lips, which gave Alex the tentative belief that it may have opened a loophole through which they could remain on that second try. The only problem was, he had a feeling they couldn't simply pick up where they'd left off, with Virgil just drinking the blood. The book had dropped, the hovering words vanishing from the pit, which led Alex to believe they would have to begin again, to ensure the spell was done in its entirety. Whether his inkling was right, he guessed they'd see soon enough.

Closing his eyes, Alex followed the familiar motions of mind control, hearing Virgil's voice reciting the words he was thinking. Each stanza danced in the air in front of them. One, two, three, four, five, six, seven, eight, nine, ten, eleven… and, finally, twelve came and went, without a hiccup. Though Alex didn't dare feel even a hint of confidence, there was something different about this try—it felt smoother, somehow, almost like it was going better than last time. Not that he'd say such a thing out loud.

Finishing the twelfth stanza, Alex felt excitement bubble up inside him. He lifted the vial, which Natalie had graciously un-stoppered, and forced the last words from Virgil's mouth.

"With the blood of my enemies, I close the circle of pain."

Making Virgil take the vial from him, Alex fed instructions into the Head's brain, forcing him to lift the vial to his lips, pour the liquid in, and swallow the thick substance. He did so, following the puppeteer, though a scarlet smear stained the Head's bottom lip as he removed the vial and handed it back to Natalie, as per Alex's mental instructions.

With that, Alex released Virgil from the clutches of the mind control, lowering him carefully to the ground. He groaned, coming around much quicker than the last time.

"What have you done?" he croaked.

"What I had to," said Alex, glancing down at the man on

the floor. However, he quickly realized there was something wrong with the image before him. Everything felt as if it had gone well, but nothing seemed to have changed. No pits were caving in; no walls were crumbling. And, most notably of all, Virgil wasn't dead. If the spell had gone as it was supposed to, the Head wouldn't be sitting up, calling Alex all the names under the sun.

Curious, Alex stepped right up to the edge of the pit to peer down into the darkness below. Was the second attempt a dud? If they used the right blood but got everything else wrong, did that mean the mist stayed below? So far, nothing seemed to be rising from the cavernous depths. He peered closer, trying to remember whether the mist had already reared its ugly head by this point, the last time they tried it. He simply couldn't remember.

A sudden, violent tremor shook the ground, sending Alex lurching forward. With the gaping mouth of the pit staring him full in the face, he knew he had been too close to the edge. His feet were no longer touching solid ground. In slow motion, he felt himself begin to tumble into the darkness, only to be snatched back at the very last moment, his body jolting upward, his neck snapping back. Virgil had taken hold of his t-shirt, while a gleaming rope of anti-magic twisted around Alex's chest, rapidly conjured from the Head's hands, allowing the skeletal man to pull Alex back over the edge of the pit, to safety. Natalie rushed to the pit's lip to grasp at Alex's flailing arm. Together, Virgil and Natalie managed to retrieve him from the edge of certain death, and for that he was eternally grateful.

"It went wrong again!" Virgil gasped, as another tremor tore through the earth below them.

"No—" Alex yelled, his words muffled by the roar of the earthquake below.

"As I was doing it, I knew something was wrong!" Virgil explained quickly, shouting over the din. "Something was missing—it was missing last time, and it was missing this time. What you said before, about the witness, it got me thinking…" he added, one eye constantly on the pit. "But right now, we need to get out of here!"

The noise of the quake was growing louder and louder, making Alex feel like his eardrums were about to burst. It was almost like pressure was building, deep below them, as something prepared to erupt.

Alex nodded, shoving Natalie toward the door, throwing the book and the vial to her. Given her wholly magical being, he knew the mist would go for her first, if that was what was building beneath the earth. As she reached for the handle, turning it and yanking the door open, a geyser of silver mist shot up through the crevasse, moving faster than anything Alex had seen before. This version of the mist was rapid, latching onto Natalie's essence like a missile. Fortunately, Alex and Virgil were already at the door, blocking its route toward Natalie, who had managed to get out into the corridor and was running for the staircase at the far end. The mist surged toward them, recoiling at the last minute. This time, it didn't seem to have much of a taste for Virgil. The mist swept out before crashing back in again, like a shark circling its victim, testing the flavor.

As it swept out again, the two men took their chance, diving out of the pit room and slamming the door shut behind them with a boom that shook the whole hallway. Glancing at one another, they sprinted for the staircase too, following Natalie up into the main body of the prison.

The mist wasn't far behind them, a door proving little challenge for this iteration of the sweeping plague. It rushed up the stairs behind them, snapping at their heels. Not pausing for a second, they raced through every floor, ducking bats and sidestepping rotting corpses, until they reached the very top level, their lungs screaming against the exertion. The mist stopped by the entrance to one of the larger common rooms, seemingly confused by the piles of dead bodies. Slithering across the lifeless forms, it snaked beneath their decaying flesh, seeking out any dregs of essence that might still be inside. This gave the trio the break they needed, and they hurried toward the turret where Storm was waiting.

She chirped in a panicked tone as they appeared. Turning around, she squatted down on her haunches, allowing them to clamber up, before hopping onto the wall and gliding off in one swift movement. As they took to the sky, Alex turned around in time to see a wave of silver undulating up through the staircase, smothering the flagstones they had been standing on, mere moments before. They'd had a very close call—too close for Alex's liking.

Nobody spoke as Storm flew. Alex couldn't stop thinking about what had happened, and what that now meant for him. He doubted he would be able to keep such a disastrous event from Julius for very long. After what Venus had said, Alex knew there were likely to be spies watching Kingstone, though whether they'd escape the mist remained to be seen. If they did survive it, they'd tell Julius what had happened, and that would signal the signing of his death warrant.

They just needed to get back to Starcross before anyone noticed them. If they could do that, Alex knew he might have a chance of evading Julius's terms of the bargain.

"Natalie, can I see the vial?" Alex asked.

"There is not much left," Natalie replied, passing the vial over, though she clung tightly to the book in case it fell.

Alex sighed. "I didn't think there would be."

Keeping one hand on Storm's shoulder handle, he lifted the glass bottle to the light. There was indeed some liquid left at the bottom, but it didn't look like there was enough for a third attempt. Peering closer, he thought there might just be five drops, but was that a risk he'd be willing to take on his final attempt? No, he didn't think it was.

"Can you pass the book?" he asked, slipping the vial carefully into his pocket.

"What if I drop it?" Natalie replied, her expression concerned.

"You won't," he encouraged.

The book passed Virgil's face, and Alex briefly feared that the skeletal man might reach up and knock it out of Natalie's hands on purpose, so nobody ever had to do the damned spell again. But Virgil didn't move a muscle, his eyes staring blankly into the distance.

Resting the book against Storm's neck, Alex conjured a thin sheet of anti-magic, and saw that the words had faded again, the lettering barely legible. *Well*, thought Alex, *at least it hasn't completely disappeared.* As long as the book remained in his grasp, he had one last chance remaining. There were now only two havens in which they could perform the spell—their options were narrowing by the day.

With a powerful flap of her broad wings, Storm sped up, causing Alex to snatch the book back up and hold it against him. Faster and faster she flew, until the world distorted and trembled around them. It was like being on a rough sea, jolted this way and that. Alex thought his head might wobble off. No matter how hard she pushed through the barriers, it was clear the Thunderbird was struggling.

Alex stroked her feathers, feeling utterly helpless. Trapped between realms, what was he supposed to do?

Just as Alex began to fear the worst, a loud thunder-crack tore through the air, and Storm emerged into a realm. However, as Alex glanced around, he realized it wasn't Starcross. Autumnal leaves fell from the trees below, and the glint of something golden in the distance caught his eye, making his heart miss a panicked beat.

They were back at Falleaf.

"No, Storm, we can't stop here," Alex pleaded, but the Thunderbird was already descending into a glade, her wings weary.

She chirped an apology, carrying them through the trees until they reached a spot near the cave. They clambered down, and Storm disappeared into the foliage, the need to rest and recuperate evidently overwhelming all else.

"Come on then, we should go back," Natalie suggested, making a move toward the cave entrance. Alex reached out and grasped her hand, pulling her backward.

He shook his head. "We can't go through the cave. If there are spies in these woods, they might see us, and that would bring Julius straight to Starcross," he warned, his voice a harsh whisper.

"Then what do you propose we do?" she asked. "If we stay out here, he will find us."

"We have to hide until Storm is ready to fly again," said Alex firmly, glancing around with furtive eyes.

"Psst!" A voice startled the trio. It was coming from the direction of some rustling bushes close to the cave entrance. From between the leaves, a head poked out. Agatha grinned at them, reaching a hand out and gesturing for them to come closer. "In a spot of trouble, are you?" she asked knowingly.

Alex nodded. "Something like that."

"How do you know that?" Virgil countered, suspiciously.

"Look at your faces! They have panic written all over them!" she explained. "Now, can I assist in any way?"

"Can you take us to that place you were telling us about? The one where Ellabell found you?" Alex asked hopefully.

Agatha beamed. "Why, certainly! I have some soup on the stove, if you're interested?"

"Soup would be lovely," said Natalie, relief washing over her face.

Leaving the cave behind, they followed the old hippie through the woods, until they came to a vast oak tree at the edge of a glade. It looked like a trap to Alex, but, as they approached, he could see that it was, in fact, a false trunk, opening onto a set of stairs that led below ground. Agatha went first, beckoning the rest of them down.

Once they were below the earth, Alex saw they were in a cottage of sorts, only it had no windows, and the entire structure was forged from hard-packed soil. There were knick-knacks and chintzy ornaments everywhere, which Agatha delighted in showing the group, though all they really wanted to do was sit down and forget about the smell of the bodies and the collapsing pit at Kingstone.

That brief reprieve was given, to their absolute relief, when Agatha went to fetch the soup.

"So, what was missing?" Alex snapped in Virgil's direction, taking a seat in an oversized armchair beside the roaring fire.

The Head seemed taken aback. "I'm still figuring it out,"

he said defensively. "All I know is, as I was doing it, it all felt wrong. There's something we're overlooking, I'm almost certain of it. We'll have to look over the book again when we get back to Starcross… I'll need some time to process things."

"You will do the spell again?" Natalie asked, her expression one of disbelief.

Virgil shrugged. "What other choice do I have? Your *friend* here would force me to do so, regardless." He cast Alex a dark look.

"I wouldn't have used mind control if you hadn't lost your nerve in the middle of the spell," Alex replied tersely, although he did feel a stab of guilt for how rash his reaction had been.

"My change of heart had nothing to do with lost nerve," Virgil spat. "As soon as I began, I knew the spell would fail. It was a gut feeling I could not ignore."

"Well, we've only got one shot left now," Alex said.

The three of them sat in silence, no one daring to voice how utterly hopeless it all seemed.

CHAPTER 18

AGATHA FED THEM BOWL AFTER BOWL OF HEARTY vegetable soup, handing them thick slices of crusty bread to dip into the warm broth, until they were so full they felt as if they might burst. Looking at the carriage clock the old hippie had perched on her mantelpiece, sandwiched between two rather frightening-looking porcelain poodles, Alex saw that more than two hours had passed in the underground cottage. How that had happened, he didn't know, but they had stayed longer than Alex had meant them to.

"We have to go," he whispered, as Virgil was finishing off his third helping. It was peculiar to see the sunken-cheeked man eating so heartily, given his appearance. For some reason, Alex had simply presumed the strange hybrid didn't eat at all, but here he was, guzzling down the soup Agatha had made.

Natalie nodded. "If we stay a moment longer, you will have to roll me out of here," she said, patting her stomach.

Just then, Agatha walked in with a tray of gigantic muffins, an equally giant grin on her face. It disappeared as she saw the trio standing up and preparing to leave.

"No, you can't leave just yet, my cherubs!" she cried. "You haven't had your dessert, and Vincent will be back from his little chitchat with Hadrian soon! He'll be so disappointed if he misses you!"

"Sorry, Agatha, we've stayed too long," Alex replied. "Thank you for your hospitality, and for the delicious food, but we really have to get going. It'll be dark in a few hours, and we want to get back before then. You'll have to say hello to Vincent for us."

Agatha frowned. "Back to your mystery world at the end of that cave?" she asked pointedly.

Alex nodded. "Yeah, back there."

"Well, if you're heading back that way, I'd watch out for soldiers if I were you—they've been all over the woods near that cave today. Like rats, ferreting about, causing a right old mess! Broke down the door and everything," she remarked. "They'd just disappeared when you arrived. It's why I called to you—didn't want you getting caught up in all that, when they got back!" She smiled proudly, handing them each a muffin. Alex couldn't focus on it, her words sinking in.

"Wait, where did they disappear to?" Alex asked, suddenly panicked.

Agatha paused in thought. "Well, I suppose they must have gone into the cave... Yes, I think maybe they did. One moment they were there, the next they were gone. Unless they're very good at magic, I think they might well have gone into that cave," she replied, rattling out the words stream-of-consciousness style.

The trio glanced at each other, knowing what Agatha said couldn't be a good thing. Perhaps, Alex hoped, the soldiers had reached the end of the cave and found only the false wall. That's what it was there for, after all, to keep the entrance to Starcross hidden. Even if they had made it through, surely Ceres's cavalry would have dealt with them swiftly?

Either way, Alex knew they had to leave now.

With a farewell to Agatha, the three individuals hurried up the staircase, back out into the forest. Running fast, though their stomachs were heavy with food, they headed for the cave entrance as quickly as their legs could carry them. Natalie was starting to limp again, her mouth set in a grim line, refusing to show any pain on her face as she raced along beside the other two.

Reaching the mouth of the cave, Alex peered closely at the ground in front of the entrance. The dirt and grass were churned up where boots had stomped the earth. It looked like soldiers had indeed gone into the cave, but whether or not they'd come back out again, Alex couldn't tell. It was hard to make out which direction the boot-prints were going in, with so many overlapping.

Alex put his thumb and index finger to his lips and whistled loudly. A second later, Storm poked her head around the side of the cave, giving Alex a look of displeasure.

"Sorry, Storm, we have to go," he explained. Her expression softened.

The trio mounted Storm's back, the Thunderbird taking a runup before soaring into the sky. She seemed to have regained some of her vitality, her neck lifted high, her wings beating powerfully once more as she swooped low over the canopy of Falleaf's forest. Curving upward, she climbed higher and higher, until the trees below were just one large patch of green. In the center, Alex could see the miniature shape of the pagoda, and wondered if Julius was still inside, plotting his revenge.

With the rocky turbulence Alex had come to expect from this particular trip, Storm powered through the barrier between Falleaf and Starcross, emerging a few moments later, the distorted world snapping back to normal, revealing the idyllic realm below. They flew along, passing over the field in front of the cave entrance. Looking down, Alex saw the unmistakable tracks of marching soldiers, the grass eroded away by their soles. As a rising feeling of concern coursed through him, Alex lifted his gaze and set it to the horizon, hoping Ceres had managed to cut the soldiers off before they could do any harm.

Reaching the encampment, Alex's eyes flew wide with horror, his heart gripping in his chest. Something was going on in the camp below, something strange and wrong. A flash of magic tore through the air like a fireworks display, energies crashing together with crackling explosions, the cries of the wounded rising beneath the din. Alex's face morphed into a mask of fury. Ceres hadn't managed to cut the soldiers off. The camp had been ambushed by a magical army, and the Starcross survivors were fighting back with all their might.

And Alex could see that their side was losing.

Glancing around, Alex tried to find Julius among the legion of soldiers, but the king was nowhere to be seen. He wasn't even sitting at the sidelines, enjoying the spectacle. Such a notable absence worried Alex—there was no way Julius would miss out on this, especially if his army was winning. No, there was something brewing beneath the surface, something he couldn't quite put his finger on. Everything felt wrong, the very air tense around him; a tiny voice in the back of his head pleaded with him to run, but he ignored it.

"Land there," Alex instructed, gesturing toward an open patch of ground at the edge of the camp, seemingly devoid of fighters. It was far enough away from the fighting that Storm wouldn't have to enter the fray, but it meant the three riders would have to sprint toward the battle.

With a delicate flap of her wings, she landed in the open

space, hunkering down to let the trio off before taking to the skies again, circling and swooping where she could, picking off any of the soldiers she didn't like the look of. Alex smiled, knowing Storm wouldn't run from a fight either.

Keeping his eye on her and the battle ahead, Alex sprinted toward the battlefield, which lay just beyond the encampment, where the two sides were clashing in a head-on attack. As he tore through the throng, wanting to reach the front lines, something strange happened.

Out of nowhere, a thick yellow fog rolled across the field, stinging the eyes and nose like mustard gas, the fog so opaque that Alex could barely the see the person next to him. It was then he realized that the enemy fighters were wearing masks that covered half their faces, keeping their noses and mouths protected. At first, he'd thought they were just part of the uniform, but now he understood they were there for a purpose. It was to keep the fog out. Whatever it was, it wasn't to be inhaled or ingested, if the soldiers' attire was anything to go by.

"Cover your faces!" Alex yelled, but his voice got lost, the fog deadening his words.

"What?" cried Natalie, but it was too late. The fog hit her.

Immediately, her body spasmed, a yellow foam frothing from her mouth, her eyes growing wild, showing the whites. Seconds later, she turned toward Alex, lunging at him with her teeth bared like a savage animal, clearly no longer recognizing him as her friend. She tore at him with her hands, knocking him to the ground, though Virgil managed to pull her away long enough for Alex to regain his footing. Scrambling to his feet, Alex conjured a shield of anti-magic around himself, protecting against her brutal advances. Letting out a scream of indignation, she conjured her own magic between the palms of her hands, infusing it with thin streaks of pale pink—dark magic.

Virgil stepped forward to try to help, but as he raised his hands to create an orb of hybrid energy, a figure exploded from the camouflage of the fog, tackling him to the earth. Alex couldn't make out who it was, but it looked remarkably like Billy Foer.

Natalie charged at Alex's shield, only to be sent flying backward. She got up again, undeterred, hurling spears of pure golden energy infused with slivers of red toward his protective bubble. One pierced through—Alex managed to duck out of the way just in time, though the movement meant the collapse of his shield, his focus knocked off guard for a moment. It was the window Natalie needed. As he struggled to regain himself, trying to put up another shield, the air was suddenly punched out of him, and he felt the bruising impact of something hard barging into him.

He fell backward, looking up to see Natalie standing over him, conjuring an enormous ball of volatile dark magic in the palms of her hands. The red center glowed. Realizing he was about to get raw dark magic hurled into his face, Alex responded in kind, letting the pressure of his anti-magic build in his hands, feeling the flow of the black-and-silver strands. He smacked his palms together with a hard slam. The resulting explosion was vast, and Natalie bore the full brunt of it. She flew through the air, landing with a sickening thud on the grass, ten or so yards from where Alex lay. Alex sat up, looking over at where his friend had landed, but she wasn't moving. He waited a second longer, but Natalie was completely still, her limbs splayed out at awkward angles.

He ran to her. "Please, no. Natalie, I'm sorry. I'm so sorry." Kneeling beside her, he saw the soft rise and fall of her chest, and felt the steady kick of a pulse, still beating, when he pressed his fingers to her wrist. She was okay, just unconscious.

Relieved, Alex scooped her up in his arms and ran with her to one of the nearest tents, at the far edge of the camp. There were some Starcross residents already inside, cowering in the corner, but their expressions of fear eased as Alex explained what had happened.

"Can you take care of her until I come back?" Alex asked. The four cowering individuals, two men, two women, nodded. A gray-haired woman, the oldest of the group, moved forward to examine Natalie.

"I will help heal her until you return," she said, looking at Alex with milky blue eyes.

"Thank you," Alex said. "Wrap cloth around her face and yours so the yellow fog can't affect you," he added, before disappearing back out the tent flap, heading for the battlefield once more.

As he ran, Alex began to understand what was happening. Julius had, at last, discovered Starcross, and had released the fog to alter the minds of the opposing side—why lift a finger to fight when he could just get his enemies to fight each other, doing the hard work for him? Yes, he had soldiers present, but they seemed to be an additional force, not the main event. Julius's intention, as far as Alex could see, was to get the Starcross inhabitants to kill and maim one another, leaving him free to sweep in at the last moment and claim victory. It was all so clear now. *That* was why he was nowhere to be seen; he was keeping away from the scene of battle until it was safe for him to arrive.

Never had Alex been more enraged by a single human being. If they ever came face-to-face again, Alex knew he'd defy everything to knock the smirk off that evil man's lips.

A short distance away, Alex made out the two figures of Aamir and Jari, fighting one another. Beside them, Ellabell and Helena were doing the same. Friends were fighting friends, but it was worse for the half-essence survivors, whose bodies and energies were already weaker than most.

Aamir appeared to be losing badly, unable to use his magic to defend himself against his friend. Bobbing and weaving wearily like a boxer in the twelfth round, the older boy avoided the golden blasts of magic surging from Jari's hands, landing punches and kicks where he could, to try to get the blond-haired boy to back off. From the sluggish way he was darting this way and that, it was clear Aamir was getting tired, though Jari was showing no signs of letting up.

Ellabell and Helena were more evenly matched, though the fight was a ferocious one. Helena was obviously more skilled in offensive magic, shooting blasts of golden artillery with incredible speed, but Ellabell matched her blow for blow, using her powerful shields to deflect Helena's attacks and send them back to their creator.

Just as Alex was about to push Aamir and Jari apart, Demeter and Ceres flew by, emerging from the fog on horseback. They had fabric tied across the lower halves of their faces, and though their eyes were streaming with tears, it didn't deter them from trying to help as many students as they could, pulling the vulnerable up onto the Kelpies and sprinting with them to the back of the camp, where the fog had yet to reach. Still, it was clearly proving to be a Sisyphean task—as soon as Demeter mind-controlled one student out of their stupor, tying material around their face, they had to come back for more. The cycle was endless; everywhere Alex turned, he could hear the sound of hooves echoing.

Then, as quickly as it had come, the yellow gas began to fade away, as though it were being sucked out, back across the field. Alex watched it go, dread flowing through his veins. If the mist was leaving, Julius would be on his way.

As it cleared, Alex got a better view of the battlefield. Around him, people were beginning to return to normal.

Aamir and Jari stopped fighting, looking at one another in pure shock. Jari had a ball of magic raised to strike, and Aamir was holding up his fists, ready to jab at Jari's face. Ellabell and Helena separated too, eyeing each other suspiciously, glancing down at their palms as if their hands belonged to strangers.

Bodies littered the grass. Some were moving, their groans rumbling across the ground toward where Alex stood. Others were still, never to move again. Those who had delivered the final blows covered their mouths in horror, seeing what they had done, yet not knowing how or why it had happened. Alex took in the devastation, feeling as if someone had taken a knife to his heart. Of all the cruel, cold things Julius had done, this was one of the worst—turning neighbor against neighbor, student against student.

Still, they were not defeated.

On the front line, there was a rallying cry, urging the fighters to take on the remaining soldiers. Seeing there were still uniformed enemies among them, the survivors sprang into action, chasing after those who belonged to Julius's militia—those who had brought this terrible fog with them. Seeing the mob swarming toward them, the army scattered, turning tail and running from the sight of the battlefield. The Starcross warriors gave chase, several Kelpie riders catching up with a few of the enemy soldiers, cutting them off in their tracks. As the soldiers crossed the river, however, the Starcross folk skidded to a halt, a whole line of eyes watching the retreating soldiers.

Soon after, a roar of victory rose from the crowd, but the triumphant sound brought only sorrow to Alex's heart. They believed they had won the fight.

Sadly, he knew they hadn't.

CHAPTER 19

"STOP!" ALEX BELLOWED, HIS VOICE BOOMING across the field. Victory died on the lips of the Starcross warriors as they turned to see Alex approaching, his friends following close behind. Virgil had reappeared too, limping at the back of the smaller group. "Everyone needs to stop cheering!" Alex shouted, drawing looks of displeasure from the crowd.

"And who are you to tell us to quiet down?" someone yelled.

"I know it looks like we've won, but we haven't!" Alex explained, his voice carrying across the warriors. "Julius planned all of this. The fog, the fighting, the retreat. He is doing it to lure you all into a false sense of security! We need to get back on our guard, and be ready for him when he strikes!"

A murmur rippled through the assembled force. They glanced toward the spot where the soldiers had run, but the uniformed army was no longer visible.

"How do you know that? Are you working for him?" a second voice called, the tone accusatory.

Alex shook his head. "I just know the man we're dealing with. He isn't done with us, I promise you!"

It was all too straightforward not to be a setup. Yes, the fights had been tough, and several people had lost their lives, but it was much too easy. Julius had something else up his sleeve, Alex was certain of it. Now, it was a waiting game. If they could be ready when he struck, they might stand a better chance of survival.

Ceres rode up to where Alex stood. "You think we should evacuate?" she asked, looking around nervously.

Alex shrugged. "I think we could try. Julius is—"

Ceres cut him off with a wave of her hand. An eerie stillness was settling across the battlefield and all who stood upon it. Her people watched her, waiting for her to speak, but she was silent, listening intently to something only she could hear.

"Too late," she whispered, her head snapping up. "Everybody, run for the trees! Get into the forest! Hide yourselves!" she screamed. There was no time to do things calmly, the group of gathered warriors looking at each other in a panic. As her words sank in, they began to run in all directions, chaos ensuing as the people of Starcross fought to escape an enemy they couldn't yet see.

"What is it?" Alex asked, trying to figure out what it was Ceres knew that he didn't.

He understood, mere moments later, as the clouds began to roll in at an alarming, unnatural speed. They gathered, swelling and frothing over one another, fluffy white giving way to deep, bruised storm clouds that loomed above the realm. A great boom of thunder shook the earth below, and lightning tore across the dark sky in terrifying forks of rampant electricity, lashing nearby trees that burst into flames.

Those who had run for the trees backed away, seeking an alternative exit, only for another bolt of lightning to hurtle in the direction they were running, cutting them off. Julius was dividing and conquering, without even getting his hands dirty.

Storm, who had been circling the battleground with her keen eyes, weaved between the forks of lightning with ease, darting this way and that to avoid them, but as one came too close to her wing, singeing the very tips of her feathers, she spiraled out of the way, retreating into the nearby forest with a squawk. Alex wanted to follow her, to ensure she was okay, but the storm brewing overhead prevented him, not to mention the warning grip of Aamir's hand on his arm.

"She will be fine," the older boy promised. "She will be

safer in there, hidden away, than she will be out here," he added. Alex nodded reluctantly; he could see the sense in it, but he couldn't bear to think of the Thunderbird alone and in pain, left in solitude to lick her wounds. Glancing at the spot where she'd vanished, he made a promise to come back for her as soon as he could.

Meanwhile, thunder growled deafeningly overhead, the roar intensifying as the heavens parted. A great glowing light shone down, so bright Alex had to cover his eyes with his arm. Once it had dimmed, he dared to look back toward the sky. A large band of elite soldiers floated to the ground the way Venus had done when they'd snatched her from Spellshadow. Julius was leading them this time, confirming Alex's suspicions that he'd simply been biding his time, waiting for the majority of the fight to be over before he made his triumphant final blow. Here were the remnants, waiting to be scooped up and destroyed for his amusement.

The King's squadron was dressed in sleek black military garb, with glistening plates covering their chests and arms, and helmets over their heads. They exuded power like electricity.

As thunderbolts shot down any attempt to flee, the Starcross fighters gathered in the center of the battlefield, turning to face the elite squad walking calmly toward them, their hands raised, rippling magic already flowing around their fingers. The energy bristling from them was like nothing Alex had ever experienced; it was tangible, emanating from their very beings. There was no way they could fight this kind of soldier—they were too few, too weak, too helpless.

One of the elite sent a thin ribbon of magic through the air toward one of the Starcross warriors who stood at the front of the gathered force. It seemed innocuous enough, but when the warrior tried to conjure a spell to protect himself, it sailed straight through and snaked beneath the warrior's skin, embedding itself deep inside. Those standing beside him stared in horror, not knowing what was going to happen next.

If they had known, they would have run.

The poor victim unleashed a blood-curdling scream, his eyes bulging outward, before he exploded into a million bloody pieces, his body splattering onto the nearby onlookers in a fountain of scarlet. The thin ribbon that had done the damage retreated to its owner, carrying a coil of pulsing red light behind it.

It reminded Alex of what he'd seen at Kingstone, giving him the feeling that this was a similarly quick, nasty way of removing essence. He shuddered, watching as the elite soldier fed both ribbon and essence into one of the black bottles fastened around his chest on a bandolier. Alex wondered if Julius was expecting to fill all those bottles by the time the fight was over.

Spurred on by the sight of the exploding man, the Starcross warriors charged toward the elite band of soldiers, ignoring Ceres's cries for them to flee. She charged after them on her Kelpie, trying to draw them away from battle, but they simply kept running, ignoring her futile pleas for them to stop and turn around. Alex agreed with her—these soldiers were simply too powerful.

Alex tried to conjure shield after shield of anti-magic to protect the others, but his defenses disintegrated at the touch of the golden ribbons. All he could do was watch in despair as explosions of scarlet went up from the crowd, bodies bursting like crimson water balloons. All a soldier had to do was flick their wrist, and another innocent life would be snuffed out. They barely broke a sweat, though the Starcross inhabitants were conjuring with all their might, their features straining under the exertion of using whatever they could muster, some of them feeding their own essence into the spells in the hope that it would make a difference.

It didn't.

"Ceres!" Alex yelled. The one-eyed royal rode toward him, tears streaming down her face, her skin speckled with red.

"This is all your fault!" she screamed at him, her eyes hard.

Alex had no time for self-pity or guilt, only action. "We need to surrender," he said. "You need to go to them and surrender before anyone else loses their life. Your people are fierce—they won't give up unless you tell them to."

"I've tried. They won't listen to me!" she cried, gesturing at the chaos.

"You have to get them to stop, or everyone will die!" Alex shouted desperately, taking hold of the bridle of her steed. The Kelpie reared back, snorting in Alex's face, but still he held on.

"You think I don't know that?" she raged, pulling back on the reins, the savage Kelpie tearing its face out of Alex's hands. It seemed the beast was infused with its rider's fury, its enormous hooves kicking out toward Alex. "*You* brought him here, Alex. I want you to look over there, at that battlefield, and I want you to remember every second of what you see," she howled, every word dripping venom, before she turned her steed around and headed for the fray.

The words struck Alex like a punch to the gut. She was right. She had always been right. He didn't want to face the truth of his mistakes, surrounded by a bloodbath he was helpless to prevent, but her words hit home, and they hit hard.

He didn't have long to wallow in his despair, however. Julius had broken away from his group of elite soldiers and was sauntering toward where Alex and his friends stood, far behind the battle that was raging. Their eyes met, and the king flashed a terrifying smile.

From all sides, Starcross warriors, seeing an opportunity, tried to lunge for Julius, but the king simply knocked them away, like they were little more than flies. A few times, just to mix things up, the smug royal sent out a stream of glittering energy, which was followed swiftly by the sounds of necks snapping, bones cracking, and lungs imploding.

Alex felt it was like watching a freight train coming

straight toward him, and he knew he didn't have enough time to get out of the way. Certain death stood only a short distance away, gaining ground. Alex's heart began to pound in his chest; there was no escape from the side of the bargain he had agreed to with Julius. With a smirk that smug, Alex was under no illusions about what the king knew—the fiasco at Kingstone Keep didn't appear to be much of a secret at all; he could see the knowledge of it written all over the Julius's face. The satisfaction of a victor, about to claim his prize.

He glanced at the friends who stood to either side of him, their faces turned toward the king, their hands raised to defend themselves until the bitter end, if that was what it took. Though fear glittered in their eyes, they would not be cowed—they were the most courageous people Alex had ever met, yet he knew this was a battle they could not win, and he wasn't ready to see his friends fall.

A moment later, however, Alex felt himself plucked out of the air. Storm flapped her wings above him, clutching his shoulders in her large talons. Where she had emerged from, he didn't know, but he was pleased to see her. A corner of her wing was singed, but she looked no worse for wear. Although he was thrilled by her arrival, he looked down in a panic, not wanting to leave his friends to the fate Julius had in store for them.

"Storm! Put me down!" he insisted, but she wasn't listening.

He looked back down in time to see the cavalry arrive.

Ceres and Demeter led the charge, circling around the back of Alex's friends. However, it didn't appear they wanted to fight Julius at all. Instead, they held out their hands, hauling Alex's friends up onto the backs of the Kelpies before turning the beasts around and heading for the forest a fair distance behind them. The only rider with no passenger was Demeter, who looked up at where Storm was flying.

Just then, Alex felt the Thunderbird jolt forward. A pained chirp trilled from her beak as a flash of something tore past her, the edge of it catching her wing. They sagged a little in the sky, but she recovered quickly, struggling to pull him higher.

Alex turned, his eyes locking with Julius's. The king was in the middle of forging a vicious-looking spear, the tip barbed with three glittering, magical blades. With a twisted grin, Julius hurled it with all the force he could muster, leaving Alex helpless to watch as it hurtled toward Storm.

This time, the spear didn't miss its mark.

The spear tore through Storm's body, and she let out a squawk of agony that made Alex's heart break. With her beak agape and her eyes glittering, she struggled to flap her wings, refusing to let Alex fall. A mournful coo echoed in her breast, but still she strove, wanting to get Alex out of there.

Alex didn't even see the third spear until it ripped through her, the momentum sending it straight out of her chest. She crumpled with a defeated chirrup, going into a tailspin, no longer able to hold up her own body weight, though she wrapped her wings around Alex in her final moments, in an attempt to protect him from the impact of hitting the ground.

"Storm! Storm, no!" he roared, trying to grip onto her.

They plummeted to the ground, her body breaking his fall as they hit. With tears running down his cheeks, he scrambled for her face, stroking the downy feathers tenderly, willing her to wake up. Her intelligent black eyes had lost their sparkle, staring vacantly up at the sky.

"Storm, get up!" he implored, stroking her desperately. But she was never going to wake up—Julius's spear had hit its target.

He turned toward the approaching king, pure hatred making his eyes burn, the way they had before, when Jari's life had been on the line at the Stillwater arena. Julius paused for a split second on the battlefield, seeing the silver shade of Alex's eyes. Alex hoped with all his heart that it reminded the king of Leander's eyes, that last day, when the Great Evil had been released. He wanted to instill fear into Julius for what he had done.

Before he could stride toward Julius, however, he felt a strong arm under his shoulder, lifting him up. Knowing it couldn't be Storm, he looked back to see that Demeter was hauling him onto the back of the Kelpie he rode.

"Let me go!" Alex insisted, but Demeter clung on, forcing Alex to either clamber the rest of the way onto the Kelpie's back or drag Demeter down to the ground with him. Not wanting another death on his conscience, Alex reluctantly clambered onto the back of the Kelpie.

Demeter dug in his heels, charging like the wind toward the forest closest to the encampment, evidently hoping to lose Julius and his cronies in there. There were six other Kelpies far ahead, bearing Alex's friends, and Virgil, on their backs, but Demeter was catching up.

"Hold on tight!" the auburn-haired teacher warned as the Kelpie sprinted along at an alarming pace.

Turning back, Alex felt his chest grip like a vise. Julius had reached the crumpled form of Storm, her wings splayed out wide, her head turned to the side, her black eyes dead, her beautiful feathers losing their sheen. The king kicked her, hard, in the side, and Alex lost it—he screamed at the wind, wanting to jump down off the Kelpie that very instant and punch the smug, disgusting smile from Julius's face.

"Save it for another day, Alex," Demeter warned. "Store it all up, and use it when you need it most."

Alex wrenched his gaze away, though it tore him up inside to do so. They were almost at the tree-line; Alex could see the shady trunks and dense canopy hurtling toward him. They were going to make it.

Something shot out of the sky, smacking Alex in the side and lifting him off the steed. He lost his grip on Demeter, the blow to his side too powerful, knocking him sideways, and his body tumbled to the ground with a painful thud. He rolled over and over, his body twisting under the momentum of the fall. As hooves thundered past him, stamping perilously close to his head, he tried to tuck himself into a ball, closing his eyes until the danger had passed.

Another blow hit him square in the back, rendering him immobile, though this one felt different. It felt sharp, then cold, the iciness trickling through his body with a feeling like brain freeze, making everything seize up and ache in the most peculiar way. Reaching up to see what had struck him, he felt the feathers of a dart in his spine. Where Spellbreakers were concerned, it seemed Julius had come prepared, knowing his magic wouldn't be as effective on someone like Alex.

As his eyelids became heavy, the dart working the rest of its magic, Alex managed to lift his head, looking up to see if his friends had made it to the trees. Their bodies littered the ground ahead, Ellabell having fallen mere inches from the edge of the forest. All of them were writhing in agony, fighting against whatever cruel spell Julius had used to knock them from the backs of the Kelpies.

"Ellabell!" Alex cried, trying to crawl toward her.

She turned, pain twisting her face up. "Alex…" she whispered, before going still.

"No, no, no, no," he muttered, trying to reach her before his body gave out. The trees loomed just ahead, taunting him.

They had been so close to the forest, but Alex realized it didn't matter. They could have been in the trees, and it wouldn't have mattered. Julius would have found them eventually. It was true, what Helena had said: Julius would find them, no matter where they went. There was no escape from him. Running was a waste of time and energy—it made sense now. No matter how far or how fast they ran, Julius would always catch up.

Straining to turn around, Alex saw that another sea of yellow fog had been let loose across the remainder of the Starcross warriors, turning them against one another, while Julius and his band of merry men walked calmly away from it, moving at a leisurely pace in the direction of Alex. The king hadn't even bothered with the rest of Starcross. Alex and his friends were the target... The rest were just collateral.

Julius grinned as he neared, kneeling beside Alex's frozen figure. "Goodnight, sweet prince," he whispered, leaning close to Alex's ear. Alex tried to speak, wanting to scream in the king's face, when a blow to the head turned everything to darkness.

CHAPTER 20

ALEX STIRRED, FEELING THE PULSE OF A HEADACHE pushing like daggers at the backs of his eyes. Blinking slowly awake, the sunlight streaming in much too bright, it took him a while to fully come around. Everything felt strange. The ground beneath him was no longer the hard-packed solidity of earth, but something softer, like he was enveloped in a marshmallow. Tucked under his chin was a warm, thick duvet cover, and beneath his head was the soft give of a luxurious pillow.

Am I still dreaming? he wondered, though much of the sleep he'd endured, when it hadn't simply been the dark stretching landscape of oblivion, had been plagued by nightmares: giant Kelpies with snapping teeth thundering toward him, Julius's laughing face looming close to his own, just a floating head in the darkness, his friends' features twisted in agony.

As the headache subsided, and his vision stopped dancing with black spots, he struggled to sit up. The motion set off a stabbing sensation at the sides of his head, like someone had rammed a red-hot poker behind his eyeballs, but that soon faded too. Gradually, he began to take in the room around him, though it was a million miles from what he'd expected to wake up to, given the events of the previous day.

Had it been a day? he thought to himself, not knowing how long he'd been out. However long he'd slept, the sun was now high in the sky, streaming through wafting cream curtains in a warm haze of golden light. Behind the curtains, he could make out a panel of French doors that stretched across the whole far right side of the room, and beyond that, the carved marble perimeter of a balcony, with rising hills undulating on the horizon.

"Where am I?" he said aloud, not really expecting anyone to answer.

A flood of panic swept through his veins as the events of Starcross came hurtling back to the forefront of his mind; there had been so much devastation, the victory snatched from their hands long before they'd even set foot on the battlefield. *That* almost seemed like a bad dream—one there was no waking up from. People had died, people had been injured, all so Julius could get his hands on Alex and his friends. How they'd found the fifth haven, Alex didn't know, though he had his suspicions.

With Agatha loitering around the cave so often, coming and going as she pleased, it only stood to reason that others might do the same. If scouts were watching the strange old hippie, wondering who she was and why she was hidden in the bushes, it wouldn't have taken long for them to realize the significance of the cave. Following her, they would have found the entrance, and closer inspection would have told them exactly what it was. Alex didn't blame her in the slightest; she probably had no idea she was being followed, or that the secret had even been discovered.

It was all a chain of events, perfectly linked. Alex could see it now. Julius had been watching the havens, just as Venus had said, but by then he probably already knew about Starcross. Alex had to give him that—the king could certainly bide his time, in pursuit of revenge. He had held back until the right moment to strike. Alex imagined that Julius had waited until he received word that Alex had arrived at a haven to perform the spell, knowing he would go ahead with the second attempt, regardless. With the blood in his clutches, why wouldn't he? As soon as word came that Alex had gone to Kingstone, that was when Julius knew to land his first blow on the realm of Starcross, leaving it in enough chaos that Alex would be disoriented on his return. It all made perfect sense, in hindsight. Alex gritted his teeth in anger; he had walked right into Julius's scheme, playing it out just as the king had, no doubt, envisioned. Perhaps, Alex thought, Julius truly did have *The Art of War* memorized.

His mind turned back to his friends. Ellabell's face haunted him—the way she had whispered his name before lying still. Glancing around, he knew he was definitely alone in the room, but the walls were so thick he could hear nothing but the rush of wind beyond the French doors. If his friends were in the rooms on either side of him, he had no way of knowing. All he had was a fragile hope that they had been brought here too, or were at least being kept prisoner at Starcross. They had been so close to reaching the trees, where they just might have lost the king and his men. It was almost worse than if they hadn't stood a chance of escape. Alex tried to picture the last time he'd seen them; they had been writhing on the ground in agony, suffering under one of Julius's brutal spells, but they hadn't looked close to death. No, not in the way so many others that day had looked. A tremor of nausea ran through him as he remembered the scarlet explosions and haunting screams.

Knowing Julius, Alex had a feeling the king was keeping his friends safely tucked away, in case he needed some extra leverage, a means by which to force Alex to do what he wanted. In that, at least, there was some relief. They were likely still alive, and that meant they still had a chance.

Slowly, his mind touched upon the sad scene of Storm's death, but he couldn't even bring himself to think about her.

It was too raw and too upsetting, and he knew he'd have to put his grief for her away in a box in his mind, just for now, until he could grieve for her properly, the way she deserved. He hoped they hadn't left her body out on the battlefield, for creatures to come and devour. He couldn't bear the thought of that.

Impulsively, Alex got out of bed and strode up to the huge double doors that dominated the left hand side of the room. Looking down, he realized he was only dressed in his underwear, and wondered, with some alarm, who had undressed him and put him to bed. It made him feel oddly vulnerable, to think someone had tucked him in, like a small child after a long journey. Shaking off his concerns, he twisted a golden handle that was molded into the shape of a mermaid and heaved one side open, peering out.

The hallway outside was impressive, with huge, glittering tapestries lining the walls and an elegant statue twirling upward every couple of feet, the middle of the floor covered in a red velvet runner that stretched away on either side. There were, however, also four heavily armored guards clutching weighty golden spears that Alex guessed were more for decoration than anything practical. Two of them flanked the door, while the other two stood opposite, their eyes glowering in the direction of Alex's peeking face.

"The king will come for you when he is ready," one of the guards opposite warned.

"You should return to your chamber," the guard beside

him added, the two making quite the menacing double act. The guards on Alex's side of the door said nothing, barely acknowledging him. Looking up at them, he decided he liked them better than the other two.

Ducking back into the room, he took in his surroundings more thoroughly. All around him, everything gleamed gold and cream, the furnishings plush and luxurious. A fireplace was carved into the wall opposite the bed, beside a small seating area, with armchairs so enormous and grand that Alex felt he'd disappear into them if he dared to sit down on one. In the hearth, a fire blazed, making the room almost unbearably hot. On the mantelpiece above, golden statuettes were frozen mid-dance, and a candelabra forged from pure silver stood in the center, no doubt with a price tag that could have paid for a student's college tuition. Even the duvet and pillow felt expensive, woven from smooth silk, both comfortable and cool on his skin.

Fluffy rugs carpeted the marble tiles of the bedroom's floor, though there was a somewhat alarming animal skin stretched out in front of the blazing fire. From where Alex was sitting, it looked somewhat like a white tiger, but the stripes were a paler color, and two large fangs, almost like tusks, pierced down from the roof of its mouth, its glass eyes staring vacantly upward. He shuddered, feeling sorry for the poor creature who had lost its life for such a ghoulish decoration. Not only that, he felt a bit of empathy toward it too, knowing he was probably going to end up in a similar state once Julius came for him.

Reminded of the king, Alex couldn't help pondering why Julius had chosen to put him up in such beautiful surroundings. Once the lights had gone out after Julius struck him in the head, he would have been certain the shivering cold of awaking in a cell would have greeted him, his body curled up on dank stones. A luxurious bedroom to rival any five-star hotel had definitely not been on the agenda.

Curiously, he padded over to the windows, wanting to take a better look at the scenery beyond, hoping to gauge where on earth he was. Drawing back the curtains, he was surprised to see that the French doors were open, leaving him free to wander out onto the balcony. As he stepped out, he realized why they hadn't bothered with this security measure. Peering out over the edge of the balcony's balustrade, he saw tumbling waterfalls beneath, plummeting all the way down into a valley that looked no bigger than a ribbon from this height, snaking away through lush green countryside. Even if he wanted to escape, there was no way out, the slippery marble walls on either side no good for climbing. The next balcony above was a long way up, with no feasible way to reach it.

Alex smiled wryly; it was a cell after all, just painted up to look pretty. Still, he had to admit he was glad it wasn't somewhere grim and dingy, where the cold penetrated through to his very bones, and the scent of fear and excrement was ripe in the air.

Gazing out at the stunning landscape, the grassy fields rolling away like green velvet to meet the softly swelling hills in the distance, Alex ruminated upon whether this was another haven, or something completely different. Holding out his hand, he let his anti-magic spiral upward, testing the boundaries to see if any magical restraints lay within. A moment later, snowflakes began to flurry around him, letting him know there was a magical barrier above, protecting the building and preventing escape.

Leaning back against the balustrade as far as he dared, Alex looked up, noticing the glint of a golden spire rising at the top of whichever wing he had been placed in. Everything was beautiful here; each carving, each statue, each tile, so lovingly, and expensively, integrated.

This must be the royal palace, Alex reasoned. Why else would it be so elegant, with no expense spared?

Upon turning back into the room, something caught his eye. Sitting on top of a small dining table, set up in the far corner of the room, was Alex's satchel. He hadn't been able to see it before, from his angle in the bed, and he simply hadn't noticed it as he'd walked past to reach the balcony. Now, however, he saw that it was sitting there, beckoning to him like a beacon.

Alex's brow furrowed in bemusement as he lifted the flap and pulled out the mostly used vial and the large spell book. Folding the pages out flat on the table, Alex conjured a thin veil of anti-magic, and watched in despair as the glyphs morphed into words, the text now all but faded away. True, the words appeared before the spell-caster, but they were likely to be dimmer too, on the third and final try, and there could be no way of studying the pages beforehand, not anymore.

"Might as well use it to wipe your backside, for all the good it's done you. Heck, it's more nuanced than I am!" a voice said suddenly, close to Alex's ear, making him jump.

Alex whirled around. "Elias! You can't creep up on people like that!"

Elias grinned, his teeth flashing. "It's the only way to approach people!" he cackled. "I love a good scare, don't you? Mind you, nothing is as scary as the mess you've got yourself into. *That* is frankly terrifying. I hear attempt number two didn't exactly go according to plan?"

"No thanks to you. You'll be pleased to know you missed out on all the heavy lifting, seeing as you've been gone so long," Alex remarked sourly. "Don't suppose you have a helpful way out of it? I mean, that's why you've been gone all this time, isn't it, to see what you can find out about the spell?" he added, remembering Siren Mave's less than complimentary words about where Elias actually was.

Elias tapped his shadowy fingers against the spot where a chin ought to be. "I'm afraid you've gone WAY past that. I said this to that awful, toady woman—I said, 'He can't be left to his own devices or he'll blow everything sky-high,' and she had the cheek to tell me I was being 'overly cautious.' Well, I guess you showed her," he taunted.

"I'm going to take that as a no, then?" said Alex, rolling his eyes. "Where have you been, if you don't have anything useful to tell me? Or not tell me, as seems to be the way with you irritating guardians."

"Hey, you know me. I'll always help out where I can," the shadow-man replied, suddenly serious. "I have been investigating, like I told you, no matter what that vile toad has said, but the rules remain the same—you have to ask me the right questions," he added, giving a dramatic wink that looked bizarre on his ever-shifting face.

Alex frowned. "I just don't know where I keep going wrong," he explained. "I got the blood wrong, but I fixed it, thanks to you. The second try should have worked—everything was in place."

Elias shook his head from side to side, little strands of shadow taking their time to catch up. "Incorrect!" he cried, making an obnoxious buzzer sound that sent irritated shivers up Alex's spine.

"So what did I get wrong?" Alex pressed.

Elias tutted. "Questions, questions, must ask the questions."

"Does it have something to do with what Siren Mave said?" Alex asked, as a sudden flash of something popped into his mind, sweeping him along on the current of an idea. In the image in his mind, there were three figures standing in a pit room, though their faces weren't clear. "Does someone else need to be in the room, to watch the spell take place? Is that what she meant by it being 'properly witnessed'?"

Elias clapped his vaporous hands together. "By Jove, I think he's getting the hang of this question game. Now, for one million dollars, what's the young man going to say next? Who might that third figure be?" He paused, a tremor of light running through his body, shattering his floating limbs with silvery veins. The shadow-man looked at Alex, panic evident on his face. "That's the trouble with bizarre loopholes—nobody knows if I've stepped over a line," he whispered, his voice thick with pain. "I think I may be in trouble... See if I can get out of this one..." He trailed off, his body disappearing in a burst of white-hot light that made Alex cover his eyes with his forearm.

Alex was left staring at the spot where the shadow-man had been, blinking away the glare of his departure, wondering if that was it—Elias's last chance. Just then, there was a knock at the door, distracting him from what might have happened to the shadow-man.

Siren Mave entered, her bright lipstick freshly applied, her cheeks even pinker than usual.

"You?" Alex gasped.

She peered at him over the horned rims of her glasses. "Yes, *me*. Does that present an immediate problem?" she remarked.

"You work for the king?" he asked, incredulous. "What, does that mean you've been on his side this whole time?"

She sighed impatiently. "I am on nobody's side, as you well know. I have always been a royal advisor and servant, which you also know, across all the havens," she explained. "And while this may not be a haven, this is the royal palace, a place in which my duties, sadly, extend to those of a chambermaid. It isn't glamorous, but there it is. Satisfied?"

Alex frowned uncertainly. Scrutinizing her closely, he began to wonder if it was possible that she was able to exist in multiple places at once. Either that, or she was extremely good at keeping tabs on him. He supposed she was supposed to be his guardian, after all, so perhaps she was simply following him around, using royal appointments as an excuse to watch over him.

"So, you're *not* working for the king?" he pressed, utterly confused.

"I am and I am not," she remarked. "But, since we're on the subject, the king wishes to see you now. Please dress appropriately from the wardrobe I have selected for you—I've made some exceptional choices, and I'd hate to see them go down the drain. Your own clothes have been taken and destroyed because, frankly, I'm surprised they didn't walk off of their own accord. He expects you in twenty minutes. I shall await you outside."

With that, she was gone, leaving Alex to fear how the king would receive him.

CHAPTER 21

AFTER RUMMAGING THROUGH THE ANTIQUE wardrobe tucked away close to the bed, Alex picked out what he thought might make him look presentable. There wasn't much to choose from, but he settled on a pair of navy trousers, a white shirt, and some dark shoes. Glancing at himself in the mirror, he knew he could do with a good shower, but twenty minutes didn't exactly give him long enough to prepare. Besides, he didn't care what Julius thought of him. After the massacre at Starcross, he wanted to make the king feel pain, and being forced to dress to the nines for him as an "honored guest" made Alex feel a fresh wave of fury.

Distinctly uncomfortable in the new, more formal attire, he went to the large double doors and stepped out into the hallway. One of the guards opposite smirked, but Alex ignored him, looking for Siren Mave instead. She was standing a short way down the hall, tapping her foot impatiently on the floor. She looked up as Alex approached, an exasperated expression on her face.

"That took you long enough, didn't it?" she remarked, tapping the clock-face of a gold wristwatch.

"I had to find something suitable," Alex replied defensively.

She looked him up and down, evidently unimpressed. "Well, I suppose you'll have to do," she grumbled, setting off down the corridor. As she walked, Alex could hear her muttering to herself. "There were some beautifully tailored pieces in there. Such exquisite suits, and he chooses that? Young people these days—no fashion sense."

He tried not to seethe as he followed her, feeling the anxiety building inside him as he hurried after the small, surprisingly swift figure. His new shoes squeaked when he walked, the stiff collar scratching his neck, the trousers slipping from his hips, being just that little bit too big. He was beginning to suspect it was all a ploy to make him feel as uncomfortable as possible before he met with the king.

At the end of the hallway, they came to a set of broad spiral stairs that seemed to go up and up to never-ending heights. Two golden statues of goddesses stood sentinel over the bottom step, and it was past these Alex and the toady woman walked, his heart sinking as he realized they were going all the way to the top. On the climb, they passed what seemed like a hundred other floors, some of them leading off to long hallways like the one Alex had come from, others simply stepping off at glass solariums where people could pause on the long walk up the stairs.

At long last, with Alex's lungs burning, they reached the top floor. Ahead of them lay an enormous foyer with an arched roof made of glass, showing the beautiful azure sky above. Aside from that, there wasn't much else in the room, just a solitary desk in the center and an imposing set of doors behind. A beautiful young woman sat at the desk, and she looked up as Alex neared. A fearful expression passed across her face, unnerving Alex even further.

"You must be Alex Webber?" she asked, her voice clipped and clear.

Alex nodded. "I believe the king is expecting me?" he replied, trying to steel himself against what he was about to endure.

She nodded. "Yes, His Royal Highness is expecting you. I would hurry if I were you—you are nearly late," she whispered, her eyes wide with concern.

"Noted," said Alex, before following the old woman toward the vast double doors at the far end of the extensive foyer.

Upon opening the door, Alex was met with one of the

most beautiful rooms he'd ever seen. A glass dome rose over the center of what he guessed to be the throne room, considering there were two very large, very ostentatious thrones in the middle. They were similar to the ones he'd seen at Starcross Castle, though these were forged from intertwining vines of gold, silver, and bronze. One was raised slightly above the other, with a golden crown placed on top of the chair's back. Julius was sitting in that one, lounging backward with a book in his hands, flipping the pages casually. The throne beside it had a smaller crown on top, sculpted from silver, and on the plush cushions sat the beautiful form of Venus, her eyes looking straight ahead at Alex, a welcoming smile on her face.

Fountains trickled crystalline water down into a small network of streams, with quaint bridges arching over them, which had to be crossed to reach the central island where the two thrones stood. In the water, beautiful fish swam lazily, their scales shining in a myriad of colors. On the walls, paintings and tapestries hung, depicting ancient battles and previous rulers. The face of Julius's father loomed at the back of the room, surveying everything. Alex wondered how that must feel for Julius, having his father's eyes on him wherever he went, considering it was Julius's fault the man was dead. Alex had a feeling the king didn't care.

Everything was decked out in gold and precious jewels, managing to be luxurious without looking gaudy. And the books—there were books everywhere. Rows upon rows flanked the walls, some of them kept away in locked cupboards, presumably for Julius's eyes only. Even on the floor by the king's throne, there were piles of tomes, stacked up, just waiting to be read. If this was the number of books in the throne room, Alex could not imagine what the king's library looked like.

Alex glanced around for as long as he dared, finding the room breathtaking despite his unease. However, it wasn't long before his attention was drawn back to Venus. If she was sitting there, Alex knew Julius must have found her at the windmill, but his worries rested not with the fact that she was back, but with the knowledge that someone had to die as a result of her rescue. As selfish as it sounded, he just hoped it wasn't someone close to him—someone like Demeter or Ceres.

Once more, his mind trailed back to the chaos of Starcross. The sad truth of it was that responsibility for what happened lay at his feet; there was no escaping it. If he had listened to Hadrian, if he had listened to Ceres, if he had listened to what they had continuously tried to get him to hear, none of it would have happened. Starcross would have continued to be a secret, and all those who had died would still be alive... Storm would still be alive. In his foolish wisdom, Alex had thought he knew better, or that he could somehow whisk them away before Julius's axe fell, but his misplaced confidence had damned them all. Worse than that, people had died, suddenly and painfully. Perhaps whatever was to come would be his redemption for the suffering he had un-wittingly caused.

One thing that surprised Alex, however, was the presence of Virgil. The skeletal man stood a short distance away from Julius, his hands behind his back. His face was battered and bruised, his lip swollen to twice its normal size, congealed black blood covering the wound. As their eyes met, Alex saw that the whites of Virgil's were covered in crimson ruptures where the vessels had burst. Julius had clearly begun his punishment of Virgil early. Alex mouthed the words "I'm sorry" in the Head's direction, causing the sunken-faced man to look quickly away, wincing at the sharp movement.

"Darling, your guest is here," Venus whispered, touching her husband's arm.

"You think I don't know that?" Julius snapped, not bothering to look up. "I will get to him when I am good and ready. I am almost at the end of this chapter."

And so, Alex was left to stand uncomfortably while Julius finished what he was reading. Siren Mave had left, and it seemed nobody else dared to speak, though Venus kept her hand on her husband's arm. Looking at the small, subtle motion, Alex realized he was likely only alive because of her strange skill—her keen ability to keep the king calm when nobody else could. Though, what had she said—if Alex were to fail on the second attempt, not even she could help him? The memory was foggy, but Alex was sure it had been something along those lines. Yet, here she was, holding her husband's arm, helping him. Well, keeping him alive at least.

Slowly, she leaned into her husband, whispering something softly in his ear. Whatever it was, it seemed to do the trick. With a loud slam, Julius snapped the book shut and turned to face Alex. A moment later, he got up, prowling across the bridge to where Alex stood. Venus followed, never less than an arm's length away from him.

"So, here he stands, the mighty Spellbreaker!" Julius taunted, eyeing him as if he were a piece of trash that had just blown in. "And here I was, thinking you a master of *The Art of War*. You certainly talked a good game, but it seems that's all it was... talk. What a disappointment you turned out to be, Alex Webber," he said in a low voice. "Quite the amateur, thinking yourself one step ahead of me, thinking I was trailing behind when, really, I was a dot in the distance, so far ahead of you, you couldn't even see me!"

"I would never presume to—" Alex began, but the king cut him off sharply.

"You will not speak until you are asked to!" he barked, his eyes flashing with fury. "You do not come into my house and presume to flap your mouth. Is that understood?"

Alex paused, not knowing whether to respond. "Yes, Your Royal Highness," he said, after a long, tense silence. He had so much anger burning inside him that it was everything he could do not to strike out at the king and damn it all.

"I have had just about enough of you, Alex Webber. You are a thorn in my side, a snake in the grass, a pebble in my shoe, and I would have seen you destroyed, had my good lady wife not persuaded me against it, for the sake of the spell," Julius continued, his mouth set in a grim line. Without warning, he darted toward Venus, violently grabbing her toward him, holding her face in a vise-like grip. "Isn't that right, darling? You wouldn't see him harmed, would you?" he snarled, so close to her face Alex thought he might bite something off. She didn't flinch. Instead, she looked into his eyes, her mouth moving, though nobody but Julius could hear the words.

"I thought he could be useful to you, didn't I?" Venus purred softly, her words louder now.

Julius nodded, his manner calmer. "You did, my darling," he said, releasing his grip on her. When he removed his hands, reddened crescent shapes began to appear in her cheeks, where he had clutched her with all his might. Again, she showed nothing on her face, the beautiful blank canvas remaining steady. "Tell me, Spellbreaker, did you think you could run away from me and not have to endure any repercussions? Did you think you could steal my blood, defy my rules, and get away with it?" the king asked, stalking back toward Alex.

Alex cleared his throat. "No, Your Royal Highness. I knew I would have to pay for my insolence," he replied, trying to be as polite as possible, knowing it might save his life, even if he wanted to tear the king's throat out.

"Did you think I wouldn't find your secret little hideaway, and all those aberrations? That vile creature Ceres certainly thought she could hide from me, stealing them from Falleaf for all these years, right under Hadrian's nose—blackmailing him!" Julius spat. "I've only kept her alive because Hadrian wants to deal with her himself. After so many years of living in fear of her, he's finally getting to be the man I always knew he could be, if he didn't have that old maverick's blood in his veins. See, why couldn't you be more like Hadrian? He knows which one is the winning side," he continued, flashing a smug look at Alex.

Alex tried not to let his puzzlement show on his face. Surely, he reasoned, Hadrian was scheming a way to get Ceres out of any predicament she might be in? If he had persuaded Julius to let him deal with his sister, surely it was because he was thinking of a way to spirit her out of there? Of all the royals Alex had met, he knew Hadrian wasn't a turncoat. No, it had to be part of a bigger contingency plan, to save his sister, if it became clear he couldn't save anyone else. Of that, Alex was convinced. Whatever Julius was spouting, it was all just smoke and mirrors made from the lies Hadrian had been feeding him.

"I don't like to get involved in family feuds, Your Royal Highness," Alex said, hoping to subtly back up Hadrian's well-constructed subterfuge.

"And yet you've managed to shoehorn yourself into our royal business, haven't you?" Julius chuckled bitterly. "First, you cause a whole world of trouble for this pathetic specimen," he continued, flicking a wrist in Virgil's direction.

"Then, you eliminate Alypia—whom nobody can wake up from whatever trance you put her in, by the way—because she was on her way to tell me what you were up to. Thirdly, you work some voodoo magic on that old loon's prison, and his own inmates dispense with him. I mean, what else were the prisoners going to do, if you gave them that slice of power? I may not have liked Caius, but he was a royal, and royal blood should not be carelessly wasted. Fourth, you bother Hadrian and try to bleed him for all he's worth, corrupting Alypia's daughter for good measure, and joining sides with that vagrant, Ceres! Then, you have the audacity to steal my wife and lock her up. I can only imagine what you planned to do with her," he growled. Venus's hand on his arm brought him back from the edge of losing his temper. He took in a deep breath. "All in all, I'd say you've gotten yourself pretty involved in our family business, wouldn't you?"

Knowing Julius would probably want his head for what he'd done, Alex wanted to spew forth every angry word he'd ever hoped to say to the king. It took everything he had not to give in to that temptation. He wanted to shout that, if Julius hadn't gone around ripping the life from young people, he would never have had to get involved, but he held his tongue, calming himself for an even response.

"When you put it like that, I suppose I have," he remarked, with just a hint of bitterness in his voice.

Julius's eyes flashed angrily. "Aren't you missing something?" he barked.

Alex smiled. "Sorry, Your Royal Highness," he said, his tone overly sincere.

"I suppose you're wondering how I found your little hideaway?" Julius crowed, strutting up onto one of the bridges, where he leaned back against the banister, evidently trying to look cool.

"It had crossed my mind, Your Royal Highness," Alex replied, giving little away.

"It was that dear friend of yours—the mad one I locked up years ago, at Kingstone Keep. After your escape from Falleaf House, she led my scouts there, carrying that pretty one of yours. All they had to do was creep in after you, and watch where you went. After that, it was a waiting game. I knew you'd go to try out the spell, though I didn't know which haven you'd pick. My money was on Stillwater. Anyway, when my guards said you'd gone to Kingstone, that was my moment," he explained. Although it confirmed many of Alex's suspicions, and disproved others, it shed no more light on the ambiguity of Venus. It seemed she truly had suggested Kingstone because she believed it to be the least dangerous haven, but there was something about the beautiful woman that perturbed Alex. He simply did not know how much he could trust behind that beautiful, serene canvas. "You've probably realized by now, I'm a very patient man. Once I knew you'd gone, I sent my men through to make the first strike. Then, as you saw, I followed." He grinned smugly.

"You took everyone by surprise, Your Royal Highness. I

have to commend you for that," Alex remarked curtly, wanting to punch the smug look off his face.

Julius frowned, clearly not knowing what to do with the compliment. "As well as a patient man, I am a fair man," he said, prowling toward Alex once more.

This was the moment Alex had been waiting for. The king kept coming, until there were barely five inches between his face and Alex's. In that moment, Alex wanted to laugh in his face, or lash out, but stern looks from Venus and Virgil stayed his hands. He certainly didn't want to end up looking like the Head, his face a marbled mess of white, purple, yellow, and bluish black.

"Since you seem so keen to keep trying this foolhardy spell, and given the mess you've made of my essence system, I'm willing to overlook the little mishap we had at Falleaf," Julius continued.

Alex knew he wasn't really forgiven at all; it was simply more convenient for the king to rope Alex into doing the spell. If it failed again, Julius could come up with a new way of destroying lives for essence. If it succeeded, Julius would become the hero of the magical realm, taking the glory. Either way, Julius was still going to get what he wanted.

"However, as laid out in the previous terms of our agreement, your life is now mine." The king paused for effect, but Alex gave him nothing. Evidently frustrated, Julius carried on. "You are to complete the final attempt yourself, in whichever place I see fit. Think of it as your execution, your punishment for all the trouble you have caused me. But, the perk is, you'll be saving a lot of people in the process—well, if you manage it, anyway," he taunted. With a look of disgust, he turned to Virgil. "Now, you may have the assistance of that wretch over there, but he won't be doing the spell this time. As foul as he is to me, he is still a royal, and you know how I feel about wastage. All sound fair?"

Alex gave a sour smile. "I suppose I'm not allowed to disagree?"

"Oh, you can disagree until you're blue in the face, but you will still be doing this spell," Julius hissed, lifting his hands to Alex's throat. Gently, he pressed his thumbs down on Alex's windpipe, until Alex felt lightheaded with lack of oxygen, the king having made him literally blue in the face.

Still standing by the throne, Virgil looked at Alex with an expression of sorrow. It was clear some choice words had been exchanged between Julius and his stepson, but Virgil seemed no less apologetic for what the king was making Alex do. In fact, he seemed more so, like he somehow felt responsible.

"Then... I... suppose... I agree," Alex gasped, his eyes bulging.

Julius released him, a victorious smile upon the king's face. "Glad I could persuade you so easily," he taunted, though Alex ignored the bait. He had bigger concerns to think about now. For a second, he thought about asking after his friends, but he didn't dare—not while he could still feel the imprint of the king's hands on his throat.

With a sudden realization that smarted like a smack to the face, Alex understood the gravity of the situation. He was going to die, one day very soon. After everything he had done to try to avoid it, performing the spell was going to rest on his shoulders anyway. There was no escaping it; this place was too well guarded, and he knew he would be under constant scrutiny. With a bubble of furious sadness, he realized that none of the in between mattered.

I was always going to end up here, he thought to himself, his whole body going numb at the thought. There was no panic; that would come later.

For now, there was only dazed disbelief. The tide had brought him straight back to where he'd begun.

CHAPTER 22

H OWEVER, IT SEEMED JULIUS WASN'T QUITE DONE
with Alex. Expecting to be dismissed so preparations
could get underway, Alex was surprised that the
king was still prowling around him, darting forward every
so often, like a predator testing to see if its prey was broken
enough yet to go in for the kill.

"Oh, and I forgot to mention," he purred. "I have another
little surprise for you."

Alex didn't want to know; he was done with surprises.
There was nothing that could come out of that man's mouth
that would make Alex feel any better, or ease his troubled
mind.

"A surprise? For me, Your Royal Highness?" Alex replied, trying not to let the sarcasm drip from his words.

Julius glowered, moving closer to Alex. "I have your friends," he whispered malevolently. "And if you speak in that insolent tone again, I will change my mind about what I have planned for them."

Alex frowned. "So they're here?" he asked, all the daring gone from his voice.

"Oh, yes," said Julius. "And I had planned something remarkably kind for them, though I'm starting to have second thoughts."

"My apologies, Your Royal Highness. I didn't mean to offend. I am simply in shock," Alex admitted, hoping to win the royal over with a little groveling. "It's not an easy thing, to learn your life has a much briefer timer over it."

For a moment, the king said nothing, his wolfish eyes scrutinizing Alex closely, no doubt trying to see if the fear was genuine. Alex was convinced Julius could sniff out the real deal, and hoped there was enough of it to convince him.

"No, I would imagine not," said Julius, finally.

"Please, tell me what kind thing you had planned—I won't speak out of turn again, Your Royal Highness," Alex insisted, adding the cherry to the top of the forgiveness cake.

Julius gave a dramatic sigh. "Well, Alex Webber, I will promise the freedom of your friends, upon the successful completion of the spell, by you," he explained grandly, clearly thinking himself the most benevolent creature to ever walk the earth.

Alex didn't know what to say. The offer seemed genuine, but he knew better than to believe anything uttered by the king, especially where good deeds were concerned. Glancing over to Venus, he saw a small smile pulling at the corners of her lips, and realized the offer must've had something to do with her hypnosis magic.

"Forgive me, Your Royal Highness," Alex began, his voice tight. "Your offer is as generous as it is kind, and it's one I would gladly thank you for, but how do I know you'll carry out your promise? After all, if I succeed, then I won't be around to..." A lump formed in his throat, but he continued through it. "...see that your promise is kept. It's not that I don't trust you, but I would like some sort of insurance, Your Royal Highness."

Venus stepped forward. "Your friends will all be safe. You have our word. It has been promised, and so it shall be done," she said softly, her voice carrying like a song toward Alex's ears.

"Thank you, Your..."

"Your Grace," Venus offered, seeing that he was struggling with how to address her.

Alex bowed. "Thank you, Your Grace. As I say, the offer is a generous one. I'll be happier going to my grave knowing they are taken care of. Not happy, but happier," he said, trying to force a smile onto his face, though he wasn't in any kind of mindset to feel pleased. All through the conversation, though

1

it was growing more promising by the second, Alex could not escape the sense of impending doom that was threatening to crush him beneath its weight.

Julius leaned into his wife, his face showing his displeasure.

"You do not speak when I am speaking," he hissed, pulling her roughly toward him by the neck. "You know this, and yet you continue to disobey. I don't like to blemish your beautiful skin, my darling, but if you persist..." The rest of the sentence did not need to be said; the intent was clear enough.

Venus took in a deep breath, her face perfectly calm as she lifted her hands to her husband's face and planted a delicate kiss on his lips. Pulling away, she held his gaze. For a moment, they were perfectly still, saying nothing, barely moving, while Venus, using whatever strange powers of manipulation she possessed, turned their full force onto her husband.

"I am sorry, my darling," Venus whispered. "I got overexcited about your grand idea, and felt compelled to speak. It will not happen again," she said. Julius appeared hypnotized by her words, his expression softening. Alex watched, transfixed to see her powers at work on someone else.

Slowly, Julius broke away from his wife, and she released her hold on his face. His eyes looked strangely placid, as if he'd just awoken from a deep slumber. He blinked sluggishly, apparently figuring out his surroundings. Seeing Alex, he narrowed his eyes.

"Where was I?" he asked.

"Your kind plan for my friends, Your Royal Highness," Alex replied, encouraged by a subtle nod from Venus.

Julius nodded slowly, as if it was all coming back to him. "Yes, your friends shall be set free, upon completion of the task before you," he repeated, before pausing, a grim smile dancing upon his lips. "If you aren't successful, however, then your friends shall suffer the same fate as you. There will be a public execution, and all of you shall leave this world together." He sighed, evidently delighted by the poetic drama of it.

Alex nodded, not daring to say anything. He would do the spell, as he had been asked, but to have his friends' fates hinge on his success seemed cruel and unjust. *But what choice do I have?* Alex thought miserably. He could only hope that Venus would ensure the promise was seen through to fruition, no matter how much power it took her to persuade her husband of mercy.

"Excellent. Then you are dismissed until I call for you again!" Julius cried, turning around to go back to his throne and his book.

Alex cleared his throat, and the king froze midway over the bridge leading to the central island. He turned in slow motion, a look of pure resentment upon his face, just as Alex opened his mouth to speak.

"What about everyone else, Your Royal Highness?" he asked brazenly, knowing it would get him into trouble. Still, if he didn't ask, no one would.

"Why, you ungrateful little beast! How dare you come in here and make demands of me! I have given you plenty, and you ask for more? You vile wretch. You're almost as bad as that disgusting half-breed, wanting everything, sucking the very life out of me with his mere presence! How DARE you!" Julius screamed, sprinting toward Alex and grasping him by the shoulders. He shook Alex as hard as he could, making Alex's brain rattle, while jabbing a finger in the direction of the shamefaced Virgil.

Alex thought he might be sick, the world juddering in front of him. "I… am sorry, Julius! I should not have asked… more of you. I am… grateful for all you have… offered. I was… simply concerned… for the people… down there, just as… you are no… doubt concerned for… them. They are… your people, after… all," he said, managing to blurt out the words between shakes.

Julius released Alex, sending him careening backward. He landed with an awkward splash in one of the streams, startling a small band of goldfish. Scrambling to his feet, he brushed the moisture from the back of his trousers, but Julius was already halfway back to his throne.

The king shrugged, not bothering to turn around. "They aren't your concern. I left them to my soldiers… though, I was tempted to escort them all through to Spellshadow Manor or Kingstone Keep and watch them all squirm as the mist took them." He chuckled callously. "Mind you, I have no control over what my soldiers do—most of those at Starcross are probably already dead," he added with a backward flick of his hand.

Alex glanced over to where Venus was standing, and saw from her face that what her husband said wasn't true. Her beautiful eyes said a thousand things, and none of them spelled out the deaths of the Starcross survivors. Whatever she knew, it was clear there was hope still for all those in the havens below.

"You can go now," Julius repeated, his tone carrying a warning. "But just so we're clear, you will pay for what you've done, and you will pay for it with your life. I will come and collect you soon, to set the ritual in motion... So you had better start saying your prayers, Spellbreaker. Now, get out, before I start making alterations to my offer," he added coldly, keeping his back to Alex.

Alex didn't need telling twice. He turned to leave, but once again Julius called him back, apparently desiring one last moment of attention.

"Oh, and Alex?"

"Yes, Your Royal Highness?"

"We're having a mighty feast tonight, and you're not invited," the king said, sounding like a spoiled toddler.

"I am sorry to hear that, Your Royal Highness," Alex remarked, wanting to leave.

Julius chuckled. "Are you? You see, Spellbreaker, I've asked that a special meal be prepared," he continued, his eyes dancing with malice. "I wonder, have you ever tasted roasted

Thunderbird?" he asked, his mouth twisting into a foul grin.

Fury pulsed in every cell of Alex's body. "Am I dismissed, Your Royal Highness?" he hissed through gritted teeth, spitting out every word as he fought back tears.

"Yes, you are dismissed," the king cackled.

Turning from the throne room, Alex ran out into the vast foyer, darting past the young woman behind reception, hurtling down the spiral staircase two stairs at a time. At every level, he thought about jumping down past the guards and finding an escape route, but, the truth was, Julius had truly cornered him. Yes, there were soldiers keeping watch over every floor, and some following him, but it didn't matter— Alex wouldn't have run, even if they hadn't been there.

The king had his friends, and there was no way he was going to let them suffer for his fear.

CHAPTER 23

ALEX RETURNED TO HIS ROOM, WATCHED BY THE keen eyes of guards along the hallways, and the ones following at his back, ensuring he went the right way, without making any detours. Although he knew he couldn't make an escape, part of him wanted to search the grand palace for any sign of his friends. But everywhere he turned, more guards blocked his path. They were here, and that would have to be enough for now. He just hoped that, wherever they were, they were safe and warm, and being treated properly. The thought of them in a dank cell while he lived a life of luxury in a plush bedroom wasn't something he wanted to dwell on, but he had confidence in the manipulative hand of Venus. With her around, he knew his friends might just be okay. Well, as long as what he was seeing wasn't simply a well-rehearsed act, made to ensnare people in her trap.

Once he had shut the double doors behind him, ignoring the sneers of the four guards outside, he let out a long, shaky sigh. His heart beat faster, his hands trembling, his mouth suddenly dry. Sinking down to the floor, he let the enormity of the meeting, and his loss, wash over him. All around him, he could feel the sand in the hourglass of his mortality hissing away, the world suddenly very small and desperately precious to him. Never before had he wanted to cling onto it so badly, knowing there was nothing he could do to hang on. Julius had signed his death warrant—now he just had to wait for his moment on the gallows.

Tears pricked his eyes, and for once he let them fall. He was alone, so completely alone, facing his mortality head on. Holding his head in his hands, a wave of nausea crashed through him. He let it pass and kept his head down, his whole body shaking. Looking up slowly, he saw the billowing curtains and the marble balustrade beyond and, just for a second, wondered if he should just vault it and get it over and done with. If there weren't something he needed to do first, he knew it'd be preferable.

"I want to live," he whispered to the vacant air.

He stayed there for what seemed like hours, crouched in front of the double doors, trying to push the thought of what was to come from his mind. Julius had deliberately not given him a date or time, of that he was certain; it amped up the panic and paranoia, just the way the king liked his torture. The tears dried, and soon all Alex was left with was a numb ache of dread, pulsing deep in the pit of his stomach.

He got up, dragging himself over to the bathroom. As he was about to reach for the door handle, there was a frantic knock at the bedroom door. Swiveling around, Alex frowned, not knowing who it could possibly be. He walked over to the double doors and tentatively opened one side, peering out to see who waited in the hallway.

Virgil stood there, glancing up and down the corridor with anxious eyes.

"You?" said Alex, dumbfounded to see the Head standing before him.

Virgil nodded. "Can I come in for a moment?"

"Why would I let you in?" Alex asked, hoping the skeletal man couldn't see he'd been crying.

Virgil rolled his eyes. "This again? Really? I thought we were over that."

Alex paused. Where there had been four guards, now there were none. "Wait, where are the guards?" he asked, puzzled.

"Look, there's no time to explain," Virgil insisted, pushing past.

Once the Head was in the chamber, there wasn't much Alex could do but close the door and go back in, although not before taking one last look at the empty hallway. There was no sign of anyone, the entire length. It was a very tempting sight, but Virgil's voice called him back to reality with a rude bump.

"Don't even think about it, Webber. There are still guards patrolling, I just managed to persuade your particular set to go elsewhere for a while," he explained.

Alex wandered over to where Virgil had taken up a seat at the small dining table where Alex's satchel still lay, deflated with the book and vial now out on the bedcovers. Up close, the sunken-faced man looked even worse for wear. Bruises and cuts had formed a camouflage pattern across his features, and there seemed to be miniature bolts sticking out of his skin, the metal a dull gray, the wounds still sticky where the awful objects had been twisted in. Virgil grimaced every so often, jumping in his seat, like an electric shock had just gone off inside him. Peering closer, Alex could see that was exactly what was happening; tiny blue sparks jolted every couple of minutes, flickering in a pathway across the hybrid's face.

"What did he do to you?" Alex asked, genuinely concerned.

Virgil brushed it off. "Nothing he hasn't done to me before. He calls this his Frankenstein torture treatment—made it just for me one time, when I was in the stable and shouldn't have been," he explained, gesturing to the tiny bolts. "It's been a while since I've endured this, I can tell you... but I'll be fine. Anyway, I'm not here for sympathy, not that I'd expect to get any from you—even if this is partially your fault."

"How is that my fault?" Alex remarked.

Virgil sighed. "I offered to take your place. I told Julius I wanted to do it. I told him I wanted to redeem myself, that I wouldn't stand to see him force you… and this was his reply," he explained solemnly.

Alex glanced suspiciously at the Head, not really knowing why he was telling him this. It sounded true, and the mottled blue and black of his beat-up face certainly gave some credence to the story, but Alex couldn't figure out Virgil's reasoning behind sharing this with him. Perhaps, Alex thought, it was the Head's way of showing that he could be trusted? If that was the case, it certainly went some way toward proving it. No sane person would come under the wrath of Julius, if there wasn't a good reason behind it.

"You really offered to take my place?" Alex asked, unable to keep the hint of doubt from his voice.

Virgil nodded. "You may never believe me, but it is the truth," he croaked.

"Was that all you came here to say?"

Virgil's eyes flitted about the room, as though he were double-checking there wasn't a guard dangling from the ceiling, or hiding in the enormous wardrobe. Once he appeared satisfied nobody was about to interrupt them, he opened his mouth to speak, leaning his elbows up onto the dining table for support.

"I came to tell you that the students still at Starcross are all fine, despite what my stepfather would have you believe," he began. "A few are injured, and those who didn't make it have been buried, but the rest are alive and well. They are under the perpetual watch of a large army of soldiers, and they have been corralled into pens, presumably so Julius can deal with them swiftly at a later date, when he can bring himself to be bothered about them. He'll probably do a quick cull at some point down the line, but we are hopeful it will never get to that." A strange smile pulled at the taut skin of his face, causing the swollen cut on his lip to bleed afresh.

Alex fetched him a tissue. "'We'?"

"Thank you," said Virgil, dabbing his lip. "Yes, we—Hadrian, Ceres, and I. Ceres and I have had many discussions in my time at Starcross, and they have been somewhat enlightening. With her words, I have found parts of myself I thought were long dead, buried with the boy I once was. Sorry, I shouldn't get bogged down in the past..." He trailed off, staring out at the view beyond the French doors.

Alex listened intently, eager to learn more about this strange man who had been his arch-nemesis not so long ago, but was now something else entirely. What he was to him, Alex had yet to figure out, but it was becoming clearer with each meeting.

"No, go on," Alex encouraged, but it was clear the moment had passed.

"It doesn't matter," Virgil said, shaking his head. "Where was I? Ah yes—so, Ceres and I had many discussions in the windmill at Starcross, and one of those was a plan of action, should the place be captured. As planned, Hadrian is still at Falleaf, under no suspicion whatsoever, because he managed to do the impossible task of getting Julius to believe he wasn't involved in any of it. That nervous tic he has is a veritable pot of gold when it comes to persuading someone you'd do anything not to be killed," he explained, chuckling softly. "So, Hadrian told the king that Ceres had been blackmailing him and taking students in the middle of the night, without his consent. Once captured, Ceres admitted to it to Julius's face, to back up her brother, in the hopes of keeping that alliance with the king open, should it come in handy again one day soon," he continued, pausing to flash Alex a curious look. "Am I boring you yet?"

Alex shook his head. "Please, continue."

Virgil nodded. "I have been told my voice can get a little soporific at times," he said apologetically. "So, while Ceres is sadly under lock and key, the good news is, she hasn't been punished yet. As you heard, my stepfather wants to let Hadrian deal with her, so we know she's good for a while. That friend of yours and hers, the redhead—he has been captured too, but he's fine," he added, almost regretfully.

Alex frowned at the skeletal man, wondering if he wasn't a bit jealous of the flame-haired Demeter, and his relationship with the fiery Ceres. If that was the case, Virgil didn't confirm it, quickly changing the subject.

"As for your friends, they are indeed at the palace. So,

getting them out is going to be a nightmare," Virgil continued. "Julius really is keeping them as collateral, and I don't think there is much to be done about that. I suppose they'll just have to hope he keeps his end of the bargain," he said, giving a tight laugh. Alex shook his head subtly, hoping that wasn't the Head's attempt at humor. If it was, Alex pitied the poor man even more. "Sorry, I realize that was in poor taste. I mean to say that there will be no other way of getting them out of this place. The palace is both a fortress and a labyrinth, and I could not even begin to guess where your friends are," Virgil added, fidgeting uncomfortably.

"So what did you mean when you said it won't come to that, for the people at Starcross?" Alex pressed, shifting the conversation in the direction he wanted it to go.

Virgil smiled his strange, discomfited smile, though it was cut short by a jolt of electricity. "Well, it has all worked remarkably in our favor. You see, all the soldiers who were formerly at Falleaf are now at Starcross, and nobody is watching Hadrian," he said, getting a touch excitable. "Hadrian is going to rally his own students, and get the survivors out of Starcross, back to Falleaf, where he will shut the portal behind them."

Alex frowned, unconvinced. "What about the soldiers at Starcross?"

"The army there is large, but they are lazy. Plus, Julius won't expect it. He won't have time to send backup—by the time he even hears they're gone, the portal will be shut and a swath of his force will be stuck there," explained Virgil. "Not everyone can do the impressive heavens-opening thing he likes to do, and only he can fly back the same way. He will be royally—pardon the pun—screwed."

Alex sat back, impressed by the skeletal man before him. It seemed Virgil had taken sides, at long last, and though it didn't wash away the sins of all the terrible things he had done, it was clear the hybrid royal wanted to make amends, no matter the cost to himself. That, irrespective of how much he could actually absolve himself of, was something to respect.

Alex whistled. "That's quite the plan."

"I'm just sorry I can't take your place," Virgil said, sounding sincere.

"Why the sudden desire for martyrdom?" Alex sniffed, wondering what had come over the Head.

"It isn't martyrdom I seek, Webber, it is redemption… as I have said," Virgil began quietly, a solemn expression on his face. "I believe the shift came when you informed me of our mutual relation—my father. I was furious; I didn't want to believe a word. To me, Leander Wyvern had always been a monster who razed villages to the ground, murdering innocents and suffocating infants as they slept—the nightmarish fables they told children to make them behave. I never, for one moment, thought to question it. I was told I was the product of an attack, though the man in question was never named. He was this spectral enemy who had hurt my mother and made my stepfather loathe my very existence." He sighed with sadness.

"Only, he wasn't," Alex said softly.

Virgil shook his head. "No, he wasn't. Stuck in those cells, in that windmill, my mother finally told me a story I had never expected to hear. It was a story about love... about a young man and young woman who loved each other more than anything else in the world, but they stood on either side of a dangerous line. They gave up their love to protect one another, only to find each other again during wartime, when they better knew their own minds. She loves him still, thinks about him still, but could never breathe a word to me about him. Julius had threatened to have us both killed, on the spot, if word ever reached him that I knew of my heritage. In fear, she kept it from me, though she had wanted to tell me, over and over, all these years," he whispered, his voice tense with emotion. "Every time she'd heard me or him say a bad word about Leander, it had torn her up inside. The suffering she has had to endure, to keep me safe... I want to be redeemed for so many things, Alex. Knowing who I am has given me a strange sense of closure. When before, I was not ready for death, now I am. I wanted to do this, to take your place, for my father, for her, for the people I have killed."

"I'm sorry you can't take my place, too." Alex laughed bitterly. "But Julius has spoken—I have to be the one to die, to pay for my crimes against the royals," he added, putting on the king's voice.

Virgil chuckled, the sound a strange, raspy thing in the back of the man's throat. "I would switch with you in the room, if I could, but Julius has insisted he be present, to ensure everything goes the way he wants it to," he explained, sighing heavily. "He's asked me to build a barrier, to protect him from any silver mist fallout there might be. I had no choice but to accept. I hope you can understand."

Alex nodded, though it was a bitter pill to swallow. Given that Julius was not the sort to change his mind, Alex realized, once again, that it was going to be up to him to get the spell right. More than that, it was going to be up to him to give his life for the cause, after everything he'd done to try to avoid it. At last, he could see why Virgil had been so afraid in the past, when he'd been forced to do the counter-spell at his stepfather's behest. A twinge of sorrow made its way through Alex's veins, making him feel a flicker of sympathy for the way Virgil had been forced to do the tasks, back when he was so much younger and so much more afraid than he was now. It seemed they not only shared a relation, but they shared the same fears too.

"I understand why you want to do the spell, but there's something I'm still not sure I get," Alex said, voicing a thought that had been troubling his mind for some time, ever since it had looked as though Virgil was changing sides.

"What is it?"

Alex glanced at the Head, scrutinizing him closely. "Why the sudden change of heart, about me? I thought you'd be glad to see me go to my death, after all the trouble I've caused you."

Virgil smiled. "If you had asked me that question some days ago, I may have agreed. But I realized..." Virgil paused, seeming to collect his thoughts. "That I had forgotten myself. Spellshadow was never meant to be forever, but the years wore away, and with them, little pieces of who I was did as well. Then you and your friends broke the system, and I could see clearly again. I almost feel like I never knew myself, until very recently. So, as annoying as you have been, I have you to thank for that clarity," he said, his eyes glittering. "Put simply, I want to lay all my ghosts to rest, my grudges included."

That much, Alex could understand, though his own ghosts were growing louder by the second.

CHAPTER 24

VIRGIL LEFT SHORTLY AFTERWARD, LEAVING ALEX alone with his thoughts once more. He padded around the room aimlessly, though impulse made him go back over to the double doors to peer out. This time, the guards were back, their warning glances telling him to stay inside. Whatever deal Virgil had brokered to make them go away, it was evidently at its end.

Reluctantly stepping back inside, Alex went to the balcony and sat out in the sunshine, enjoying the warmth on his face, wondering how many more times he would feel the sun's soothing rays upon his skin. Looking up at the sky, he thought about his poor mother, waiting at home, not realizing the danger he was in. Doubtless she thought he was already dead, since he'd been missing for so long, but it didn't make it any easier to deal with. He wanted a moment with her, just a moment, to say goodbye. Perhaps, if he wrote a letter, he could ask Virgil to deliver it? It seemed unlikely, but he knew he had to try.

Sifting through the cupboards, back inside, he came across a small stack of smooth cream vellum and a pen and ink, stowed away at the back of a gold-handled drawer. He pulled them out, took them over to the dining table, and sat down, dipping the pen in the inkwell before holding it poised above the paper.

Where could he even begin?

Mom,

I am writing this to you in my last moments. I never intended to leave you—I was trapped by a strange man, in a strange place, and now I'm afraid they are going to...

A knock at the door made him stop, though he knew the words he had written would go straight in the trash. He didn't want to frighten his mother, or bring her more sadness than she had already suffered. No, he would write something else, something lighter, something that might bring her peace in the dark days to come.

He was halfway to the door when Siren Mave burst in impatiently. He had been half expecting to see Virgil again, but the sight of the toady woman made him halt in his tracks, a sudden shiver of panic running through him. Was this the moment? So soon?

"Don't you worry, Alex, I'm not the executioner," she muttered. "I'm just here to take you to a meeting that has been prepared."

Alex nodded, though fear had rendered him silent. He tried to put one foot in front of the other, but he was frozen to the spot, unable to move, his heart thundering in his chest. With an unexpectedly kind smile, Siren Mave came up to him, taking his arm like a kind grandmother, leading him toward the door of the bedroom. She kept hold of him all the way to their destination, helping him along the gilded corridors and hallways, though Alex saw little of their beauty. It was all he could do not to break away from her and jump through the nearest window.

They stopped outside a pretty solarium, the glass sides revealing a veritable forest of beautiful plants and flowers within and a view of a golden city beyond, leading Alex to realize they must be on the opposite side of the palace, overlooking whichever royal city Julius held home dominion over. Two lemon trees grew on either side of the entrance, and there were slender plants everywhere, some sprouting long-flowing purple flowers, others bearing the most striking red flowers, the petals almost as long as Alex's hand. Fluttering butterflies swept elegantly from blossom to blossom.

In the center of the solarium, several rattan sofas had been set up in a circle, with figures sitting in them, but Alex's view of their faces was blocked by the wall of greenery.

Heading through the entrance, he saw them as clear as day. His friends were sitting there, awaiting his arrival, sipping tentatively at glasses full of peculiar purple liquid. Alex could sense Venus's influence in this unexpected meeting.

Aamir, Jari, Natalie, and Ellabell looked up at him as he entered, their faces relaxing into expressions of relief. Helena wasn't with them, however.

"Helena has been locked away in a different part of the palace, to receive a punishment more fitting of her royal heritage," Natalie explained, evidently seeing Alex's puzzled expression. "We have not seen her, but we know she is safe," she added quietly.

"They worried you're going to up and run?" Jari teased, gesturing toward the large cluster of guards that had appeared beyond the glass walls of the solarium. There were even some standing out on the balcony, through the French doors that lined the front of the room.

Alex smiled. "They know I have a thing for diving out of windows," he joked, though the laughter felt tight in his throat.

"Have you already met with the king, then?" Aamir asked solemnly, concern in his dark eyes.

"Yeah, we've had words," Alex said wryly, trying not to let his emotions overwhelm him. Still, he knew he'd looked away too slowly; they had seen the fear in his eyes. The room fell silent. It was clear they had been expecting the worst, but to understand how real it was, was a different beast entirely.

"You're not getting out of this?" Ellabell whispered, though she would not look up, her hands balling into fists.

"Doesn't look like it," Alex replied quietly.

"Do you remember when you first arrived at Spellshadow, and Jari was looming over you, bouncing around like a little kid?" said Aamir suddenly, cutting through the tension.

Alex frowned, the memory bringing a small smile to his face. "I do remember that," he chuckled.

"I had to stop him from trying to shove you awake. He thought that if he could roll you off the edge of the bed, the impact of you hitting the floor would make you wake up quicker," Aamir continued, laughter glittering in his eyes. "He wouldn't listen when I said it might knock you out. If you hadn't woken up when you did, I wouldn't have been able to stop him."

Jari grinned. "Hey, it was a good idea! It would have worked, too, if it hadn't been for you pesky kids," he said, putting on his best gangster voice.

"And that first lesson, when you could not do the aura! Derhin was so disappointed in you!" Natalie chimed in. "But when I made you crackle, it was like you had run a marathon—he was so happy for you."

Alex nodded, that memory somewhat tainted by the thought of what had happened to the professor after. "And that duel on the front lawn was pretty epic," he said, flashing a knowing look at Aamir.

The older boy smiled sadly. "It's just a shame it led to so

many terrible things."

"Yeah, your moment of victory didn't last very long," Jari said, nudging his friend. "You were a total boss though, when you were fighting. Sneak attack master! It's the one time since I've known you that I've actually thought you had a hint of cool in there somewhere."

"I fear I may have used up all my cool," Aamir replied, laughing.

"I think we have all done some terrible things and some cool things in our time here," Natalie added, looking slightly sheepish.

Jari nodded. "Yeah, Natalie, we definitely all thought you were going psycho at one point, but you came through it."

"The curse, the dark magic. You've been through a lot," Alex agreed, looking at the French girl with warmth in his eyes. "And while we haven't always seen eye to eye, you've always been a good person. Power is tempting. I know it now."

Natalie smiled shyly. "I have been a bit of a nightmare at times, haven't I?"

"Understatement of the century!" Jari whooped, eliciting a swift punch in the arm from Natalie. "See, there you go again," he teased, as Natalie's laughter rippled across the room. It was a beautiful sound, and one that Alex had not heard in too long.

Aamir laughed. "We had no idea what was coming, back then, did we? I mean, do you remember that Christmas—how happy we all were? It feels like twenty Christmases should have passed by now, right?"

The others nodded.

"I just remember thinking you didn't like me very much," Alex admitted, glancing at Aamir.

"You mean, when I took you up to the hill and had a go at you?" he asked, grinning.

Alex smiled. "That's the one."

"I thought you had potential, but I didn't think you were taking magic seriously. Can you believe that?" Aamir said, shaking his head. "How wrong I was. It was all simple back then, wasn't it? It was class and teachers and students, no different from being at high school. I think we thought, if we pretended enough, things would be okay." His face took on a dreamy expression. "When you're young, you think school is the world—you think it dictates everything you are, and everything you will be. It's only when you're out that you realize there is a whole other world awaiting you, and you have to deal with life as it comes, adapting and changing," he added, a tinge of sorrow leaking into his words. "Without you, Alex, we'd have stayed there. We would never have reached beyond that idea of accepting it was our only choice, our only world; we would never have tried to leave."

So far, they had managed to avoid actively talking about what Alex was being made to do, but there was a peculiar undercurrent running beneath their talk of memories—good times and bad. It was their way of saying goodbye, without having to say the words.

"Dude, way to bring down the mood." Jari whistled, but there was a smile in his eyes.

Aamir laughed. "Sorry, time in a cell, however plush, has made me somewhat philosophical," he apologized, trying to bring the levity back.

The only person who had yet to speak was Ellabell. She was sitting in her seat, her head down, her nails digging into her palms. An aura of angry sadness emanated from her. Even her body language was prickly, her shoulders hunched, a muscle in her cheek twitching where she was gritting her teeth. Alex couldn't bear for her to be silent a moment longer; he wanted to hear her voice.

"Ellabell? Do you remember when we first met, and you told me all about Jari's attempts to woo you?" Alex asked, trying to involve her in the conversation.

She lifted her head. "I remember everything," she said simply, her eyes strangely blank.

Aamir stood. "The three of us should be going," he said, flashing the other two a knowing look. They stood quickly, though Natalie's eyes were filling with tears.

"Don't leave on my account," Ellabell murmured.

"We aren't, but there are discussions that aren't meant for our ears," Aamir replied kindly, resting his hand on Ellabell's shoulder. She flinched, refusing to look up at him. Taking her point, he removed his hand and moved toward Alex instead. Without saying a word, he pulled his friend in for a tight hug, thumping him hard on the back. Alex gripped him hard too, unable to prevent a smile from creeping onto his face, despite the looming sadness.

As Aamir released him and stepped back, Jari swooped in. "You're the coolest guy I know!" he said, squeezing Alex hard before letting him go. "Honestly, a true hero." He lifted his hand in a salute, forcing a wide grin onto his face, though it didn't reach the eyes that were brimming with tears.

Natalie was next, though her embrace was softer. She wrapped her arms around him, and he returned the gesture. "I am sorry I got you into this," she whispered. "Jari is right—you are a true hero. For all the times I doubted you, please forgive me."

"There is nothing to forgive," Alex said, letting her go.

She turned her face quickly away, hurrying to where the boys were standing. Both Jari and Natalie leaned into Aamir, appearing to draw strength from his stoic demeanor, though the older boy's face was undeniably sad. With a final, awkward wave, they left the solarium, two guards flanking them to escort the trio back to their chambers.

Now alone, Ellabell stood up abruptly. "I should be going too," she said.

"Ellabell, you can't go like this," Alex insisted, reaching for her arm to prevent her from walking from the solarium, and out of his life forever. He could see she was already hardening herself against the pain and suffering that was to come, becoming colder in order to survive. The defiant expression on her face reminded him a little of Ceres, another woman forced to guard herself against emotion, to protect herself from the pain that would undoubtedly come.

"I don't think we have much more to say to one another." Ellabell sighed, her eyes steely.

"Come on, please don't leave this way," he said. "I don't want this to be my last memory of you."

She smiled strangely. "Would you rather I was a mess on the floor, crying my eyes out, tearing out my hair, begging you to run, to hide, to do anything to get out of this? Would you rather I was clinging to you for dear life, wanting to change places with you, with every fiber of my being? Would you rather I fell into your arms like a damsel, and kissed you until the whole world faded away?" she asked, digging her nails ever harder into her palms.

"No, Ellabell, I don't want any of that," Alex whispered, moving closer to her, though she took a step back. "I just want you to know that you are loved. I love you, and you will be there with me, when the moment comes, and for that I will be glad," he said softly, reaching for her hands.

"I love you too, but I can't stay here giving you the sweet, loving goodbye you want. I won't stay and be broken by the loss of you. Otherwise, I won't make it," she replied, squeezing his hands tightly for the briefest moment. No tears glittered in her blue eyes, and though she reached up to kiss him momentarily, it was a hard, cold kiss.

The soft side of her seemed to be fading before his very eyes, and though he hated to think of her that way, so spiky and distant, he knew it would serve to pull her through the impact of his death. Many people would fall apart—even Natalie had been on the verge of tears—but Ellabell would not be broken by it. No, she would become stronger in the face of adversity, because that was what survivors did; they found strength they never knew existed. They adapted and they changed to match the cold world that met them.

"I have to go," she said, moving toward the entrance to the solarium. She turned back, her face an expressionless mask. "I wish you luck."

And with that, she was gone.

CHAPTER 25

ALEX STAYED IN THE SOLARIUM FOR A WHILE longer, until one of the guards came in and told him it was time to leave. He went without a fuss, his mind full of Ellabell and his friends. Thinking of her, he felt troubled; he wanted to find her, to make her soft and sweet again, to take away everything that had made her heart turn to stone, but he knew he couldn't. He had to hold onto the memories they'd shared, and hope they'd be enough to see him through the task that lay ahead.

Once more, Alex arrived at the double doors of his bedroom and went inside, walking over to the edge of the bed, where he sat down, holding his head in his hands. It was lonelier than ever within the silent walls of his pretty prison.

Before long, shadows began to trickle from the ceiling.

Alex looked up, half glad, half exasperated that the shadow-man was arriving just when Alex needed company most. It wasn't exactly great timing, considering the red rims around his eyes, which the vaporous man would no doubt comment on, but Alex was pleased not to be alone anymore.

"They didn't blast you back into the ether, then?" Alex asked as the shadow-man stretched into his full form, a yawn spreading from the cavern of his black mouth.

Elias grinned. "Not this time. When one is a master of wriggling out of tight spots, one finds you can talk your way out of just about anything," he explained, giving a low, dramatic bow. "Flashing a face of pure innocence doesn't hurt, either," he added, putting on his best naïve expression.

Alex gave a half smile. "Glad you got out of it. I thought you were a goner for a moment there."

"Takes one to know one," Elias retorted.

"I take it you heard about my meeting with dear old Julius?"

Elias gave a slow nod. "Oh, yes, I had a feeling it would go down like a granny on a frosty morning. That man gets ideas in his head and there is no shifting them. Who in their right mind turns down an offer from a much-loathed stepson to willingly take himself out of the picture? Honestly, if Virgil were my stepson, I'd have jumped at the chance," he said, a hint of amusement in his strange voice.

"Nope, it looks like I am the chosen one," Alex said bitterly.

"Hey, let's not be getting ideas above our station," Elias replied. "I'd say you're more like the unlucky one in this scenario..." The shadow-man's expression became briefly uncomfortable. "I am sorry it's come to this, you know? As much as we've had our little frictions, you've grown on me—like an unsightly mole, or a rash, or the first few flecks of gray in one's hair."

Alex wouldn't give Elias the satisfaction of saying he'd grown on him too, especially given the actual scale of their "little frictions." What Elias had done to Alex's father had not been forgotten; it had simply been put on the backburner of his mind.

"Wasn't this the whole point of you being my guardian, though?" Alex asked, voicing something that had been bugging him for a long while. "Wasn't this your objective, to find me and get me to do the spell?"

Elias tilted his head from side to side. "Yes and no. Once we knew what you were, there was an element of that, but it was only ever supposed to be a voluntary act. I would never have made you do it, and with Virgil still around, I always hoped you'd make him suffer by getting him to do it instead, just like old times. It made my day when you said that was precisely what you had in mind—all my little drip-feeds paying off handsomely. Well, until they didn't," he said, gesturing at the room.

"Why do you hate him so much?" Alex asked.

"Actually, I don't. We have somewhat buried the hatchet, in the brief interim since last we met," Elias explained, shrugging with languid arms. "Well, I say that—we may have tied a ribbon on the fruit basket of our differences, but a lifetime of hatred is a tough thing to shift completely. I'll always keep a little spot in my heart for my secret loathing of him," the shadow-man chuckled.

"I'm sure he has one for you too." Alex sighed, incredulous of the idea of Elias and Virgil no longer at odds.

"Hey, I never did anything to him. *He* was the guilty party in all of this," said Elias, wafting his hands in front of his vaporous body. "I'd still be a solid man if it weren't for Virgil's idiocy. We were friends, back in the day. It wasn't me who caused the rift." He pouted.

Alex smiled, pleased to have rattled the shadow-man. "Regardless, I'm sure you annoyed him enough to warrant whatever he did to you," he teased.

"I've a mind to show you precisely what he did," Elias grumbled. "Instead, I shall bring you vague news, in the hopes it'll exasperate you enough to satisfy me."

Alex frowned. "What news?"

"Well, I stopped off by our old chum on the way, and we decided enough was enough, where our feud was concerned. But, we also had a little chat about you," Elias began. "He's got something up his sleeve—something to do with what we were discussing when I got snapped away. I would show you the image again, but I don't feel like pushing my luck. Anyway, Virgil has it all worked out. He has a plan, and he's putting it into action as we speak, though he's told me not to tell you," he continued, putting on the voice of a petulant schoolchild. Alex felt as if Elias were about to say he couldn't sit with him at the lunch table.

"Elias, what did Virgil say? What is he planning?" Alex asked firmly, not in the mood for funny business. "Does it have something to do with the third person in the vision you showed?"

"Maybe... Maybe not." Elias sighed, stretching out his long, vaporous arms. "I can't say any more on the subject. All you need to know is that it's worked out."

Alex felt a wave of irritation prickle across his skin. He was tired of people keeping important information from him, yet again. Surely, if it was something to do with the spell, he had a right to know?

"If I'm supposed to be the one doing this spell, shouldn't I know if I'm missing something glaringly obvious?" Alex pressed.

"Well, it can't be that glaringly obvious if you haven't figured it out," Elias bit back, smiling sardonically.

Alex glared at the shadow-man. "Elias!"

"Okay, okay, I didn't want to be the one to tell you this, but the reason Virgil has explicitly said you are not to be told, is because you can't be trusted," he said, holding up his misty hands in defense, though it was clear he was reveling in every second of Alex's torment.

Alex almost choked on the words. "*I* can't be trusted?"

"That's what he said." Elias shrugged. "Or perhaps he said it was to protect you, in case Julius tried to torture you, and you accidentally let something slip? I forget. This old mind is like a sieve—a great big, foggy sieve. It's nothing bad, though. It's just something he needs to keep secret. Or so he claims, anyway."

"And he told you all of this?" Alex pressed, still in disbelief over the idea of the two of them being buddies all of a sudden.

Elias smirked. "Oh yes, he's quite the chatterbox once you get him going. We discussed your upcoming task, and what happened in the throne room. He told me he'd come to you after, to speak with you, which I thought was a nice touch." He sniggered. "Yes, he called to me, I was curious, and we spoke. There was tea and a quartet and unicorns too," he said, with a wave of his shadowy fronds.

"If both of you want me to succeed, I don't understand why you won't just tell me what it is Virgil has in mind," Alex snapped, exasperated. "You almost told me yourself, before you got dragged back into the ether. Why not just tell me now? I won't say anything."

"Can't, shan't, won't," said Elias petulantly.

"This is ridiculous!" Alex was almost shouting now.

Elias's face grew stern. "I'm not the one making the rules, Alex. Virgil has asked me not to say anything, and I happen to agree with him, in this case. It is for your own good," he insisted, his voice serious.

"Then why even bother coming here to feed me these stupid, annoying little tidbits? You do it just to get under my skin, don't you?" Alex was really going for it now. "You come here to flounce about and irritate the living hell out of me. That's all this is—this is the Elias show! You just want to prove how amusing and witty you are, but you're starting to grate on me. Actually, you started to grate on me a long time ago. What use are you, if you can't tell me things that will be legitimately *helpful* to me?"

Elias put up his hands. "I don't want to start an argument, Alex. I just wanted to let you know that Virgil is coming up with something that will *help* you, but you can't know about it. It is to protect you," he reiterated, but Alex was having none of it.

"Protect me? Don't make me laugh," Alex snarled. "Your whole purpose was to protect me, and look at the great job you did at that! I am going to *die* because of you, Elias. I am going to die because you didn't do your job. I am going to die because none of you would tell me anything that could have prevented this. Everything that comes out of your mouth is worthless. It's just vague, worthless crap!"

"Alex, you should calm down," Elias said softly.

He shook his head. "I am way past the point where I need to calm down. I am sick of you! I am sick of this world! You think you can come and go as you please, without even asking if I want to see you. And then, and here's the best part, you don't even do anything useful! You're a smug, self-centered ass, and you deserved what happened to you. I want you out of my sight!"

"Alex, I am sorry... I didn't mean to—" Elias began, but Alex cut him off sharply.

"No, you never mean to do anything, do you?" he snapped. "I am so sick of you I don't even have the words. If you have nothing useful to say, then GET OUT!"

"I'm sorry, Alex," said Elias, who was beginning to disappear up into the shadows in the corner of the room. "I'm trying to help. You will see..." His disembodied voice trailed off as his wispy form evaporated into nothingness.

Alex stared up at the corner of the ceiling for a long time, wondering if the shadow-man was going to reappear, but as time wore on, Elias remained absent.

It eventually began to plague Alex that they had parted on such bad terms. Yes, the shadow-man was annoying, but perhaps there had been something worthy in what Elias had been saying, and he'd just said it in the wrong way.

Virgil was trying to protect him, but from what?

There was nothing Alex could do to take back the words, and that made it worse. His mind raced with all the things he should have said, not only to Elias, but to everyone. Though they'd had their goodbyes, there hadn't really been a proper farewell. They had spoken of memories and old days, but nobody had mentioned the elephant in the room—not really.

Panic coursed through him, combined with a strange numbness, a dull dissatisfaction in the way he had parted with everyone. He was going to die, and there was so much he still wanted to say. More than that, there was so much he still wanted to do. He ought to have his whole life ahead of him, to indulge in all the things everyone else got to do and see, but that path was closed to him now.

It was all too late. With so many goodbyes, Alex had a feeling that D-Day was coming much sooner than he was prepared for. Not that he could ever be prepared. Time was running out; he could hear the death knell sounding.

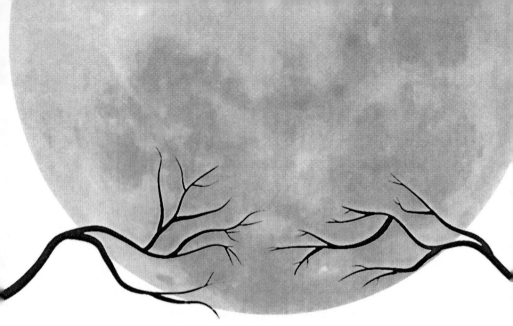

CHAPTER 26

ALEX DIDN'T REMEMBER FALLING ASLEEP, BUT THE rough shove of hands stirred him abruptly from his brief slumber. Blinking awake, he saw Siren Mave loitering beside the bed, her gnarled hands shaking him into consciousness.

"Ah, he's alive," she crowed.

"What is it? Has something happened?" he asked, regaining his bearings.

She shook her head. "No, nothing so dramatic," she tutted. "The king has demanded another audience with you, that's all."

Alex felt like snapping at her. That was all? The last time

he'd met with Julius, it hadn't exactly gone well for him. Still, he knew he couldn't defy the king's orders. If Julius wanted to meet with him again, so be it.

"Why does he want to meet me?" Alex asked, getting down off the bed. The covers were still in place; it seemed he hadn't managed to get under them.

Siren Mave flashed him a withering look. "You think I know the inner workings of the king's mind? I'm just the messenger, and if you don't hurry yourself up, I will be in trouble," she barked, rushing off to the wardrobe to pick out some clothes for him to wear. "He did say you were to bring the book, however," she said, not bothering to turn as she pulled a dark gray three-piece suit out of the wardrobe and laid it out on the armchair by the fire.

Alex frowned, both at the clothes and the request to bring the book. "I'm not wearing that," he said firmly.

Siren Mave sighed, smacking her overly painted lips together. "Just put it on and be happy I didn't choose something flashier," she instructed, pulling out some shoes to go with it. "I'll be outside—you have five minutes," she added, before scuttling from the room.

Reluctantly, Alex walked over to the clothes and put on the shirt and trousers, leaving the waistcoat, jacket, and tie she had put out. There was no way he was going to dress up for Julius again. Once he had the clothes on, he picked up the book and the mostly empty vial and shoved them into the depths of the satchel that still sat on the dining table. Slinging it over his shoulder, he went out into the hallway, where Siren Mave was waiting. She eyed him as if he were an unsavory vagrant who had just traipsed into her home, but Alex didn't care.

"Why do I even bother?" she mumbled to herself, before leading the way toward the spiral staircase.

They had reached the halfway point when Siren Mave stopped and got off on the middle level, turning to ensure Alex was following. They walked down a long, beautifully decorated corridor, toward a door at the very end. It was here that she stopped, knocking lightly on the gold-and-cream door before hurrying away.

"Come in!" Julius's voice bellowed.

Taking that as his cue, Alex pushed open the door and stepped inside. Beyond lay an enormous dining room, with a table longer than any Alex had ever seen running down the middle, capable of seating more than five hundred guests, by the looks of it. Painted on the ceiling was a fresco that reminded Alex of the Sistine Chapel, with gods and cherubs floating above, playing instruments and lounging upon clouds.

Julius and Virgil sat up at the very top end of the table, with Julius at the head. Seeing just the two of them, Alex was a little anxious that Venus wasn't there to offer her soothing influence. Still, that wasn't what drew his attention.

Laid out on the gleaming marble surface, a very civilized breakfast had been prepared. It looked delicious, the scent of sweet muffins wafting up from the table. Alex paused, wondering if this was some kind of last supper-type deal, especially as there seemed to be everything he liked spread out before him. They even had a stack of strawberry pancakes, just like the ones his mother used to make. The sight of them was almost more than he could bear, making him lose any remaining appetite he had been clinging onto.

With his life on the line, he didn't particularly feel like eating. In fact, the sight of so much food made his stomach turn. Julius was watching him closely, no doubt expecting him to refuse the glorious meal he had prepared, just so he could pretend to be affronted, or could gain some smug pleasure in the fact that Alex was too scared and too broken to eat. Well, Alex wasn't going to permit that. No matter how sick he felt, he wasn't going to give the king the satisfaction. Sitting down in the chair opposite Virgil, Alex picked up his knife and fork.

"Is this for us, Your Royal Highness?" Alex asked brightly.

A flicker of disappointment passed across Julius's face. "It certainly is. I thought you could use a hearty meal to restore your strength before the big event. I'm just sorry we couldn't save you any of the delicious roast we had," he said, recovering quickly. The king's jibe stung Alex to the very core, but he refused to react, no matter how much it pained him. He had to try very hard not to show how the words "big event" jarred in his head, too—if Julius had put on this meal before the "big event", that meant it was today. With Virgil there too, it

291

only confirmed Alex's suspicions. Still, he wasn't going to let the king see his terror, not if he could help it.

"How very thoughtful," Alex remarked. "This is so generous, Your Royal Highness. Do you mind if I dig in? I'm starving," he said, laying it on thick.

"By all means," Julius replied, having a harder time keeping his emotions off his face. Alex could see the very act of him eating was irking the king, and that pleased him greatly.

Reaching forward, he took up two enormous waffles, drenched in a bright amber syrup, and brought them to his plate. With one eye always on Julius, Alex forced the food down, though it got stuck in his throat. Gritting his teeth, he swallowed, taking bite after bite and going back for more, simply to prove a point. He ate apple slices coated in cinnamon and sugar; he ate blueberry pancakes; he ate thick slices of toast drenched in dark jam. He ate hash browns; he ate omelets with cheese; he ate a myriad of things he'd never seen before—little pinwheel pastries stuffed with green, jelly-like goo, and steamed buns with savory fillings. He ate as much as he could, washed down with orange juice and black coffee, until he felt like he really was going to be sick.

"That was delicious," Alex said, patting his stomach. "You are most kind, Your Royal Highness. I know you didn't have to do this for me. You have my thanks."

Julius stared at Alex, in disbelief of the amount of food he had just polished off. "Yes, well, I try to cater to my guests as best I can. It is a royal duty, to see people are well taken care of within the palace walls," he said, still staring at the empty plate in front of Alex, and the chunks he'd taken out of the feast. "Are you sure you are finished?" he asked, sarcastically.

Alex nodded. "Oh yes, I couldn't eat another bite, though I might get hungry in a bit."

"Then we should begin preparations," Julius remarked. "I trust you brought the book, as instructed?"

"Yes, Your Royal Highness," said Alex. He brought out the book and laid it on the table, pushing his plate away with a spine-tingling scrape to make room.

"Very good. I would like you and Virgil to go over the spell until you know it back to front," he insisted. "I will not have another slip-up. Is that clear? Although, you know the consequences for your friends if you fail." He smiled cruelly, drawing a line across his neck with his index finger.

Alex wanted to roll his eyes, or at least tell the king how clichéd he was, but he held his tongue. Such comments would get him nowhere.

"Of course, Your Royal Highness," Alex replied.

"As you know, you only have one chance left to get it right, so make it count," Julius added, the remark falling somewhat short of a pep talk.

"Of course, Your Royal Highness," Alex repeated.

With that, Alex and Virgil set to work. The skeletal man came around to Alex's side of the table so they could work at closer proximity to the book. The atmosphere was tense, with Alex constantly aware of Julius's eyes upon them, perhaps wondering what they were discussing. When Alex conjured up a thin veil of anti-magic, by which they could read the words on the pages, Julius's face twisted into a mask of utter disgust—it seemed the very sight of something Spellbreaker caused a kneejerk reaction of displeasure. Alex tried not to smile.

"I'm still not sure where it went wrong the last time, though I know it had something to do with it not being 'witnessed properly,' whatever that means," Alex began, pointing at the section in the spell where the line was mentioned. The words were very hard to make out, but he could discern the phrase he was looking for. "Yeah, here: 'Two sides of a coin must witness and see, for the grip on the realm to be finally free.' I was thinking about this part yesterday, and thought it might have something to do with it."

Virgil nodded. "I had been thinking about that too."

"Do you know what it means?" Alex asked innocently, testing Virgil's dedication to secrecy.

Virgil glanced at him oddly. "I have an idea, but it's not something I can share," he whispered.

"Why can't you share it, if I'm the one doing the spell?" Alex pressed, feeling a strong sense of déjà vu.

"I can't explain now, but be sure it is all in hand," Virgil breathed, making sure Julius couldn't hear.

Alex shook his head. "No, this is stupid. If you know—" His words were cut off by the hasty arrival of the young woman he'd seen upstairs sitting at the desk, the whites of her "eyes showing her fear. She rushed over to where Julius was prowling, handing him a letter on a silver tray. Julius plucked it up, turning it over and opening the seal. The young woman didn't stick around to see his reaction, but scurried away through the door, practically slamming it behind her in her rush to be out of there.

As the king read the letter, everything froze. His eyes flickered across the slender sheet of vellum, the color draining from his face, his lips curling more with every sentence he read. Reaching the end, Julius balled the card up and hurled it toward the table. Without Venus to help, there was nobody to quell the king's temper.

"You!" he roared, picking up a butter knife from the table and rushing at Alex. "You did this!"

Alex tried to get up and back away as quickly as he could, but his foot caught on the chair leg, stalling his retreat. Julius ran at him, the knife raised.

"What did I do, Your Royal Highness?" Alex asked, lifting his hands to protect himself from the blade. In Julius's hands, even a butter knife seemed like a deadly weapon.

The King tapped the blade against Alex's arm. "You and your band of do-gooders have caused me another calamity!" he snarled, the spittle flying into Alex's face. "I have just been informed that Stillwater House has been engulfed by the silver mist because there was no essence left in the pit. Nobody bothered to pour any down, and nobody bothered to tell me! It could have been avoided, Alex Webber, if one of you had simply spat it out!" He yanked Alex's arms out of the way. "But this was your plan, wasn't it? You thought you could keep it secret, just to aggravate me. Isn't that right? Well, your little scheme worked—we found out too late, and several of my men have died because of it!" he bellowed, bringing the knife to Alex's throat.

"Your Royal Highness, I apologize for causing you more trouble," Alex began calmly, trying not to feel the cold bite of the blade every time he spoke. "We didn't know that would happen. We had friends there too," he said, half lying.

Julius paused, removing the blade slightly. "You had friends there?"

Alex nodded. "Not everyone from Stillwater managed to escape. We had allies trapped there. If the mist engulfed Stillwater, then we have lost people too, Your Royal Highness," he explained, hoping to appeal to some twisted sense of justice in the king's moral code.

"I hadn't thought about that," Julius mused, taking the knife away.

"I know it is an inconvenience to you to have lost your men, but I am going to pay for the hassle I have caused you soon enough," Alex added, pleased to see Julius's face relaxing.

The king took a step back, moving toward the head of the table again. "Indeed you are. I suppose a handful of men is a small price to pay, in the grand scheme of things," he murmured, a smug expression on his face. Alex felt disgusted that the king could dismiss lives so easily—not that he was surprised in the slightest. "Go ahead then, get back to whatever it was you were doing. Quick as you can," Julius instructed, pulling a small book out of one of his pockets and settling down to read it.

As the minutes wore on into hours, however, the king grew more and more impatient, every look and sigh showing his annoyance at the length of time it was taking. Alex and Virgil had been at it for a long while, trying to iron out any kinks, though Virgil still refused to spill the beans on what he had planned. It irritated Alex deeply, but he knew he wasn't going to get the skeletal man to break.

The slam of a vial on the table interrupted their work, making them both jump. Through the glass, Alex could see blood sloshing around, ready to be utilized.

"Hurry up!" Julius demanded. "Why is this taking so long?"

Virgil spoke up. "We want to ensure we have everything right, Your Royal Highness. As you said, we don't want any slip-ups this time."

"Well, do it quicker," Julius barked, returning to his book.

"Yes, Your Royal Highness," said Virgil, turning to Alex with an apologetic expression upon his sunken face. It was clear they couldn't stall anymore—the moment was upon them. "In fact, I believe we are ready to go," he added. The king looked up in surprise.

"Oh, you are? Excellent." He pocketed his book. "Then

gather your things and follow me," he said, jumping up excitedly.

Alex put the Book of Jupiter back in his satchel, while Virgil took up the fresh vial of blood. With that, they nodded for Julius to lead the way. Like the Pied Piper, the king practically danced down the hallways, knowing he was about to get the very thing he wanted the most—glory, at no cost to himself. Up and up he led them, until they reached a fairly innocuous-looking door. Pushing through it, he gestured for Alex and Virgil to step inside.

It opened onto a small room with a bronze dome, speckled with glinting diamonds made to look like stars, bending above. There was a design etched into a gold plinth in the center, showing a ring with four dots, a gemstone marking each one, encircled by a larger ring containing five dots, though these no longer bore gemstones.

All around the room stood portals, though most were blocked off. Crouched down beneath three of the still-working ones were two men, their magic flowing through the gateways, clearly trying to shut them down. The two that remained untouched, however, seemed to open out onto wide expanses of sky. No buildings or trees or ground, even, could be seen through them. Alex realized this was likely how Julius did his heavens-opening arrivals, but the thought of having to plummet through the air wasn't exactly comforting. Besides, he didn't have the same floating abilities that mages had. If he jumped through that portal, he knew he'd end up falling to his death.

"Do you want us to go through these, Your Royal Highness?" Alex asked.

"Why else would I have brought you here?" Julius sneered.

Alex glanced at Virgil. "We're going to have to do our whooshing travel thing," he said, to which Virgil nodded.

Julius grinned. "I don't think so." He chuckled coldly as two guards stepped up.

Grabbing Alex roughly by the arm, one of the guards led him up to the lip of the chosen portal, gripping him hard as he stepped through. Alex was pulled along by the momentum. For a moment, the air rushed up to meet them, and Alex thought he was going to end up a squashed mess on the ground. But then things slowed, the guard holding Alex as he used his magical abilities to float down. A flurry of snowflakes fell from Alex's arm where the guard was clutching him, but aside from that, they managed to soar downward and land with little difficulty.

Brushing off the remaining flakes of snow, Alex looked around. He had seen where they were headed from the sky, and realized it was the only place that made sense. Falleaf remained the sole haven without any mist rising from it… for now, anyway.

Virgil landed beside him, followed swiftly by Julius and a handful of extra guards. Once everyone had regrouped, they set off toward the pagoda, where Hadrian was standing at the main entrance, awaiting their arrival.

The nervous royal gave Alex the subtlest of nods before turning to Julius.

"Your Royal Highness, and guests, I welcome you to Falleaf House," he said, the muscle in his cheek twitching with the effort it was taking him not to stammer. "Please, f-follow me."

With that, Hadrian led them up to the third floor, ushering them through into a wide gallery that reminded Alex of the one a few floors above, the tapestries shimmering with movement as the group walked past. At the end of the room, hidden away in a recess in the wall, stood a silver statue of an owl. Hadrian twisted its head, and a door slid back to reveal a staircase, the steps going all the way down beneath the earth. It was similar to one Alex had walked down before, in this very building, only this went even deeper. A door opened out onto a rough-hewn rock hallway, gut-wrenchingly familiar, with a set of looming gates ahead.

The pit lay beyond, and with it, Alex's fate.

CHAPTER 27

T HEY ENTERED THE PIT ROOM, VIRGIL LEADING THE way. Hadrian had remained above, standing beside the silver statue, promising to keep guard over the staircase. It all looked the same, the gold bird flapping slowly above the gaping mouth of the cavern.

Julius entered last, stepping in with surprising tentativeness. An expression of uncertainty passed across the king's face upon seeing the crevasse.

"Where would you like to stand, Your Royal Highness?" Virgil asked, gesturing toward the solid boundary that surrounded the pit mouth.

"I think over here, perhaps," said Julius, moving toward

the widest stretch of ground. Virgil followed him, opening out his hands as if to begin weaving a spell. The bristle of silver and gold, the Head's particular brand of energy, rippled out over his skeletal hands, forming a swirling orb. However, the king paused beside the wall of the cave. "Yes… here, I think," he said after a moment of silence.

Virgil nodded and began to forge a barrier around the king and his guards, who had taken up position behind their royal leader. It swelled out across the small group, forming an almost liquid sheen between them and what lay below the earth, distorting their faces until it was like seeing someone through the thin film of a bubble.

"It is complete, Your Royal Highness," said Virgil. "The barrier will hold back any mist that might come, giving you the chance to escape, should you need to."

From the uncertain expression on his face, it was clear the king was having second thoughts. "Actually, perhaps I would be best outside the pit room? Yes… I think I will leave you to it, and wait for you on the other side. There's no real need for me to be here, is there?" he asked, his stern voice overcompensating for the fear he evidently felt. Alex smiled—the pit tended to have that effect on people, and it was nice to see that even the king wasn't immune.

Virgil spread his hands. "But, Your Royal Highness, pardon my boldness, somebody will need to write a book about the undoing of the Great Evil, and what happened here today. If things go well, surely you will want to be the one to see it—to witness it, firsthand, and write the tome decreeing its destruction? I imagine it will truly be a moment that will live long in the memories of the people of our world," he encouraged. "Who better to write a firsthand account than our great king? It will be your triumph, after all, should it succeed."

Julius eyed Virgil thoughtfully, and Alex frowned as he watched the scene play out. Whatever Virgil was up to, his powers of persuasion were proving just as impressive as his mother's. Alex also noted the small team of soldiers behind Julius—if the king were to bow out now, they would see his weakness. Perhaps, if Julius waasn't careful, news of his cowardice would spread.

"I can see you are trying to regain my favor with blatant flattery," Julius replied at last. "However, you are correct that I am the best person to record such an heroic tale. It must be well documented. It is a story that begs to be told." He nodded to himself, as if it had been his idea all along. "How does that sit with you, Alex Webber? You may die today, but you will be immortalized in my book," he chuckled, grinning in amusement.

"I guess that is all any of us can ask for, Your Royal Highness," Alex replied, though he was distracted by Virgil's behavior. It wasn't like the Head to be so insistent where his stepfather was concerned, yet here he was, daring to suggest something that scared the king. More than that, Julius appeared to have taken the bait.

"Ha! Quite right, Alex Webber, quite right," Julius mused.

"With this book, I too shall be immortalized."

Alex held his tongue, wanting desperately to say that the king already was immortalized in the annals of history, playing the villain of the piece—the murderer of an entire race. With Alex's death, the circle would close; there would be no true Spellbreakers left in the world. Julius's initial vision of a cleansed magical world would come to fruition, at long last, and the thought made Alex sick.

"Are you staying, then, Your Royal Highness?" Virgil asked. "If so, I shall make some final adjustments to the barrier, and then we can begin."

Julius nodded. "Yes, I shall stay, along with my guards," he said, gesturing to the small squadron behind him. They exchanged nervous glances, evidently not sure what they'd signed up for. Alex felt sorry for them, dragged into something they had no say in. He wanted to hate them for assisting the king, but knew they were as helpless as he was. To fight back meant certain death.

"Excellent! Then I shall continue my shield, Your Royal Highness, to ensure your safety," Virgil replied, weaving more hybrid magic into his hands and layering it into the barrier he'd already built.

As Virgil worked, Julius remained oddly quiet, his eyes simply staring toward the great, gaping mouth of the pit, and the slow-flapping bird above. It had him transfixed, his fear almost palpable. Even the guards looked down at him with curiosity, having never seen this strange, silent side of him before. Virgil was unusually silent too, his hands twisting and turning as he layered more and more energy into the barrier, reinforcing it. Alex watched him, wanting to know what was going on, but unable to ask. He knew there was something the Head wasn't telling him, something to do with the third person in the vision Elias had shown him. Was the third person Julius? If so, why was Virgil bothering to protect him with a barrier? The mist would never be able to penetrate such a shield, forged by half-Spellbreaker hands, so having Julius present was pointless. Unless, Alex thought, it just had to be witnessed by the king? Was that the missing link in the spell? Recalling the words of the line he had pored over, it began to make sense. Two sides of a coin—Alex was one side, Julius was the other. Both of them had to be there in order for the Great Evil to be destroyed.

That was it. Julius had to be present. He had been the missing piece all this time.

Before he could give it any more thought, however, Julius's voice bellowed across the cavern, echoing from every wall.

"Are you going to get on with it anytime soon?" he asked.

"I am putting the final layer of anti-magic into the shield, and then we will be secure enough to proceed, Your Royal Highness," Virgil said nervously, doing just that.

"And you're certain it'll hold back any mist?" Julius demanded.

Virgil nodded. "That amount of anti-magic should hold

back any force of magic, Your Royal Highness," he confirmed, before stepping away, moving toward Alex. "Do you have the book?" he asked.

Alex couldn't speak. Instead, he gulped, pulling the tome from his satchel and handing it to Virgil.

"You will succeed, Alex," Virgil said softly. "You are scared, and I don't blame you, but you will succeed where everyone else has failed. I will be here, helping you through. You can do this. I know you do not want to, but that choice has been taken from you. Now, you must do what you have to, to save everyone else," he continued, never breaking eye contact with Alex.

"I don't understand why it has to be me," whispered Alex sadly. "I didn't ask for any of this. I didn't ask to be born this way. I didn't ask to be a savior." Tears pricked his eyes, his teeth gritting as he struggled to force them away.

Virgil smiled wanly. "Nobody who is a true savior asks for it, Alex. Yours is an honest sacrifice. Your fear is valid, but you must use it now to see this through," he replied, his tone apologetic. "Shall we begin?"

"I guess we have to," Alex whispered, his breathing coming in short, sharp bursts. He refused to break down, though all he wanted to do was shout and scream at the injustice of it all, and have it all disappear in the blink of an eye. But that was never going to happen. He would not break. His head was swimming, his heart was pounding, his vision was blurry, and there was no escaping what was to come.

Taking the cue, Virgil moved into position, opening the book to lie flat in his hands and holding it up to Alex. It was a simple movement, to place his palm flat against the page, but it felt like climbing Everest. Taking a deep breath, he lifted his hand and placed it down on the appropriate spot. Everything inside his body screamed at him to run, but he remained rooted to the ground, unwilling to give in to his fears.

The time had come.

With a sudden burst of light, the book began to glow, far brighter than it ever had before. The writing on the pages soared upward, twisting in a tornado of words, before falling into line above the mouth of the pit, spelling out the sentences he needed to speak. The glowing letters had faded, their luminescence far paler than they'd been before, but Alex could just about make them out. Whether or not he'd actually be able to open his mouth and speak them aloud remained to be seen.

Taking a shaky breath, he began to say the words that hovered before him. At first, his voice shook, barely audible to anyone but Virgil. Gradually, however, as he moved through the incantation stanza by stanza, each one disappearing as it was completed and replaced by the next, he settled into the flow of the words, the rhythm calming him. Line after line went by, his voice growing stronger with each one, until he saw only the spell, the looming pressure of his mortal existence fading away into the background.

It seemed like it was going far better than any of the previous attempts, the air crackling strangely, the atmosphere tense with anticipation. This time it really did feel different, like it might just work. Having learned his lesson the last two times, he hardly dared to think it.

Finally, the twelfth and final stanza appeared before him. He knew this part well.

"With the blood of my enemies, I close the circle of pain," he said, the words sounding strange in his own voice.

Virgil, with a concerned smile, handed Alex the small vial of blood and watched as he lifted it to his lips, downing the disgusting, viscous liquid in one. It tasted metallic and sour, and it took everything Alex had not to gag. He swallowed it, feeling it ooze down the back of his throat. Wiping his mouth, he removed his hand from the book's page, looking down to see that the text had been restored. Did that mean it had worked? He didn't know. But he was still alive.

Just then, the ground shook violently, rocks tumbling from the walls of the cavern. A great roar like crashing waves erupted from the depths of the pit, battering the eardrums of everyone who heard it. Alex covered his ears, glancing at Virgil, whose eyes were wide in terror.

"What is it? Did it go wrong?" Julius shouted from his bubble-prison.

"I don't know, Your Royal Highness," Virgil called back. "We must wait and see!"

"Well, I'm not waiting a moment longer! I must leave

this place!" snarled Julius, pressing his palms against the liquid sheen of the barrier in an attempt to shatter it with his royal powers. "Come and break this thing down at once!" he demanded, realizing he was going to need help. Virgil had made it extremely strong.

The whole cave was shaking. Alex staggered back from the edge of the pit in case he fell in again. Virgil grasped his arm, helping him.

"Did it go wrong?" Alex asked.

Virgil shook his head. "I don't know. I really don't know."

No sooner had Virgil spoken than the silver mist shot up from the ground in a roaring geyser of glittering light, but this was like no mist Alex had seen before. The Great Evil had arisen, taking on the form of slender, wispy creatures with feminine faces, their misty hands reaching toward Alex. Moving through the air like liquid, they danced in his direction.

"*Give us your sacrifice,*" they whispered.

Soon, they stood before him, a seething mass of misty faces, their clawing hands grasping at him, sinking their misty fingers deep inside his flesh. The grip of their greedy hands was excruciatingly painful. A jolt of agony tore through his body like a thunderbolt, the pain searing again with every clawing grasp they made. It enveloped him, and the mist consumed his body until he could see nothing but silver. He could feel it tearing at his insides, though he could no longer see individual hands seeking out his life. It was one mass of gripping, grabbing, tearing creatures.

Dragging air into his lungs, Alex knew he was about to die. The mist was like water around him, suffocating him as it took his life.

Something tugged at his hand, fingers squeezing his fingers. It wasn't the mist, whatever it was.

"With the blood of my enemies, I close the circle of pain." Virgil's voice cut through the deadening silence of the mist. Peering through the silver haze, Alex could make out the skeletal man's figure beside him, lifting the vial to his lips, drinking the remnants.

Alex felt something pull on his other hand, a cold feeling spreading through his arm. Looking down, he saw the unmistakable black vapors of Elias's hand, grasping his as best he could, given his form.

"With the blood of my enemies, I close the circle of pain," Elias shouted, drinking from the old vial that had been used in the second attempt.

The mist, now utterly confused, swooped between all three, swirling in and around them, engulfing them, grasping and clawing and taking what it could. The pain was immeasurable. Alex and Virgil's cries echoed around the trembling walls of the cave as wave after wave of pure agony ripped through them. It was never-ending, the pain growing worse with every passing second, the tearing hands of the mist feeling as if they were shredding Alex's insides. Glancing down, though his eyes were running with pained tears, he was convinced he was fading away, his skin growing translucent.

Alex knew the end was coming. No person could suffer so much and not feel the warm hand of death upon their face, come to take them away from all the pain.

Yes, death was close.

CHAPTER 28

ALEX FELT SOMETHING TEAR INSIDE HIM, LIKE A part of him had been ripped away, the acute searing pain that followed eliciting a scream from his lungs. Virgil gripped his hand tighter, but it was no good—the pain was like nothing he could describe, so unforgiving he could barely catch his breath. It ripped again, feeling like his soul was splitting in two, the sensation so strange and unnatural that he could do nothing but roar through it, hoping it would end soon. In truth, he just wanted it to be over. No thoughts of friends or family could take the pain away, and had they felt what he felt, he doubted they'd have wanted to live much longer either.

With a sudden jolt, Alex's eyes rolled back in his head, his world turning inward. Flashes of light disrupted his vision, and, deep inside him, swimming through his veins, he could feel energies moving that didn't belong to him. The flashes persisted, the blank bursts of light morphing into something else. At first, they were blurry, showing shapes and the vague outlines of landscapes, but then the visions sharpened, becoming fully fledged images, flickering across his eyes like slides on a reel.

Only, the images didn't belong to him either.

A flash of a small boy, running through walled gardens with two friends. The boy was smiling, and the two friends were smiling too, but their expressions shifted a second later, with the arrival of a fourth child. She was older, by the looks of her, with a rock held in her hand. Alex tried to peer closer at the images, but he couldn't hear a word any of them were saying. Their mouths were moving, but he had to guess the intent. It became clear when the next image showed the small boy on the floor, his forehead bleeding, while the female friend he was with stood in front of the cruel fourth child, raising her hands as if to fight. Alex realized it was Ceres, Hadrian, Virgil, and Alypia when they were kids. It must have been the time he'd heard Virgil and Ceres talk about, when she came to his aid, protecting him from his older sister's wrath.

With a jarring flicker, the images moved to those of an older boy, standing at the edge of a pit, tears running down his face, blood trickling from the corner of his mouth. All around him, rocks were falling, while silver mist rose in a torrent before him. The next vision showed him fleeing the scene, with the horrified faces of the haven's inhabitants flashing past, the mist snatching at them, engulfing them, leaving the young Virgil helpless to do anything for them.

Another image showed Virgil standing in the vile chamber with the dangling manacles, where he had removed the essence of so many students. Only, the man in chains was no student, by the looks of his black cloak. He had a striking face, somewhere between handsome and strange, though it was twisted in a grimace of pain. His piercing brown eyes told of a burning hatred, and his jet-black hair was plastered across his forehead with sweat. He was tall, with broad shoulders and a clean-shaven face, making him look younger than Alex had imagined, though he'd glimpsed him before. That was Elias dangling from the manacles. In the frame that followed, Virgil was reading from a red-bound book, magic twisting up around Elias, though the man was clearly shouting for Virgil to stop. Elias's magic met Virgil's, and a billowing black cloud engulfed everyone within the room, including the crouching figure of Derhin, who had sneaked in to watch. When it receded, Elias was the shadow-man, and it was Virgil's turn to grow angry, having failed again.

Later, it showed the Head pacing his office, reading a letter from Julius that told him he was to fetch more essence.

The skeletal figure sat down in his chair, holding his head in his hands, then tore up the letter and threw it into the trash. Silently, the man wept, his shoulder shaking. On the desk beside him, he looked over a list of names, moving his finger down the line, mouthing the name of every person whose life he'd been made to take. Over and over, he repeated them, not wanting a single one to be forgotten.

For a moment, the images flashed back in time again, to a much younger Virgil running through the labyrinth beneath Falleaf House. There were two men running beside him, one younger, one older, their eyes set dead ahead. The younger one was clutching a handful of letters. This one, Alex didn't recognize, but the other, the older man... With an astonishing realization, he knew him to be Malachi Grey. As vile as Finder had been, Alex knew the pair of them had started out on good terms—he had seen it, in their conversation in the grounds of Spellshadow, when Malachi had agreed to let Virgil do whatever he needed to do, to find more essence out in the real world. However, the younger man was of more interest to Alex. Seeing as there were only three of them, Alex guessed it was the younger who had given up his life so Virgil could take the book from the vault.

More and more images flashed in quick succession, showing moments in Virgil's life. It seemed the Head's life had, for the most part, been a stretched-out tale of woe. Despite all the dark memories Alex held of him, it was hard not to pity the man who had been lied to since the day he was born. What chance had he had to be more than what Julius had made him? As more images flashed into Alex's mind, interspersed with some of his own, Alex realized that the mist was taking some of Virgil's soul too, the energies mingling inside Alex's head before being torn away. How it was happening, he didn't know, but he had a feeling Elias was somehow involved, perhaps acting as a buffering agent and preventing the mist from taking the whole soul from either of them.

It was a peculiar and painful sensation, having half of himself forcibly ripped out of his body, slicing out of his skin, being drawn through by the clawing hands of the mist creatures. But with the images, the pain faded somewhat. The more that flashed through his mind, the less he felt the agonizing tear of his soul's removal.

Still, Alex was ready for it to be over.

A loud explosion boomed through the cavern, the roof splitting, the rocks cracking all around, the ground rumbling louder than it ever had before. Alex began to panic, convinced this was the final step in the Great Evil's ploy to free itself. His legs were shaking, his ears filled with the roaring crash of the earthquake trembling beneath his feet.

Suddenly, the mist cleared, and Alex saw the ground ahead begin to cave in. More images flowed unbidden into his head, but these were not of Virgil's life, nor his own. They were of the other three pits, their gaping mouths filling with rock and debris as they folded in on themselves, the released mists rushing backward, disappearing back down into the ground, where they could do no further harm to anyone. Parts of the havens were crumbling too, in response to the destruction of the Great Evil. Large cracks ricocheted up the sides of the Stillwater villa, while the roof of the library collapsed at Spellshadow, and two turrets plummeted into the dried-up moat of Kingstone Keep. The tremors rippled through all the havens, showing him the crumbling walls of buildings he'd never even seen. They belonged to old havens he'd never visited, each quake sounding a victory for the spell Alex had done.

Finally, the flashing images slowed, and the shaking ground came to a standstill, just for a while. The whole world twisted away, swirling upward in a kaleidoscope of stretching shapes and colors, like the moment before Storm burst through a barrier between realms. When it snapped back, the world around Alex was a completely different one, though Virgil was still standing beside him, gripping his hand.

Rolling away to either side was the battlefield where the Great Evil had been created in the first place. Troops of weary mages were standing in clusters, their eyes fixed upon the gallows on which Alex and Virgil now stood. In front of them, Leander Wyvern hung from chains, his burning, silver eyes looking straight into theirs, a smile playing upon his lips.

"For our people... for my children... for all those who

perished," the great man whispered, before bowing his head.

As soon as the last word was spoken, the world turned inside out again, the landscape racing sharply back to the pit room with a jolt. It didn't seem like anyone else had seen them go. The vision of Leander Wyvern was reserved exclusively for them. Regardless, the sight of the great Spellbreaker had made Alex understand what they had done.

They had completed the spell, and rid the magical realm of the Great Evil. Not only that, but it looked like he and Virgil might just live to tell the tale.

The only problem was, the silver mist had yet to dissipate. From the quaking ground, the flashing images, the tearing of his soul, and the vision of Leander Wyvern, Alex was almost one hundred percent certain they had achieved what they set out to do, but he could still feel strands of misty energy writhing inside him, flowing through his veins. The Great Evil had been defeated, but it didn't seem to be going anywhere.

Perhaps there were more trials still to come? Alex hoped not.

With a violent tug, Alex felt the energy within him pull away, a darker silver mist gathering in a cloud above his head. Howling faces emerged from the mist, black mouths opening in a piercing scream that shook the very foundations below. As the scream faded, the cloud surged toward Julius, the paler mist following suit.

Alex felt a connection still linking him with the mist. He

closed his eyes, focusing on it, leading it in the direction of the one who had made Leander Wyvern release the spell in the first place, bringing the Great Evil into being. Another scream pierced the air as his mind connected with the cloud of mist, showing it what his heart wanted more than anything. In his head, he rewound the flashing image he'd seen, flicking it back to the burning eyes of Leander Wyvern, and the hatred his ancestor had felt for the king who stood nearby. He understood now that this was the final step.

The silver mist hurtled through the barrier Virgil had made, which had no protective effect whatsoever against the ferocity of the Great Evil's last stand. It whirled around Julius's head, constricting him like a shimmering boa, swallowing him up. He howled in pain, but the mist had him now. His body collapsed onto the stone floor. A few seconds later, a ghostly form rose from where the mist had torn Julius's spirit away. With its clawing hands, the mist dragged the spectral form down into the pit, and though the wispy fingers of the phantom king struggled to grasp at solid ground, there was no escaping the Great Evil.

As soon as the torn spirit was pulled below, the rest of the mist rushing backward with it, another thunderous blast shook the pit room. The earth cracked as boulders tumbled from the roof—the cavern was falling in around them.

"GO!" Virgil yelled, shoving Alex toward the door.

Though he had little energy left, Alex ran as fast as he could, diving headfirst into the hallway and not stopping until he reached the staircase at the far end. Virgil arrived a second later, followed by the straggling soldiers.

They turned, just in time to see the corridor collapse, sealing the pit forever.

CHAPTER 29

THE ROAR OF THE COLLAPSING PIT ECHOED IN THEIR ears, fissures tearing up the sides of the pagoda. Alex and Virgil, trailed by the guards, stumbled upstairs. Hadrian was nowhere to be seen, having left his guard post, but Alex didn't mind—he was too exhausted to think about anything but what had happened in the cavern below.

Alex sat down against one of the still-shaking walls, too weary to move. The guards who had made it out sprinted past, heading for safer ground.

"We need to leave the pagoda," Virgil commanded.

"Need a minute to… catch my breath," Alex said, shaking his head. His whole body felt weak, every limb numb, as if he'd been leaning on them and they'd gone to sleep.

Virgil hauled Alex back to his feet. "Not yet. You may rest soon, but we must get out of this building."

Reluctantly, Alex allowed Virgil to drag him along, though he leaned heavily against the skeletal man's frame, unable to hold his own body up.

"Did you know that was going to happen?" Alex asked as they hurried toward the pagoda's exit, the whole building still trembling around them.

"Know what was going to happen?"

Alex clawed a breath into his lungs. "The mist taking Julius?"

Virgil smiled. "I thought something might happen, although I didn't quite know what. Given the failed attempts, I knew a key ingredient was missing, and when we read that passage, and you told me of your friend's warning, I came to a conclusion. Julius had to be present too," he explained. "I knew I had to get him to stay, no matter what. With you there, I thought it'd be easier. He wanted to keep an eye on you, make sure you did it properly, which gave me a window of opportunity. I didn't know it would kill him... Let's just call that a perk."

"Why wouldn't you tell me that was what you had planned?" Alex asked, feeling as if his body were about to crumble around him, just like the pit.

Virgil sighed heavily. "If I told you, and Julius were to practice some of his favorite torture treatments on you, I knew you might break and tell him what I had planned," he began. "You might think you're strong, but you don't know Julius's definition of pain the way I do. I have had years of it, and have developed something of a tolerance, but you haven't. Moreover, I had nothing to lose, whereas you have your friends and allies. In all honesty—and I envy you for it—you had too many weaknesses he could prey upon. I couldn't risk it. Keeping it secret was the only way I could ensure his presence during the spell."

Alex could understand that—not that it made him any less irritated that he'd been kept in the dark. What if they hadn't been able to keep Julius at the pit? What would have happened then? He thought about asking the skeletal man, but he was too tired to get into it. Already, his eyelids were drooping and his shoulders felt heavy. It was all he could do not to curl up into a ball and sleep for a thousand years.

"I became the mist, in those last moments," Alex said sleepily, hoping Virgil would understand what he meant.

"I felt it too." Virgil paused for a moment, leaning against the wall, still clutching Alex. "The spell is designed purely for regicide against a cruel ruler, so it makes sense now that it had to be the king's blood that broke the spell. An elaborate eye for an eye kind of deal."

"Did it take half of me?" Alex gasped, his lungs burning.

Virgil smiled sadly. "Yes, I think it did. It took half of me too. We split the load—I think Elias stepped in to ensure it only took half of each."

They had reached the main foyer of the pagoda, the room dripping with dark corners, just the sort Elias liked to hide in. Alex looked around for the shadow-man, but he wasn't there. "Did Elias get out?"

"I think that man can get out of anything." Virgil chuckled wryly, though the laugh turned into a cough, a few splatters of blood landing on the Head's pale palm.

"You okay?" Alex asked, helping Virgil over to the banister of the staircase.

Virgil shrugged, coming to the end of his cough. "I feel strange, as if there's something missing inside, but I guess we won't know the true damage until later," he replied. "How are you feeling?"

"Like hell," Alex said grimly. "Everything hurts. But at the same time, everything feels numb."

"Hopefully, it'll ease with time," Virgil whispered, clutching his chest.

Alex thought about the survivors of Starcross, and how some of them had wandered through the camp like zombies, their eyes vacant, never recovering from the loss of their stolen half. He wondered if he'd end up like them.

"Elias!" Alex called, searching inside himself for the piece of soul he'd accidentally taken. The pulse of it was weaker, the connection seeming to fade by the second. When he could no longer feel it, he began to panic. "Elias, are you there? Elias?"

Movement in the rafters above drew Alex's attention. A waterfall of shadow poured down, and Elias appeared before them. Only, he was not quite the shadow-man he usually was. The black vapor of his being had thinned, the stars dimming across his galactic skin, bright flashes exploding inside his being, like suns turning into supernova before burning out completely. His starry eyes were dull and listless, his flowing form barely hovering above the ground.

"Elias, is that you?" Alex whispered.

The shadow-man flashed a faint grin. "Still here, *mon cher*... just about. Who knew death could hurt this much? I've avoided it for so long, I thought it would be easy when the moment actually came," he wheezed.

"Elias, you're not going to die," Alex said. "You used a lot of energy to save us both, but you'll recover—you always do."

Elias shook his head slowly. "Not this time, amigo. I think I hear a bell tolling, and it's tolling just for me," he murmured, still smiling.

"You can't go," Alex insisted, feeling a flutter of panic in his chest.

"Ha, I knew you'd come to like me, Alex Webber," Elias teased. "It took me stopping that mist from tearing you to pieces, but we got there in the end. You love me, you really love me!" he cried dramatically, putting on his best spoiled-actress voice.

Alex chuckled, though he was too sad to give it much energy. "Maybe I'll even miss you a little bit, one day, when I'm by myself, expecting you to drop down from the ceiling unannounced," he teased halfheartedly.

"You never know, I might just be watching," Elias said with a wink. But Alex knew he wouldn't be. Where Elias was going, there was no coming back.

Siren Mave appeared a moment later, pushing through the front door. With a sigh, she shuffled over to the spot where Elias floated, her eyes watery, her mouth set in a sad line. Sniffling, she pushed her horn-rimmed glasses back up the bridge of her nose.

"Come on, you wastrel, it's time for us to go." Siren Mave spoke softly, conjuring an orb of black magic between her palms. It held the stars inside, the constellations swirling in a bright white stream that melded into a circle as the orb span faster. "In fact, it's time for all of us to go," she said, ushering them all outside, where nothing was about to tumble down on top of them.

"Thank you for finding me," Alex said, choking on the emotion that clogged his throat. "You might have been vague and annoying, but we did it, didn't we?"

Elias grinned, his teeth flashing. "We sure did, kiddo."

"You did an excellent job, Alex," Siren Mave chimed in. "We couldn't have asked for a better charge. Nobody thought you'd ever walk through that gate, and none of us could have known you'd be precisely the one to finish this, for good," she added, flipping the orb onto one hand, while reaching out her free hand to shake Alex's. He took it wearily, a shiver running through him as he felt her deathly cold palm.

Meanwhile, Elias was fading away, turning almost

entirely see-through, until Alex could see the water gardens through his body. Their time together was at an end, and though it had been a turbulent journey, to say the least, Alex was sorry to see the shadow-man go. Siren Mave too. The world would seem just that little bit too quiet without them.

"Alrighty then, let's get this show on the road while there's still something left of me to sashay away with," Elias said, his voice barely a whisper.

"Quite right. Wouldn't want to rob you of your dramatic exeunt, would we?" Siren Mave teased.

"Never," Elias replied.

"Siren Mave?" Alex piped up, finding his voice.

The squat woman glanced at him. "A final request?" she asked.

He smiled. "Something like that… I was just wondering, what do I do with the book? It didn't return to the vault on its own." He gestured to the tome tucked under Virgil's arm.

"Ah, yes, the book. You may keep it, or put it back—it's up to you," she said. "It is yours, in essence, to do with as you please. Is that everything?"

Alex hesitated, having so much more to say but little time to put his thoughts into words, as Elias was fading more and more by the second. "That's everything," he said finally.

Elias had faded into almost nothingness, and his voice was like an echo. "Find peace, Alex Webber."

With that, Siren Mave's orb grow bigger and bigger, until it blocked them from view. It spun faster, sucking their bodies into the center, before closing in on itself with a loud snap, sending out a blast of air that swept Alex's hair back.

Looking at the empty space where Elias and Siren Mave had been, Alex refused to cry, though a bubble of emotion welled inside him. He would let it all hit him later, when the dust settled and he could accept that it was actually over. Instead, he thought about what Siren Mave had said about the book, and the potential it held, with all its mighty spells. It might be handy to keep around, he reasoned, but knew there was too much temptation between its covers. As powerful and useful as it might be, Alex wasn't sure he wanted to keep it.

"So what are you going to do with it?" Virgil asked, handing it to Alex.

"Put it where it belongs."

He was going to return it to the vault and lay its curses to rest.

CHAPTER 30

A SMALL CLUSTER OF SOLDIERS HAD GATHERED AT the far edge of the water gardens outside, chattering anxiously among themselves. It seemed the guards who had come up from the pit had spread the word about Julius's demise, and no longer knew what to do with themselves without his leadership to guide them.

"Is the king dead?" one asked as Virgil and Alex walked toward them. It was surprising to see that it was still daylight, the sun hurting Alex's eyes. He'd thought they'd been down in the pit for hours and hours, but only a few had actually passed.

Virgil nodded, propping Alex up. "King Julius has died,"

he said, a strange look passing over his face. "As the son of the rightful queen, Queen Venus, I will be aiding her in her duties as ruler of our nation. She will be firm but fair, as you have come to expect, and she will make an announcement when the time is right. In the meantime, you should all return to your families, wherever they are, and await further instruction," he continued, his voice gathering strength.

Alex glanced at the sunken-faced man, surprised by his quick thinking. It was best to get the idea of Venus ascending to the throne into their heads as soon as possible, to prevent any ideas of a coup d'état on the soldiers' parts, or on the parts of any other royals who might deem themselves worthy.

The soldiers looked at one another in confusion, but Virgil was still a royal. Given his heritage, they did not dare defy him, even if they thought him the runt of the litter.

"Spread the message as far as you can," Virgil added, before hauling Alex forward. "And dispense with as many of the traps in the forest as you can, before you leave."

"We need to go to the vault," Alex insisted. The hybrid nodded and changed direction. The walk was a longer one than Alex remembered, the sun dappling the ground as it glanced through the canopy. Birds tweeted, seemingly oblivious to the quake that had shaken the earth. The pagoda remained standing, to Alex's surprise—and was relatively unscathed, with only a few split planks and broken windows to show for the chaos that had ensued in the cavern beneath. For that, Alex was glad. Of all the havens, he'd always liked

Falleaf best.

At last, they arrived at the side door of the vault. It was sealed shut, just as it had been the last time. But as Alex neared, clutching the book to his chest, the door sprang open with a rusty creak. Unaided, Alex walked into the warm, cozy light of the library. It was little changed since the last time he had visited, except for one notable difference: a skeleton lay on the ground, curled up by the fireplace, the bony knees tucked up beneath a bony chin.

Alex shuddered, knowing whose skeleton it was. After the promises they had made to return in time, it appeared Alex's fears, and the immediate loss they had felt, had been right—they would never have reached Lintz before the specters did. Even if they had, the ghoulish creatures would still have devoured him. It was like the professor had said—once a person had looked one in the eye, there was no escape. They would travel to the ends of the earth to take what was owed.

The true loss of Professor Lintz hit Alex hard, adding to the losses that already weighed heavily on his chest. They had all come here together; they had all walked this path together, and he was losing them one by one. Gaze, Lintz, Storm, Elias, Siren Mave, and countless others, falling along the way.

"I'm sorry, Professor," he whispered, struggling to keep himself together.

Solemnly, he left the skeleton and walked up to the diorama of the solar system that still ticked its steady rhythm. A few of the smaller planets had moved since he was last here, but Jupiter had barely moved at all. Climbing the ladder to reach the largest planet, he wrapped his hand around the orb that represented it, waiting for it to glow. A moment later, it pulsed beneath his palm, the empty drawer popping open beneath.

His limbs felt sluggish, like he was wading through molasses, but he managed to clamber back down the ladder and wander toward the drawer. After taking one last look at the book, smoothing his hand across the leather cover and flicking through to see the glyphs that covered the pages within, he placed it in the compartment and pushed it shut with a quiet click. There was a satisfaction in knowing nobody else could get their hands on it, not without Hadrian's say-so, anyway, and it was unlikely the nervous royal would ever let anyone run the gauntlet again. Hopefully, with the Great Evil quelled, and no imminent threat upon the magical world, there would be no need for such a book ever again.

"Dear boy, I was wondering if you'd be back." A voice spoke softly from behind.

Alex whirled around to see the ghost of Lintz hovering before him, though the professor was no less sizeable in his phantom state. He wore a smile upon his face, his moustache twitching at either end, but the glitter in his eyes showed a silent sadness beneath.

"Professor?" Alex choked. There was no mistaking Lintz's death now. At long last, the professor would get to return to the sister he had sought all these years. Alex just wished they had been able to meet one another again in the real world, with all their futures laid out before them. Julius, and his hold on the magical realm, had robbed so many of that gift, and though he was now gone and his tyranny with it, that didn't change the devastation that had already been wrought upon so many lives.

"Looking a lot lighter than the last time you saw me, I'll bet?" Lintz tried to joke, though his heart evidently wasn't in it. "Goodness me, you look as if you've been through the wars," he remarked, peering more closely at Alex's face. Given that Alex hadn't looked in a mirror since he'd left the palace, he had no idea what he looked like. He could only guess it was just about as ghoulish as the way he felt.

"Something like that... Let's just say it didn't get any easier," he admitted, nodding toward the drawer of the diorama, and the book within.

"No, I didn't think it would, dear boy," Lintz murmured sorrowfully. "Then again, I always knew you'd be the one to do it. As soon as I knew what you were, I wondered if you'd do marvelous things. Although, seeing as you're here, did that mean the spell went awry?"

Alex shook his head. "No, the spell was a success. Julius is dead. The Great Evil is gone. And, somehow, I'm still breathing... more or less," he said. "It's a long story, and I doubt there's time for me to tell it."

"No, perhaps not," Lintz agreed. "Something is troubling me, dear boy, and it would be remiss of me not to mention it.

It seems there is something missing within you. I can sense it—a vacant space where something ought to be. Goodness, the things you have endured, my dear student. It should never have rested on your shoulders."

Alex shrugged. "Better a half-life than no life, right?" he tried to joke, before realizing what he'd just said. "Sorry, Professor, I didn't mean..."

"No, no, you're quite right, dear boy," Lintz said, an amused expression on his face. "So, tell me, what do you plan to do now?"

"To be honest, I thought I was going to die today, so tomorrow still seems like an alien concept," Alex admitted.

Lintz nodded. "Mm, quite right. Just promise me you'll take your time fixing yourself? Don't go back out into the real world until you're ready. I know it is no doubt calling you, and believe me, I understand the temptation, but you will want to return to your loved ones with as much of yourself intact as possible, no?"

"I wouldn't want my mother to see me like this, if that's what you mean." Alex sighed, his eyelids growing heavy again.

"Look at you, dear boy." Lintz tutted. "What have they done to you?"

Alex smiled tearfully. "I think they broke me, Professor."

"I think you are too strong to be broken, my boy. You have already proven that," Lintz replied. "If I could give you a bear hug right now, I certainly would."

"Thank you. I could probably do with one of those right about now." Alex laughed tightly. It was all much too sad.

Lintz's expression softened. "Promise me you will take some time to put yourself first—you have given enough to others, for now."

Alex grimaced. "Why do I get the feeling you're trying to say goodbye?"

"Oh, my dear boy, it is not what I want, but I must go now. I have had a good run, but my time is through," Lintz replied with a sad shrug of his ghostly shoulders. "I have been in this world far longer than I should have been, but because of you, I can go free. There is someone waiting for me, wherever I am going, and I shall be gladder than you know to see her." He beamed, one side of his moustache curving upward. "So, you take care of yourself, and I hope I won't see you for a very long time. Live a good life, Alex. You are owed that much."

"Thank you, Professor, for everything," Alex murmured. "None of this would have been possible without you."

"I shall be sorry not to see the wonderful human beings you all shall no doubt blossom into," Lintz bellowed. "I have already seen hints of it, and it warms my old heart."

Alex smiled. "Then I guess I should say goodbye."

"Adieu, dear boy, adieu," Lintz said, bowing low. A second later he was gone, vanishing into the air like smoke on the wind.

With his tasks completed, Alex left the library, the side

door of the vault slamming shut behind him. As he stepped back out into the cool shade of the forest, a wave of nausea crashed over him. He stumbled into the grass, his hands breaking his fall. He tried to get up, but his head was spinning.

He felt like a ghost himself.

With Virgil's help, he managed to pick himself up off the ground and walk the long path from the pagoda to the cave, hoping all the while that the portal hadn't been closed.

At several points along the way, Alex fell down, his knees buckling. Virgil tried to insist he stop for longer, but Alex wasn't having any of it. He wanted to get back to Starcross. Only then would he be able to figure out what to do about his friends. After all, he had kept his end of the bargain—he wanted to believe Venus would honor her husband's.

Reaching the slim entrance to the cave, Alex ducked inside, moving swiftly past the shelves of glass bottles until he arrived at the narrow opening at the far end. To his relief, the oval of the portal glowed ahead of him, its rippling surface showing the rolling fields of Starcross beyond. Not wanting to pause for a moment, though he no longer felt like any of his limbs belonged to him, Alex pressed on through. It was only when they began to walk toward the first field that Alex realized the journey to the camp was beyond him. He was too exhausted, every single part of him drained.

"I can't do it," he whispered.

Virgil crouched down, his bony knees cracking. "Can't do what?"

"I can't walk all the way to the camp. I don't have the energy," Alex explained, though he could barely spit the words out.

Virgil nodded. "Then you should wait here, get yourself rested, and I will return with Ceres. I won't take no for an answer," he insisted, seeing that Alex was about to protest.

Eventually, Alex relented. "Fine, but if you're not back within the hour, I'm coming to find you."

"That sounds fair," Virgil said, smiling. "Now, you stay here, propped up against this rock. Do not move, understood?"

Alex sighed. "Understood."

Satisfied that Alex wasn't about to give up on life before he got back, Virgil took off across the field, disappearing into the horizon, his black cloak flapping behind him. He looked like a menacing scarecrow, put among the flowers and plants to keep birds away. Alex watched him until he could no longer see his retreating figure, wishing he had the strength to get up and run. How Virgil was doing it, Alex had no idea. Perhaps the spell had done something different to the skeletal man? All he really knew was that it had taken more out of him than he'd ever thought possible. In truth, part of him wished it had killed him, so he wouldn't have to feel like this.

That's the tiredness talking, he chastised himself, knowing he was getting dangerously close to self-deprecation territory.

He let his mind wander toward thoughts of the people he had left behind at Starcross. There was no telling what Virgil would find when he arrived, but Alex allowed himself a sliver of faith, just this once.

If Hadrian executed the plan, then they are all safe, he told himself. *They are all safe. They are all safe. They are all safe.*

He repeated the mantra, hoping that if he believed it enough, it might come true. Then the silent, dreamless sleep of the world-weary took him in its arms, letting him rest at last.

CHAPTER 31

HE WAS AWOKEN BY THE SOUND OF APPROACHING hooves. Still in a half asleep state of semi-consciousness, he was convinced it was Julius and his soldiers, coming to exact revenge for what he had done. When he felt hands grasp his arms a few moments later, he flailed them wildly, trying to fight back against his aggressors.

"Alex, it's just me and Virgil," Ceres spoke, coaxing Alex out of his nightmare with a rough shake.

He blinked his eyes rapidly until his vision cleared. Sure enough, crouched on the ground before him was Ceres, peering at him with her one good eye, while Virgil stood in the background, leaning over her shoulder.

"He found you?" was all Alex could say.

Ceres smiled, though it didn't quite reach her eyes. "Yeah, he found me. We've come to take you back to the camp," she said, a little standoffish, though she offered her hand to help him up. He took it gladly, using her as a lever to haul his whole body up to a standing position. Even then, his legs wobbled slightly.

"You may have to help me," he said reluctantly. She nodded, taking his arm and placing it around her neck, her arm gripping him tightly at the waist.

"Lean on me. I can bear your weight," she assured him, softening slightly. Alex did. It was a relief not to have to hold up the weighty bones of his own body by himself. The brief sleep had somehow left him feeling worse. Still, he had to keep going, at least until he saw that everything was right with the world again.

With some difficulty, Ceres helped Alex up onto the back of her Kelpie before hopping up behind him and taking the reins. Virgil had volunteered to walk back, though there was definitely room for him on the extensive back of the huge beast.

"You sure you won't ride with us?" she asked with a knowing smile.

Virgil nodded. "I prefer to walk," he said, stepping back as the Kelpie snorted loudly in his direction. Horses were evidently not the Head's favorite animals.

Leaving Virgil behind, Alex clung on tightly as the beast

thundered along the fields. His senses perked up as they passed the rows of beautiful lavender, the scent wafting up into his nostrils, clearing his head for a brief time, as if he had just sniffed smelling salts. It was by no means easy to cling onto a charging steed, considering his arms and legs felt like jelly, but somehow he managed it, even admiring some of the pretty countryside that flashed past.

"Ceres, I wanted to apologize," he began, mustering the courage to say what needed to be said. She didn't turn, but he could tell she was listening. "I know what happened here was my fault. If I had listened, if I had just—"

"You don't have to apologize, Alex," she said, cutting him off. "I was angry with you. We lost a lot of people that day, and I won't lie—I blamed you for it. But when the dust settled, I realized my blame was misplaced. Julius did this… He did all of this. Yes, things could have been done differently, but if nothing had changed, nobody would be free. You aren't to blame, Alex, and I was wrong to say those things to you."

Alex shook his head wearily. "I still accept responsibility for my actions. I know where I made mistakes, and I'm so sorry for your losses," he replied, unable to accept her full forgiveness until he could accept it in himself.

She smiled. "One day, I hope you manage to let go of the guilt, before it eats you up inside," she murmured.

Before long, they arrived at the edge of the encampment, the bluish smoke of the fires rising over the roofs of the tents and shanties. The corral pens were still up in the fields beyond the camp, but the people who stood inside them were not Starcross folk. No, it seemed the survivors had rescued their own, putting the soldiers in the pens instead, where they could keep an eye on them. People were wandering about as if it were any ordinary day, fixing broken parts of their homes, chatting happily to one another, and warming themselves by the fire.

Farther afield, many people were lifting and carrying covered bodies toward a graveyard that had been fenced off. The camp already had a cemetery, but it was much too small for the number of dead. Some individuals were digging, while others buried the deceased. Friends stood by, saying kind words and a prayer over the fallen, to send them on their way to the afterlife. Alex watched the sad scene, saying a silent prayer for them too.

As they trotted through the makeshift avenues, Alex saw the central square up ahead. In it sat more clusters of soldiers, magical ropes tied tight around them. Hadrian was there, going around the groups of militia and taking notes. He looked up as the Kelpie approached, an expression of relief falling across his face as he saw Alex.

"Alex!" he cried. "You're alive!"

The nervous royal tried to rush forward to give him a hug as Alex clambered down from the back of the enormous beast, but Ceres stopped him in his tracks, shaking her head. A subtle look passed between them, Hadrian's brow furrowing as he looked from her to Alex, and back again.

"It's okay, Ceres, I won't break," Alex said, forcing a smile upon his face. Even so, Hadrian did not attempt the hug he had been going for. Instead, he stepped forward and patted Alex lightly on the shoulder.

"It's good to see you alive and well, though you'll have to tell me how you managed it," Hadrian said, all hint of his stammer gone.

"Perhaps later, when I've gotten some rest," Alex suggested. "Right now, all I want to hear about is what happened to this place. I was expecting to find a warzone."

"Here, let's get you sitting down, and I'll tell you all about it," he agreed, helping Alex over to a nearby bench, where he could warm his hands by the fire. "So, when I left you at the statue, I waited a short while, then came straight here with a small army of my own students. None of the soldiers here were expecting it, and we ambushed them. As soon as we got the corral pens open, they were done for," he began triumphantly. It was nice to see the nervous royal so animated, without a hint of a tremor anywhere. "That's not the best part, however. I have some even better news for you, which I'm sure you'll be thrilled to hear!"

Alex smiled. "Go on."

"Well, Venus is here too," Hadrian explained. "She was the true mastermind behind the release of the Starcross survivors. My army was good, and we fought well, but we would never have won if she hadn't arrived, demanding the soldiers stand down."

"The queen is here?" Alex asked, incredulous. Perhaps he had misjudged her, believing she'd stay in her ivory tower until the whole thing had blown over.

"Oh yes, but there's more. She helped me in my plan, after Virgil explained to her what it was I had in mind. But, when she arrived, she brought guests." He paused for effect, grinning broadly. "Your friends are with her, Alex. She got them out of the palace and brought them here, where they would be safe."

Alex frowned. "Why would she do that? If I'd failed, her neck would be on the line."

Hadrian smiled. "It's love, Alex, or so she told me—something about honoring a former flame."

Alex had thought he was past being surprised by anything in this world, but that admission left him gloriously speechless, for just a moment.

"So they're here?" Alex asked. "My friends, they're here?"

Hadrian nodded. "Indeed they are, Alex. In fact, let me go and fetch them. You wait here—I'll be back in a moment," he promised, jumping up and disappearing between two tents.

"I don't have much choice," Alex muttered, holding out his hands to the warmth of the flames that danced in the fire-pit before him, flickering against the warm breeze that rippled through the makeshift town. Suddenly, he felt a shiver of panic, though he couldn't pinpoint why.

When they came tearing around the corner, his fears

soon faded. Natalie saw him first, happy tears streaming down her face. Aamir and Jari followed, broad grins breaking out upon their lips. Ellabell came last, moving shyly around the corner of the tent, but her relief was unmistakable.

"You're alive, you sly devil!" Jari beamed, throwing his arms around Alex.

Alex grimaced, the impact making everything pulse with pain. "Good to see you too," he gasped, waiting for the stabbing sensation to cease.

Ceres, seeing what was going on, came up to the group. "He's been through a lot," she said. "Maybe go easier on him, okay?" she suggested, though not unkindly.

Jari glanced at his friend, suddenly concerned. "Sorry, dude, I didn't realize," he murmured, patting Alex lightly on the back instead, before sitting down near him.

Alex smiled. "It's really okay, I'm just a little tender," he assured them, though his insides felt as though they were on fire. Looking up, he caught a sympathetic look from Ceres, but she duly backed off, giving him his space. Nothing was going to ruin this reunion, not even the sensation of every cell spiking at his flesh.

"You look like you've been through hell," Aamir remarked, giving Alex a careful hug.

"It's not as bad as it looks," Alex replied, brushing off his friend's concern. Even now, he didn't want to appear weak in their eyes. In front of Lintz and Virgil, it hadn't been so bad, but he couldn't show his friends how much he was hurting.

It would only worry them, and that was the last thing he wanted.

"It is wonderful to see you here, living and breathing," Natalie gasped, planting two air kisses on either side of Alex's face.

"It's good to see you all too," Alex said, the relief washing over him. "I didn't know how I was going to get you out, but it seems Venus kept her promise."

Ellabell nodded, stepping forward. "Yeah, looks like she was on our side this whole time." A smile spread across her face. "You should have seen her—the way she came barging past the guards, shouting at them to get out of her way. She came for us almost as soon as you had gone."

"She's quite a woman," Alex agreed, wondering why Ellabell hadn't tried to hug him. He remembered her face when they had last parted, and the cold kiss she'd left him with. Had the rest of her heart turned to stone, in his absence?

Slowly, she approached him. He opened his mouth to speak first, but before he could say another word, she bent down and kissed him tenderly on the lips, holding his face in her hands. He could feel her shaking as he put his arms around her, so he held her tighter, giving the last threads of energy he had to holding her.

"I'm sorry," she whispered, pulling away slightly.

"You have nothing to be sorry for," he replied, kissing her again.

Remembering they had company, Alex and Ellabell

separated, and the curly-haired girl sat close beside him on the bench. The others chattered excitedly about what had happened, wanting to know more about the events that had brought Alex back to them. He recounted as much as he could, though his heart wasn't in it. In fact, his heart wasn't in any of it. He was thrilled to see his friends again, but he couldn't muster the emotion he knew they wanted to see from him. Glancing away for a moment, he saw Ceres standing nearby, watching him closely. Her concern made sense to him, given that she was used to dealing with his sort— the half-life survivors who had no idea what to do with themselves.

Still, he pressed on with the story, knowing he owed them that. He could hear his voice lulling, becoming a tired mono-tone, but he refused to give in to the weariness that was penetrating down to his very bones. He wanted to be the hero his friends thought he was, but he felt about as heroic as a slug.

"So, Virgil left me at the portal and came to fetch Ceres," Alex finished, his mouth dry from all the talking.

"Whoa, dude, you're a total legend!" Jari whooped enthusiastically.

Aamir nodded. "Even I have to admit, that is pretty impressive," he said. "Although, I would never have expected such an act from Virgil. Who'd have thought, after all this time, he'd switch sides?"

Alex shrugged. "I'm not sure he ever really knew whose side he was on."

"How is he? Is he injured too?" Natalie asked curiously.

"He's in better shape than me," was all Alex could say on the matter. As much as he wanted to stay with his friends and talk some more, he could feel himself fading. His eyes burned, his face ached, and every movement sent a thousand shooting pains through his body.

"Is it really that bad?" Ellabell pressed, her eyes wide with concern.

He shook his head. "No, it's not too bad. I just need to sleep it off, I think."

"I am not sure you can simply sleep off the loss of half your soul," Natalie said solemnly.

"No, indeed, you can't," Ceres cut in, walking over to the group. "You're exhausted, Alex. I know you want to keep up the pretense, but you're in a lot of pain, and I think it's time you got some rest," she remarked, offering her hand to him, to help him up.

He didn't have the strength to protest as she hauled him to his feet, leading him toward the entrance to a nearby tent. The others stayed where they were, upon Ceres's instruction, and watched him go, their faces morphing into masks of worry. He hated doing that to them, but it was clear he needed help. He had no idea what was going on inside his body, but Ceres seemed to understand.

Once inside the tent, which appeared to be vacant, Ceres led Alex over to a pile of furs that lay stacked in a comfortable nest shape at the far end of the space. There, she made him lie down, while she went off to brew some tea. The furs embraced him like the softest mattress in the world, easing the jolts and jars that spiked through his body. Already, he could feel himself falling asleep, but Ceres made him stay awake a while longer, shaking him gently just as he was drifting off.

"Drink this," she insisted, handing him a steaming mug of something sour smelling.

"All of it?" he asked, wrinkling his nose.

"Yes, all of it," she replied sternly, taking a seat on a stool beside the furry nest.

Pulling a face, he lifted the hot drink to his lips and sipped tentatively. It tasted as foul as it smelled, but the warmth soothed the pains in his chest, making him feel more relaxed. Taking sip after sip, until the whole mug was gone, he began to feel marginally better—not a lot, but a fraction less grim.

"What was that stuff?" he asked, wiping the remnants from his mouth.

Ceres smiled. "You really don't want to know. Herbs, mostly."

"It tastes like pondwater," he complained.

"You're not far off," Ceres chuckled, stirring something in a pot beside her. "Anyway, you're probably wondering what's going on with you, inside, right?"

Alex nodded. "I feel about as close to dead as it's possible to feel," he admitted.

"That's not uncommon," Ceres replied, lifting her hands

to Alex's face and pulling back his lids to check his eyes. "I'm not entirely sure how it works in someone like you, but I'm guessing it's the same state the mages came to me in. Half of your life essence has been removed from you—or your soul, if you prefer. As you can imagine, that comes with a lot of suffering, and the need for a lot of recovery. There are magical exercises that you'll need to do to help repair the damage inside; I'll guide you through them. They'll help you breathe and focus, and put the pieces back together again. It will not be a quick fix, nor will it be easy, but if you rush it you'll suffer more. These things take time, and you need to understand that," she continued. "Even the swiftest recoveries can take months. Like I say, I don't know how your body will respond, but I am certain of one thing—you're in no state to go home yet," she said, her voice laced with sorrow.

They were the words Alex had been dreading. Lintz had hinted at it, but he had chosen to ignore the professor. The thought of having to wait longer to return to the real world was almost unbearable. His mother was still waiting out there, and the longer he stayed, the longer she had to wait.

"I know it's not what you want to hear," Ceres said softly. "But we have to begin treatment right away. It starts with tea and sleep, and then the hard work begins. You'll need to relearn a lot of what you used to take for granted, but if you focus and you apply yourself, you may just get back to a normality you recognize," she explained. "It will never be the same, but you can get pretty close."

Alex sighed wearily. "How come Virgil isn't reacting like this?" he asked, feeling as if some great injustice had been done.

"Virgil is a different case entirely, considering he's half and half," Ceres said thoughtfully. "He told me what happened. Not only that, but he told me what the spell did to him."

Alex frowned. "What did it do?"

"It left him more or less the same, which is the good news," Ceres explained. "The bad news is, he has no Spellbreaker power left. The mist took it all, leaving him only with his magical side—he's surprisingly disappointed."

Alex laughed at the irony. After everything the hybrid had been through in his struggle for acceptance, he was now as normal as any other mage.

CHAPTER 32

T HE NEXT DAY DAWNED, AND WITH IT, GOOD NEWS.
Alex stirred to find Aamir sitting on the floor beside his bed, sipping a mug of green tea and talking
quietly with Ceres, who was toasting bread over a small fire.
The smoke rose through a gap in the tent's roof. It smelled
tantalizing, and Alex's mouth watered as he struggled to sit
up.

"Breakfast?" Ceres asked brightly.

Alex nodded. "Please," he croaked. Although the sleep
had done him some good, and his mind was clearer, his body
still felt broken, the numb ache inside him ever present.

"How did you sleep?" Aamir asked, turning to him.

"Like the dead," Alex said wryly, shuffling up into a better position, shoving some cushions behind his back to prop himself up.

Aamir gave a worried smile. "How are you feeling?"

"Like the dead," Alex repeated, trying to muster a chuckle. It was clear the secret of Alex's true state was out. Ceres's words had no doubt put the seed of concern into the minds of his friends, and had blossomed into a true account of what had happened to him.

"You don't look as bad as you did yesterday," Aamir reassured him, an irreverent twinkle in his eyes.

"Charming," Alex rasped, rubbing his face. "What brings you here, anyway?"

It wasn't that he didn't want to see Aamir, but the conversation he'd witnessed had seemed like a pressing one, Aamir's face animated with passionate discussion. Ceres had been smiling too, a pleased look on her face, but those happy faces had morphed into expressions of solemnity upon Alex's awakening. He hated that. It was why he hadn't wanted anyone to know how much he was suffering, in case they treated him in precisely this way—walking on eggshells, unable to be themselves.

"Well, we have exciting news," Aamir said eagerly.

Alex perked up. "Really?"

"Indeed. This morning, we are gathering everyone from the real world who wants to leave, and taking them through to Spellshadow," he explained. "Some have chosen to stay, for a number of reasons, but we are returning those who want to be returned. There's a mix of Spellshadow students and Falleaf students going, since Hadrian opened the offer up to his students—the ones whose families still live out there. Some might come back, and the door will likely always be open, if they want to return."

The news warmed Alex's heart. The Great Evil was gone, and the students were going home. It was everything he had hoped for, and yet he couldn't bring himself to feel the elation he knew he was owed. He wanted to scream and shout and dance around in triumph, but all he could do was smile and nod. Even that wore him out.

"That's wonderful news," he said, knowing it barely covered the scope of emotion he wanted to show.

"It is, Alex—and it's all possible because of what you did," Aamir replied, gripping Alex's hand and giving it a squeeze. "I know you're suffering right now, and everything feels wrong, but one day you'll get to celebrate the way you deserve, and we'll be waiting to celebrate with you."

"I hope so," Alex sighed. "Are you going with the rest of the students?" he asked, suddenly realizing what the exodus entailed for his friends.

Aamir nodded reluctantly. "I think so," he said. "All of us are going through to the manor, leading the rest, but I don't know what the others are thinking just yet. I know I need to go, even if it's just for a while, to let my family know I'm okay. I've been gone for over five years—I want them to know I'm alive, at this point, you know?" he added, almost apologetically.

"You don't need to sound so sorry about it, Aamir," Alex reassured him. "I'm happy you get to go back to them. Plus, there's no way you're all going through to Spellshadow without me." He flashed a mischievous smile, causing Ceres's expression to darken.

"You're not strong enough to go with them, Alex," she insisted.

He shrugged. "I started this with them, and I'm going to finish it with them. If I can heal here, I can heal at home," he said firmly. It was something he had been thinking about the night before, as he'd drifted off to sleep. What difference did it make, if he was here or back at home in Middledale? As long as Ceres told him what he had to do, he was confident he could get better.

Ceres shook her head. "It doesn't work that way—because you are of magical, or anti-magical, origin, you can only heal those injuries within this realm. The exercises required for you to get better are magical exercises—if you try to do them out in the real world, they won't work, and you won't heal. It requires the sewing up of all the gaps the torn essence left, through prolonged magical therapy of the mind and body that need to be guided by someone like me. Like any new skill, it needs to be taught. Or, in your case, relearned. Plus, you have to consume a lot of medicine, and the potions that will heal you are only beneficial when consumed in this realm."

"I need to go with them, Ceres," he replied, adamant now. "You can either help me get to Spellshadow, or you can step out of my way, and I'll go there anyway, with my friends."

Ceres sighed deeply. "Fine, but you'll be setting yourself back by doing this."

"Then I'll just work harder to fix whatever else I've managed to break," he insisted.

"Are you sure you should be pushing yourself, in your state?" Aamir chimed in, a worried expression furrowing his brow.

Frustration prickled at Alex's nerves. He wasn't an invalid; he was just exhausted after the events of the past few days. Yes, he'd lost half of his soul, but he was still Alex. He was still strong enough to see the journey through to the conclusion they'd all agreed upon.

"I know my limits," he said slowly, trying not to snap. "I'll be fine."

Aamir left a short while later, with a promise to come back for Alex when the time came for them to return to Spellshadow. It left him alone with Ceres, who continued to insist he should rethink the matter, while forcing pieces of buttered toast and endless cups of herbal tea into his hands. Alex tuned out her sage words, knowing there was no pain on earth that could prevent him from going with his friends. They had waited too long for this moment, and he wasn't going to be the one absent from the pack when it came to closing the circle of their path together.

Around midday, the quartet of friends arrived at the entrance to Alex's new abode. Helena still wasn't with them, nor had he seen her the day before. It was strange not to see the silver-haired girl standing beside them; she had become such an integral part of the group that her absence was almost jarring.

"No Helena?" Alex asked.

Natalie shook her head. "She has returned to Stillwater House, to see what she can salvage," she explained. "She left after Venus freed us. I'm sure she would have come if she'd known you were still alive."

"How is your romance blossoming, anyway?" Alex wondered, flashing Jari a knowing glance.

To his surprise, Jari gave a casual shrug. "A man like me can't settle for just one dame, dude. I've got to see what's out there, you know?"

Natalie giggled. "What Jari is trying to say is, things did not exactly work out. I believe Helena just wants to be friends, correct?" she teased.

"Yeah, something like that," Jari muttered. "Ah well, plenty more fish in the sea, right?"

"I'm sure there'll be someone out there who can deal with you and your outlandish displays of love, Jari Petra," Ellabell chimed in, an amused smile on her face.

He winked. "Yeah, we can't all be like you two."

Rolling her eyes at the blond-haired boy, Ellabell walked up to where Alex was sitting and helped him to his feet. Aamir moved around to his other side, pulling his arm around his neck. With their support, he hobbled over to the tent's entrance, and stepped out into the bright sunlight. The scent of bonfire rippled through the air, reminding Alex of Halloween and summertime campfires by the river. Many of the Starcross inhabitants were still milling about their make-shift homes, but a notable number were elsewhere.

As they moved toward the edge of the encampment, Alex saw where they had gone. Standing in the field just beyond the perimeter, a swarm of people were chattering and laughing, slinging bags over their shoulders and clutching their limited belongings to their chests. Alex felt his own chest swell with pride; these people were going home today. He noticed there were a few older individuals in the crowd, the years having flown by for them. They weren't royal or elite; they were ordinary mages, whose lives had not been extended by their magical ability. Instead, they had grown old in the usual way, the years graying their hair and lining their faces, all of it exacerbated by the loss of half their life essence. In his mind, they were the bravest souls, choosing to return even though the outside world had changed immeasurably since they were last there.

A few cheered as Alex approached, the news having spread that the Great Evil had been vanquished because of what he had done. Virgil was already there, passing a conspiratorial nod in his direction, but Alex almost didn't recognize the sunken-faced man. If he hadn't been standing next to Ceres, he would have missed him entirely. The Head was no longer dressed in the hooded robe Alex had always seen him in. Instead, he wore a smart suit with a high collar, the fabric flowing smoothly over his thin form.

"Right, everyone keep it friendly—no pushing, no shoving," Ceres bellowed, jumping up onto the back of her Kelpie.

"Come on, hop up," said a familiar voice, as hooves trotted up behind Alex.

Demeter was sitting astride his own Kelpie, holding out his hand to haul Alex up. With the help of Aamir pushing, he made it onto the back of the beast, where the auburn-haired man turned to look over his shoulder and grinned at Alex.

"Long time no welcome," he chirped brightly. "I hear you've been defying all kinds of magical challenges, Alex Webber."

Alex smiled, the auburn-haired man making him feel calmer. "Yeah, you could say that."

"Ceres tells me you're being as stubborn as a box," he said, grinning.

"I'm just ready to go home." Alex sighed, wondering what else the one-eyed royal had said about him.

Demeter nodded. "I can understand that, just don't push yourself. You don't want to really break, you know?" he warned. "Anyway, sorry I wasn't there to welcome you back last night. As soon as the news broke that the Great Evil had gone, I went through to Spellshadow to get things prepared for today. I only got back this morning."

"Hey, I'm just glad you'll be around for the farewell," Alex said as they set off at a slow trot across the fields, toward the portal to Falleaf, where they would all head through to Spellshadow's gateway. From there, they would be heading for home, and Alex was jittery with anticipation. "What's your plan for the future, anyway?" he asked.

Demeter gave a casual shrug. "The current plan is for Hadrian, Ceres, and I to join forces, to make Falleaf House into a real school, with a voluntary student body. We might liaise with Helena at Stillwater, and share the load, as it were. Anyone who wants to come, can come, with no fear of death at the end of their time there. I'll be caretaker of this place too, ensuring the people who have stayed have everything they need."

It sounded perfect, everything falling into place. Helena had Stillwater. Hadrian and the other two had Falleaf, with Starcross as a bonus. It seemed unlikely anyone was going to take up the reins of Spellshadow again, with Virgil heading up to the golden city of Angel's Roost to rule beside his mother. That seemed like the most fitting end, that Spellshadow Manor should be left to rot, a crumbling monument to the cruelty that had gone before, and should never be allowed to prevail again.

It took a longer time than expected to get the large crowd through the portal to Falleaf. Then, of course, they had to traipse through the dappled forest, watching out for traps, though the soldiers there had done a decent job of clearing them, under Virgil's instruction. Upon reaching the portal at the other side of the forest, the one that led to Spellshadow, Alex began to feel nervous. They'd had to leave the Kelpies behind at Starcross, and even though Demeter and Aamir had stepped in to help him on the lengthy walk, Alex was beginning to feel weak again. His breathing came short and fast, and he could feel Ceres's watchful eyes upon him, the words "I told you so" teetering on the tip of her tongue.

Eventually, they made it through, crossing the barren wasteland of the smoking field beyond the sickly woods. The wispy snakes had vanished, the ground split in places, cracked apart by the vibrations of the Great Evil's final quake, giving them a swift route to the hill. After passing through the crumbling wall, they walked through the desolate gardens, until they reached the front lawn of the manor. The gates stood closed, wreathed in gray ivy. Alex looked at them curiously, wondering what it would be like to see them swung open, at long last.

Virgil stepped through the crowd and stood on the top step, opening out his arms to address the masses below.

"Those of you who spent time here, I know you will

struggle to trust me. I have mistreated so many under the jurisdiction of the king—you did not know him, but believe me when I say he was a cruel, callous man who made many people do terrible things. I ask for your forgiveness, on the steps of the school where you were kept prisoner," he said solemnly. "If you cannot forgive, I understand. But, please take this final gesture as a show of my goodwill, and my desire for redemption. I shall open the gates, returning you to your homes. Wait here a moment, and you shall see it happen," he added, before disappearing into the shadowed building. Alex and the others followed him, watching as he hurried along the hallways, lifting away clusters of ivy to reveal grates in the ground. Inside them lay small, flat golden discs. He crouched beside each one, opening the lid to reveal ticking clockwork, a barely visible sheen of something flowing through them.

Alex realized they were like the cylinders at Kingstone Keep, making the barrier flow, even when there was nobody to conjure it. The Head broke each one, the cold feeling in Alex's stomach dissolving with each destruction.

"Mind helping me with these?" Virgil asked, turning to look over his shoulder at the group of friends.

Jari and Natalie volunteered, along with a few other former Spellshadow students. Alex assumed that they would be running along the corridors, seeking out each barrier, using magic and force to break the clockwork within. Every time Virgil moved a pile of ivy, he inhaled sharply, letting Alex know that the draining power of the plants was still at work.

It took a fair while, but eventually Virgil paused, a satisfied expression on his face. As he dusted off his hands, a tight smile stretched the pallid skin of his mouth.

"Now, to open the gates," he announced, heading back the way they had come.

Rushing down the steps, he glided toward the looming gates. His face twisted in a grimace as he tore down each vine, the power of the ivy sapping his energy, but still he persevered, until there was not a scrap left on the gates. The remnants lay in a messy heap around his feet.

From his pocket, the Head pulled a large key and placed it in the lock. A loud clunk echoed across the silent lawn as he turned it. Nobody dared to speak, their eyes set on the gates, and the hope that lay beyond them. Virgil grasped one of the bars and yanked it with all his might, the gate giving with a reluctant squeal of ancient metal. Once one side was open, he pulled the other, until both swung wide, revealing the long road with the crumbling, derelict buildings at either side.

The street no longer looked grim and gray, however. Instead, it was as if someone had gone along the rows of buildings, coloring them in, in preparation for this day.

A roar of victory went up from the crowd, but Alex could not join in. His breathing was becoming difficult, his limbs shaking, his mouth dry. He wanted so badly to be able to whoop and holler with the others, but he simply lacked the energy.

"You are free to return home!" Virgil shouted.

With that, the crowd swarmed toward the gate, walking along the road to the very end, where the camouflaging magic of the manor gave way to the real world. The glamor to keep the magical realm hidden was still in place, but the school's barrier was long gone.

It was a happy moment, and one that the five friends, flanked by Demeter, Ceres, and Virgil, watched together.

Finally, Alex could feel that the time had come for more goodbyes, though he didn't know if he'd be one of the people leaving. As much as he wanted to damn everything and stride down that road, it was becoming clearer by the second that he wasn't capable.

"Okay, well, I guess we should get going, right?" Jari spoke first, breaking the awkward tension.

Aamir nodded. "Yes, I imagine we will have to figure out a route home, and who knows how long that will take."

Alex shook his head, feeling his chest tighten. "I won't be going with you, just yet," he said quietly.

The group looked at him.

"Dude, you have to—this is what we've been waiting for!" Jari exclaimed, the disbelief written across his face.

"I can't... I have to stay and recuperate," Alex explained miserably, hating every word. "Right now, I feel like a zombie. If I go home to my mom like this, I'll never forgive myself. I want to see her so badly it literally hurts my heart, but I'd rather she got her son back than this feeble mess." Bitter tears glinted in his eyes as he balled his hands into fists against the sorrow he felt.

Natalie put her hands on his shoulders. "I think you are making a very wise, very brave choice, Alex," she said. "And I suppose it is a good moment to say that I will not be returning either—not yet, anyway. Helena has asked that I join her, taking up the role of Deputy Head of Stillwater House, and I plan to accept."

"What about your family?" Aamir asked, dumbfounded.

Jari nodded emphatically. "Yeah, don't you care?"

"Of course I care, Jari. I am not as heartless as you seem to think," she snapped, but her tone quickly calmed. "The truth is, I will see them again soon enough, once I have everything settled at Stillwater. This is simply something I must do first. I feel as if this is my life now. I belong in the magical realm—perhaps it was always meant to be this way."

"This is insane!" Jari barked. "You're all coming home, right now."

"No, Jari, we are not," Natalie said, stepping toward the blond boy. "We will go when we are ready, and we will see you again, but we have our reasons for staying. Alex needs to recover, and I need to figure out a life for myself."

"Ellabell, tell me you're not buying this madness?" Jari sighed, turning to Ellabell.

The curly-haired girl couldn't meet his eye. "I will stay too, for a short while, to assist in Alex's recovery," she murmured quietly.

"This is a joke, right? You're all in on this?" Jari asked, his eyes wide. "Come on, this has to be a joke!"

"It's not a joke," Ellabell replied simply.

Alex gazed at the young woman standing beside him. "Ellabell, you can't stay here. You have to go back to your family. There is a life waiting for you out there," Alex insisted, feeling a twinge of guilt that he was somehow responsible for making her stay.

She smiled. "And it can wait a little longer. You won't change my mind."

"Ellabell, you have to go. I'll come and find you when I leave here, but you can't stay for my sake," he said, desperate not to see her give up this opportunity.

"Like I said, you won't change my mind," she repeated. "Where you go, I go. I've waited a long time for these gates to open... What's a few months more?"

Alex swallowed hard. "And what if it's longer than that?"

"Then we'll cross that bridge when we come to it," she said, taking his hand in hers.

Aamir and Jari shared a defeated glance. It was bitter-sweet; they had expected to walk through the gates together, but the group was splintering. It had done so before, under more strained circumstances, but it did not make the separation any easier. There was no telling how long it would be until they saw each other again, and the sad atmosphere that settled across them revealed that they all knew it.

"Looks like it's just you and me for now, Petra," Aamir

sighed, forcing a smile onto his face.

Jari shook his head. "I can't believe this."

"We'll see you again, both of you," Alex promised.

"Yeah, you'd better! If you don't, I'll hunt you all down and make you," Jari said, clearly trying to sound threatening, even though his voice was thick with emotion.

"Come on, Jari. We will return in due course. No need to worry," Aamir encouraged, taking the tone of an older brother. Which, Alex reasoned, he kind of was.

They hugged and swore to meet again one day soon, until finally, there was no more to say. Shifting their gaze toward the horizon, Aamir and Jari walked down the long road to freedom, turning back every so often to wave and smile. It was sad and happy, both at once, and tears rolled silently down the faces of everyone present.

It was an image that would remain with Alex for the rest of his life.

CHAPTER 33

I N THE AFTERMATH OF THEIR FRIENDS' DEPARTURE, LIFE changed quickly for all those who remained. Natalie went to Stillwater, as promised, to help Helena set up a new school, much like Falleaf, where students were free to learn without fear. It would not only be for the elite anymore, either, with mages of all kinds coming to study there. They sent regular updates through to Alex at Falleaf, for him to read while he continued with his recovery.

Among that news was the more startling fact that Alypia had died in the mist that claimed Stillwater. She was buried with honor in the royal vault, the ceremony overseen by Venus and Virgil, who had swiftly taken charge of the magical realm, officially abolishing the essence system and initiating new laws to help with the establishment of the schools. Alex had been too unwell to make the journey to the funeral, but Ellabell had come to tell him all about it later, describing the beautiful music, Helena's moving eulogy, and the sorrow the former Stillwater students had felt, despite what Alypia had done. When all was said and done, she had been a victim of her father too, whipped into being as cold and calculating as he was, in a bid to win his affection. Plus, no matter what sins she had to her name, she had still been Helena's mother, and the silver-haired girl had loved her deeply, as any daughter would, so Alex's heart went out to her.

Hadrian, Demeter, and Ceres made good on their promise to turn Falleaf into a better school too. Moving everyone to Starcross for a couple of weeks, they had refurbished the dorms and classrooms to appeal to the new starters. A fresh system began to take shape, and the students were moved back in, where they began lessons under the kind rule of Hadrian. Agatha and Vincent remained within the grounds of Falleaf, in their subterranean cottage, coming up to teach the students there. Vincent led a class on the darker side of magic, though he never strayed too far into anything potentially catastrophic, while Agatha taught students the art of healing, showing them how to make poultices and potions and pills, and how to reinforce their natural power with magic. She also told one or two choice stories, to make the students gasp in awe of the life she had lived.

Alex loved to hear these tales of how the magical realm was changing for all of their acquaintances. Usually, the news came from Agatha and Vincent, who visited him often, given that they were pretty much neighbors. Alex had been put up in a treehouse close to their underground dwelling, and most days Agatha would come over with food and tea, to ensure he was properly nourished. Vincent came with her on occasion, using his powers of necromancy to try to rebuild some of the broken strands that lay torn within him. Ceres visited often, becoming a kind of anti-magical physiotherapist. Each day, she would get him to focus on constructing shapes and objects with his anti-magic, and then she would ask him to search within himself, and use that skill upon the threads of his ripped soul. Piece by piece, he sewed himself back together, under Ceres's instruction. His mind needed healing too, and with that came more tasks. Some of them were focusing exercises, while others were intended to help him piece together the memories and abilities he'd lost. In the first few weeks, he was clumsy, having lost some of his motor ability, but it gradually came back, with help from Ceres's mental exercises, repairing the damaged neurons and anti-magical receptors.

She usually brought food too, in great big boxes, to wash down the vile taste of her potions, leading Alex to worry that he'd be ten times the size he'd been when he started, by the end of his recovery.

Ellabell often had bits of news for him too, whenever she

went up to the pagoda to see how things were coming along. What pleased him most was to hear that Demeter had begun to teach Spellbreaker lessons, to ensure the new mages knew about both sides of the magical spectrum, and the histories that had divided a nation, long before any of them were born.

And, over time, Alex began to return to something close to normal. With the help of everyone around him, his strength slowly returned, his mind ceasing to wander aimlessly, and the vacant expression began to fade from his eyes. Demeter accompanied Ceres sometimes, offering up his use of mind control to assist with the fixing of any broken memories he found in Alex's head. Having half his soul torn out had left some gaps, but Demeter proved to be a deft hand at filling them in again. It was like a game of connect the dots, joining up the numbers until the whole picture emerged.

Sometimes, Elias would pop into his head, and he would feel the poignant loss of the shadow-man all over again. It was strange to look at shadows on the wall and not have them manifest into a floating guardian, but that was something he had to get used to, alongside everything else that had changed. Slowly but surely, he stopped expecting to hear a voice whispering in the darkness, Elias fading into nothing more than a bittersweet memory.

Day by day, things improved, though they had started poorly.

For the first month, Alex had continued to feel weak and weary, his mind foggy and useless. Even simple tasks were too much, his brain unable to concentrate on what he was supposed to be doing. Short walks made him breathless and wobbly, and even talking for long periods left him exhausted. All he had seemed to do was sleep and eat and drink herbal tea, on an endless cycle that frustrated him deeply. Every time he awoke and saw Ellabell beside him, he hated himself for keeping her there. What fun was it to sit and watch someone sleep, their body and mind too useless to even chat awhile? He pitied her, his pity turning to bitterness. He had known he was hurting her with the cold things he said, and yet she had refused to go.

"I know what you're doing," Ellabell had said one day, sipping from a cup of coffee.

"I'm not doing anything. In case you hadn't realized, I'm bed-bound," he'd snapped.

"It won't work, Alex," she'd retorted. "You can push and push and push, but you won't get me to go."

After that, he'd endeavored to be nicer to her, remembering that she was there because she loved him, and he loved her. Accepting her assistance instead of resenting it, he had found himself feeling better. It wasn't an instant fix, but the comfort of having her there had improved his mindset, allowing him to focus better on functioning like an ordinary human being, instead of using her as his verbal punching bag to vent his frustrations upon.

Shortly after that, he and Ellabell had begun to take more walks together. Soon, he could walk to the pagoda and back, with little trouble from wobbling limbs or strained breath, and he found he could go through a whole day without needing to rest. His energy improved, his appetite grew, his weakness faded, and his mind returned to him, slowly but surely.

A while later, Venus came to visit him. She had been so busy in her queenly duties that it had taken her a while, but when Alex saw her, he thought she looked happier than he'd ever seen her. There was a flush in her cheeks and glitter in her eyes, the ripple of fear no longer prevalent beneath them.

"And how is the wounded soldier?" she asked, smiling pleasantly as she sat beside his sickbed, neatly folding her legs beneath the chair, her hands resting on her knees.

"Getting there, Your Grace," Alex replied, remembering the correct term. For some reason, though she was still strikingly beautiful, he didn't feel the same magnetic pull he'd felt before.

She picked up a basket of fruit that Ellabell had brought for him, plucking a grape off its vine and rolling it between her fingers. "Nice to see people still bring fruit to the sick," she said, amused, as she popped the grape into her mouth.

"Why did you do that for us?" Alex asked, skipping past the pleasantries.

"Do what?" she replied coyly, her eyes twinkling with irreverence.

Alex laughed. "Why did you set my friends free, and get the guards to stand down? If I hadn't succeeded, you'd have been in a world of trouble."

The queen gave a delicate shrug. "If you think I still feared my husband's wrath by then, you are not as smart as I thought you were. Death would have been a kindness, had you not succeeded. Freeing those people would have been worth every foul word, every lash, every beating he gave as punishment."

"How did you endure it? Julius as your husband—how did you get through it?" Alex wanted to know, in awe of her strength.

"I had a place in my mind where I would go when things became dark," she admitted. "It was a place that was just for me... a place where Julius was nobody. My Leander was there, always there, standing by my side. After all this time, my loyalty to him never waned, even through the cruelest moments my husband could conjure up. Leander was my true love—you only get one of those, you know?" she said, with a quiet chuckle. "My life, and my marriage, were frightening and loveless after Leander's passing, but I had the memory of him to keep me warm, and to give me strength when I had none left."

"So you did it for him?" Alex pressed, wanting to have it clear in his mind.

She nodded. "My son and you share his blood—how could I not step in to assist, when you both needed me?"

She didn't stay much longer, simply wanting to check on how he was, but Alex was glad she had come. With her words, he had been able to put his thoughts of Leander Wyvern to rest. Venus had loved him, and it was that love that had set his friends free.

He had just passed the three-month mark in his recovery, when Ceres came to visit him.

"Anyone home?" she asked, tapping on the front door of the treehouse.

"I'm in the kitchen," Alex called back. Ellabell had ordered him to bake some cookies for Agatha, while she went to visit Hadrian up at the school. It was a focusing task in itself, but a fun one that meant everyone got to eat something delicious.

"Ellabell got you making cookies again?" Ceres said, amused, as she walked into the small kitchen area that Hadrian had installed.

Alex grinned. "She thinks it keeps my mind steady, going through the recipe, measuring things out. What she doesn't know is, I just like to lick the bowl," he chuckled.

"I hope you don't do that before you've spooned the mixture out," Ceres teased.

"With everything you people keep feeding me, I don't need to," he remarked, patting his stomach. "What brings you to this neck of the woods?"

"News that you'll be pleased to hear," she said, taking a seat on one of the high stools that sat by the kitchen door.

Alex turned to her, raising an eyebrow. "Oh?"

"I have decided to test whether your recovery is complete," she said, smiling kindly.

Alex frowned. "Sounds painful."

"Not painful, it just requires focus," she said, chuckling softly. "Now, I'm going to place my hand on your chest, and I want you to reach inside, to find your soul, and let it rise to meet my palm. Focus your mind, and it should come easily," she encouraged.

He did as she'd asked, closing his eyes as he felt her palm on his chest. Once upon a time, such a task would have been simple, but now it was a real strain to seek out the pulsing coil of his essence and coax it into action. Reaching it, he focused hard on lifting it, feeling as the tendrils twisted up through his ribs, pushing toward the hand pressed just above.

"And, relax," said Ceres.

Alex smiled nervously as he felt his essence descend back into the depths of his body. "How did I do?" he asked.

"You're done," she replied, grinning. "There's nothing more we can do for you. You have your strength back, your mind is as focused as it's ever going to be, and the little pieces that were broken have been tied off, as it were. Demeter and I have been discussing it, and we think you're ready to go home. That test proved it."

The spoon in Alex's hand clattered into the bowl, splashing unfinished cookie mixture up the sides. Without a word, he reached out and pulled Ceres into a tight embrace, his shoulders shaking from happy laughter. She laughed too, the sound infectious, as she patted him on the back. It was a well-known fact that she wasn't exactly a hugger, but it was evident she was making an exception for Alex.

"I'm really good to go?" he asked, pulling away.

She nodded. "You're really good to go."

When Ellabell returned, he told her the good news, scooping her up into his arms and spinning her around, both of them whooping with excitement as they danced around the kitchen, eating half of the cookies that had been intended for Agatha. It had been a long time coming, and both of them were eager to return home.

"What will you do when you get home?" Alex asked, once they had come down from cloud nine.

Ellabell shrugged. "Depends who's there when I get there," she said sadly. "My parents probably won't be home, with how much they work. My neighbors, if they still live there, might be happy to see me, though."

"You only saw your parents every few weeks, right?" Alex asked, remembering the stories she had told him of her lonely childhood, in the many long conversations they'd had together.

"Yeah, I was the ultimate latchkey kid," she said with a tight smile.

"Perhaps things will change, seeing as you've been gone so long?" Alex encouraged, putting his arm around her.

"Perhaps... but I think it might be too little, too late," she sighed. "I just want to see them to let them know I'm okay, and then I'll leave again. If they'd been home, Finder never would have kidnapped me."

"But if he hadn't, you'd never have met me," Alex teased, wanting to coax a smile back to her face.

"Every cloud, eh?" she murmured, giving him a playful shove in the ribs.

The following afternoon, Ellabell and Alex met with Natalie on the front lawn of Spellshadow Manor. They had sent had a message through to her the day before, explaining what had happened, and she had sent one back, asking if she could come with them.

She looked sleek and sophisticated, dressed in silver trousers and a white t-shirt, her black hair slicked back into a high ponytail. Whatever she had been doing at Stillwater, it agreed with her. She looked happy and healthy, a big smile on her face.

"I suppose we should do this at last," she said as the duo approached, gesturing toward the wide-open gates.

The spells that concealed the place from ordinary eyes were still up, but the barrier remained absent, the clockwork discs all broken to pieces.

"I suppose we should," Alex agreed, turning to look at the looming figure of Spellshadow one last time. "I can't say I'll be sorry to see the back of this place," he muttered.

"Nope, not one bit," Ellabell chimed in, taking Alex's hand.

"Goodbye, Spellshadow!" Alex yelled, his voice echoing all the way around the crumbling walls.

"Goodbye, Spellshadow!" the girls howled, grins spreading across their faces.

With that, they walked out of the school, not giving it a second glance. It might not be the last time they returned to the magical realm, Alex reasoned, but he never wished to set foot inside the manor again.

As they walked, Alex turned to Natalie. "What are you going to tell your family?" He had given it some thought during his long recovery, but had not come up with anything particularly plausible. The real explanation seemed too outlandish, even for him.

She smiled. "I am going to tell them I slipped and fell into the ravine after messing around up there—typical teenager mischief—and suffered a bout of amnesia that made me forget who I was. I shall say you were in there too, and when the two of us came around, we couldn't remember a thing, so we traveled all the way up to Alaska, hitchhiking most of the way, believing that was where we were from," she began, the whole thing apparently carefully thought out. "Then, I will say my memories were restored after eating strawberry pancakes at a truck stop in Juno, and we hurried back as fast as we could."

Alex whistled. "You mind if I use that too?"

"I was counting on it," Natalie chuckled. "It will not work if your story is different!"

Alex laughed. "That's very true. So, accident, amnesia, Alaska, strawberry pancakes?"

"That is about it," Natalie replied.

Faced with the passageway that led into the real world, Alex began to worry. The door would always be open for a return journey, he knew that much, but he felt as if he were in a strange kind of limbo. Part of him never wanted to set foot in the magical realm again, but then the other part knew that the real world would seem strange and unusual to him now.

How was he supposed to deal with ordinary life, having lived through the things he had?

CHAPTER 34

ANXIETY SETTLED ACROSS THE GROUP AS THEY stepped over the threshold between realms, emerging into the world beyond. For a moment, Alex was confused, wondering if they'd come out in another part of the world. With the way the horizon had shifted scenery, seen from the library window at Spellshadow, he knew the gateway didn't always lead out to the ordinary streets of Middledale, Iowa. This time, however, it seemed they'd hit the jackpot, timing it just right. He recognized the landscape instantly. Yes, this was definitely his hometown; there was no mistaking the quaint streets and uniform houses. The roads were quiet, although an elderly gentleman, in the middle of putting out his trash, eyed them curiously as they passed by.

Do we look different from normal people now? Alex wondered, feeling suddenly self-conscious.

The memories of the night he had followed Natalie and the raggedy gray phantom came flooding back as they walked along the streets, and Alex's heart began to pound harder when he realized they were almost back at his family home. Turning onto the very road he had known all his life, nausea gripped his stomach like a vise. What if his mother was worse? What if the sight of him sent her over the edge?

Picking up a newspaper, left discarded on a neighbor's lawn, he checked the date and was surprised by what he saw. If it was correct, only six months had passed since he had gone missing. Enough time to cause worry and distress, but not nearly as long as he had actually been away. He passed the paper to Natalie and Ellabell, pointing to the date.

"Is this today's?" Ellabell asked.

"Even if it's not, it's recent," Alex replied, looking again at the newspaper. It hadn't browned, nor had the print faded. In fact, it looked fairly fresh off the press.

"How is that possible?" Natalie wondered, a nervous expression upon her face.

Alex shrugged. "Time must move slower here."

Finally, he could put it off no longer. Standing at the gate that led up to his front door, he paused, his knuckles white on the latch. All he had to do was lift it up and walk along the path to the porch, but he was frozen to the spot. Moving beside him, Ellabell lifted the latch for him, swinging the gate open.

"You've got this," she said softly, placing her hand lightly upon his arm.

Taking a deep breath, he put one foot in front of the other, forcing himself to make the short journey to the front door. Hesitating for a second, he knocked on the wooden surface and took a step back, waiting for the familiar face of his mother to appear.

Only, the person who answered the door wasn't his mother. A large man stood in the doorway. Gray eyes peered at them curiously, set in a grizzled face, his dark hair short and flecked with silver at the sides. Alex's heart sank, convinced something had happened to his mother, and this was the new resident of his childhood home. A moment later, however, the man's eyes went wide with understanding.

"*Alex?*" he gasped, in utter disbelief.

Alex nodded. "Who are you?"

"I'm Detective David Cartwright," he said, holding out his hand to shake Alex's. "I'm a... friend of your mother's. I've been helping with your missing person's case," he explained hurriedly, almost shaking Alex's hand clean off. "And you must be Natalie?" he asked, spotting the French girl standing behind Alex.

Natalie nodded. "That is me."

"Well, come in, come in," the cop said, ushering them

quickly inside. "Your mother is in the den. I'll be with you in a moment; I just have some calls to make," he added, looking over them again as if they were figments of his imagination. His gaze paused on Ellabell, like he wasn't sure what to make of her, but urgency sent him toward the phone without saying another word.

Alex braced himself as he walked toward the den door. Quietly, he knocked on it, not wanting to burst in and give his mother a shock.

"David?" his mother's voice asked.

Alex felt tears brimming in his eyes as he pushed open the door and stepped into the room. His mother was sitting on the sofa, clutching a pillow to her chest, her eyes listlessly watching the television in the corner. She looked up as the trio entered. For a minute, nobody said a word. Then, his mother screamed, jumping up from the sofa, before running into Alex's open arms. She grasped at him, pulling him to her with such ferocity he felt she might crush him, but he understood the impulse. She wanted to make sure he was real. Wrapping his arms around her, he held her tightly, hearing her sobbing in his ear.

"Alex, Alex, Alex," she whispered. "Is it really you?"

"It's me, Mom," Alex said gently, tears falling from his eyes. "I'm back."

"Oh, Alex… Where have you been?" she breathed, hugging him tighter. "Where did you go? Who took you?"

He smiled, knowing the story was going to be long one.

"I'll explain everything later, but I think David has phoned the cops," he said.

She pulled away. "You met David?" she asked, brushing the tears away from her eyes.

"Yeah, he seems like a nice guy," Alex replied, not really knowing how to broach the subject of a strange man in his house, not when there were so many other things to discuss.

"Where have you been?" she asked again, more desperately this time. "You've been gone for six months. The police told me you were likely dead somewhere. I never believed them, but when you didn't come back, I started to fear the worst." She rattled off the words, as if she'd been storing them up for a long time.

He smiled, planting a kiss on her forehead. "I promise I will tell you everything later," he said, and the funny thing was, he meant it. If anyone could understand the bizarre world he'd been living in, it was his mother.

"And Natalie! You're here too! Everyone has been so worried!" she shrieked, finally noticing the two others in the room. "And you, I don't know you, but you are very welcome here," she cried, enveloping both Natalie and Ellabell in a warm embrace.

"I am back, Mrs. Webber," said Natalie. "And we have quite a story to tell you, once the police have gone."

Alex's mom nodded. "I have been on the phone to your family every day, trying to encourage them not to give up on you. I just knew you would walk back through that door one day—I just knew it!"

"How are they?" Natalie asked sheepishly.

"They are distraught, as you can imagine, but I know everything will be forgotten once they see you again, and hold you again," Alex's mom replied.

Natalie smiled nervously. "Perhaps I should call them?" she said, but Alex's mom shook her head.

"I would wait until the police have been and gone. They will have a lot of questions, I'm sure. David has been keeping me up to date with the investigation, and they will be very intrigued to know where you have been all this time, just as I am," she explained, coming back over to wrap Alex in another hug. "I can't believe you're home," she sobbed.

"I was always going to come back to you," Alex swore, holding her close. As she let him go, he realized she looked healthier than she had the last time he'd seen her. There were blooms in her cheeks again, the dark circles beneath her eyes no longer as prominent, her whole figure less skinny than it had been before. "How are you feeling?" he asked, puzzled by the change in her.

She smiled. "I am better, my darling boy. My treatment is working. David has been helping me, but I am on the road to recovery," she told him, fresh tears pouring from her eyes.

"That is the best news I've heard in months!" he cried, clutching her hands and squeezing them tightly. After all the worrying he had done, his mother was getting better. She hadn't been sitting at home, wasting away, getting sicker by the second. No, the universe had seen fit to offer her some hope in all of this. He couldn't believe it—she was going to be okay.

A short while later, the police descended on the house like a swarm of flies, buzzing around the place in sharp suits, wielding notepads and pens. Some were there to take statements; others were there to take DNA samples and fingerprints, with one taking photos, while the rest stood around doing nothing, drinking Alex's mother's coffee and eating her cookies.

They set up a makeshift interview room in the kitchen, bringing Natalie and Alex in individually to ask them for their version of events. They tried to interview Ellabell, but seeing as nobody knew who she was, or where she had come from, the information they got was fairly useless to their particular case.

Once it was Alex's turn to enter, the detective in charge of interviewing scrutinized him closely. Natalie had gone first, flashing him a wink as she came back into the den. Alex sat down in the familiar chair, putting his hands down flat on the kitchen table. He didn't know why—he simply reasoned it made him look less guilty, if the cop could see his hands at all times.

"Would you like to tell me where you've been?" the detective asked, pressing the nib of her pen down onto the notepad she had laid out on the surface of the table.

Alex nodded, recounting the tale they'd agreed upon. It

tumbled from his mouth easily, the words well rehearsed in his head by that point. The detective barely looked up as he spoke, scribbling it all down onto the paper. When he finished, she finally lifted her gaze to his.

"Amnesia?" she said, giving him a withering look.

"Amnesia," Alex confirmed, trying hard not to smile.

She glanced over the notes she'd made. "And strawberry pancakes triggered your memories?"

Alex nodded. "My mom used to make them, and the taste of them must have brought something back."

The woman sighed. "Very well. If that's all you have to say to me, then you can go."

Alex jumped up from the table and hurried back into the den, where everyone was waiting anxiously for his return. He said nothing, not wanting to give anything away while the police were still in the house. Instead, David was called out into the hallway, where the detective greeted him. Alex could see them through the crack in the den door, but he couldn't hear what they were saying. Whatever it was, it seemed the detective was at the end of her tether, her expression showing her exhaustion. She gestured at the den, but David put his hands up, shaking his head. Finally, the detective shrugged, shoving her notepad and pen into her bag.

"Teenagers go missing all the time," she said, her voice just loud enough for Alex to make out what she was saying. "Some come back, some don't. Your new friend is just lucky those two did come back. If they're going to tell us lies, there's nothing we can do. If they're okay, they're safe, and they don't seem to be hurt, what more can I give to this investigation? It was a missing person's case. Those missing people have been found. As far as I'm concerned, my job is done," she continued tersely, gesturing for her team to gather their things and leave.

Alex and the others remained in silence, absently watching the television, until the squad of police had gone, their cars disappearing from the road outside. The detective was the last to leave, poking her head into the room, a look of displeasure on her face.

"I have informed your parents, Natalie," she said. "There will be a flight booked tomorrow afternoon, with your name on it. You too, Ellabell, though we couldn't get through to the number you gave us. Please, try not to go missing again before then, okay? They are worried sick," she added, her tone spiky.

Natalie nodded. "Thank you, Detective. I won't."

With that, the woman turned on her heel and left, giving the door a good slam on the way out. It was evident she felt like Alex and Natalie had wasted her time, and had no doubt been off gallivanting somewhere, having the time of their lives, giving little thought to their families at home. Even from the interview, Alex could tell the detective hadn't believed a word of their story, but what she had said was true—if they were going to lie, what else could the police do?

"I'm just going to go down to the station, see if I can help with any paperwork," David said, rising from the sofa, a suspicious look in his eyes. "Let me know if you want me to pick up anything on my way home," he added before disappearing out the door.

At last, the trio was alone with Alex's mother.

She looked at them expectantly. "Well, where have you been then, if it wasn't Alaska?"

Alex smiled, inhaling deeply, as he began his tale. Natalie and Ellabell chipped in bits and pieces along the way, though some of the things he said surprised even them. After all, they hadn't both been around for everything he'd been through in the magical realm. Ellabell blushed when he mentioned her, and how they had met, but Alex's mom seemed thrilled by the prospect of a new love interest for her son.

"And so beautiful too!" she chirped excitedly, smiling at Ellabell.

"She is very beautiful," he agreed, embarrassing Ellabell even more. "Now, where was I?" he asked, before continuing with his story, running through the months he'd spent at Spellshadow, followed by their escape into the domain of Stillwater House. Running back a step, he told her all about Elias, and how the shadow-man had helped, in his own kind of way, from day one, before switching to the journey they had gone through with Helena. He explained what happened with Alypia, and all the things they had endured at the villa. He pressed on, recounting how they had escaped to a fearsome prison named Kingstone Keep, full of psychopaths and murderers. She didn't like that part, a gasp of horror rising from her throat, but she was too enthralled to interrupt. He spoke of Caius, and how things had ended horribly for him, despite his best intentions, leading them to move swiftly into the world of Falleaf and through the gauntlet to obtain the Book of Jupiter. Ignoring another gasp from his mother's lips, he spoke to her of the kind soul, Hadrian, they had met there, and how they had come to meet the people of Starcross. Finally, he told her all about Julius and the final battle, though he left out the part about his sacrifice, and how he'd spent a short while in recovery afterward, not wanting to worry her too much.

"And that is about it," Ellabell said, finishing the story for him.

Alex's mom sat back, absorbing all the information she had been bombarded with. For what seemed like an age, Alex was certain she was going to sit up and scold him for making things up, but then her expression changed from dubious to understanding.

"I knew you were alive," she said softly. "I just knew you were out there somewhere, watching over me. I knew you hadn't been kidnapped or killed and dumped in a ditch somewhere—they tried to tell me, but I knew I was right. It's funny, sometimes it did feel as if you were walking in another plane of existence, looking down... and I suppose, in a way, you were."

"Wait, you believe me?" Alex asked, dumbfounded.

She nodded. "You forget, Alex, you're my son. I know you. If you wanted to lie, you would have come up with something far simpler," she explained, a faint smile lifting the corners of her lips. A chuckle began in the back of her throat, growing louder and more infectious as it took hold of her body, shaking her shoulders, making her eyes stream with happy tears.

The others laughed with her, getting rid of all the bad energy that had built up inside them, for so long. It was good to laugh.

But, more than that, it was good to be home.

EPILOGUE

AFTER THAT DAY AT THE HOUSE, NATALIE AND Ellabell had boarded their flights the following afternoon, the trio sharing a tearful farewell at the airport. Ellabell and Alex had stolen a private moment together, taking the opportunity to have one last kiss, before everything changed forever.

Alex had waved them off, returning to his home, with no idea what the future would hold. His mom had given Ellabell an open invitation to return whenever she wanted, and Ellabell had promised to keep her to that, but he didn't know how long it would be until he saw her again. Natalie, too.

In fact, after returning home to find her parents away

on business, with a message on the answering machine to say they'd heard she was back but they couldn't be there to greet her, Ellabell realized she no longer felt like herself in the home she'd grown up in. Alex heard about it straightaway, as Ellabell called him as soon as she heard the message to tell him how lonely she felt in the big, empty house, and what had happened when she got back. Her parents had said they had just presumed she'd run away to do the things some teenagers did, and only realized it was something else when the police called. Still, they said they couldn't come home just yet, promising to return when they'd finished their business trips. Saddened by their absence, and the thought of continuing to flit about the empty home, Ellabell had written her parents a note and boarded the next plane to Iowa, less than a week later. With her return, Alex's life truly did change forever.

It felt like five years had passed in the blink of an eye, as the group gathered together again at Stillwater House. A reunion was afoot, in celebration of Alex and Ellabell's engagement. Much had changed, but the six friends remained as solid as they ever had been, regularly seeing one another, and keeping in touch through letters with those they couldn't see as often.

Clinking glasses around the table that had been set up on the sparkling banks of the Stillwater lake, they toasted the happy couple, who kissed beneath the stars.

After realizing, in those first few months back in the real world, that it wasn't for him, Alex had returned to the magical realm to take on the role of Spellbreaker teacher at Stillwater House. He explained to his mother where he was going, and though he went back home most weekends to make sure she was okay, his mother loved to visit the villa when the impulse took her. From time to time, he returned to Spellshadow to check on the colony of Thunderbirds that had settled there. They were thriving in the ruins of the manor, which had crumbled into dereliction without anyone to take care of it, and been reclaimed by nature. Alex trained a select few mages on how to ride the winged beasts, wanting to keep Storm's legacy alive, even if there were no more Spellbreakers to uphold it.

Helena had taken up the mantle of Headmistress, in her mother's stead, and had turned the place into a wonderful center for learning, producing some of the magical realm's best and brightest mages, who never had to fear death at the end of their education. It was remarkable what she had done with the place, and they often had intercollegiate matches and competitions with Falleaf, to see who would come out on top. It was always friendly, and it was nice to see the arena being used for good, instead of evil.

Natalie returned from France shortly after her first visit

back to the real world. Her family had believed the amnesia tale, but they had been a little reluctant to let her go and "study abroad," which was what she had told them she was going to do. However, being the headstrong young woman that she was, she went anyway, though she kept in touch frequently, having to duck out of the magical world in order to call them. They'd gotten over the shock of it after the first year, knowing that she was safe and thriving.

Aamir and Jari remained in the outside world, both of them heading to Harvard to study engineering, where they shared a dorm for the second time in their lives. Aamir had never quite recovered from the mist that attacked him; his magic was always weaker after that, whenever he dared to try it, but in the real world he didn't need it. Despite that, he visited the others often, usually with Jari by his side. Jari had simply never desired to come back to the magical world. He enjoyed his powers, but the realm still left a sour taste in his mouth. Alex could understand that, and though it was sad not to see more of his former dormmates, he was glad they were happy, out there, doing their own thing. By all accounts, Jari had been quite the hit with the ladies when they reached college, though Aamir had often had to rein him in when it came to wooing them. Even at college, a room full of kittens was too much—and way too expensive when they couldn't be conjured out of thin air.

Ellabell, who was excitedly showing her sparkling engagement ring to Natalie, had taken an entirely different path.

Knowing there might be young people out there, harboring magical powers, she had decided to take on the role of a kind of voluntary Finder, seeking out new recruits who might want to be taught in the ways of magic. Each time, she would lead them to the border between worlds, where she would make her pitch. Either Alex or Demeter usually went with her, so they could erase the memory of the potential student if they decided not to take up the offer. After all, they still wanted to keep the magical world a secret. Such a rare and wonderful knowledge would boggle the mind of an ordinary human being, and they didn't want that on their consciences. If the student accepted, a scholarship letter was sent out, inviting the young person to study at a private boarding school for talented students, to ensure the parents didn't worry. The parents were even invited along to visit, though Demeter and Alex usually stepped in at the pickup to make them believe they were traveling to somewhere else in the country, rather than a different realm. In just under five years, they hadn't had a single slipup—a statistic the pair of them were hugely proud of, much to Ellabell's amusement.

The friends talked long into the night, sitting around that table by the shore, discussing the memories that had brought them to this point. They talked of each other's current lives, and how each of them had been shaped by the events they had endured. More than that, they talked about their friendship, and how it would live long into the future. An engagement brought people together, and it had certainly brought them all back to one another.

The path to get there had been a long, hard, brutal road, with so much loss and suffering along the way. Whenever they met at Christmas and Thanksgiving, they said a prayer for those who were no longer with them, wishing they could be. But there had been good times too, and with every year that passed, the bad faded, and the good pushed its way to the front.

Just as nature reclaimed beauty from dereliction, so life sprang from hardship... and love conquered all.

The End.

Dear Reader,

Thank you so much for following Alex's journey through to the end. It means a lot to me, and I sincerely hope you enjoyed the conclusion.

Love,
Bella

P.S. Turn the page for a list of my other Young Adult stories.

P.P.S. Sign up to my VIP email list and I'll send you a personal heads up when my next book releases: **www. morebellaforrest.com**
(Your email will be kept 100% private and you can unsubscribe at any time.)

P.P.P.S. I'd also love to hear from you—come say hi on **Instagram** (@ashadeofvampire) or **Twitter** (@ ashadeofvampire) or **Facebook** (@BellaForrestAuthor). I do my best to respond :)

READ MORE BY BELLA FORREST!

THE GIRL WHO DARED TO THINK (New!)

The Girl Who Dared to Think (Book 1)
The Girl Who Dared to Stand (Book 2)
The Girl Who Dared to Descend (Book 3)

THE GENDER GAME (Completed series)

The Gender Game (Book 1)
The Gender Secret (Book 2)
The Gender Lie (Book 3)
The Gender War (Book 4)
The Gender Fall (Book 5)
The Gender Plan (Book 6)
The Gender End (Book 7)

A SHADE OF VAMPIRE SERIES

Season 1: Derek & Sofia's story

A Shade of Vampire (Book 1)

A Shade of Blood (Book 2)

A Castle of Sand (Book 3)

A Shadow of Light (Book 4)

A Blaze of Sun (Book 5)

A Gate of Night (Book 6)

A Break of Day (Book 7)

Season 2: Rose & Caleb's story

A Shade of Novak (Book 8)

A Bond of Blood (Book 9)

A Spell of Time (Book 10)

A Chase of Prey (Book 11)

A Shade of Doubt (Book 12)

A Turn of Tides (Book 13)

A Dawn of Strength (Book 14)

A Fall of Secrets (Book 15)

An End of Night (Book 16)

THE SECRET OF SPELLSHADOW MANOR

The Secret of Spellshadow Manor (Book 1)
The Breaker (Book 2)
The Chain (Book 3)
The Keep (Book 4)
The Test (Book 5)
The Spell (Book 6)

A SHADE OF DRAGON TRILOGY

A Shade of Dragon 1
A Shade of Dragon 2
A Shade of Dragon 3

A SHADE OF KIEV TRILOGY

A Shade of Kiev 1
A Shade of Kiev 2
A Shade of Kiev 3

DETECTIVE ERIN BOND (Adult thriller/mystery)

Lights, Camera, Gone
Write, Edit, Kill

BEAUTIFUL MONSTER DUOLOGY

Beautiful Monster 1
Beautiful Monster 2

For an updated list of Bella's books, please visit her website:
www.bellaforrest.net

Join Bella's VIP email list and she'll personally send you an
email reminder as soon as her next book is out:
www.morebellaforrest.com

CPSIA information can be obtained
at www.ICGtesting.com
Printed in the USA
LVOW07s2346110118

562803LV00003B/230/P